KU-091-523

Being Sally Cartwright

Being Sally Cartwright

Mario Borazio

Copyright © 2022 by Mario Borazio.

Library of Congress Control Number:		2022909143
ISBN:	Hardcover	978-1-6698-8864-2
	Softcover	978-1-6698-8863-5
	eBook	978-1-6698-8862-8

All rights reserved. No part of this book may be reproduced or transmitted in any form or by any means, electronic or mechanical, including photocopying, recording, or by any information storage and retrieval system, without permission in writing from the copyright owner.

This is a work of fiction. Names, characters, places and incidents either are the product of the author's imagination or are used fictitiously, and any resemblance to any actual persons, living or dead, events, or locales is entirely coincidental.

Any people depicted in stock imagery provided by Getty Images are models, and such images are being used for illustrative purposes only.
Certain stock imagery © Getty Images.

Print information available on the last page.

Rev. date: 05/20/2022

To order additional copies of this book, contact:
Xlibris
AU TFN: 1 800 844 927 (Toll Free inside Australia)
AU Local: (02) 8310 8187 (+61 2 8310 8187 from outside Australia)
www.Xlibris.com.au
Orders@Xlibris.com.au
841117

CHAPTER 1

I READ SOMEWHERE THAT people close one eye when they're holding the barrel of a gun to their temple. Why was that? This conundrum was definitely worth pondering as my bus meandered its way through the choked city streets.

I arrived at work at precisely 9 a.m. and applied the prerequisite amount of bum glue before sitting at my desk. I sighed heavily, for I knew nothing could possibly move me away from my computer until lunchtime. Except maybe if a fire broke out and we were forced to evacuate the building, which was an extremely unlikely event. This has never happened in the four years, two months, and seventeen days that I have been working here.

I'm a data analyst for a medium-sized graphic design company in the centre of Melbourne. This is the one and only job I've ever had since graduating from university. I like working here, even though it boils down to nothing more than eight hours of drudgery. Some days the best part of my job is the swivelling chair.

My work day is based on routine. I know precisely what time things happen, when I get a break, what I have to do. It's this routine that keeps me going. Just.

I'm in the back office, so I don't get to use the fancy software like the workers who occupy the front office space. But I don't mind. I'm not one who craves attention. In fact, the opposite is true.

My name is Sally Cartwright. I'm 26 years old and an only child. I'm a little bit different; I tend to see the world through a different lens than most people. I feel like I'm always swimming in the deep end and wrestling with what the world expects of me. You could say that I struggle with imposter syndrome, mainly through a lack of self-confidence.

I'm also a bit of a loner. Not the enigmatic, crazy type of loner.

I'm more the quiet, stays-out-of-everyone's-way type. I would often get home from work on a Friday afternoon and not see another human being until catching the bus to work again the following Monday morning.

I don't fit in anywhere and don't have any friends. I've never been one to dream to be that popular person or part of some cool gang or be invited to every party happening. It's so easy to watch the cool kids and think they have it all, but appearances can be deceptive. I'm sure many of them are just as insecure as I am; they're just a whole lot better at hiding it.

Most weekends I lie in bed trying to think of reasons to get up, but none are convincing.

Loneliness seems to be the quintessential taboo these days—a shameful and embarrassing scourge. I have learnt to cope with solo dining, paying for everything myself, and not having anyone to comfort me after waking from a horrifying dream (of which I've had a few). But the predicament I find myself in is not really my fault. You see, Mummy took me to see a nice doctor when I was 3 years old and he diagnosed me with autism, a quirk of hard wiring in my brain. I was never the classic regressive type. I was never running around banging my head against a wall or flailing my arms. I'm only on the mild end of the spectrum, which means that I can function normally for almost all things except social interaction. All social interactions are challenging for me. They cause me great anxiety.

Social interaction, in my opinion, is just a form of acting. I wouldn't be good at acting. I'm generally not good around people. All I've ever been was Sally Cartwright with her insular rules, routines, and rituals.

I am predictable Sally.

I am boring Sally.

I recently watched a documentary on poverty in Africa. It showed, quite graphically, starving children forced to live on the streets and resort to prostitution to survive. By the end of the programme, I decided there and then to give up my tedious day job and dedicate the rest of my life to working for a humanitarian organisation. In the end, I worried about how I was even going to get to Africa and decided to put off my quest indefinitely.

I don't know how to deal with change. I'm used to things staying the same.

You wouldn't want to look through my mirror. I have never once felt the flood of somatic sensation that screams 'I'm alive'. If I could have one wish, I would erase my entire past.

I have trouble associating with intimacy; it feels awkward to be in any sort of intimate situation. I've only ever had one boyfriend. We met at university, and his name was Lars. He was studying philosophy and was rumoured to be a maths genius, which was what initially drew me to him because I am good with numbers. He had a way of telling stories that entranced me. I hung on his every word, trapped within a heady whirl of giddiness.

On one occasion, he invited me to a lecture where serious-looking people were debating serious topics. One such topic was the antithesis of art and nature. I was totally uninterested and felt terribly uncomfortable sitting in that room. I'm not good in crowds.

Lars was also an activist in the student union. Please don't get me wrong: everyone has the right to speak their mind. Some people do it to convey a personal message, while others do it for the perceived good of the world. In no way was I inclined to broadcast any message of any kind to anyone. This, among other reasons, was why our relationship was doomed from the start. Lars's position in the union meant that he was obliged to attend numerous meetings and rallies. It soon became painfully clear to him that my lack of social interaction was cramping his style. Isn't style just another form of acting? I'm much more comfortable being myself, thank you very much. I am respectable Sally

Respectable is just another word for *dull*.

My relationship with Lars only lasted a few weeks. Nothing physical happened during our time together. It was purely platonic. Or almost. Only once did I allow him to kiss me on the cheek and explore the underneath of my blouse. I stopped him at that—the electric spark of near discovery. For some reason, I just couldn't cross the line into physical intimacy. I find the whole contact thing between a man and a woman unedifying. It's anathema to me.

You may be wondering if I'm gay. Well, I can tell you resoundingly that I'm not.

As you may have guessed, I'm still a virgin; but there's a good reason for that, which I'll explain later.

Mummy told me not to worry when Lars broke it off. 'Love only lasts forever in the movies, dear,' she told me. I found that comment to be a rather strange one. Movies only go for about two hours.

Most mornings, the pile of folders on my work desk is higher than it was the previous evening. It's as though an elf or a pixie comes in during the night and leaves them there. But I know that can't be true because I don't believe in fairytales, although it can be a fine line between the magic of imagination and the numbness of reality.

I'm a firm believer in routine because predictability is safe. I'm a paragon of efficiency in everything I do.

I am unvaried.

I take an hour for lunch at exactly the same time every day. That's the beauty of my job; the only thing I have to answer to is my computer. I don't usually talk to anyone either. Not even my boss. I detest office politics and all the idle chatter and interminable dross that go along with it—people telling each other the same story over and over, just changing details here and there. Pointless conversations about banal subjects: 'And then he says to me—I swear it, it's true. He turns around and says to me …' Endless drivel enunciated in an oddly excitable tone. They see it as a wonderful way to pass time. I see it as a stupendously mind-numbing waste.

I've learnt to avoid gossip and just zone out.

The employees I share my office space with—Rob, Casey and Wilma—are all capable of histrionics in their own way, which I have learnt to tolerate to some degree. They know to give me my space too. It's not personal with any of them. I don't really hate them. Except Rob.

I love routine. I always go to the same café for lunch: the Fancy Chef. I can't tell you if the chef lives up to the name bestowed upon him because I've never actually met him. The café is barely a block away from work, which is extremely convenient on days of inclement weather. It is a sort of a refuge for me, my 'safe place'. I can make believe that the people here care about me, but in reality, they are only nice to me because I am a paying customer.

I always sit at the same window table. It's sort of reserved for me nowadays, which I think is kind of special. I always order the same meal: a garden salad with a bottle of water. The only annoying thing about this arrangement is that the ingredients are not always the same. I love cherry tomatoes, radishes, and cucumbers. Sometimes they substitute these items with things that I'm not particularly fond of, like celery ribs, green onions, and chopped avocado. I don't totally despise eating these foods, but a little more consistency would be appreciated. I've often thought about mentioning this to the staff behind the counter but have never had the courage to do so.

In the end, today's offering was a trifle disappointing: no cherry tomatoes and not enough dressing. At least the bottled water was consistent.

As I mindlessly stabbed the last slice of soggy cucumber onto my plastic fork and thought about heading back to work, I took one last look through the window. It was a depressing scene, one that I thought was a clear representation of the discombobulated culture that has infiltrated all levels of our society. I watched mostly miserable-looking people in miserable-looking clothing scampering along the sidewalk. They looked languid and ambled along with metronomic gaits, as though they were robots. They are so monochrome, so lukewarm. So like me in many ways.

Some possessed vacant looks, pretending to be pondering extremely important world issues. The few well-to-do women who passed by were all busy adjusting tight-fitting designer clothing as they trotted quickly in high heels. Their nails were polished pink or red or even black, and their hair was always perfect. They swung expensive-looking handbags, and I wondered if their lives mirrored one of their newly purchased bags: glamorous on the outside but empty on the inside.

Most of these people were 'regulars' who passed by on most days. They occasionally looked in through the smeared glass. If they ever caught my eye, I was always quick to look away or pretend I was picking up some food on my fork. It seemed odd, even strange, that not one of these people had ever acknowledged me with a wave or even a raised eyebrow during our micro interludes. They must all be in a hurry to be somewhere else.

It's not as if I'm unattractive or anything, or so I think. I'm tallish for a female, slim, with an elegant figure. I have bright blue eyes, which I figure I probably inherited from the father I've never known because Mummy's eyes are a deep brown colour. My hair is naturally blonde and neatly styled down to my shoulders. I don't use a lot of makeup because I don't think I need to.

Today would prove to be different to the mundane travails of yesterday and the day before that. I was in such a strange mood and couldn't work out why. For the first time in the four and a bit years I've been coming here, I didn't leave the café at the time I always did. I dithered, breaking the tines on my plastic fork one at a time, starting at one end, and proceeding systematically to the other. This took me about five minutes. Even if I left now, I thought, I would be late for the resumption of my work duties by approximately five minutes and forty seconds. I find lateness so disrespectful. Being late is like saying that you consider your time to be much more valuable than someone else's. Wilma, Casey, and Rob are always late for work; but I've become acquainted with their tardiness, and it doesn't irk me as much as it used to.

Knowing that I would be late back today should have bothered me, but strangely enough, it didn't.

With the plastic fork successfully disassembled with surgical precision, I checked the time on my phone and decided that I definitely should start heading back to work now. Mike, my boss, may be worried as to my whereabouts although I know he won't ring me. He never has. Does he even have my number?

As I got up to leave, an elderly gentleman I'd never seen before and who appeared decidedly unkempt pressed his face against the glass and was staring directly at me. I instinctively deployed my default strategy of averting my gaze and speared my tineless fork into my empty plate, but the man remained steadfast, as still as a photograph. I became a little nervous and glanced up at him. In one hand, he held one of those white polystyrene cups, and I knew he wasn't just asking for a cup of coffee. Normally, a beggar was on every corner in these parts. Many worked the same 'beat', and a few passers-by even bothered to get to know them. Most, though, like me, always avoided them. Even so, I often wondered what life-changing event determined them a life of such destitution. I think about any loved ones they may have lost or left behind: a wife, a son, a daughter.

With all the courage I could muster, I forced myself to keep on staring into this man's eyes. They were sad and lonely eyes. I know the kind all too well. He had a toothless grin and hollowed cheeks. He was unshaven, and his greyish hair looked like it had been electrocuted. His hands appeared roughened by weather, and his fingernails were filled with grit. Ingrained dirt settled on his frown lines and was easily discernible against his pallid skin. He wore a shabby coat with a large hole at the front as though his heart had been ripped out of his chest.

Still, he kept staring. This man who did not know the soothing feeling of lying on a warm bed or sitting in a comfortable armchair or taking a long hot shower. The saddest thing was that no one seemed concerned whether he ate right or if he even ate at all. He had become human surplus, literally resigned for the scrap heap. He reminded me of an old dying tree.

I averted my gaze again, but the man was persistent. He didn't budge. I noticed that a small crowd had gathered to watch our little impromptu rendezvous. I'm not the most together person in the world, and it doesn't take much to make all my wheels fall off. Feeling immense embarrassment at this point, I did something quite out of character for me. I reached into my purse and pulled out a few coins before stepping outside and dropping them into the man's cup. The man grinned widely, extolled effusive praise upon me, and wished me a happy life. Was this how it worked, then, successful social interaction? It gave me an immediate rush as well as an uneasy feeling in the pit of my stomach. The whole episode felt awkward, making me momentarily dizzy. I was like an actor in a play or a fairytale, but then I reminded myself that I would never be a good actor and that I don't believe in fairytales.

The man bowed his head and began walking away ever so slowly. His shoulders moved like potatoes in a sack as he trudged across to the other side of the road, swaying from side to side like a pendulum. I stood and admired him, not because I felt sympathy for him but more because he was prepared to persist and was duly rewarded for his efforts. There's a lesson somewhere in that, I think.

I watched him approach a young mother pushing a pram. The mother stopped, and the man lowered his head into the pram to look at the infant while thrusting his cup under her chin.

Just at that moment, my phone rang. This startled me because my phone never rings. The only two people on my speed dial are Mummy and Mike. I've never had to ring Mike.

'Hello, is this Sally Cartwright?'

The female voice was totally unfamiliar as was the number.

I hesitated. I knew never to talk to strangers, but this would be different because I would be talking into an electronic device. Relatively safe. Still, I procrastinated.

'Hello?'

Just like the beggar, this woman appeared to be persistent. 'Is this Sally Cartwright?'

'Yes, this is Sally Cartwright,' I eventually enunciated through a croaky voice laced with anxiety.

'I'm calling from YouTube Australia. Congratulations, Sally. Your video post has had over 300,000 hits in the past week!'

I was distracted enough by the excessive joviality in this woman's voice to not fully comprehend what she had just told me. 'Excuse me?'

'You have qualified for a Creator Award.' The woman's tone was more measured this time. It was a soothing tone. Like honey and smoke.

I remained silent.

'The video you uploaded where the beggar gets blown up has gone viral, Sally. You're a big hit!'

I couldn't believe what I had just heard. I had to remain level-headed about this. Was I dreaming?

'Sally?'

I wasn't dreaming. 'I'm still here,' I said.

'Did you hear what I said, Sally?'

The world went still. I could barely breathe now. It wasn't just my hands that were shaking; it was my whole body: my shoulders, my middle, even my legs. I felt like I was going to collapse. Just for a second, I still let myself believe that this could not be happening. But I knew it was. Frantic with fear, I allowed my eyes to search for my beggar man. He had left the woman with the pram and was heading back this way. Then some innate survival mechanism kicked in. Yes, autistic people have survival mechanisms too. I dropped my phone and began running as fast as I could. Some might say my decision to flee the scene was a level-headed one. But *level-headed* is just another word for *cowardice*, in my opinion.

It wasn't until I reached my office building that I heard the ear-splitting explosion.

CHAPTER 2

I T WASN'T UNTIL I got to work the next day that I realised my phone was missing. Until very recently, I thought the only mechanical device that would serve any purpose in my life would be a smoke alarm. That was, of course, until I moved out of home and realised that I needed a convenient and reliable form of communication to keep in touch with Mummy, and so I belatedly purchased a mobile phone.

I rummaged through my bag one last time without success. Could I have left my phone on the bus? I doubt it because I never look at it while travelling. I'm not one of these Gen Ys, who need real-time information. Perhaps I left it at home. That was also an unlikely scenario. The only time I used my phone at home was to call Mummy, and that was always only on a Saturday.

'Well, well, she's alive!'

Rob's voice caught me off guard, and I cringed. Isn't *cringe* just another word for *embarrassment*? I sensed him standing quite close behind me. My suspicions were confirmed when I forced myself to turn around and noticed a hairy hand resting on the back of my chair.

'Did you end up seeing the doctor?'

The incongruous nature of the question forced me to stare briefly into his eyes, but the question I wished to ask back never made it out of my mouth.

He continued to hover like a moth over a bright light. I forced myself to maintain eye contact, but his unresponsive face saddened me. Rob is a few years older than me. He has aged a little too prematurely in the time that I've known him; his hair has thinned considerably in that time, and he has acquired the beginnings of a paunch. When I first started working here, he would often bring in a block of watermelon and a packet of corn chips for his lunch. He would squeeze crushed corn chips between two thick slices of the watermelon and nonchalantly sit at his desk devouring this gastronomic incongruity. The grotesqueness of this practice unfortunately mirrors the man.

I don't find him as unbearable as I once did, though. In fact, I almost admire him. I suspected he wanted us to be an 'item' when I first started here. He would occasionally invite me to join him at the movies. I don't patronise the cinema in any way, shape, or form, especially after I realised that Rob had a predilection for the more violent variety of the moving image. He hasn't asked me to see a movie for over a year now, so I think that penny has finally dropped.

Nobody around here likes him much, but no one really dislikes him either. I think his mannerisms are due more to ignorance than to any intent to be objectionable. He is a man incapable of being embarrassed, a man with no real conscience. He doesn't pretend to care about anyone other than himself, which I suppose at least makes him honest. This is the reason I find it rather strange that he should be enquiring about my well-being this morning.

The silence between us was eventually broken by the sound of shuffling feet. Wilma and Casey stood either side of Rob. I was feeling quite uneasy now. Electronic communication between us in the form of email was about to give way to verbal exchange, which I certainly wasn't expecting or ready for.

Wilma touched the top of her head with her hand and rubbed it. 'Does it still hurt?'

'What?' The word came out easily enough.

'That was quite a knock you got yesterday.'

I gently touched the top of my head, and it did hurt. There was a lump the size of a golf ball. 'What … what happened to me?'

Wilma and Casey looked at each other briefly before breaking out in childish laughter. Were they more amused by the fact that I wasn't following what they were saying or that I actually opened my mouth and strung some words together? They are quite immature for their age, those two. Rob gave them an incredulous look. I think he also finds them immature.

'Ladies, a little more respect for our colleague, please. She obviously can't recall what happened.'

I read somewhere that curiosity is the hunger of the human mind. What had 'happened' to me was obviously of grave-enough concern for my colleagues to care, these being the same people who had been conditioned to ignore me daily.

I was allowed to be curious too. 'What are you all talking about?' I asked.

Casey looked at Wilma and nodded. The two usually rub each other like sandpaper, which is one reason I can't stand their near-constant squabbling. But they were as one now, and I guessed from their nonverbal communication that the responsibility of conveying what had happened to me had been placed squarely on Wilma's shoulders.

'There was an explosion about a block away from here yesterday afternoon,' she began. 'When we all rushed out to see what was going on, we found you on the pavement near our doorstep.'

'Yeah, you fell and knocked yourself out,' Rob added dryly.

I must have had a disbelieving look on my face, and I shook my head ever so subtly. My colleagues were anticipating a response, but I remained as quiet as a lamb.

'Sally, don't you remember any of this?'

The tone in Casey's voice was one of genuine concern. Hearing it gave me an uplifting feeling and empowered me to enunciate more words. 'No. All I remember is waking up this morning and coming to work.'

'What about the doctor? Didn't you go?'

'What doctor?'

Wilma chimed in, 'We bought you inside once you came to, and Mike insisted you go to the doctor and get checked out.'

I tentatively touched the top of my head again and assessed the swelling in more detail. There were, in fact, two lumps, one smaller than the other. If I hadn't physically confirmed the existence of these lumps, I would have had genuine cause to consider this whole thing a practical joke, which really isn't the norm around here. Everyone knows I don't enjoy being either the instigator or the recipient of such puerile

MARIO BORAZIO

behaviour. It would have been much easier if they just ignored me as usual. 'I honestly can't recall anything,' I said and immediately blinked twice before blushing. The blush was initiated by the realisation that this was the longest conversation I had had with anyone outside of Mummy for as long as I can remember. It felt awkward but at the same time exhilarating.

Rob disappeared for about five seconds before returning with a newspaper in his hand. 'It's all in here, Sally.' He pushed the paper onto my desk. 'Read it.'

News of the explosion was front page. I began reading the main article, but the presence of my colleagues hovering over me like hungry birds made me feel awfully uncomfortable, and my mind wasn't registering any of the words. Rob sensed my hesitation and proceeded to fill me in on the details, a tinge of empathy evident in his expression. Perhaps I had been too hasty to judge him all this time.

'The bomb was found strapped to a homeless man. The cops reckon it was planted on him, or how else could a homeless man get a bomb? He can't even afford to feed himself for fuck's sake.'

I was used to hearing the odd profanity escape Rob's mouth, but the tragic circumstances of what he'd just told me made his choice of words less palatable on this occasion. As a general rule, I am against the use of profanities. It may be an acceptable source of mirth in certain social settings, or inside your own head, but I think that swearing is just a way of demonstrating an individual's poor grasp of the lexicon of his or her language. There are more suitable and cultured ways of expressing oneself.

I'm all for temperate language.

'That's awful,' I said spontaneously, which surprised me.

Casey shook her head. 'It is,' she said morosely as her eyes darted towards the newspaper. 'Lucky no one else died. It says in there that there was a kid in a pram close by.

'Apparently the bomb went off near that café you always go to. What's it called? The Handsome Chef?'

'The Fancy Chef.' My mouth was now on autopilot.

'You were lucky you weren't walking out of there at that exact moment,' Rob added.

I indeed was lucky if the timeframe conveyed to me by my colleagues was accurate. My brain stuttered for a moment as I tried to comprehend how things could have turned out so differently. What if this homeless man approached just as I'd left the café and detonated the bomb at that instant, right in front of me? I'd be dead. Would anyone miss me? Maybe Mummy would. Or maybe she wouldn't.

I shook my head, and my eye caught my bag on the floor near my feet. 'Has anyone seen my phone?'

My colleagues all appeared dumbstruck and looked at each other before staring at me in unison. 'Your phone? We didn't know you had one,' Casey said almost apologetically.

Their reaction wasn't so out of place. From what they know of me, which is not much at all, I believe they've never actually seen me with a mobile phone in my hand. 'Yes, I have a phone,' I said a little defiantly. Sometimes I wondered whether I really needed one, though. I could just as easily call Mummy on a payphone. But then how would she call me back? Wait. She never does.

Rob shook his head. 'It couldn't have fallen out of your bag. We would have spotted it on the pavement where we found you.'

That was a safe-enough assumption. I sat back and took in a deep breath, momentarily forgetting the presence of my colleagues.

'Sally!' The shout came from across the room. Mike Cosgrove, my boss, had seen the commotion around my desk and was making his way over. His gait was awkward due to his size. The medical fraternity would categorise him as beyond the clinical threshold of obesity, and he bulged in whatever he wore. But I hate it when my colleagues gossip behind his back. I refuse to put people down because of any medical condition they may have acquired. If they want to talk about what a great boss he is, I'm all ears. A boss can be professionally nice or professionally unpleasant. Mike was always the former.

I genuinely like Mike. I still remember the day I got this job. Six of us had applied for the one position. As we all sat in the waiting area in anticipation of our interviews, I'd already convinced myself that I wasn't going to be the successful applicant. Later, when Mike welcomed me into the company, he told me the reason I was successful: 'Out of the six applicants, Sally, you were the only one who wasn't fixated on your phone before your interview. It showed me that you were focused!'

Being a loner can have its advantages sometimes.

'I'm surprised you're even in today,' Mike continued. 'Didn't the doctor give you any time off?' His eyes were wide and shone the colour of crystal-blue water. A sincere smile flashed across his face from beneath wisps of thinning white hair.

I found myself fixing my gaze on him. 'Hello, Mr Cosgrove.' The words came out as awkwardly as I felt saying them. I could have closed my eyes and looked away again, as I'd always done around my boss in the past. Around anyone. Instead, I found strength inside me to maintain my gaze. It was a novel sensation. 'Ah, no, I think I …' my thin voice trailed off ineffectually, leaving a lingering air of confusion.

Wilma eventually broke the awkward silence. 'What Sally is trying to say is that she never made it to the doctor's surgery, or at least she can't remember going.'

The lines on Mike's face deepened, and he wore a puzzled expression, almost a grimace. 'You didn't go?'

This time, I closed my eyes and stared down at my knees. 'I don't remember. Anyway, I'm fine now.'

Mike screwed up his eyes as he examined the two rocks on my head. 'Wait here.' Without another word, he turned on his heels and tottered back towards his office. Rob, Casey, and Wilma proceeded to amble back to their workstations too. For the next few minutes, office machinations reverted to their normal political and sociological steady states.

Mike returned soon after holding a piece of paper. 'I've made you an appointment, Sally. There's a nice female doctor where I go, and I'm sure you'll get on well with her.' Before I even had the chance to breathe, he placed the appointment details on my desk and looked at his watch. 'It's in half an hour, so you'd better get moving.'

And with that, he was gone. He was a no-fuss kind of guy. I assumed that that was what made him a good businessman.

I stared at the piece of paper but didn't pick it up. In one way, I viewed Mike's actions as a personal affront. I have always taken great pride in managing my life alone—my unique modus operandi. I'm a self-contained biological unit. If I needed a haircut, I organised it. If anything needed fixing in my flat, I organised that too, although I would make myself scarce as soon as the tradesman arrived. And if I ever needed a doctor …

I've never needed one until now.

CHAPTER 3

I'M GOOD NOW. I can feel it right inside my bones that I've got what it takes to do this. The only other time I ever have reason to attend a prearranged appointment is when I visit the hairdresser, which is precisely every two months. I don't mind going to get my hair done nowadays although this wasn't always the case. I can still recall vividly the first time I visited a salon. I remember it being a vast establishment, which was way too bright, had way too many mirrors, and was high on scent and noise. I felt like a trapped animal and was about to make my escape before I was corralled onto a chair and had my hair pulled every which way by a young female who, without introducing herself, asked me, 'So what are we doing today?' *Cutting my hair, you moron!* That was the answer I wished to convey to her, but instead I remained silent and timidly pointed to a glossy picture on their wall, which depicted a glamorous young blonde sporting a more-than-acceptable hairstyle.

'Good choice!' she beamed in a falsetto voice.

I just nodded and left the girl to do her work in silence. Fast forward to the present day and my hairstyle, just like my lunch order, never changes.

The social interaction I engaged with my work colleagues this morning, although marked by brevity, had left me feeling upbeat and could well be the beginning of a whole new chapter in my life. I may look back on this one day and laugh; a knock to my head had proved the catalyst for my evolution into a new and exciting social stratum.

Those days lay ahead, but first, I had to deal with the here and now. I'm standing at the door of the doctor's surgery, procrastinating. If I don't go in, Mike will be angry with me; I don't want to let him down. Besides, his reasoning is very sound. I've had a nasty blow and need to get it checked out by a medical professional. What if there's a bleed on my brain? I don't feel unwell, don't even have a headache. But

I've watched enough medical reality shows on television to know that symptoms and signs don't always match up.

What's holding me back? Nothing, apart from the fact that I will most likely be asked to divulge personal and sensitive details about myself. I'll have to mention my autism, of course, as well as my hip accident when I was 13 years old, the result of which has left me with an ever-so-subtle limp whenever I walk. You could call it an accident. I think of it more as a cruel childhood souvenir but more on that later. Anyway, I don't get what my previous medical history has to do with my head knock. All I needed was to be reassured that my brain wasn't going to leach out of my head.

And that my memory loss wasn't going to be permanent.

The surgery was located on the ground floor of a tall modern building only a few blocks away from work. I approached the entrance cautiously and peered in through the glass doors. The waiting area appeared empty, which presented me with one less excuse to abort. I took a deep breath and pushed the door open, being immediately confronted by a wave of warm air. There was a distinct floral theme to the décor: large prints of brightly coloured flowers adorned every wall, and a few large potted palms lived in the corners. I recognised one as a fishtail palm and another as an areca palm. These are familiar to me because Mummy kept a lot of palms in the house when I was growing up, and I used to imagine them as my play friends because I wasn't allowed to have any real friends. The carpet was, you guessed it, floral. It looked like it belonged in some sort of grand palace.

'Ms Cartwright?'

The receptionist wore a friendly smile. She must have ESP because how else would she know my name? I nodded and looked at her briefly. What struck me most was her pale skin and red hair.

'Please fill out this questionnaire and bring it back here when you're done.'

I was handed a clipboard and a pen before being told to take a seat in the waiting area. Feeling relieved that no one else was occupying a seat, I sat down and began my 'exam'. It was like being back at school all over again. For a brief moment, my whole body shuddered. My memories of school are not pleasant ones. But more on that later.

The form wasn't as daunting as I expected. I had to provide details about my age, address, occupation, current medications (proudly none), and any surgeries I'd had. I felt a huge relief when I finished filling everything out, although I didn't mention anything about my hip surgery. There are some things I'd rather keep to myself, thank you very much.

'Sally?'

A thin young female wearing a white coat poked her head around a corridor that I hadn't even noticed was there. I had just handed my exam paper back to the receptionist when I found myself following the doctor into her room.

'Come through, Sally. Take a seat.'

The doctor's room appeared dingy and was poorly lit compared to the reception area. There were no windows. A solitary framed print of some abstract theme, which I found strangely offensive, hung on the wall behind her desk.

'Good morning. I'm Maria.' She smiled at me. 'It's a pleasure to meet you.' Pleasant enough, I thought, until she began staring at me with searchingly intense eyes. For a moment, I pictured her as a medium who was supposed to work out what was wrong with you without having access to any clues. I wouldn't mind that because it would mean that I didn't have to speak. But I don't believe in mediums.

I sat forward on my seat and slotted my hands under my bum cheeks to stop myself from fidgeting. I'm sure that to a trained professional my nervousness would be as obvious as the nose on my face no matter how much I tried to hide it.

Maria pressed some keys on her computer. 'OK, I think we'll get started.' She read some notes on the screen. What notes? I haven't been here before. Perhaps she really does have ESP. 'Your boss made the appointment for you. Is that right?'

I nodded. She looked at me and must've been wondering if she's examining a mute. 'Yes, that's right,' I said. My voice was surprisingly pleasant and strong.

'He's filled us in on some details already. He said that you had a fall yesterday and hit your head. Is that correct?'

It must be, but I still don't remember it. 'Yes, apparently, I did have a fall, but I can't recall it.'

Maria nodded and turned her attention back to her screen. 'He also said that there were witnesses who saw you running quickly in a state of panic just before a bomb went off close by.'

I wondered if she'd read this morning's newspaper. Of course, she would have. Doctors like to keep up with all the news, the same as ordinary folk.

What would I have been so panicked about? My mind immediately harked back to the conversation with my colleagues earlier this morning. Me being in a 'state of panic' was a part of the story I was not told about.

'Can you recall if you were scared, Sally?'

I honestly couldn't. 'No. It's as though nothing happened.'

Maria stood up and came around behind me. 'Except that something did happen,' she said before cradling my skull in her hands and gently palpating the two lumps. 'Any pain?'

I shook my head. She proceeded to massage around the lumps.

'What about there?'

'No.'

'Any headaches, vomiting, blurry vision, dizziness, ringing in the ears?'

No, no, no, no, and no. I answered all five of Maria's queries simultaneously with one economical shake of my head. She then proceeded to check my pupils and eye movements and did a quick hearing test by clapping her hands near each of my ears in turn. Then she got me to squeeze her hands tight and stand on one leg, both which I found to be rather strange requests. Then she did some tests of memory and concentration, which I easily passed. When she'd finished, she sat back down and began tapping the keys on her computer with fury. 'You've had a mild concussion with retrograde amnesia. I don't think it's necessary to order any tests.'

I was relieved. One medical appointment was about as much as I could handle. 'What about my memory of the incident? Will it come back?'

Maria shrugged. 'It should. Usually a bit at a time, like completing a jigsaw puzzle.'

I don't do jigsaws. Just give me the goddamned finished product I say. But at least Maria was giving me hope. The memories were buried for now, but they should eventually resurface. I wondered if there was something significant that I was forgetting, something that would allow me to make more sense of everything. It was all so frustrating.

Maria began fiddling with the pendant around her neck. It looked like it had been made by a child. I figured by her age that she wouldn't have children old enough with the requisite knowledge and motor skills to construct such an intricate piece of jewellery. It might be a gift from a niece or nephew. I never received any gifts, not even from Mummy.

'When was the last time you had a physical exam, Sally?'

The question caught me completely off guard. I unhooked my hands from underneath my bum and began fidgeting with my nails. Thoughts of any physical exam bring flashbacks of pushes and prods and insertions of things in orifices, which should not be interfered with under any circumstances. I had to think fast. 'A few weeks ago, I think.'

Maria pulled out a pen and notepad. 'What's your doctor's name?'

I felt a hot flush shoot from the top of my head all the way down my back. My pulse quickened. How did I end up in this situation? I had never lied before in my life. Mummy always told me that nothing good ever happens to liars. That was so hypocritical of her but more on that later. I rubbed my head and put on the best expression of puzzlement that I could muster. 'I'm sorry, did I say weeks? I think it's been years, actually.' I sighed and felt a pressure slowly lifting from my chest.

Maria raised a quizzical eyebrow and then smiled. 'Sally, you've had a concussion. Your memory may be foggy for a while. In time, I think you'll be thinking more clearly.' She opened another page on her computer. 'I'm going to measure your blood pressure now, and I'm also sending you for some blood tests so that we have everything up-to-date.'

Another appointment? My social life had just gotten a lot more hectic. Maria handed me a pathology form and swung her chair around so that she wasn't behind her desk anymore. Our chairs were facing each other with only air separating us now. I felt an urgent need to tuck in my hands again but restrained myself. Just as well because she grabbed at my left arm and had the blood pressure cuff around it before I could even blink.

'Blood pressure's normal,' she declared quite nonchalantly before removing the cuff. 'Tell me about yourself, Sally. Married? Do you have any kids?'

'Neither.' I answered but still couldn't look her in the eye. Would she think I was lying?

'Have you had any major health issues? I notice you have an uneven gait.'

How did she—of course, she's a trained professional. Now I was forced to reveal my little secret, a secret that only Mummy, Dr Rickards, and the nice people at the hospital know about. For over four years, I've even managed to hide it from my work colleagues. 'I had an accident when I was 13.'

'Oh?' Maria's tone was inquisitive. I hesitated, and she immediately sensed my unease about discussing the topic. 'I can assure you, Sally, that anything that you divulge in the confines of this room will be held in strict confidence. I'm a member of the Australian Medical Association and have to adhere to a strict code of conduct at all times.'

She was waiting for some kind of response, but none was forthcoming from my end. I merely nodded. She sunk lower into her chair. 'That's all right. You don't have to talk about it if you don't want to.'

Suddenly I felt that I *did* want to talk about it. Here was someone, a stranger, who had taken an interest in me, albeit only on a professional level; and I was refusing to divulge anything about myself to her. 'I …. I …' The words wouldn't come out. Maria sensed my continued frustration.

'Are you alright, Sally?'

'I'm also autistic.' This time, the words flowed out of my mouth as freely as a torrent of water raging through a flooding river.

'Excuse me?'

I didn't know if she hadn't heard me, so I repeated myself a little louder.

'I have autism. I was diagnosed when I was 3 years old.'

Maria knitted her brow. 'That's a long time ago. Have you been reassessed since that diagnosis?'

I shook my head. 'I'm only on the mild end,' I declared.

She picked up my exam paper. 'It says here that you're a data analyst. How long have you been working for, Sally?'

'Just over four years.' I wasn't willing to divulge the exact time to the hour; she might think I'm a real nut case.

'Same place?'

I nodded and looked down at the faded floral carpet. 'It's the only job I've ever had.'

'I see.' Maria's voice was becoming a little more animated, making me feel more uncomfortable. 'And did you attend university?'

I nodded again. Maria swung her chair around and typed something else before turning back to face me. 'Sally, I want to send you to a psychiatrist who specialises in behavioural disorders. I think you will find it worthwhile.'

A psychiatrist? Isn't that someone who crazy people are sent to see? I'm definitely not crazy. Suddenly I felt empowered to convey this assertion to Maria. 'But, Doctor, I'm not some crazy woman. You can see that, right?'

She sat back and sighed heavily before bombarding me with a volley of short but confronting questions:

'Do you live alone?'

'Do you have trouble sleeping?'

'Are you in a personal relationship?'

'Do you have many friends?'

'How is your relationship with your family?'

'How is your relationship with your co-workers?'

I thought I'd escaped having to expose this personal information. I slumped back into my seat, panting like a prize fighter who had just been floored by a knockout blow. Maria had taken me by surprise with her astoundingly accurate appraisal of my life. I feared she already knew the answers to her own questions.

I hate doctors' ESP.

My silence did nothing but confirm what Maria had suspected—that I was a miserable loner. I stared at the door, willing it to open up and suck me out of the room.

'Sally, autism has a specific range of behaviours, and I think you should—' She saw my expression and stopped in her tracks. She knew that I understood what she was implying. I felt a chill in my blood, the coldness bringing my brain to a momentary standstill. My legs began to tremble. I cleared my throat to say something, but nothing came out. I'm new to this conversation caper and still trying to get the hang of it. Suddenly everything fell quiet. I heard voices coming from the reception area, people laughing. I imagined them laughing at me.

'Sally?'

I thought back to Mummy's house. A memory kept recurring. A memory of being inflicted with the greatest pain imaginable followed by a bloodcurdling scream loud enough to peel paint off walls.

CHAPTER 4

D R MARIA'S WORDS filled me with conflicting emotions. In one sense, I should feel rage and bitterness enough to make me want to explode. In another sense, I should feel elation because there is a distinct possibility that I may not be autistic. Imagine that. I couldn't until now. I tried not to think about it too much. All will be revealed once I see my psychiatrist. I hate that word *my*. Nobody has the right to own anybody else. Anyway, he's not my psychiatrist yet because I haven't even met him. Or will it be a she?

Dr Maria signed me off work for a week. She said that my concussion had affected my thought processes and ability to concentrate, which would impact on my ability to carry out my work duties in a proficient manner. I think she's right. I didn't sleep well last night, and not recalling the whereabouts of my phone was probably a stark reminder that it's best I take it easy for a while.

I live in a ground level one-bedroom flat in the inner Melbourne suburb of Collingwood. It will never make the cover of any lifestyle magazine, but I work hard to maintain it presentably, even though I never have any visitors. It has a double bed, a tatty patterned carpet, and a small Formica table. The estate agent who first showed it to me described the apartment block as being on the 'good side' of the tram tracks. I've never quite grasped this concept: doesn't it depend on which direction you're coming from?

I am not far from the famous Smith and Brunswick Streets district with its hipster pavement cafés, its graffiti-daubed walls, and all the shops run by people who speak with foreign accents. There is a constant air of dereliction here, but the hipsters still insist on calling it 'trendy'. As you may have guessed, I have never embraced this view or its culture; I could never tolerate the fakeness of it all.

The people who do embrace it may think they are fashionable

and up-to-date, but in reality, they are just ephemeral and superficial beings lured by faddish appeal. It is my opinion that these individuals go against the very fabric of authenticity. That being said, I like where I live. Almost everything is within walking distance, and it's fairly safe; no one feels they have to pull a trigger for accolades. My neighbours tend to leave me alone too, which is nice.

That being said, the sense of alienation I felt when I first moved here has not waned one bit over time. That's just me; it has nothing to do with where I live.

I pondered what a week of idleness would look like for me. In all my working life, I have not once had reason to call in sick. Like I said, I don't do doctors. I have a solid constitution, physically at least.

What will I do with my week? As far as I can deduce, I have a few options. I could spring clean my flat; heaven knows it's in dire need of it. The carpets haven't been steamed since I moved in, and some walls have succumbed to a malady of mould and damp.

I could call Mummy, but it's not Saturday. I always only called Mummy on a Saturday because she's too busy to talk during the week. To say that her social life sits a rung or two above mine would be the understatement of the year.

I always hoped the day might come when I could think about Mummy and feel gentle warmth. I'm not asking for harp music or a cosy fire. I just want to be accepted for who I am. I keep hoping for a normal mother-daughter relationship, for ordinary times like a nice lunch together on Mothers' Day or a night out at the theatre. Sadly, these activities will probably forever remain distant dreams.

Since I moved out, she has collected an impressively inventive and colourful panoply of insults which she steadily keeps hurling towards me.

Whenever I think of Mummy now, all I see is her hand dangling over the arm of her favourite chair, an ugly Linnea recliner she bought at a fire sale, her fingernails painted bright red, her cigarette trailing grey-blue smoke, and her bottomless wine glass poised near her pouty lips.

I can just imagine she'd be doing something similar right now, sitting in a swank pub or in a club smoking a cigarette and drinking gin in an aristocratic sort of way while her carefully sourced audience watched on and admired. Mummy craves affection. She just doesn't know how to return serve. I think this anomalous imbalance in her behaviour has to do with the fact that she is a heavy drinker—has been since I can remember. 'There's nothing demure in doing that, Mummy,' I would say as I watched her going about her business with a wine glass permanently attached to her hand. She would always shake her head and throw me a scornful look. 'Demure? You wouldn't know the meaning of the word!' she'd proclaim.

The first thing I did when I got home was to search for my phone. My flat is small; and I estimated that it would take approximately twelve minutes to sift, probe, scour and comb through every nook, and cranny in the place. I was done in seven, proud with my level of efficiency but at the same time disappointed that the item in question had not been recovered.

My fruitless search had forced me to reprioritise my tasks for the day. Buying a new phone had now become an exigent function. My last one was bought online. This method of purchase has its advantages as well as its disadvantages. Lack of social interaction was an obvious tick. Not having an opportunity to ask a professional for advice on the device best suited for my purposes was a big cross.

Knowing that there was a possibility that I may not be autistic had given me just enough confidence to choose the latter purchasing option this time around. I was going to wing it, and the thought of that filled me with a small level of exaltation.

The shopping mall was quiet, which I was mighty relieved about. I headed straight to the technology section of a big department store. I considered this a safer option than visiting one of the many free-standing mobile phone kiosks scattered around the mall.

A tall young man with an oversized wrinkled white shirt and a loosely hung black tie worn with the top shirt button undone was staring at a laptop while fiddling with a phone, presumably his own. A name tag indicated that he was more than likely a member of staff.

I approached him from behind and decided to give him the courtesy of completing his current task before gaining his attention. Besides, it would buy me some time to work out how I wished to phrase my opening question to him.

Before I could even begin to formulate anything in my head, he swung around and we were face-to-face.

'May I help you with anything today?'

The young man portrayed a confident deportment, but that wasn't the first thing I noticed as I stared at him in silence. He had almost-translucent skin, which made his acne stand out like strawberries atop a bowl of whipped cream. I wondered if he was as self-conscious about this as I would be. I kept staring for a few more seconds while trying to enunciate some words. He returned my stare with eyes that suggested he needed more of a connection with me.

'Are you after a phone?'

'Yes, I am, Thomas,' I eventually said as I squinted at his name tag.

The mention of his name saw him take half a step back for some reason. Had I overstepped the mark? Judging by his reaction, I think I had. We don't even know each other for goodness' sake. I was about to apologise for my misplaced amicability, but he beat me to the punch.

'A smartphone?'

I certainly didn't want an unintelligent one. 'I think so,' I said.

'Do you prefer iPhone or Android operating systems?'

I had no idea what he was talking about. May I inform you, Thomas, that my life so far has been lived exclusively underneath every microchip known to mankind. That's what I should have told him.

'I haven't purchased a phone before. I'm new to this.' The look he gave me was one that screamed he couldn't believe that any twenty-something-year-old human being still breathing anywhere on this planet could possibly function in any conceivable capacity without a personal phone.

Thomas nodded before pulling at the collar of his shirt. 'What will you be using it for?' he asked without making eye contact. *Are you kidding me? It's a phone!*

'I need to call my mother and maybe my boss sometimes.' And

there it was. I had involuntarily divulged to this stranger the entire list of my social contacts.

'I see,' he intoned slightly apathetically. 'What about memory?'

I nodded timidly. My memory's not the best at the moment due to my head knock. I wouldn't be here if it was in normal operating mode but thanks for asking. That's what I felt like saying but thought it best not to embarrass myself any more than was absolutely necessary. I just nodded timidly and sensed Thomas's impatience growing with my shallow responses.

'What about the camera? Do you want a dedicated camera button?'

'What type of headphone connection do you prefer?'

'Do you require a Bluetooth modem?'

'Wideband adaptive multi-rate?'

'Near-field capability … expanded memory …'

He paused for a moment before continuing. 'Would you like me to explain the relative merits of these features as they pertain to iPhones compared to Android devices?'

I felt like cornered prey about to be devoured by a voracious predator. Now it was my turn to step back. 'I don't think that will be necessary, Thomas. I'm sorry, I just need a basic phone for making calls.'

'And texting.'

Thomas probably assumed that he was finishing my sentence, but I hadn't even considered the texting option. I had never texted anyone before. You may think that, given my reluctance to interact verbally, sending a written message would have been right up my alley. The sad truth was that, other than sending the odd email at work, I preferred not to interact at all.

After thanking Thomas for his help, I paid for my new phone with my debit card. I don't own a credit card. Credit card spending can lead to spiralling debt. Debt is like quicksand: it's easy to get into but hard to get out of. Call me old-fashioned, but if I don't have the money to pay for something upfront, I won't buy it.

I left the department store slightly unbelieving at the amount of money I parted with. I was corralled into signing up for features I knew I would never use, let alone understand.

Back home on my couch, I took out my new phone from its carry bag and leafed through the setup manual. The length of the manual made me a little apprehensive until I realised that the same instructions were written in six different languages. I then examined the phone itself. Its sleek design made my old one look like it belonged in another epoch in history. Setting it up was more straightforward than I'd imagined it to be. I was done in ten minutes.

My first task was to inform all of my contacts that I have a new number. Lucky I kept Mummy's and Mike's numbers written down in case of an emergency which is definitely what my current situation was.

As I was staring at the shiny keys of my brand-new phone, it suddenly dawned on me that calling them may be a futile exercise. Mike may be too busy to answer, and I can understand that. Our relationship is purely a professional one, and this would be more of a social call. Mummy's situation is on a whole different level, though. I have grown tired of her excuses: 'I'm too busy!' or 'I'm swamped!' as well as 'I'm running in a hundred directions!' These cop-outs just don't cut it with me anymore. Am I, her only daughter, not important enough? It's all about manners. If the situation were reversed and Mummy was doing most of the calling, I'm sure I would feel compelled to pick up the phone every once in a while. Or at least I'd think about it.

In the end, I realised that my hesitancy was just a flash of emotion to cover for my weaknesses.

No, calling them would be the most appropriate course of action.

But today isn't Mummy day, and as I've already mentioned, Mike is probably too busy.

I know. I'll send them a text!

Hi Mummy, this is Sally Cartwright
speaking. My new phone number is
0444 280281

I sent Mike the same message.
The power of texting! Succinct, to the point, and without the need

to talk. I sat back feeling emotionally charged and wondered why I hadn't used this mode of communication before.

I was enjoying basking in my monumental achievement until I suddenly felt a level of worn-out-ness. It was like a leech had crawled inside me and sucked out all my ability to think and to keep my eyes open. My head lolled from side to side as I fought back sleep. Dr Maria informed me that drowsiness might rear its head at some point as a result of my concussion.

I dragged myself off to bed. Soon the only two things I was aware of were the soft mattress underneath and the smooth sheets around me. My eyelids finally surrendered.

I had a nightmare.

I am confronted in the street by a homeless man with bare feet. In his left hand, he brandishes a large knife, and he stares at me with heavy lidded eyes and an evil smile. In a blind panic, I begin running as fast as I can. But no matter which path I take, I always end up seeing the homeless man in front of me. His face grows angrier until he finally pleads with me to help him. Strangely, I don't feel the urge to run away anymore. I touch his arm, which feels as cold as ice. It is then that he lunges forward with the knife. The last thing I remember is feeling an obliterating pain.

CHAPTER 5

THE UNPLEASANTNESS OF the dream woke me, and I noticed I was perspiring. My brain felt like it had been shot at, and I had a mild headache. My heart was beating fast, and there was a buzzing in my ears—panic with jump leads. How long had I slept? Sunlight streamed in through the curtains. I guessed it to be late afternoon.

I went to the kitchen for a glass of water and pondered what the last twenty-four hours had looked like for me: a homeless man was blown up, and the explosion apparently caused me to hit my head resulting in a concussion that has made my mind hazy. More than that, I have no recollection of the event whatsoever. I conversed with my work colleagues, visited a doctor who told me to rest up, bought a new phone, and had a disagreeable dream. That was it in a nutshell. It left me with a feeling of detachment in a way as if I were a figment of my own imagination. Except that everything I experienced had indeed been real.

What does all this mean? Am I just expected to carry on with my life as if yesterday never happened? I desperately wanted to recall the events that transpired before the explosion and why I was apparently so panicked. Dr Maria said it might all come together slowly one piece at a time like a jigsaw puzzle. Now I regret never doing one of those.

I took a shower and immediately felt better. I don't do baths. The water gets cold and dirty quickly. Some people swear by them. I've even heard someone compare a hot soothing bath to being baptised in the holy waters of the Jordan, but I think that's taking it a little too far, especially given that I don't have a religious bone in my body.

No, give me a shower any day. There are few things in life more relaxing than standing under a hot shower. According to research, it can wake you up and boost your creativity. I wasn't feeling exactly creative, but I definitely felt more relaxed as soon as the first drops touched the top of my head. It was like being draped by a soothing cloud. Even my headache disappeared.

After my shower, I decided to watch some television because I couldn't think of anything else to do. Television is not my favourite pastime because almost all the content is just plain garbage: sex, drug use, infidelity, race, religion, eating disorders, profane language, and a smattering of anything else you can imagine offensive or illegal. And don't even get me started on reality shows, which are so far from real life that it's not even a point of contention. When exactly was it that television decided to scrap the idea of programmes that truly entertain and make you think for yourself?

I channel surfed and passed at least a dozen stations until I found something palatable. It was a wildlife documentary by David Attenborough, which followed the true stories of five of the world's most celebrated yet endangered species. Each was fighting for survival against predators and the forces of nature in their particular environments. I could definitely relate to that.

At the conclusion of the documentary, I was feeling a little flat and pondering dinner when suddenly my new phone pinged and made me jump. I stared at the illuminated screen. I just received my first-ever text reply!

Thanks for your number, Sally. Hope u r resting up.
Regards, Mike.

I was inspirited by Mike's clear and concise message and wondered whether a counter reply was in order. Should I respond to let him know that I received his message? I thought about this for a while. If every person sending or receiving a text message were to adhere to this practice, then messages would be sent ad infinitum. I put my phone back down on the coffee table.

It began to irk me that Mummy hadn't replied yet. Then again, she wasn't obliged to. Mummy's not like Mike. I'd say she was just as self-centred as Rob. It would make sense if those two were related. The thought of that being even a remote possibility made my stomach hurt, but then I remembered I'd skipped lunch and was famished.

Mummy never taught me how to cook. The limited culinary skills I possess were all gleaned from recipes in newspapers and magazines as well as from watching the odd cooking show on television.

When I first moved out on my own, I cooked small meals on the fly but soon realised that this was not the most practical or economical way to operate. These days I cook for a crowd. That is to say I make a big batch of something and then package it into single servings for the freezer. Whether it's vegetable beef and barley soup, pesto penne, bean and rice bowls or chicken fajita burritos, they're all favourites of mine.

The trick with solo eating is to ensure that the portions you are making are consistent in their effective satiety. Using the right container can make or break the meal too. One has to ascertain how filling a meal is before deciding on the size of the container it is destined to occupy. As a general rule, anything involving meat will require a smaller container than a purely vegetarian meal. It's not rocket science.

I ensure that my food storage containers are all clean and in good condition. I'm always checking that the lids are tight-fitting and free of any holes or cracks to minimise potential staleness or contamination.

I never eat out and hardly ever order takeaway. I pride myself on eating healthily and maintaining my figure even though I'm not really out to impress anybody. I guess I'm lucky that I never put on weight no matter how much I eat. I feel sorry for all these young girls, and some boys also, who feel constantly pressured by a society that asks human beings to try to reshape their bodies to conform to unrealistic and largely unattainable standards. Body shaming is surely one of the greatest modern scourges on our society.

I don't exercise. The thought of joining the gym or some exercise class has never crossed my mind.

Given that I'd skipped my usual garden salad lunch today, I settled for a dinner of vegetable beef and barley soup. As I systematically and slowly ingested the vegetable pieces in order of descending size, I pondered whether the staff at the Fancy Chef would have realised I wasn't in today. I'm sure they're not really missing my six dollars and seventy-five cents. But did they really miss *me*, Sally Cartwright?

As I was finishing up my meal and pondering another night of bromidic television, my doorbell rang.

I wasn't expecting anyone.

CHAPTER 6

I DROPPED A SPOONFUL of soup on my bathrobe at the sound of the door chime. There was a feeling in my gut that said, "No, you mustn't answer it," but another in my head that said, "Yes, if you want to usher in the new Sally Cartwright, you must do what normal people do and answer it." I should choose to be brave instead of being a puppet of fear. My recently acquired social interaction skills, albeit exiguous and rudimentary, would surely stand me in good stead.

I adjusted my robe to ensure that I was appropriately covered before standing at the door as still and as silent as death itself. In the past, my breath would have got caught in my chest, and stratospheric levels of fear would have gained on me faster than a cheetah hunting down a lion cub. All sorts of bad thoughts would have raced through my mind: what if it's a thief? Or a murderer. A rapist even. I tried to block out my pessimism and drew a deep breath. I think I'm going to be brave, just as I was in the department store today.

'Yes?'

The man standing before me was about my height, young, early thirties I'd say, with short curly hair, a fair complexion, and blond facial stubble. His eyes were a piercing deep-blue colour, which stared into mine briefly before shifting their gaze down to my midriff.

The soup stain!

'Hello, are you Sally Cartwright?' His voice was controlled and pleasant.

The whole world seemed to know my name today. 'Yes, I am,' I answered in a soft voice.

'I'm Declan.' He thrust out his right hand for me to shake. My reaction was a lamentable snub of modern human comportment. I moved back a couple of steps, and the puzzled look on Declan's face was plain to see. 'I'm sorry to disturb you.' His demeanour portrayed no hostility. 'I believe this belongs to a friend or relative of yours.' He held a mobile phone in his left hand. I immediately recognised it as the one I'd lost.

'That's my phone!'

'Yours?' His voice developed a disbelieving hoarseness.

'Yes, it is.' There was an awkward silence, which seemed to go on forever. I knew the ball was in my court. The easy thing would have been to take my phone, politely thank this kind man, close the door, and go back to my regular evening of watching banal talk shows. Conversely, this was the perfect opportunity for me to take a big leap out of my comfort zone. Why not give it a try?

I ushered him in and offered him a seat on the couch. I cleared my soup bowl and sat opposite. 'I suppose I need to thank you. Where did you find it?'

Declan cleared his throat. 'In the city. It was in a gutter.'

I surmised that I must have dropped it on the way to the bus stop. I took the phone and inspected it for damage. It seemed to still be in working order and didn't appear marked in any way. As I placed it on the coffee table and wondered how I was going to continue this conversation, Declan emitted a spontaneous laugh.

I was embarrassed but didn't know why. I hadn't said or done anything funny, but then again I was still new to the machinations of human emotion and interaction. 'Is anything the matter?' I asked feebly.

Declan wrinkled his nose and shook his head. 'You've got another phone?' I followed his eyes onto the coffee table, and my face immediately flushed a crimson colour.

'Sorry,' he mumbled. 'I didn't mean to pry.'

A brief smile stretched across my face. I don't believe anyone has ever said sorry to me for anything before. I felt compelled to explain myself and drew a deep breath. 'I bought a new one today.'

Declan nodded. 'Can't do without one for even one second, right?'

I was tempted to inform this man that I am not a member of the modern generation whose phones have become a part of their anatomy, always keen to share everything with the world, from what they had for breakfast to the very important issue of their last bowel movement. I don't understand how people can continue to interact on social platforms when they invariably get bad stuff said about them.

'I thought I'd never see my old phone again, so I decided to purchase a new one,' I eventually said.

'That sounds logical.' Declan proceeded to crane his neck around the room. 'Do you live alone?'

The question caught me by complete surprise. I simply nodded and pretended to look calm. I realised that I needed to change the topic before he asked any more personal or sensitive questions. Think, Sally, think! It came to me like a lightning flash. 'How did you know where I lived?'

'Easy. May I?' Declan scooped up my old phone and pushed a few buttons. 'I looked up the ICE contact.'

In case of emergency. Yes, I remember that. I'd thought about putting Mummy's number in there but knew she'd think it a great burden if she was ever called upon to save her only child's life one day. That only left Mike. I didn't want to bother him; he has his own family to worry about.

Declan's laugh returned. This time, I was pretty sure what he found so humorous. He turned the screen around to show me. There was a name followed by an address.

I'd put myself down as the ICE contact.

'It would be pretty hard to call yourself if you were dying,' he mused.

I couldn't disagree, but once Mummy and Mike were eliminated as viable candidates, my options were very much limited. Once again, I didn't wish to share that fact with Declan. 'I didn't want to trouble anyone,' I said.

'You must be a caring person, Sally.'

I was taken aback by the sound of my name. Had Declan overstepped the mark just like I had with Thomas earlier today? Not really. He already knew my name.

'Yes, I think I am caring, Declan.' I gave him a very small smile, and he returned serve with a probing stare that made my heart skip and also made me feel uncomfortable.

MARIO BORAZIO

'It seems strange, though. Your contact list only has two numbers. I would have thought such a caring person would have a multitude of friends.'

You thought wrong, mister. And what the hell are you doing going through my contacts? That's what I wanted to say. That's what I should have said. But I didn't. I remained silent and sensed from his expression that Declan was aware that he had overstepped the mark.

He shook his head and slapped his thigh. 'Hey, there I go again. I didn't mean to stick my nose in. I only opened them up to try to get more information and return the phone to its rightful owner.'

I appreciated the effort and shouldn't really be bitter towards him. 'I forgive you,' I said and then added, 'Anything else you looked at?'

'Only one other thing.'

Huh? There *was* nothing else. I don't even know why I asked the question. 'Oh?' I was trying hard not to overplay things.

'That video's a scream. I don't know how you got it, but it's so unique.'

A video? Of what? Myself maybe? I've never taken one. Never even used the camera. I hate selfies. I hate people who take them too. It's the height of excessive hubris as far as I'm concerned.

I instinctively folded my arms and averted my gaze. My heart started thumping, and I could feel myself hyperventilating. Declan leaned forward, and I sensed his eyes burning holes in me.

'Are you alright, Sally? Was it something I said?'

No, I'm obviously not alright, and yes, it was something you said. I took a few deep breaths, which calmed me a little, but I still felt as though all the storms in the world had conjured to come together and dump on me in one final world-ending calamity. Social interaction can suck sometimes.

Declan stood up. 'I think I'll be going now.'

Good idea. I took another deep breath and showed him to the door.

'By the way, is Mike your boyfriend?'

What an odd question. 'No ... no, he's my boss.'

'Oh, I see. I'll see you around then!'

I very much doubt it, I thought, as I thanked him and closed the door. I slouched down on the couch and waited for my heart to resume its normal rhythm before pondering what just happened: I got my phone back but realised that there was more to this social interaction caper than I thought. Whoever said that we were born to need social bands and a sense of others was a very good liar.

Declan was the third person today who'd discovered the unedifying world of Sally Cartwright. From now on, Sally Cartwright will be her singular entombed entity. I think I'll stay home tomorrow. Spring cleaning never seemed so appealing.

My phone pinged again. Except this time it was my old phone:

Hi Sally, I hope you're OK. How about meeting up for coffee tomorrow?
Regards, Declan.

I dropped the phone onto the floor before the text message could fully penetrate my brain. This can't be right. A man I don't know and whom I had barely spent five minutes with was asking me out. I think they call it a date. Or was it really just coffee? I'd be naïve to think that in this context caffeine was the sole tangible that would connect us if I were to accept Declan's offer.

And he'd felt it appropriate to put my number into *his* phone!

I stared down at my old phone, not sure what to think. It doesn't seem even remotely conceivable that anyone could have feelings for me. Especially not this man who I'd discourteously thrown out of my flat just a few minutes ago.

If I don't reply, he'll think I'm a total jerk.

CHAPTER 7

I STARED AT DECLAN'S message for what seemed like hours. I was tired but found it difficult to sleep. My thoughts seemed to float by in slow motion. As the sun prepared to raise its head, my brain begged for unconsciousness just at a time when I needed it to be at its most lucid. It's not as though I was afraid to text. I'd already used this mode of communication with Mummy and Mike. It's that I didn't know what to write. Not replying wasn't an option either. If the roles were reversed, I think I'd be pretty annoyed if a response wasn't forthcoming.

I contemplated that the decision whether to see Declan again would be a monumental one in my life so far, even though there is something liberating about being alone. Once you realise that there is no one else in your life, you can concentrate all your resources on looking after yourself. That said, I do sometimes wonder what it would be like to have another person to lean on you in times of need, someone who cared and looked out for you.

Mummy has never been that person for me.

I closed my eyes. Time must have passed, but it didn't feel like it had. I think I eventually slept for about two hours. Thankfully, there were no nightmares. I got up and felt as flat as a dead battery. The exertions of last evening seemed to drain all life out of me. I decided right then and there to postpone my spring cleaning.

The phone lay on my bed, but the battery was flat. I would have to wait until it was charged up again before responding to Declan's message. I'm usually not a procrastinator. I view procrastination as opportunity's assassin. There is nothing as fatiguing and irritable as the eternal hanging on of an uncompleted task.

I breakfasted on raisin toast with honey as I do each and every morning. I realised I was hungry because I only had a few mouthfuls of soup for dinner. The remainder had been incorporated into the fabric of my dressing gown.

While my old phone was charging, I got on with some basic household chores, thinking ahead to the moment when I had to sit down and compose my response to Declan. Just as I was loading my bathrobe into the washing machine, my phone pinged again. Which one? I was getting the sense that having two phones would not be an easy task to manage.

It was my new phone. Mike:

> Hi Sally, just checking that u r still OK and to tell you to keep resting.
> Rob and Casey have taken up your workload.
> Regards, Mike.

The message filled me with a sense of uneasiness. On the one hand, Mike was showing concern. On the other, he was hinting that I was potentially expendable. Will there still be a job waiting for me in six days? Do they even want me back? Mike knows that my productivity is far greater than anyone else's. Surely, that fact alone should sway things in my favour.

Now I had two new problems: Declan and Mike. Life surely wasn't meant to be this complicated.

I decided to text Mike back right away and knew I had to play it cagey:

> Dear Mike, I'm doing fine and glad that all is well at work.
> I will be back soon.
> Yours truly, Sally Cartwright.

I don't believe this message in any way portrays my anxiousness regarding the security of my employment.

I sat down and stole a furtive glance at the phone being charged. The indicator light was green. It was time. I yanked the phone out of the charger, took a deep breath, and stared at the screen. Would it be considered too early to text someone at ten o'clock in the morning? Probably not. From what I'm led to believe, the mobile phone texting world is an all-hours operation.

Trying to block out the rump-rump sound of the washing machine, I thought about how to begin my message and what would or wouldn't be appropriate to include. The conundrums of the modern heterosexual dating scene. (Yes, I'd convinced myself that this really was going to be a date.) Also, how much enthusiasm should I express? I'll only get one chance at this, and it had to look good.

No pressure, right?

My fingers hovered over the screen. This was the moment. Something so simple yet my heart was racing as fast as a scared kitten's:

Dear Declan, this is Sally Cartwright, the girl who lost her phone.
Yes, coffee would be nice.
Regards, Sally Cartwright.

I gasped as I pushed the send button. Had I said enough? Or too little? With a shaking hand, I put the phone down; but no sooner had I done that than it pinged again. My neck instantly craned around towards the screen like some Pavlovian response:

Hey, that's great! What time?'

I deduced two things from this reply: Declan hadn't changed his mind about our date, and he was an extremely fast typist. I too am a fast typist and pride myself on it; but typing reports for Mike, sometimes many pages long, seemed a far easier task than the one I was confronted with here and now. Immediately my heartbeat increased again as I sent my reply:

Two o'clock is good.

I didn't include my name this time.
Him straight back:

Sounds good. How about the Bowl and Spoon on Smith Street?

Me straight back:

OK. See you there.

Even though I've lived in the same place for over four years, I have never heard of the Bowl and Spoon establishment. I often strolled down Smith Street but always with my head down. Now I chastised myself for not paying more attention and familiarising myself with the businesses of the area.

I know. I'll look it up on the internet! Thomas was kind enough to include this feature with my exorbitantly priced phone plan. I'd never had cause to use the internet for personal reasons before. It has always been taboo to me. I imagined it taking me to the darkest and deepest corners of the underworld, sucking me into places I wished never to visit and being forced to communicate with mainly nefarious types. That thought scared me. It's the main reason why I don't own a computer.

No. As far as I was concerned, the internet was a life of extremes, not at all representative of what life really was meant to be like.

I can now see that there may be exceptions to this edict.

I typed in Bowl and Spoon café, and my screen immediately filled with information pertaining to the establishment in question. The internet was indeed a beautiful and wondrous place of magic! There was an invitation to visit a website as well as images and a 'blog post', whatever that was. There was also an expandable map, which showed me that the establishment was within walking distance and would be relatively easy to locate.

I sat back, filled with a decent amount of pride as I reflected on what I'd achieved this morning and what it all meant. There was a light in my heart that, though really only a flicker, was missing yesterday. Perhaps it's a sign of hope, optimism, and anticipation of good things to come. It's a feeling as foreign as it is welcome.

My next task was to work out my look for the date. As a strict rule,

I don't use much makeup. I believe that, for some women, makeup is just armour for hiding away imperfections both on a physical and an emotional level. I'm not too keen on wearing jewellery either. Or 'bling', as it's referred to these days. I don't get the concept of jewellery. Personal ornaments such as rings, necklaces, or bracelets should never be a symbol of who you are as a person. Mummy never bought me jewellery. That's one of the few things I'm grateful to her for. It's probably the only thing.

The disdain I have for jewellery also applies to clothing. Eccentric or outrageous outfits, which can sometimes even go against the grain with regard to gender expectation, aren't my thing. Or the sight of lurid costumes that make people look like clothes horses. No thank you.

As it was going to be a mild sunny spring day, I went into my wardrobe and decided on a pair of well-fitting, slim-fit dark-wash denim jeans with a nice lemon cotton blouse, which was kind of see-through but only against strong light. I finished off with a pair of newish strappy sandals.

My body was built for slim clothing although I don't count myself in any way privileged to have inherited thinness.

A lot of young girls yearn for a glamorous modelling career. They are willing to beg, borrow, or steal to get silicone implants or buy sexier clothes that will accentuate their figure.

Not Sally Cartwright.

In a culture notorious for demanding conformity to a narrowly defined body image and irrationally championing this as perfection, most people are made to feel insecure about their bodies. I feel this is so wrong.

I decided long ago that I will never under any circumstances have any 'work' done on my body. You read so many stories of plastic surgeries gone wrong. No, my body will forever remain untouched. No one would ever think of putting a balcony on the pyramids.

My makeup would be minimalistic, and I'd wear the only piece of jewellery I owned: a double-knotted pearl necklace, which I bought myself for my twenty-first birthday.

I put on my outfit and looked in the mirror. I don't usually stare at myself in the mirror. It is not because I feel the image looking back at me is an unsettling one. As I mentioned before, I think my appearance is very acceptable for my age. I have honest-looking eyes (I think), full-bodied lips, and unblemished skin.

I did a little twirl. Yes, I looked quite presentable.

I unloaded the washing machine and was disappointed to discover that the soup stain on my bathrobe hadn't been fully removed. Then I had an idea. The internet might provide me with advice on an effective remedy for my predicament. Bingo! I was truly convinced now that the internet wasn't a big a scourge on society as I'd thought it was. The procedure involved using dish soap, baking soda, and a toothbrush. I made a mental note to pick up some baking soda on the way home from my date. Date ... oh golly gosh!

I looked up at the clock above the kitchen table. I had two hours and fifteen minutes until my meeting with Declan. I started to feel butterflies in my stomach. I don't think lunch would be a good idea today.

To pass the time, I thought I'd familiarise myself some more with my new phone. I had a cursory glance through the features yesterday, but it was time to go over things with a fine-tooth comb.

Thomas had ensured that my desktop was ready to go. I looked at the icons I hadn't used yet: email, iTunes, calculator, weather, calendar, camera, photos.

The video! I threw my new phone onto the table and retrieved my old one. Declan had mentioned something about a video, which I'd totally forgotten about. It's not like me to forget things, but I think that under the current circumstances I could be forgiven.

I shakily opened the photos icon. There was one item only. It was a picture of city buildings with a time stamp on the bottom right corner. As I tapped it, a video began playing.

CHAPTER 8

THE VIDEO DISTURBED me so much that I felt disconnected from myself, like I was a completely different person. But it had to be me who took it. Why would I have taken it? My thoughts danced in random directions. I seriously considered cancelling my coffee appointment with Declan. Here was my first opportunity since Lars to engage meaningfully with a member of the opposite sex, and I was thinking of calling it off.

That would be poor form.

No, I'm getting too grand now. Life is all about seeing the obstacles in front of you and dealing with them accordingly. I wish Mummy had taught me that.

I will keep my appointment.

I left the flat with both phones in my tote bag. I shouldn't have any trouble finding the Bowl and Spoon café, but it was comforting to know that I could rely on my new phone for assistance at any time if required. I was beginning to see how one could so easily come to view such devices as indispensable.

I looked up at the crystal-blue sky and breathed in the balmy air. There was not a breath of wind, and I could feel the sun stinging my exposed arms and the back of my neck as I turned onto Smith Street.

As I walked towards the café with my head down, a hurricane of thoughts invaded my brain. I knew nothing about the man I was about to meet, although the fact that he went to the trouble of returning my phone gave me reason for optimism. But even with my limited knowledge of human behaviour, I was well aware that this action alone may not be a true indication of his overall character.

I also reflected on potential topics of conversation. While I believe I have a good grasp of most world events and the workings of society, in general, I think I would be found wanting on the subjects of sport, movies, or current trends in music. Those just aren't my thing. And what if he asks me about that video? Or more personal stuff?

Best to park those thoughts for the moment.

In the end, I decided it was probably best to expect nothing from Declan. I figured that if you expect nothing, you never get disappointed. That's how it always was with Mummy.

I also kept reminding myself that I am worthy of love and a better life. That's why I have to take this chance.

My mouth went dry and my heart ricocheted off my rib cage as I approached the front of the Bowl and Spoon. I paused at the doorway, letting my eyes roam around to give my brain a few moments longer to prepare. Could I do this? I quickly pushed the door open before second thoughts could get the better of me.

As soon as I entered, my bowels began moving faster than trains through dedicated tunnels. Panic hit. I looked around. The café was empty. Normally, this would fill me with glee but not today. Declan was nowhere to be seen. The clock on the wall said two o'clock exactly. I'm always punctual.

Have I been stood up? I think that's what they call it when your date doesn't show. Panic with jump leads now.

'Table for one?' A young girl wearing a long black apron and holding a large laminated menu the size of an Egyptian papyrus materialised out of thin air. She looked tired and bored.

I was determined not to let my anxiety get the better of me. 'For two please. Can I use your bathroom?'

'That way.' She motioned to the back of the café without shifting her gaze.

While sitting on the toilet and waiting for nature to take care of my gastric earthquake, I checked my old phone. No messages. I reflected on this: I'd had too many disappointments in my life so far, and whilst one more wouldn't be catastrophic, a phone call or short text message from Declan informing me that he had to cancel our meeting would have been nice. No, courteous. Even given my fears and apprehensions, it was disappointing to think that all the trouble I'd gone to would be for nought.

With my gastrointestinal tract now in sync with my brain, I walked back into the main café area and noticed that the young waitress was seating a customer at a table. It was Declan. A quick glance at the clock revealed that he was six minutes and twenty seconds late.

'Hello, Sally!' He stood up as I ambled towards the table, trying hard to disguise my limp. I think he wanted to pull my chair out, but the waitress beat him to it.

He looked me up and down, making me feel instantly uneasy. 'Well, you certainly know how to get a man's attention,' he said as I was sitting down.

At first, I thought his tone was laden with inappropriateness, but then I realised that my blouse as well as the top of my jeans had been splashed with water from the washbasin in the toilet. I sat in silence, frozen. My head began to spin; and I imagined the cruel laughter clowning around inside Declan's head, even though his expression was impassive—first the stained dressing gown and now the dripping clothes. This girl must not care much for personal cleanliness.

I tried my best to appear stoic, self-assured. 'I was just in the toilet,' I remarked matter-of-factly. Declan nodded. To his credit, he didn't break out into one of those forced bouts of laughter like a lot of people do when they're trying to impress someone.

A sudden pause in his natural expression gave way to a nonchalant gaze and a weak smile. 'Don't you hate those taps? Happens to me all the time too.'

I smiled back, contemplating that to be an appropriate response. I was good at not speaking. I remember Mummy once saying that the most powerful words are sometimes those not spoken. That's one of the few constructive things she ever said.

'How's your phone?'

'It's all fine now.' My voice was cavernous and deep, like a man's. I'm sure Declan sensed my nervousness. You'd have to be deaf and blind not to. I forced myself to look at his face. I was struck anew by his looks. He was more handsome than how I remembered him from last night. He had light-brown hair, a chiselled chin, white straight teeth, and eyes that drew you in like magnets. Something deep inside of me moved, but I didn't quite know what it was.

Is this what love is?

'Shall we order? How do you take your coffee?'

I don't drink coffee. My body is especially sensitive to it. One time, when I was 12 years old, Mummy allowed me to drain the dregs of her coffee cup before sending me off to bed. I lay awake all night, my eyelids refusing to budge and my ears buzzing like beehives. Then I read somewhere that consuming high doses of caffeine can lead to, among other things, hormonal imbalance. It was also around this time that I got my very first period, and that's when I decided that coffee just wasn't for me. Or tea for that matter.

I thought it best to be upfront. 'Um, I don't drink coffee.'

I sensed Declan had an awful impulse to laugh, and his mouth curled up at the corners. 'But you agreed to meet me for coffee.'

So it really was just coffee. I often overheard Wilma and Casey talking about meeting friends for coffee. My understanding was that this phrase was a generic term encompassing all manner of social connection between two or more people. The word *meet* was key and the only one of real significance. I decided not to promote my views on the matter. 'I'll have something else.'

Declan nodded and called over the waitress, the same one who greeted me on my arrival. Her features were more discernible against the window light. She had a stern, sinewy face with no makeup and an expression that yelled she'd rather be somewhere else. She unenthusiastically handed us each a menu before ambling off, her flat shoes dragging along the linoleum floor like a seal or walrus trudging through soft sand. I held my menu awkwardly with the top half resting on the table and the lower half neatly and conveniently hiding my still-damp blouse and jeans.

'They do a mean celery juice here.'

I didn't know if Declan was being facetious, but just to cover myself, I examined the beverages section of the menu. A cursory glance failed to reveal anything even remotely resembling celery. 'I don't think they have it today,' I said matter-of-factly. His laughter this time was like a

MARIO BORAZIO

waterfall—so free and pure, so childish despite his adult years. I could do nothing but blush a little and join in.

'I'm only joking!' he said after his fitful spurts had abated. 'Don't take me seriously, Sally. Believe me, I'm not a serious guy.'

Okay, so he wasn't the serious type. Did that also mean he wasn't as thoughtful or as caring as I'd thought? Did he view life as just one big carnival where he gets to ride the merry-go-round and is free to get on and off as he pleases? I stored these titbits of doubt in the recesses of my brain just as a squirrel judiciously stores nuts.

'I knew you were joking,' I lied. 'I didn't think an establishment such as this one would serve such fare anyway. Perhaps if instead we had gone to an environmentally friendly, plant-sourced organic café, then celery could well have been on the menu.'

It was the longest sentence I had spoken, and Declan appeared a little shocked. He stared at me with his mouth agape. 'Yes, I suppose you're right. The reason I mentioned the celery juice was because I thought you'd be into the health drinks, given your svelte figure.'

Declan was flirting now. I knew this because Mummy told me that if a man you just met pays you a compliment, that's flirting. She also said that most men treated women like they had an expiry date. I don't think Declan is that kind of man. But then again, what do I know?

I gave him an awkward smile and continued perusing the menu. 'I'll have an orange juice. Thanks, Declan.'

He scanned the near-empty café for the waitress, like a seaman looking out for land. She eventually extricated herself from near the kitchen door and sauntered over to take our order. In stark contrast to her listless manner, the order was handled expeditiously, and we had our beverages in front of us within a couple of minutes. Declan took a large gulp of his cappuccino, and I saw that he was poised to ask me a question. 'So, what do you do? Work wise.'

In all my adult life, no one has ever asked me about my status of employment. 'I work in an office,' I offered.

'Oh. What kind?'

I knew my answer hadn't been specific enough. *Working in an office* can have many guises: running errands, doing the photocopying, being a mail clerk, doing data entry (which is really just tapping a keyboard), or making important business decisions. Declan's piercing eyes were drawing me in even further now. I felt momentarily giddy, and a flutter of electricity ran through my body. For the first time in my life, I felt locked in with someone. 'I'm a data analyst for a graphic design company. I analyse trends in what people are looking for to help them promote their businesses.' That wasn't totally accurate because I don't actually talk to the clients, but it was about as exciting as I could make it sound. Declan seemed impressed. I think he was genuinely interested in what I had to say. 'And you?' I asked.

He took a much smaller sip this time and leaned forward with his hands clasped together. 'I work for a computer network engineering firm in town.' A faint smell of coffee trailed his words.

Wow, he must have attended university. I thought about mentioning that I too had gone to university but decided against it. 'That's an important job.'

Declan shrugged. 'It pays the bills. Has to when you're on your own.' I nodded back, not for one second thinking that by doing so I had revealed that I also lived alone. Then I remembered that I hadn't given Declan an answer when he asked me about that same subject last night. There was no point hiding it now. 'Yes, I know the feeling. After paying for rent and groceries and for—' Hang on. There *was* nothing else that Sally Cartwright paid for.

'And for coffee,' Declan added. He looked at me, and I think he saw an expression of oddness. He held a hand up as if stopping traffic. 'Hey, no stress. This is my shout.'

Mummy told me that a woman should never be expected to pay on the first date. I was prepared to debunk this decree purely on the premise that paying for Declan's coffee would be an appropriate symbolic gesture of my appreciation for him returning my phone. It would be a way of balancing the scales of justice. 'No', I started in a voice as thick as molasses, 'I insist on paying. It's the least I can do as a gesture of goodwill for you returning my phone.' Goodwill? Now I was beginning to sound like a real estate agent trying to sell a business.

'That's very kind of you, Sally. I appreciate your gesture. Thank you. I always try to do the right thing by people too.'

Suddenly I felt the urge to tell Declan everything about the real Sally Cartwright. He won't mind if I'm autistic, timid, not worldly, and able to disguise the greatest pain one can ever know.

I stayed silent.

'Tell me about that video.'

My ears pricked up. I knew the subject of the video was going to be brought up sooner or later. For a moment, I thought about chastising him for looking through my private stuff, but I didn't have any private stuff for anyone to look through.

Declan spoke again. 'You must have known, right?'

I heard the sound of my heart beating through the silence. I was too embarrassed to tell him that I knew nothing of this video and decided to play dumb instead. I was good at that. It came naturally. 'Must have known what?'

'That the homeless guy was going to blow himself up. That is, unless you get off filming homeless tramps.' Declan gave an expression suggesting that he had overstepped the mark, that he was being judgemental.

If he was intimating that it was degrading and in no way appropriate to film people less fortunate than ourselves, then I would agree with such an assertion.

I'm going to lie again. This was becoming a disturbing trend. 'I felt sorry for him, that's all. I didn't know he had a bomb. I must have dropped the phone when it went off.'

'You're one lucky person to still be alive.'

I knew I was. I could just imagine myself pausing, probably scared to death, realising that this guy had a bomb, and then running away in a panic.

I told Declan about my fall but not about the amnesia. He nodded but didn't ask for any more details.

I decided to deflect the topic away from myself. 'Have they worked out yet why he had a bomb?'

Declan shrugged his shoulders. 'Not yet. If you want my opinion, though, I reckon it was some militant group. I'm sure they'll come out and claim responsibility soon. I mean, how easy would it be to strap a bomb onto a homeless guy? He probably didn't even realise it.'

Declan was being degrading again, but I could see his point. With my limited knowledge on politics and world terrorism, I decided to just nod in silence.

He caught me looking up at the clock. 'You gotta be somewhere else? Work?'

No. I had concussion and was given the week off by Dr Maria, and I have never spent more than five minutes talking to anyone, and I'm feeling edgy. That's what I should have said. 'Day off' was all I could manage.

'Me too!' I thought the joviality in Declan's voice was misplaced. 'Are you meeting your boyfriend later?'

It would have been so simple. If I'd told you straight up that I had a boyfriend, you'd get it: we'd get a coffee and move on with our separate lives. But then you'd think I'm a little stuck-up, and you'd also be asking yourself why on earth I would agree to meet you for coffee if I had a boyfriend. Then it would end up being too complicated, as complicated as, well, perhaps marriage.

'I don't have a boyfriend.' There was a long drawn-out silence before I spoke the words, like a stammer.

Declan propped himself up with a startled expression. His eyes darkened, inviting me in. 'No way. Are you playing with me?'

I remember him saying that he was never serious. Was *he* playing with *me* now? 'No I'm not, Declan. I've never had a boyfriend. Honest.' I wasn't going to mention Lars. I think I just told what is called a white lie although I'm not a devotee of the term. The word *white* signifies something pure, and there's nothing pure about lying.

He cocked his head to one side and slapped his palms lightly on the edge of the table. 'I cannot believe you've never had a boyfriend.' His face formed the expression of a confused newly neutered dog. 'Who are you, Sally?'

The tears burst forth like water from a dam, spilling down my face. I felt little furnaces were burning at the back of my eyeballs, and my chin was trembling. Declan was finally seeing me in my collapsed, totally fallible state. Without a word, he handed me a dry napkin. As my tears began to subside with each laboured breath, I felt the heat of another face near mine. There was a tiny lapse before I pulled away. What I said next felt so right.

'I have to see a psychiatrist.'

Walking home, I kept shooting impatient glances at passers-by for no apparent reason. Some shot glances back. As I walked, I reflected that I'm not built to withstand stress. Declan saw me for who I truly am today. Baring one's soul was supposed to be calming, therapeutic. I'm sure that's what the psychiatrist will tell me. What I felt today was anything but calming.

I felt empty. I had no safe harbour away from the storm. I was unsheltered, a ghost in my own machine. I read somewhere that some things stay the same only if they change. If they don't change, they don't stay the same. I don't really know if I agree with that.

I agreed to meet Declan for dinner on Saturday night; my fallibility wasn't going to win this time. Perhaps there was a safe harbour for me after all.

I got home and plonked myself on the couch, thoroughly exhausted. I glanced over at my bathrobe resting gracefully over the armchair, like a military flag draped over a coffin.

I forgot to buy the baking soda.

CHAPTER 9

'NO MORE TALK about school. You're all I have. I won't lose you to them. No more talk about school. Do you hear me?'

Mummy's words still ring in my ears.

My memories of school are not pleasant ones despite always knowing that I had what it took to be a good student. The thoughts of classrooms and teachers excited me even before I'd begun formal schooling. Images of notebooks with lined pages, columns of numbers, pens of different colours, the heady smell of heavy markers. How I longed to place a ruler on a page and add up numbers and then show my teacher what I had achieved.

When I was in fourth grade, a teacher asked the class to share what item we'd want if stranded alone on a deserted island. When it was my turn, I answered immediately: 'A dictionary. So I would never get bored!' Everyone burst out laughing, and I felt myself melting under the humiliation.

School wasn't fun anymore after that.

I can still recall my first-ever report card: *Sally is as sharp as a tack, brilliant with numbers. She tends to play by herself, but I see that a lot in creative kids. She has real potential.* I beamed with pride as I highlighted the word *potential* and showed Mummy. She looked at me derisively before slapping the card down on the table and walking away.

I still occasionally find myself thinking about my classmates and what they're up to these days. I wonder how many are doing well in their lives. How many are bankrupt. How many are lonely like me. I don't want to think about them too much because thinking about them gets me down.

I still often have nightmares about my school years. Two unsavoury incidents stand out in my mind, and I will never forget them. The first occurred in primary school. A new girl in my class handed me an envelope with my name neatly printed on the front. Inside was a carefully decorated card cut into a perfect circle. It read, 'You are cordially invited to the ninth birthday party of Isabella Smith.' I rushed home all excited and eagerly showed it to Mummy. I'd never before seen such a sharp expression in her eyes. She snatched it from my hand and proceeded to tear it up. 'You don't even know this girl,' she said. Before I could ask why she had forbidden me to attend Isabella's party, she'd already turned away and stormed off.

The second incident occurred when I began secondary school. I remember the day ever so clearly. It was a hot, dusty afternoon, making me sweaty and dry-mouthed. I got off the school bus and walked towards the house. Mummy was sitting on the front porch, watching me. I found that strange because she never waited for me outside the house. She must know, I thought. After an initial shutting off of my breath caused by fear, calmness set in, and I walked slowly past our gate to the front door.

'Hello, Mummy,' I said.

Mopping her brow, she watched me like a hawk but didn't say anything as I stepped inside. I heard her follow me in, her footfall heavier than usual. 'You got something to tell me, young lady?'

I had made a friend, my first ever, just a few days after commencing my secondary education. All through primary school, Mummy never allowed me to have friends. She said that autistic people didn't deserve friends because we were 'a bad influence' on people.

'Well?' Her mouth was pouted, and she had her arms on her hips like a two-handled teapot.

I couldn't bring myself to tell her about Ravi although I came pretty close a couple of days before. Mummy got into one of her gloomy moods, and the moment passed.

'I got a phone call from Ms Sarah today and you know what she told me?' I stood as still as a cadaver with my eyes down. 'She told me that you went to a boy's house after school last week. Why did you do that, sweetheart?'

I hated Mummy calling me sweetheart because I knew she didn't mean it.

Ravi was a boy in my class who had juvenile arthritis. Sometimes his joints swelled so much he could hardly walk. Or write. On this particular day, his fingers were extra painful, and he couldn't finish the maths problems Ms Sarah had set us. As maths was my best subject, Ravi asked me if I could help him complete the problems after school. He had such honest, caring eyes that I couldn't say no.

'I was helping Ravi with his homework,' I said in a soft voice.

The fact that her daughter had made an effort to help someone should have made Mummy beam with pride. Instead, all I saw were clenched fists and a face red with rage. She spoke with rancour in her voice, 'I'm not having a trollop for a daughter, do you hear? How dare you do that behind my back!' I didn't exactly know what *that* was; but before I had the chance to explain myself, she grabbed my arm, marched me upstairs, and forced me into bed. She drew the curtains, preventing the summer rays from providing me with at least a sliver of comfort. She didn't even come up to see how I was. I missed dinner, and that made me really angry. I thought that, feeling the way I did, I would have cried—but I didn't. I was getting angrier and angrier the more thinking I did. The anger brought out sorrow hidden deep inside. I was starved of the love I craved. Not once in my childhood did I hear Mummy say the words 'I love you'. Not once did I feel her arms wrapped around me in a loving, warm, motherly embrace.

I had had enough, and my stomach was growling. I got out of bed and opened my bedroom door. Mummy, on seeing me on the landing, sprinted up the stairs. 'Oh no, you don't! Get back in your room!' she screeched. Suddenly I was overwhelmed by the futility of everything I'd been through. So many times I've wanted to fight back, wanted to shout, have a tantrum, and beat my clenched fists on the ground like a rambunctious child. But something always held me back and my anger would subside. It was like a raging fire that would always burn out all too quickly.

The fire kept on burning today. 'You can't control me, Mummy. Not anymore.' I pushed past her; but just as I was about to place my

MARIO BORAZIO

foot on the first step down, Mummy grabbed my arm. 'No, you can't stop me!' I shouted and tried to yank my arm free. But Mummy had a strong hold. With one firm push, she thrust me towards the handrail, and my feet went scampering under me. I took a couple of small steps to try to regain my balance but started hurtling downwards instead. Taking a deep breath, I closed my eyes and heard the thud of my body hitting every rise and run of the stairs. When the rolling stopped, I heard my name being called. The first thing I felt was an intensely sharp pain around my groin.

I began crying and tried to get up but couldn't put any weight on my legs before I collapsed on the floor. The pain in my groin had spread to my hip and was getting more severe. My cries had now become wails.

I'd fractured my hip. Mummy didn't believe me at first but eventually called Dr Rickards, who put me in hospital that night.

The surgery, according to the medical report, was a complete success, although the legacy of the subtle limp I'm still left with has made me doubt that assertion.

*

Conversations with Mummy always went like this:
I'd say hello politely.
She'd say hello back, much less politely.
She'd ask me what I'd been up to.
I would always offer a stock standard reply: 'I've been working all week and just relaxing at home.' Mummy never asked for any more details. After four years, she knew there was nothing more.

I'd ask her about her week, and then she would start: 'Mavis annoyed me because she was acting childishly at the bridge club. Dr Rickards gave me a hard time about my weight. Tony the barman kept stealing furtive glances at my breasts.' Mummy talked about such things as though they were affairs of the utmost importance. It was always all about her.

What was there for Mummy and me to talk about if not for this petty stuff? We never talked much when I was living at home. We never had lively conversations about current affairs over the dinner table. We never really talked about anything. It didn't matter because I didn't matter.

I imagined this silence going on for the rest of our lives. I'd always listen without interrupting. I'm a good listener because I don't like talking much.

Until the other day with Declan when my tongue was loosened and my social fears were somewhat alleviated.

Maybe I'll surprise Mummy today with a verbal barrage.

'Hello, Mummy.'

'Oh, it's you.'

'Hello?' I said, somewhat tentatively. Mummy's voice sounded as dull as dirty dishwater.

'Yes, I'm here, Sal.'

'Is anything wrong? You sound as though there is.'

A petulant silence before 'Sal, darling, you don't need to hear my problems. I can cope quite well on my own.'

I was fully aware that the opposite was true. Mummy had a way of making you feel guilty if you didn't ask her to elaborate on her problems. She was hard and implacable that way, as cunning as an old fox. And even if you did ask about something, she had a way of making you feel obsolete, of inferring that no matter how hard you tried, there was no way you could possibly help her.

What made me the saddest was that she was so intransigent about important things like being a good mother, as if trying to justify to herself that such things weren't really important. She was, if the truth be known, an extremely fragile woman.

I cleared my throat. 'Mummy', I said, 'please tell me what's happened. Maybe I can help.' I tried my best to keep my voice even.

Her instantly raucous laughter was almost unbearable. 'That's gold, darling. It really is. I'm sorry for laughing, but I can't see how an autistic child living a world away from me can be of any help.'

Not too subtly, Mummy was making the point that I don't visit her as often as I should. She lives in Colac, a small town in the western district of Victoria, approximately 150 kilometres south-west of Melbourne.

'I don't have a car, Mummy. You know that.'

'Haven't you heard of trains? They've been around for centuries.'

I had no comeback for that, but trains have a lot of people in them. It was bad enough catching the bus to work.

There was an awkward pause before Mummy continued, 'Anyway, I have diabetes now. Yes, that's right. Are you happy? I bet you don't even know what that is.'

I know perfectly well what diabetes is. 'You have diabetes?' I tried to sound surprised, but deep down I knew that this day would inevitably come. Smoking, not eating the right foods, and putting on weight through lack of physical exercise were all cardiovascular risk factors that put the body under an immense stress that could lead to diabetes.

I heard her breathe in and then the distinctive wheeze as she released the air from her smoke-affected lungs. 'Dr Rickards told me that my last blood tests came back suspicious. Then he got me to drink this vile-tasting liquid and told me that I have diabetes. Just like that, Sal. I mean, me, of all people. It's not even in our family.'

I wanted to inform Mummy that poor lifestyle choices can lead to serious systemic disease irrespective of robust bloodlines. But I didn't. I sighed quietly. 'Did Dr Rickards give you any tablets?'

'He did. And you know what else? He wants me to go on a special diet, to stop smoking, and to cut down on my drinking. Can you imagine that?'

Quite frankly, I couldn't imagine Mummy doing any of those things. For her, such draconian measures would be worse than death by a thousand cuts. I honestly cannot fathom why she even visits doctors if she's not prepared to heed their advice.

I always found Mummy's drinking repulsive. It wasn't so much what entered her mouth that was evil. It was what came out of it later that was.

I felt like a deflated balloon. Today would have been the perfect opportunity to tell Mummy about my meeting with Declan and about the exciting fact that I might not be autistic. But she had stolen my thunder yet again. 'Mummy, you must follow Dr Rickard's advice. It's for your own good.'

There was a brief pause before she spoke, 'My, you are chatty today, and I haven't even asked anything about you yet. Are you alright Sal?' That voice—I remember it from childhood. It's still in my nightmares sometimes. Mummy was very adept at changing from antagonistic to charming in the blink of an eye. She was a moraliser when she wanted to be but a seeker of perverse pleasure the rest of the time.

I'd suspected for a long time that she wasn't well mentally. I didn't know too much about it when I was younger, but thinking back, I think she's been bipolar for as long as I can remember. As far as I know, she was never diagnosed and never had any treatment. I think people get labelled too easily sometimes; but even if Dr Rickards gave her some pills for it, I know she wouldn't have taken them.

'Anyway', she continued, 'God will decide my fate. I'm not going to be here forever. It's not as though I'm hanging out for a grandchild or anything. There was a time when I used to get rather impatient at the thought but not anymore. I know it's not going to happen, right, Sal? No man in his right mind would ever want you to be the mother of their child.'

Once Mummy started throwing these poisoned darts, there was very little time to duck for cover. I always remained quiet, waiting for the storm to abate.

'And furthermore, you know you're worthless, don't you? I wish I never had you.'

I'd heard those words many times before, and they still cut me as deep now as the first time. It was more than a pain. It was an existential ache. Sometimes I wondered if Mummy's malicious words were just an exaggerated form of self-preservation of power over her daughter. 'Don't say that, Mummy. I know you don't mean it. Anyway, I might have some news to tell you soon.' My breathing quickened.

'Ah, I knew something was up. I'm all ears, Ms Chatterbox.' Her voice was as sweet as a rose now. But then, 'You're not pregnant, are you?'

I couldn't believe Mummy would in one breath claim that no man would ever want me to father his child and then virtually in the same breath ask me if I was pregnant. Being pregnant was a stomach-churning thought for me. Pregnant women often get praised for how glamorous they look during this magical time in their lives. 'You are glowing!' and 'Wow, you look amazing!' are endearing terms that have no physical basis whatsoever. These women should just accept themselves for what they really are: bloated, unattractive, and always testy. I know it's only for a finite time, but I wouldn't put my body through that for even five minutes. And don't get me started on the birthing process. I know it can get really messy. It's animal husbandry at best.

'No, Mummy, I'm not pregnant.' *I'll never forget what you did.* 'What made you think that?'

'I know what you young people get up to. I may be old, Sal, but I'm not stupid.'

I was tempted to remind Mummy that I was still a virgin, but she probably wouldn't believe me or care.

'There's really nothing to tell, Mummy,' I eventually said after an awkward pause. I just couldn't pluck up the courage to tell her anything at all because I knew that, more than likely, she would find fault in some trivial detail, and I didn't want that spoiling my upcoming dinner date with Declan. Her barbs would be stinging me all night.

You had to pick your moments with Mummy.

'You don't have to hide anything from me, darling,' she continued, her voice sly, hushed. 'You can always talk to me about anything. Or anyone. It's impossible to destroy a bond as close as ours. You know that, don't you?'

Such audacity. The moral bafflement of her alternately affectionate and rebarbative tones riled me because I knew her lovingness was only ever portioned out for personal gain.

The sentimental plots she concocted in her little brain from time to time always had an inevitable mawkish ending.

My hands began to quiver, and blood was roaring through my veins like a freight train. I sighed as quietly as I could and heard the gross hiss of exhaled cigarette smoke over the phone.

In a way, I felt sorry for Mummy. I felt sorry for the dull vision of love she'd invented for herself. Yes, Mummy. You're absolutely right,

Mummy. My life is completely worthless, even though I have recently become consumed with matters I wish so dearly to share with you, but the strong force field you've erected around yourself makes it too hard for me to get even remotely close. You may believe it harnesses your aura by adopting this persona, but I'm afraid the opposite is true. You're incapable of projecting love. I think you're only projecting weakness and guilt.

I see you.

I sometimes want to destroy you.

I am woman.

'Okay, we'll keep in touch, Mummy. I'll call you next week,' I said with an audible strain in my voice.

'You do that,' Mummy replied dryly.

It wasn't until I hung up that I realised I'd been crying.

CHAPTER 10

RATHER THAN FEELING sorry for myself after my unproductive conversation with Mummy, and to distract my mind from some of her abrasive comments, I decided to spend the afternoon spring cleaning my flat. After a quick lunch, I ventured to the supermarket and purchased a range of cleaning supplies as well as some baking soda for my bathrobe. I find it repulsive to think that, by sticking the words *green* or *natural* or *sustainable* or *organic* on a product, it gave someone the right to price it much higher than its non-eco-friendly competitor. Most people wouldn't even know what *organic* means. I'm not a great believer in these products anyway. Logic would tell you that if a cleaning agent has had any harsh chemicals removed from it in order to save the planet, then whatever you're trying to clean may need to be soaked or scrubbed for a longer period to achieve a comparable outcome.

I wasn't in the mood to save the planet today; I just wanted to clean my flat.

As soon as I got home, I examined the contents of my moderately sized cleaning caddy: a plastic apron, some rubber gloves, a scrub brush, as well as various sponges and a squeegee. Then I unpacked my shopping bag full of economically priced generic-branded products: an all-purpose cleaner, hospital-grade disinfectant, detergent, household ammonia, and carpet cleaner. The label on the carpet cleaner alleged that it smelled like the fragrant white flower of the buckwheat plant. I'll have to take their word for it. I read somewhere that buckwheat contains a host of healthy nutrients. I just hope my carpet will appreciate all the goodness it is about to receive.

It took me the best part of two hours to clean and disinfect every surface in my flat. While I was at it, I also decided to unclutter the living and storage areas. I ended up filling a large community sack with a disorderly assemblage of old clothes and an assortment of next to useless knick-knacks and trinkets that I'd purchased sporadically over the past four years, usually on a whim in order to make myself feel better. I think they call that retail therapy.

It was an eerie feeling to see how much more spacious my flat looked when I'd finished.

I looked around and tried to see my home through the eyes of a visitor. I believe it would appear very welcoming, especially now that it was uncluttered. The furniture was simple, inexpensive, but perfectly functional. I didn't see the point of lavishly upgrading anything, seeing as I'm the only one living here. Yes, this was a place in which a visitor would feel safe and comfortable.

I made myself a hot drink of milk with Milo and plonked my weary bones on the couch. Cleaning can be tiring work. My thoughts turned quickly from matters of domestic cleaning and household décor to Declan and our dinner meeting tonight. It occurred to me that neither of us had specified a meeting place or time.

Text time:

> Hi Declan, it's Sally Cartwright.
> Just wondering what time and where to meet tonight.
> Regards, Sally Cartwright.

There was no reply for twenty minutes, and I began to regret my impulsive decision to send the text message. It made me feel very anxious. I suspected Declan was either very busy or … or what? Did he have another date?

I felt queasy and kept looking up at the clock. Just as I was contemplating sending another text informing him that we could make it another night if that was more convenient, I received a message back:

> Hey, hi Sally. Sorry, I've been busy.
> About tonight. How about I pick you up around seven?

Pick me up? I hadn't factored that action into tonight's agenda. I'd never been picked up before, mainly owing to the fact that I never went out.

I realised that Declan hadn't mentioned the venue. I decided not to press him on that point.

I sent off a reply straight away:

That would be great. Thank you.

I didn't put my name this time.
A new message right back:

Great, cu then

I had just over a couple of hours to get ready. My makeup would be minimalistic as usual. What should I wear? Should my outfit be governed by the type of restaurant we'll be attending? I assumed Declan would have informed me if there was a formal dress code involved. Judging by some of the bohemian and shabby-looking diners I often see sitting in posh city restaurants on my way home from work, I don't think I need to stress too much about it.

Should I have purchased a new outfit? Such a strategy would most likely have backfired; for if I never see Declan again after tonight—and that was a highly likely outcome—I'd feel as though I'd wasted my money.

Even though the evening promised to be a balmy one, I felt it would be inappropriate to wear anything too revealing. For Sally Cartwright, it would be akin to false advertising. No, nothing low cut in the front and definitely not backless. I don't own anything like that anyway.

I decided on a knee-length black leather skirt, a long-sleeved soft knit, and flat patent leather shoes. This is a combination I often wear to work.

Put the nerves, the hair, the makeup, and the outfit together and I'm already flustered, not to mention just a little sweaty.

It was five minutes past our assigned meeting time, but I decided it was best not to pass comment on Declan's tardiness when he eventually got here. The streets outside were eerily quiet for a Saturday night. Then I heard the sound of a moaning car engine nearing my driveway.

He wore low-hung denim jeans with a pale-blue patterned shirt and brown leather shoes. I think the modern vernacular is that he was *well turned out*. 'Hi, how are you?' he said with a broad smile accentuating the nooks of his stubble beard. 'You look lovely.'

A warm, fuzzy feeling began to permeate my skin, and my cheeks were kissed pink like a spring rose. 'I'm fine thank you, Declan. I appreciate you coming to pick me up.' I invited him in, and he took a seat on my freshly deodorised couch.

'So what's the game plan, Sally?'

I had no idea what he meant, and my facial expression portrayed as much.

'What I mean is have you decided where we are going to eat?'

I hadn't banked on being tasked the responsibility of deciding our dining locale. Maybe it was custom for the female to decide such things, but I was too embarrassed to ask if this was a correct assumption on my part.

I wasn't at all familiar with the local dining options. 'I'm not fussed. I'll let you decide, if that's all right.'

'Sure.' He shrugged his shoulders and flicked his phone open. Within minutes we were booked into a local Italian restaurant for 8 p.m. I wondered why he hadn't insisted on an earlier arrival time, seeing that the restaurant was only about five minutes away.

Suddenly my nerves jumped all together; I was forced to entertain Declan here in my flat for almost an hour. 'Would you like a drink?'

'I'd love a beer thanks.'

'I'm afraid I don't have anything alcoholic.'

Declan's eyes boggled at me, as if frightened by something. 'You're not serious, are you?' I nodded and sensed that at any moment he would explode with laughter and mock me as others would have. But to his credit, his face remained as lifeless as a worn stone. 'That's okay. Do you have any Coke?'

I don't buy Coke or any other fizzy drinks as a rule. They're full

MARIO BORAZIO

of sugar and can cause an array of physical ailments. Not to mention Coke's caffeine content. 'I'm afraid not. I've only got juice.'

'Okay.'

The impasse was broken. As we sat opposite each other separated by two tall glasses of cloudy apple juice, I noticed Declan looking at me in a way I didn't think was appropriate. It was the same look I recalled seeing in an SBS documentary once about rabbinical elders who secretly coveted women with burqas.

Declan took a sip of his juice and leaned forward. 'Tonight I want to find out who the real Sally Cartwright is.' He said it in a way that implied he was on some kind of fact-finding mission.

I could have saved him the trouble and just announced, as I had partially revealed already, that I am a 26-year-old virgin who leads a boring single life with a boring mundane job. I have no friends, low self-esteem, and an alcoholic mother who wishes her daughter dead and that I have to see a psychiatrist now to find out if I'm crazy or not.

Did I miss anything?

Oh yes, I don't own a car and don't even have a licence.

One thing I learnt from watching truckloads of humdrum TV dramas was that the best way to deflect attention from yourself was to pretend that you're interested in the other person's affairs. 'What about you, Declan? I'd like to hear something about you.'

Declan looked puzzled and mildly amused. He leaned slightly more forward and interlaced his long bony fingers. 'Alright, I'll go first then. I live on my own a couple of suburbs away. I recently broke up with a girl, and so I'm single again, but you already know that. I work for an engineering firm, and I like gaming. That's it in a nutshell.'

I was relieved on two fronts: he wasn't presently seeing anybody else, and he didn't come across as a crazed axe murderer. All positive so far. 'That's certainly interesting,' I said.

'I'm glad you find me interesting, Sally. A lot of people don't.'

I didn't know what was implied by that last comment but wasn't willing to ask him to elaborate.

'Now it's your turn. What about you?' he asked again.

I looked down at my bright buckwheat-cleaned carpet. 'Oh, my story's way more complicated than yours.' My voice was thin, lightweight.

'Whenever you're ready. I'm not rushing you.' He took my hands in his and squeezed them ever so slightly, and I felt a gentle heat being transferred. My first instinct was to withdraw, but then I thought of Mummy's force field, and I didn't want one of those surrounding me tonight.

I felt an alluring comfort as Declan kept his hands on mine. It felt like the gentleness of something opening, like a flower at first morning light. I was fully aware what was really happening. Maybe, just maybe, there was a miniscule part of my heart that wasn't scarred, a part just big enough to let in a morsel of affection. 'I want to tell you more about myself—I really do—but ...' At that instant, Declan's face fell faster than a wrought-iron hang glider, and his childlike expression changed to a supple grin. I was afraid I was going to cry.

'You don't have to tell me anything yet if you're not ready.'

He squeezed my hands tighter as I fought, and won, my battle against impending tears. I looked up at the clock. 'I think we'd better get going.'

We drove in thick traffic in silence and arrived at Michelina's restaurant ten minutes after our preordained time. This was the first time in my life that I'd ever been late for anything. The staff didn't seem to be too put out by our tardiness and promptly showed us to our table.

I was relieved that my bowels were behaving themselves tonight.

The waiter greeted Declan by name when he brought the menus. At first I thought that Declan must be wearing a name tag like Thomas had, but then the two of them began talking and laughing in a way that suggested they'd known each other for a long time. The waiter introduced himself as Joe and informed me that he and Declan were old school buddies. He appeared to be older than his friend, was unkempt, had scruffy hair, and was apparelled in a shabby white shirt and poorly fitting trousers. The other staff all seemed to have the same general appearance.

While Declan and Joe continued their banter, I allowed myself to survey the surrounds. The place was almost full, with most patrons dining in pairs. I wondered how many of these couples were also out on their first date.

The lighting was dim. I think the modern terminology for this is *ambient*. There was soft music playing in the background in a foreign language I assumed to be Italian. Our table was one of the smaller ones and was covered with a sheet of plain white paper. I wondered whether they changed it after every meal. The fact that it looked spotless and not creased probably implied that the answer was yes. The chairs we sat on were ordinary wooden ones with no cushions. I could already feel my bony buttocks pressing against the textured wood grain.

The décor appeared dated and grubby. I contemplated whether they ever spring cleaned.

The silverware and glassware appeared old, as if they were discarded wedding presents that were belatedly afforded a new home.

Joe poured us some water from a cylindrical steel decanter and promptly left. Declan picked up his menu. 'Shall we order?' I nodded and perused the fare on offer. My knowledge of Italian cuisine was quite limited. I made up my mind quickly to show that I was all over this task.

'I think I'll have the mushroom risotto.' I was less likely to spill, splash, or wear risotto. After my experiences at the Bowl and Spoon, I wasn't taking any chances.

'Good choice,' Declan said. 'I'm having the cannelloni.'

Waiting for the food to arrive was an awkward time. I wasn't sure how much dialogue a couple was supposed to engage in during this hiatus in proceedings or if it was incumbent on me to even initiate it. I noticed most other diners were looking at their phones, but I was determined not to do that. Other than that video, I had nothing else to look at anyway. I tried not to play with my hair and not to touch my face either.

Then Declan spoke up, 'May I ask you something, Sally?' He slurped his water and gently placed the glass on the table. I nodded and instinctively looked away. 'How long have you been seeing a psychiatrist?'

Suddenly the place was a cacophonous din, everyone seemingly feeling the urge to talk at the same time.

'Well', I said in a slightly raised voice to make myself heard, 'I haven't actually seen one yet. The doctor I visited after my head injury thought it would be a good idea.'

'Ah, the head knock. Must be pretty serious if you have to see a specialist about it.'

It may have been a bit serious, but it's not the reason Dr Maria recommended I see a psychiatrist. I should have made Declan aware of this fact but decided not to. My reasoning for adopting this stance was this: If I'm officially diagnosed as *not* having autism, then no one needs to ever know that I had that label bestowed upon me for the best part of 23 years.

I was beginning to make shrewd decisions. Savvy Sally.

I could tell that Declan wanted me to expand on the nature of my head injury, but I wasn't prepared to do that. I was saved this dilemma by the arrival of our food. 'Here we are,' Joe announced cheerfully as he placed the plates down. 'Enjoy!'

Declan thanked Joe, who returned him a warm smile. I was ravenous and began devouring my food as if it were the last meal I'd ever have. Declan admired me with what I sensed to be a level of amusement. 'Hey, slow down over there. We've got all night.'

I managed to extricate my mouth from my spoon. 'Sorry, I don't usually eat this late.' It was almost nine o'clock.

'That's okay. I'm quite famished too.' Declan also began attacking his cannelloni with fervour as we both ate in silence.

My risotto was superb, but I think everything tastes good when you're hungry. I remember many times complaining to Mummy when she made something bland for dinner. 'You'd eat rocks if you were really hungry,' she'd say.

The noise around us had died down considerably as other diners were also busy negotiating their meals. The clattering sounds of cutlery on porcelain dominated the airwaves. Declan sat back and wiped his mouth, his napkin making a soft grating sound against his stubble. 'That was nice.'

'Mine too,' I offered.

'Do you know what else is nice?' he said. 'It's nice to talk to someone about something other than data communication and wireless networks or even gaming.'

It was virtuous of him to say that, but we really hadn't talked about much at all. 'Can I ask you something, Declan?'

'Sure, anything,' he said, smiling as he played with his napkin.

'Will you accompany me to my psychiatrist appointment?'

CHAPTER 11

I COULDN'T HELP MYSELF. The day before my appointment with the psychiatrist, I opened Dr Maria's referral letter. As I've already mentioned, I've never been a big advocate for the wonders of the internet world, but this was another occasion when I anticipated it could be utilised to my advantage. *WikiHow* showed me, in four easy steps and with devastating clarity, how to steam open an envelope and reseal it so that no one would know it had ever been tampered with.

Dr Maria had confidently stated in her letter that I was suffering from depression and that medication and psychotherapy may be beneficial. The investigation of my autism was only mentioned in the last paragraph, as if it were an afterthought.

The nature and tone of the letter disappointed me, and I was forced to reassess my opinion of Dr Maria. How could she deduce from a single consultation, and from only a few scant details she'd gleaned from me, that I was depressed? And sticking in autism only at the end made it appear as if it were a trivial matter. It wasn't trivial to *me*. In fact, it should have been stated right at the top, in bold red ink, that it was the *only* reason for the referral.

Dr Maria's letter also stated that formulating a treatment plan was an essential step in making me 'normal' again, whatever that meant.

Declan drove me to the appointment. He had been a real gentleman, and I was beginning to realise that not all men were after only one thing. After insisting on paying for our meal on Saturday night, he drove me home and even escorted me to my front door. It was comforting to know that chivalry still has a place in modern society. As a show of my gratitude, I invited him in, but he said he was too tired and had things to do in the morning. That eliminated any uncertainty or tension that may have eventuated if he had accepted my proposal. I slept well that night.

The main reason I wanted him to drive me in today was so that I'd be less tempted to change my mind and not keep my appointment. I'd been feeling jittery for a few days, and not solely because of Dr Maria's letter. The thought of pouring out my thoughts and emotions to a complete stranger was still an unpalatable scenario but one I knew I had to endure if I was to obtain the answers I so eagerly craved.

The doctor's name was Gail Eisenhuth. The surname sounded German. Her office was located on the fifth floor of a modern office block on the outskirts of the city. Declan accompanied me into the bright open waiting area, but I'd already decided there was no way I was going to allow him to come into the consulting room with me.

To my relief, I wasn't required to complete an exam paper this time. The waiting area was empty but for me and Declan. We sat in silence. Eventually, Declan got bored and took out his mobile phone. I assumed he was playing a video game, probably one of those brainless ones where people go around slicing each other's heads off for some baseless pleasure. I threw him a furtive glance. His brow was creased under immense concentration, and his eyes seemed to be burning holes into the screen. I wondered if he was still aware of my presence.

As we waited, I was filled with a state of almost-euphoric realisation that I was finally going to do this.

'Ms Cartwright?'

'Do you want me to come in with you?' At that instant, Declan managed to dissociate himself from the onerous task of saving the world from impending doom to honing in on Dr Eisenhuth's voice.

'I'll be fine,' I whispered.

Dr Eisenhuth stood at the door, smiling. She was a stout middle-aged woman of average height with shoulder-length auburn hair, dark eyes, and an erect posture, almost graceful. 'I'm Dr Eisenhuth, but you can call me Dr Gail or just Gail. I don't mind either. It's a pleasure to meet you.' Her voice was pleasant enough, calming even. It was a voice that said I'm not going to talk above you, that I won't talk in platitudes you won't understand.

'Hi. You can call me Sally.' My words bungled out as thick as molasses. I took a seat opposite.

Dr Gail looked intently at me from across her desk. 'Have you ever seen a psychiatrist or psychologist before?'

'No. Never.'

'Alright then,' she said firmly. 'Let's get started.' She pushed a box of Kleenex eucalyptus tissues towards me. I never got how a tissue impregnated with tree oil was somehow more beneficial than the plain variety. All you did was blow your nose into it.

Dr Gail settled in her chair and began reading Dr Maria's letter. 'You're suffering from depression.' It was more of a statement than a question. 'How long have you been feeling this way, Sally?'

I had to clear the air right away. 'Is that what Dr Maria wrote?' I said, trying my best to sound surprised. 'No, I don't think I'm depressed.'

The doctor's expression assumed somewhat of a hardened quality. 'Excuse me? Your GP says in her letter that—'

'I don't care what she says. I'm telling you that I'm not depressed.' My voice was wrapped in sandpaper. I believe this was the first time I had ever interrupted someone midsentence. Even with all the vitriol that has flowed from Mummy's mouth over the years, I never once stopped her short on anything.

Dr Gail maintained her hardened expression. 'Was there something in particular that led you to seek help from your GP?'

Firstly, Dr Maria is *not* my GP. Not anymore. Secondly, she didn't mention anything about my head knock in her letter. And to think we put these champions of society up on a pedestal. 'Well, yes, there was.' I told Dr Gail all about how I hit my head on the pavement outside work and how I lost my memory and about how I was told that I was running away from a man with a bomb when this whole thing happened. I felt comfortable telling her all this.

'Do you remember any of that now?'

I shook my head. 'Not a thing.'

'And this was how long ago?'

'Eleven days precisely.'

'I see.' Dr Gail continued reading to the end of the letter. 'Autism?'

The way she enunciated the word reminded me of the way a prosecuting lawyer in a crime show reacts when finding out that the accused has been acquitted. I think I watch too much television. 'Yes. My mother, Mummy, took me to a doctor when I was 3 years old.'

'But you said you've never been to a psychiatrist.'

'Not a psychiatrist. She took me to our GP back home. Dr Rickards.'

'Dr Emerson Rickards?'

'Yes, I think that's his name,' I said. Dr Gail wrote something down.

'Tell me, Sally, did you ever consider getting a second opinion?'

'No, I didn't. Mummy trusts Dr Rickards.'

Dr Gail nodded enthusiastically. 'There are quite a few issues that have already piqued my curiosity here, Sally. First and foremost, I'd like you to tell me about your parents.'

No way! All I need to hear from you right now is that I'm not autistic. Then I can pay you your two hundred dollars, and we can go our separate ways, and I can get on with continuing to live my mundane life. You don't need to know what I think about Mummy.

That's what I wanted to say, but of course, I didn't. Folding my arms, I looked down at the carpet. 'I'd rather not talk about Mummy, Gail, if that's okay.'

'What sort of relationship do you have with your mother?' I don't believe she was listening to me. Is this how all shrinks operated, unrelenting until they broke you? She continued, 'You two don't get along then?'

It was a leading question.

Suddenly I wished that the tissue box between us would materialise into a giant wall of eucalyptus trees. But something deep inside was urging me to answer. 'Mummy's too controlling. That's why I left home, and now I live on my own.'

'What about your father?'

I threw my head back and let out a sigh. 'I've never met my father. I don't know who he is. It's only ever been me and Mummy.'

'Did your mother ever talk about him?'

'She'd always make it a kind of game whenever the subject of my father came up, which was rare. It was her way of trivialising the whole subject.'

Dr Gail nodded. 'I see,' she said. 'What about siblings?'

I shook my head. 'Like I said, it's only ever been me and Mummy.' The emotion of talking about this stuff was starting to get to me. Tears threatened, and I reached for a eucalyptus tissue. Dr Gail pushed the box closer towards me.

'Okay,' she said, measured. She opened up a folder and handed me some sheets of paper stapled together. 'I'd like you to fill these out.'

Damn! Just when I thought I'd escaped the exam.

I fought rising panic as I scanned the list of questions. Some of them were rather confronting, and I couldn't hide my vexed expression. 'Do you want me to answer all of them?'

Dr Gail nodded. 'As best you can. You have got to be honest with yourself, Sally. You would only be cheating yourself if you are not.'

So no cheating. And no lies either. I swallowed down my frustration, took a deep breath, and got to work. When I finished, my brain felt like it had been flattened by a road grader. Dr Gail studied my answers while playing with her hair, which I found curious. She lifted her head slowly. Her eyes widened, and her forehead furrowed just a little.

'I think we'll finish up for today, Sally. I want to see you regularly. Once a week to begin with. I need to delve deeper into your childhood and also try a few exercises that might help you get your memory back.'

Fuck! Fuck! I don't make a habit of internalising profanities, but I think I could be excused on this occasion. Not only had I to come back for more visits and relieve myself of more of my hard-earned money, but I was also going to be coerced into talking about my painful past, about emotions that had been buried deep inside for many years. I would be forced to dig up things I've been trying to outrun for most of my life. And I'm still not even sure if I'm autistic.

No harm in asking, I thought. 'What about my autism?'

Dr Gail slid open the top drawer of her desk and handed me a glossy pamphlet. 'This is what I think you're suffering from, Sally. You definitely don't have autism.'

Fuck! Fuck!

CHAPTER 12

*Y*OU DEFINITELY DON'T *have autism.* The words kept ringing in my head like incessant church bells. I was beginning to see that opening up to Dr Gail could have an upside. She might be my gateway—the portal to all my possibilities.

I sat on my couch and began reading the pamphlet that she gave me. It was about a condition called emotional behavioural disorder, or EBD for short. I glanced down the list of things that characterised this condition:

- A general feeling of unhappiness
- Feelings of fear and anxiety related to social or personal matters
- Inappropriate actions or emotions under normal circumstances
- Internalising behaviours such as poor self-esteem
- Depression

That last one hit me right between the eyes.

Then there was a section on the causes of EBD:

There are often overlapping factors that predominantly relate to a troubled childhood resulting in abnormal conditioning.

Finally, a treatment section listing three things:

- Medication
- Psychotherapy
- Social skills training

I felt my throat constricting and tightening with tears. Finding out that I wasn't autistic was meant to be my holy grail. But now I have this. What was I meant to do with this new piece of information?

I looked again at the pamphlet in my hand. They may as well have called it the Sally Cartwright disorder, or the SCD for short. It really did summarise me. And what about the depression? Was I just in denial all this time?

Can you have depression without knowing it? On reflection, there have been some days where I'd felt the sadness build and build. Some days when it blindsided me and stopped me dead in my tracks, and I was at a loss to explain what exactly was happening.

I suppose there may be some signs recognised by professionals only. Perhaps I was presumptuous in judging Dr Maria.

The next day, I went back to work after more than a week away. I dressed in a floral blouse and dark pants that I'd purchased last year but never had the pluck to wear. I looked confident, normal.

Beware the new non-autistic Sally Cartwright!

The beginning of a fluttery panic in my chest wasn't what I needed as I approached my office building. Suddenly I was having second thoughts. Was I ready to face my work colleagues again? Although everyone knew why I'd been off, I was wary of any unsubstantiated rumours about me that may have begun to circulate during my absence. I was scared that I might not be able to focus on my assigned tasks.

My fears were allayed somewhat when I reached my desk. Mike had left an impressive bunch of bright-pink chrysanthemums in a vase. That was all the confirmation I needed: I hadn't been made redundant and was still a valued member of the company. He'd kept his word.

I'd never told anyone at work that I was autistic. Not even Mike.

The office appeared somehow different to how I remembered it. The waste paper bins seemed to be not ideally positioned. Three of the five desks were angled in a way where you had at least one colleague in your line of sight while you were looking at your computer screen. This could easily lead to unnecessary distraction and decreased productivity.

Maybe the bins and desks were moved by the elves and pixies while I was away. I had to remind myself that I didn't believe in the existence of such things.

'Sally!' Mike stood behind me. 'Welcome back! How's your head?'

I swivelled my chair around faster than an ice skater doing a pirouette. 'I'm fine now, Mr Cosgrove.'

'Hey, I love your new outfit!'

I was in no mood to explain. 'Thank you for the flowers, Mr Cosgrove.' Even with my newfound confidence, I still couldn't bring myself to call my boss by his first name.

He took in a sharp breath, and his nose wrinkled. 'Sally, the department has been falling apart without you. Rob hasn't the foggiest about drawing up a client profile, and as for Wilma and Casey …'

Mike was snorting his words, which was always an indication that he was frustrated or irate. I must admit it gave me a kind of perverse pleasure knowing how poorly my colleagues had performed in my absence. 'Don't worry yourself, Mr Cosgrove. I'll fix up any anomalies their work practices may have created.' Mike's face beamed but also showed surprise. He wasn't used to me stringing so many words together.

'I like the way you think, Sally. Keep up the good work!'

'And if you don't mind', I continued, 'I'd like to move the desks back to their original positions.'

Mike looked around and nodded. 'Of course,' he said before tottering away.

Oddly, Rob, Wilma, and Casey didn't say much to me that morning. Perhaps they'd known that Mike was going to inform me of their ineptitudes. Or perhaps they were just carrying on as before, leaving Sally Cartwright to herself. Either way, it didn't faze me.

Declan had noticed the changes in me too. I hadn't disclosed anything to him, of course. Even when we left Dr Gail's rooms last week, he'd stayed as quiet as a church mouse, pretending to still be interested in his stupid war game before driving me home in silence. I think it was his way of being respectful.

'You wanna go out tonight?' It was a Tuesday, and Declan rang me. I guessed calling was a natural progression from texting if one felt that the relationship was moving forward. I also guessed that he wanted to spend more time with me. How much was I prepared to give back? With this new EBD diagnosis hanging over me, how normal was I really?

I'd have to wait at least until my next visit with Dr Gail to find out.

'Where to?' I asked nonchalantly.

'There's this new punk band playing tonight at a pub nearby. I've heard they're really avant-garde.'

I've never been enamoured of music, in general, especially the punk variety. Punk conjures up scenes of distasteful body piercings, multicoloured hair, putrid body odour, black lipstick, black leather, tattoos, and angry distorted faces. The music is often overly loud and invariably politicised beneath a hostile façade.

No. Punk was not for me. 'I'm sorry, Declan, I—'

The new Sally Cartwright had to be bolder, be prepared to take the odd risk. 'I'd love to come. What time?'

'Seven-thirty. I'll pick you up.'

'Great. What will I wear?'

'Black's good.' What a surprise.

I got home around six. A full day's work had exhausted me. I managed to clean up some of the mess left by Rob, Casey, and Wilma. Their failings made me reflect that I was better at my job than I'd ever given myself credit for.

I defrosted a container of pesto penne and scoffed it down in less than five minutes. Dressing for tonight's occasion wouldn't need much ingenuity. I already had the black skirt and shoes. All that remained was to find a dark top. I vaguely recalled throwing one into the community sack.

I opened up the sack and began scooping out items of clothing. Voila! One stained, slightly damp, and crumpled black top. I wasn't too concerned about the stains, as no one would probably notice. I'm led to believe that most music venues are quite dimly lit.

We reached the venue and there was a long queue waiting to get in. I was actually enjoying the atmosphere. It wasn't that long ago that just standing between two people, like at a supermarket checkout, would evoke annoyance and anxiety. But now it felt kind of homely, as though there was a kindred spirit that we all shared. Declan's presence was of considerable comfort too.

We were inside by eight o'clock. Declan informed me that the real 'action' wouldn't get underway until just before nine. That made me wonder why we rushed to get here.

The support band was coming to the end of its set. They finished to cheers and stomping from a worked-up audience. Frankly, I couldn't see what all the fuss was about. I hope the main band is in possession of a little more talent.

'Would you like a drink, Sally?'

I shook my head. 'No thank you, Declan.' Before I knew it, he was off to the bar, and I lost him through a wall of dense humanity and low-hanging smoke.

A few minutes later, the entire venue was, as I'd anticipated, plunged into near darkness. There was a hum of noise permeating throughout the room, both male and female voices, and lots of laughter. By now I'd gotten used to all the noise, the smoke, even the people. All of them seemed to have mastered the task of holding a drink, talking, and attending to their phones simultaneously. I wondered how many were socialising with others whose company they didn't particularly enjoy, or even despised, but were forced to endure. I'm sure that would happen quite frequently in social settings such as this one.

A few minutes later, a voice rose up as if from nowhere. 'Lots of cowboys out tonight!' Declan had sneaked up behind me and was holding a large plastic cup filled with beer. His unanticipated greeting had scared me. My mind immediately filled with visions of Mummy's house. More on that later.

'It was hard to find you!' Declan had to shout.

Yes, I was dressed in black, and so was everybody else in this stink hole that I didn't want to come to but only agreed so as to improve my social status in life.

'We can watch from here if you like.' Declan drained a portion of his beer and gave me a smile.

I nodded. 'Yes, this is a suitable spot I'm sure.' We were midway between the stage and the back wall. 'Do you know where the toilets are, Declan?'

He pointed to the far-right corner, indicating to me that he was more than likely a previous frequenter of this establishment. 'I'll wait here for you!' He had to raise his voice again to be heard.

I snaked my way through a collection of sweaty bodies, their personal odours mixed with the smell of cigarettes, beer, and spirits. It wasn't my bowels this time—it was my bladder. The toilet area smelled of stale air and vomit. As I held my breath and prepared to enter an empty cubicle, I spotted a group of young girls taking group selfies by the wash basins. What a bizarre sight. Who in their right mind would want to photograph themselves inside a public toilet?

As soon as I'd relieved myself, my phone buzzed. It was my old phone. 'Hello?'

'Hello, is this Sally Cartwright?' The female voice was totally unfamiliar, as was the number.

'Yes, this is Sally Cartwright. Who is this?'

'I'm calling from YouTube Australia. Congratulations, Sally! Your video post has had over 300,000 hits in the past week. You're up for another—'

'What on earth are you talking about? Is this some sort of joke?' My tone was slightly abrasive.

'I can assure you, miss, this is no joke. You posted a video on your phone.'

'I didn't post any video.'

'It's from this number, miss.'

My mind immediately conjured up images of the video of the homeless man and the bomb. 'Does this video pertain to a homeless man?' There was a brief silence.

'What? No. It's the one where a group of people are watching a band in a bar and a large disco ball falls from the ceiling, killing five.'

All my life, I'd rehearsed my response to theoretical moments of peril, most of those scenarios involving Mummy. In my imagination, I stopped her wielding a knife, ran away from a beating, or just shut myself in my room until she'd calmed down from a fitful rage. But now that a situation had presented itself outside of those parameters, I became panicky and was momentarily paralysed.

I felt the panic begin like a cluster of sparks in my chest. I closed my phone and sprinted out as fast as I could before barging my way through the crowd like a stampeding bull.

'Declan, let's go! Please!'

CHAPTER 13

I WOKE UP COLD as a tomb. Sleep didn't come easily, and I must have thrown off the blankets while tossing and turning during the night.

I sat back and just stared up at the ceiling. To say that the events of last night were chaotic would be a gross understatement. 'I'm bleeding, Declan. I need to leave now!' I'd said, panting with fear. Declan looked me up and down before adopting an expression of equal parts confusion and helplessness.

'Where?' he'd asked in a mild panic.

Do I need to spell it out? There is a considerable amount of discharge of blood and mucosal tissue from the inner lining of my uterus through my vagina. 'I've got my period!' I'd yelled.

He drove me home in silence, completely oblivious to the goings on in my brain. I had told another white lie. It was the purest of white lies. It was so pure that each one of my words was delicately infused with disinfectant. My period wasn't due for a couple of weeks. I didn't have the heart to tell him the truth—that we would have been in grave danger had we stayed to see the band. Or at least that I thought that. He took the sudden and unexpected curtailment of our evening's entertainment quite well. For the majority of men, understanding what women go through in this monthly ritual would be akin to cracking the Da Vinci code. *Glad I'm not a girl,* they'd all be thinking.

What made me an expert on men all of a sudden?

My phone rang, and my heart immediately jumped. It was Declan.

'Good morning, Sally. Are you alright this morning?'

I lifted my head off the pillow and squinted out at the bright new day. 'Yes I'm fine now.' My voice was creaky.

'Have you seen the news?'

I don't watch morning news, and I never buy the newspaper. I find that I can't respond to constant negativity adequately. I'm of the opinion that every time you're watching or reading the news, you're filling your mind with unnecessary fear and anxiety, and I certainly didn't need any more of that in my life right now. 'No, I haven't. Is there anything interesting to report?' My words were forced, as though being passed through a meat grinder.

'You bet! There was a big accident at the pub after we left last night. Apparently, one of those big heavy mirror balls fell from the ceiling and killed five people.'

'Oh my.'

'It could have been us, Sally. I believe we were standing right near that ball. We could have died, but we're still alive, thanks to you.'

'I got my period, that's all.'

'It's more than that, Sally. I believe everything happens for a reason. Call it fate, destiny, or whatever.'

Declan's line of conversation was slightly unnerving. 'What do you mean?' I asked in a controlled tone.

'It's obvious, isn't it? First I find your phone, and now you save me from near-certain death. It's our serendipity. We were meant to be together.'

Those last words stung me. Emotional warfare was being waged on my brain on a global scale. I had been trapped in an iceberg that took the best part of twenty-six years to form. Now another person was bringing a gentle flame nearer and trying to melt it little by little. How could I even contemplate investing myself further into this relationship if I wasn't prepared to be totally honest? Isn't honesty supposed to be the cornerstone of personal fulfilment?

I recalled something I read once: 'If it's not right, don't do it. If it's not true, don't say it.' I had been living with this edict until very recently.

'Declan, I need to tell you something.'

There was a long pause as if the line went dead. Declan eventually spoke, but his voice was tinged with sadness. 'Don't you believe we were meant for each other, Sally?'

'It's not that. I mean, I don't know.' I hated how I was being noncommittal.

The silence made my blood feel cold. 'Declan?'

'Is something else wrong?'

'Nothing's wrong. It's just that—' I couldn't bring myself to say it.

'It's just what? You can tell me anything, Sally. I'm here for you. I feel like we've known each other for longer than we have.' His voice slid down my spine like a draught.

'Can you come over tonight?' was all I could say.

We arranged to meet at seven.

CHAPTER 14

I WASN'T ABOUT TO blot my copybook. Especially now that I'd become aware just how valuable a commodity I was to Mike. No, the notion of Sally Cartwright 'pulling a sickie' was an inherently implausible one. An abhorrent thought even.

As the bus slowly meandered its way through the thronging morning traffic, I pulled my old phone out. I steeled myself and opened up my photo and video library. While I normally wouldn't condone using my phone on the bus to work, I felt vindicated under the circumstances.

There they were—just the two videos. I'd already watched the first. My shaky hand hovered over the screen, and I eventually opened the second one. The scene showed a bevy of sweaty-looking, black-garbed people standing stiffly, all thrashing their heads in unison like bobble toys as their ears came under attack from a thunderous and repulsive noise that some would loosely label as music. The next bit of the video could only be described as apocalyptic. The repulsive noise suddenly ceased and was replaced by a cacophony of screams and shrieks as people pushed, scrambled, and clambered out of shot. Eventually, all that was in shot was a pool of reddened bodies lying lifeless on the floor covered by shards of glass. Then the screen turned black.

That's all there was.

I sat, staring blankly and rethinking the events of last night. Who was this woman who'd called to forewarn me of this tragedy? She mentioned something about YouTube. I knew this to be a video-sharing platform where people put up videos for others to view. With some trepidation, I opened up my YouTube app and typed in *mirror ball kills five people*. Numerous short videos about mirror balls for sale popped up but none about a falling one. My video wasn't there. Then I typed in *homeless man blown up by bomb*. There was one very short video of a news report of the incident outside the Fancy Chef. Most of the other videos were about homeless men who had been hurt by pranksters hurling firecrackers at them. Again, my video was nowhere to be seen.

I checked my call records. Nothing.

It seemed that everything was spinning away and driving me to the brink of thinking that I was going crazy. Or was it just the depression I didn't think I had that was manifesting itself in some weird way? And all this just after finding out that I'm not autistic.

It wasn't fair. The fortunes of life seemed not to be metered out evenly or by choice.

My morning's work was spectacularly unproductive. I dare say even rivalling that of my colleagues. Snapshots of the disturbing video kept flashing before my eyes every time I looked at my computer screen. A little voice kept telling me to ignore them, to act naturally. After all, no one here knew I was out last night—Sally Cartwright never goes out.

I didn't go to the Fancy Chef today. I wasn't particularly hungry. Instead, I walked the streets trying to make sense of all this stuff that was happening to me. Who filmed that video? It couldn't have been me because I wasn't even there. And what about the other video of the homeless man? Was there a connection between the two? How could I have filmed a homeless man being blown up yet escape being blown up myself? I can't answer that because I can't even remember it.

The wind was icy, and I took refuge inside the foyer of a large modern hotel. I sat on a Poltrona Frau armchair located in an isolated corner far away from the bar and reception areas. I gazed around at the lifeless brown walls dappled with mildew. Sadness drained through me.

Dr Gail will make me better. I decided to call her office.

'I'm sorry, Ms Cartwright. Dr Eisenhuth isn't in this afternoon' was the brusque reply.

'Does she work evenings?' I could go there straight from work, I thought.

'I'm afraid not. Your scheduled appointment isn't for a couple of days. I suggest you wait till then.'

I didn't care what this person suggested. 'But I need to tell her something. It's important. Please.' I didn't think my tone was near urgent enough.

The secretary's sigh sounded weary. I wondered how many similar calls like this one she had to field every day. 'The best I can do is text her your number. But I can't promise she'll call you back. She's very busy.'

I thanked her and hung up.

Work was so unenticing. I had one eye on my phone and the other looking out to see if anyone was staring at me, so my computer screen got to have a well-earned rest. I found myself looking up at the clock and willing the hands to shake off their lethargy. If Mike knew the state my mind was in right now, I'm sure he would have wished he had made me redundant.

My phone rang. It was an effort to switch my brain to alert mode, and it took me a few seconds to answer it. Rob, Casey, and Wilma all craned their heads towards me like chickens trying to push through cage wire.

'Hello, Sally Cartwright speaking.'

'Hello, Sally, this is Dr Eisenhuth. Gail. You wanted to talk to me?'

'Yes, can you hold a second please?' Never having taken a personal call at work before, I was unaware of the standards and principles involved. Should I continue conversing at my desk or move to some place more private? I had often seen my colleagues taking calls at their desks, but on occasion, they also moved elsewhere to talk. It probably depended on the person calling and the nature of the call. As my reason for contacting Dr Gail was of a personal nature, I decided to step outside. 'Hello, Gail. Thank you for returning my call.'

'Is everything okay, Sally?' There was genuine concern in her voice.

'Yes. No. Well, sort of.' All bases covered.

'Something is troubling you. What is it?'

'Something happened last night,' I explained. 'There are things happening to me that I'm not sure about. Things that I don't even know if they're real or not.'

'I see. Can you tell me how you're feeling right now?'

'I feel a bit sad, I think.' I heard some rustling noises like someone shuffling paper.

'Are you at work, Sally?'

I looked up at the clock, buoyed by Dr Gail's enthusiastic tone. 'Yes. I finish in fifteen minutes.'

'Can you be at my office at five-thirty?'

'I can do that.'

She was dressed casually, but there was nothing accidental about it. Pressed khaki pants, brown polished ankle boots, and an open-necked pale-blue woollen shirt—the perfect balance between relaxed and professional.

It was only the two of us, Dr Gail explained. Her secretary had already left for the day. I felt more at ease knowing that we were alone.

'I want you to feel totally safe here, Sally.' We sat in the same chairs as last week. The eucalyptus tissues were well within reach. 'I'd like you to tell me, slowly, exactly what happened to you last night. You can go back even further if you think it's important.'

I drew a deep breath and began explaining the circumstances of how Declan and I met and how he asked me to a musical performance and how when we got there I received this strange phone call telling me about the terrible accident that hadn't happened yet and how then I'd grabbed Declan and we both left in a mad panic. I didn't put in the bit about faking my period. She didn't need to know about that.

'And then this video appeared on my phone. That's all I can tell you …' I heard my voice trail off.

Dr Gail took my phone and proceeded to watch both videos. Then she sat back and opened her notebook. 'Could anyone else have taken your phone?'

I shook my head. 'It was in my bag the whole time.'

'Okay … there are a few things I'd like to unpick in all of that. Firstly, you are aware that if, as you say, your phone was in your possession the whole time, then the only person who could have taken those videos was yourself.'

'But I wasn't there when they happened!' Dr Gail stopped writing, and there was an awkward pause before she spoke again.

'Right …' she said. 'So how do you think the video got there, Sally?

Do you happen to carry a miniature time machine in your back pocket wherever you go?'

If this was some sort of attempt at humour, it was a poor one at that and certainly didn't work. The fact was that my mind was all over the place, and I didn't know what actually happened. Was it a crime to not be thinking clearly under those circumstances?

I shook my head again.

There was a long pause. It was exhausting, talking about what I thought happened and worrying whether I came across as dumb or naïve.

Dr Gail sat back in her chair and began studying the notes she had written. 'I want to run something past you, Sally. Let's just say, hypothetically, that you *did* stay to listen to the music and you *did* take that video last night. Wouldn't it be plausible to suggest that you were merely recording the performance, and in all the panic that followed, you took Declan's arm and ran out of the venue at the same time as everybody else did when the tragedy was unfolding?'

I stared at her but said nothing. Staring suddenly seemed a natural thing to do.

Dr Gail continued, 'So in all the mayhem, you got your timelines all mixed up. You unknowingly recorded the accident. The human brain sometimes doesn't understand the passage of time, Sally, especially when it is confronted with fear. It processes our thoughts in strange ways.'

I slumped back in my seat. I'd come here for help, and all Dr Gail could do was point the finger of blame straight back at me. I know what I heard and what I saw. Declan does too. 'Gail, Declan can verify the chronology of events. He even thanked me for saving his life.'

'I suppose on some level you both want to believe the whole thing was just as you say it was.'

I failed to see what angle Dr Gail was taking. 'Can you explain that please?'

'In all the mayhem, Declan would have been just as confused as you. It is not hard to see how he could have followed your lead and reached the same conclusion.'

I tried to gather my thoughts into some sort of coherent response, but it was difficult. 'What about the video of the homeless man?'

Dr Gail nodded encouragingly. 'Yes, that will help us once you begin remembering what actually happened. That event is just one of the many issues I'd like to suggest we explore over the next few sessions.'

'But aren't these two events connected? I mean, the only way I can figure this out is to view them as possibly premonitions.'

'Premonitions?' I could see by her tone of voice and her expression that Dr Gail was totally dismissive of my theory. 'Premonitions are feelings that something is going to happen. Most people experience premonitions to some degree. The phone rings, and you have a strong feeling in your gut about who it is, even though you may not have been expecting that person to call. Sometimes it's not even as specific as that. Something happens, and you think to yourself, "I knew that was going to happen." No, Sally. What you experienced weren't premonitions.'

I listened but didn't respond. Dr Gail looked at me consolingly before continuing, 'None of us can foresee the future with absolute certainty because it hasn't happened yet.'

I knew that everything she said was logical and made perfect sense, but I still wasn't convinced. I wasn't prepared to argue the point, though.

There was a lull before Dr Gail resurrected the session, 'Did you read the information I gave you on emotional behavioural disorder?'

I nodded.

She went on to explain about EBD. 'There are many overlapping factors involved that predominantly relate to childhood: neglect, abuse, turmoil, instability, those sorts of things.'

Damn. There was my childhood rearing its ugly head again. Perhaps Mummy should stand in for me during these sessions. She'd have all the answers at her fingertips.

Dr Gail took out a prescription pad and began writing. 'Do you take any medications currently, Sally?'

I shook my head. 'None whatsoever,' I announced proudly. She handed me a prescription. 'What's this?'

She hesitated for a few seconds before seemingly going off on a tangent. 'Life is not all waterfalls, butterflies, and unicorns, Sally.'

I was okay with waterfalls and butterflies, but couldn't quite see the analogy with the unicorns.

I allowed her to continue. 'Today's session crystallises the EBD diagnosis in my mind. We don't have a drug that specifically targets that condition. We often use drugs that we know can at least address many of its common symptoms. I've given you a medicine called Tofranil, which I'd like you to take daily. You won't notice an immediate effect, but in time, I'm confident it will help you.'

Help me with what? I was too embarrassed to ask, and Dr Gail sensed my apprehension. 'Sally', she said softly, 'adverse childhood experiences can cause long-term health issues. Improving your mind is the first step in your recovery process.'

I'm sure I now looked even more anxious. Dr Gail reached out and touched my hand. 'You can't fight this on your own,' she continued. 'It's like trying to swim against the tide. If you struggle, you end up facing the wrong way and get into even more distress.'

That was a disturbing analogy; I never liked water.

'You must be patient, Sally. I'm here to help you. I think you want to be happy, don't you? We can work together in this room to achieve that goal. It won't be easy but it'll be worth it, trust me.'

Trust her? I imagined myself buying a used car from this woman. 'Okay', I said. 'do you still want to see me on Friday?'

'Yes. We have a lot to discuss.'

She refused to take any payment for today's session, which I appreciated. I was almost out the door when she called me back in. 'I almost forgot. I called Dr Rickards the other day. He and I are old acquaintances from medical school. He said he remembers you. He also said that he can't recall ever telling your mother that you have autism.'

CHAPTER 15

THE BUS RIDE home was just one big blur. All I could think about was Mummy. How could she lie to me all these years? *Why* did she lie to me? 'Nothing good ever happens to liars,' she'd say. What a hypocrite.

I hated everything about my childhood, but mainly I hated the way I was pigeonholed. I had lived my life without having an opportunity to discover the many other Sally Cartwrights who lived inside me and who would have been a lot more interesting.

Back in my flat, I sat on the couch feeling utterly exhausted and kept staring at Dr Gail's prescription. I'd never heard of Tofranil. What sort of drug was it? I know. The internet will tell me! I picked up my phone.

Chemical name: imipramine hydrochloride. A tricyclic antidepressant and a member of the dibenzoazepine group of compounds ... blah, blah, blah.

So it's official: I'm depressed. In a way, I'm grateful that Dr Gail had been sensitive enough not to press this point too much.

As I'd never taken any drug before, I thought it prudent that I familiarise myself with any adverse reactions that may accompany the consumption of this medicine.

I began reading the list of potential side effects: insomnia, appetite reduction, abnormal heart rhythm, tremors, muscle twitch, decreased libido, seizures, diarrhoea—the list went on. The last couple of items hit me right between the eyes: depression and suicidal ideation.

Medicine is a bit like reading Shakespeare: you hope the tricky words will make sense from their context. There were no tricky words here.

You're kidding me, right? Are they intimating that I could become more depressed or even try to kill myself if I take this drug? Why would anyone ever contemplate taking it? More importantly, why would any doctor prescribe it?

I promptly scrunched up the prescription and tossed it in the bin before sitting back down on the couch and reflecting on the day I'd had: First, Dr Gail tells me my mind could be a bit scrambled and that I'm making things up. Then she gives me some dangerous pills because I'm depressed. Then she tells me, rather nonchalantly, that I was never diagnosed with autism.

That's a lot to take in.

I felt like screaming or throwing something at the television. But then what? I'd have to buy a new television. No, I had to tame the volcano within. I had to learn to suppress the quiet rage knotted up inside me. Being angry never solves anything. I found that out the hard way over many years of witnessing Mummy's many diatribes.

The doorbell rang, and I looked up at the clock.

I'd forgotten that I invited Declan over and was thrown into a mild panic. Before my consultation with Dr Gail, I was convinced that the best way forward was to tell Declan the real reason why I insisted on leaving the club early last night. Tell him about the phone call and that I wasn't really bleeding and didn't need a pad. But Dr Gail had planted seeds of doubt in my mind.

I don't think it would be a good idea to tell him at this point.

The doorbell rang again. 'Sally?' The voice was muffled. I felt an urge to run, to escape and hide. But where to? I was a prisoner in my flat. How ridiculous.

'Declan, I need to ask you something about last night,' I said nervously as we sat opposite each other on the couch.

He sat back and nonchalantly took a sip of his beer, which I could see he was enjoying. I visited an alcohol shop for the first time yesterday. When I requested a moderate quantity of beer, the acne-faced young man behind the counter pointed exasperatingly to an area behind me. 'Which one, miss?' he asked in an annoyed tone. I walked out with six small bottles of an imported beer the name of which I can't even pronounce and a price that was, in my opinion, jaw-droppingly excessive.

'Ask away.' Declan took another sip of the liquid gold, and his brow was knitted with intense concentration.

'This might sound crazy, but did we leave before or after the musicians came on last night?' Declan's face puckered, and I could see he was trying hard to suppress a laugh. He looked away and then looked back to see if I was being serious. 'It was before, of course.' The corners of his mouth curled upwards. 'I think getting your period must have *cramped* your style!'

Sexism comes from a lack of sensitivity and respect for the opposite gender. It has no place in modern society. Especially when mocking a woman's menstrual cycle. Men should stop acting like giant babies. They should be educated more thoroughly on the entire biological process. I can't speak for women in, general, but for me, periods are highly unpleasant and inconvenient bodily processes. An evolutionary glitch.

My menstruation started when I was 12.

It will probably end when I am 52.

That's 40 years of periods.

That's 480 periods lasting an average of five days each.

That's 2,400 days or approximately six and a half years of blood emissions.

What a depressing statistic. I honestly believe that those happy girls in tampon commercials are mythical creatures.

I know I should have been cross with Declan for what he said, but I wasn't because I knew how ludicrous my question must have sounded. Instead, I pretended to appear bemused. 'That's funny, Declan. But I'm only seeking a factually accurate summation of what happened last night, that's all. The mind can play tricks on us in situations like the one we were confronted with.' Perfectly played, I thought. Straight out of the Dr Gail playbook.

Neither of us spoke for a while.

'Sally', he said eventually, 'this is serious. If you hadn't come over when you did and insisted that we leave, we might both be dead. I can recall what happened as clear as day.'

I couldn't counter Declan's logical and very believable synopsis.

Declan, you must be wrong because there is a video of the tragedy on my phone, and I'm the only one who could have taken it. That's what I should have said but didn't. 'Alright', I said. 'I concede that I may not have been in the best frame of mind to recall exactly what took place. Thank you for clearing that up for me.'

I could see in Declan's expression that he was more than a little curious as to why I was placing so much importance on the chronology of last night's events. 'I hope that's made you feel better,' he said. 'And I'm sorry about the period joke.' He reached out and put a hand on my arm and squeezed it tight. It was a strong hand. I could feel the heat growing in my cheeks, and I turned my head as if to hide in the most subtle of ways.

This could have been a watershed juncture for me—an inaugural evening of intimacy with a member of the opposite sex. But I wasn't ready for that just yet. If I were to lose my virginity, it had to be at just the right moment. Tonight wouldn't be that. Besides, Declan still thinks I have my period. Any physical intimacy under such biologically adverse circumstances would be akin to sunbaking on a cold and rainy day.

I stole a glance into Declan's eyes. He probably felt like he knew me by now, like he had a pretty good handle on the person I was. But he didn't know me at all. I will tell him things about me later, things I haven't told anybody else before, just to show him that I've endured the rough end like almost everyone does from time to time and that I too can feel hate. I might even let him into the events of my dark childhood so that he can appreciate why I am like I am. I'm not perfect. No one is, and anyone who tells you they are is living a lie.

The subject of dinner was to prove a tension breaker. When Declan commented that he hadn't yet eaten, I suggested heating up some soup, but he'd insisted on ordering a pizza. I have never in my entire existence eaten a pizza and wasn't about to broadcast that fact either. When Declan asked me what kind I would like, I wheeled out my newly discovered "you choose" line. I wasn't fussed. I was willing to give pizza a try. To be a little bit daring.

The pizza base was an inch thick and as white as office paper. The sauce tasted like it had come straight out of a can—and a cheap one at that. The inconsistently portioned pepperoni slices were hidden underneath pools of grease interspersed with dollops of gooey cheese. The only colour was provided by a few shards of red capsicum on top. I poked my piece with a fork, and it seemed to poke right back at me, such was the rubberiness of the dough.

It looked about as appealing as a bowl of Mummy's cold porridge. One bite was enough. More than enough actually. I couldn't fathom how the majority of people regarded this fare with admiring deference.

I think my pizza eating days are well and truly behind me.

Declan played with the pizza box, trying to crush it small enough to fit into my moderately sized bin. 'What's this?'

There, on top of a pile of apple peelings, was my Tofranil prescription. I swooped down as deftly as an overzealous seagull determined to procure the last discarded chip. 'Oh, that's just an old script for my period pain,' I casually explained. 'It expired, so I threw it out.' I slid the crumpled paper into my pocket. Declan's expression changed to one I had no hope of reading. He remained silent, fully aware that any further discussion about my period was strictly off-limits tonight.

After dinner, we sat on the couch watching an old Seinfeld episode. It was the one where George Costanza's girlfriend gets sick and he's told they can't have sex for at least six weeks. Declan seemed to enjoy the mirth much more than I did. I don't understand why anyone would ever make light of such a sensitive issue.

Declan kissed me when he left. First he leaned close and softly caressed my neck. Our foreheads briefly touched. I froze, more out of fear than excitement. I wanted to pull away but couldn't. I suppose it was that primal desire that lives in all of us. 'Sally,' he whispered slowly. At that point, I managed a half smile, my heart fluttering. Never before had my name sounded so wonderful. He pulled me closer, and I inhaled sharply as he pressed his warm lips against mine. Strangely, the unfamiliar smell of his breath didn't disturb me.

When we broke apart, his expression told me everything I needed to know.

CHAPTER 16

THERE ARE DAYS I wish I were dead, and this was one of them. A sudden gush of pain, sharp and nauseating, jolts throughout my body. My arms lose tension, and my legs begin to weaken. I try to cry, but the only sound is a pitiable moan from deep in my throat. Mummy's grip on my hair is so strong that I can't break away. Her anger grows from nowhere into a violent storm. I cannot match her rage, not even to save myself. 'Keep still, you silly girl!' Her shrill tones electrify the chilly, damp air.

It is blurry. Not exactly blurry but I have a hard time focusing on anything.

There are noises around me that I don't understand, and I can sense that I'm strapped down. I remember everything: the colours, the smells, the dirty hands, the blood. The man holding the knife gives me a predatory smile, and his nostrils flare wide. I squint hard. I have never seen such an ugly animal in my life. He pulls me up and unstraps me before hoisting me onto the table again. Then he blindfolds me, and lifts up my dress. I feel hands all over me, holding down my arms and legs and covering my mouth. Someone sits on my chest. I hear voices all talking over each other. I can feel cold steel pushing between my legs as I beg and plead for them to stop. There are vague impressions of pain, of clawed hands grabbing me, but they could just be dreams or hallucinations. I can feel panic bubbling up in me. The steel gets colder and presses harder against my skin. I am drowning in panic now; and with all the strength I possess, I push out my legs and kick someone hard. I hear Mummy yelling and calling me a silly girl again. My legs are then bound with rope again, and I lie helpless in a maelstrom of fear. I try to absorb the pain. I scream. My body suddenly becomes rigid, and my eyes roll back. I am frothing at the mouth. I become intensely tired and eventually pass out.

Mummy never warned me. It was the biggest betrayal and deceit I have ever encountered. The height of moral degeneracy.

I was circumcised at 8 years of age.

*

'Sal! It's so good to hear from you, but you normally don't call on a Thursday. What's up?'

I needed to talk to Mummy before seeing Dr Gail tomorrow. 'Oh, nothing,' I said casually. 'I just rang to see how you were.' That wasn't true.

Mummy spoke quickly, 'Listen, I can't talk for too long today. I have an appointment.'

Such difficult emotions. I see them as flotsam and jetsam scattered along a river and unable to be stopped. Before I could begin my rant, which I'd practised in my head ad nauseam last night, Mummy spoke again, 'Aren't you going to ask me where I'm going, darling?' Her voice was sickly sweet.

'Where are you going, Mummy?'

'Dr Rickards wants me to see a heart specialist. He says my ticker's not right. I don't think it's been right since you left me, Sal. You wouldn't understand, of course.' The jagged edge in her voice and the mention of Dr Rickards sent a current down my spine. I pictured Mummy pressing a sharp needle into my back, her face contorting with pleasure.

I should show empathy and be able to comfort her like any normal daughter would. But I'm not just any normal daughter.

'Did Dr Rickards tell you anything else, Mummy? Did he mention anything about me?'

'About you? Don't be silly, Sal. Why would he do that? He hasn't seen you for God knows how long.'

I had to pluck up the courage now before my thoughts tumbled unabated into the abyss. 'Mummy, I need to ask you something. Something important.'

'What on earth could be important?' Such coldness. I had no choice but to ignore it.

'Did Dr Rickards really tell you that I'm autistic?'

'What? Why ask me this now? How strange, Sal.' Her voice was a lot quieter now. I felt my heart quicken and sweat trickle down my back.

'It's just that I have reason to believe that I may not have autism.'

'Sally Cartwright, don't be daft!' Mummy laughed nervously as if trying to amuse herself.

Blood was pounding through my temples. I don't know where I found my courage. 'Mummy, you lied to me. You lied about me having autism. Dr Rickards never told you any such thing!'

'Sal, darling! I think living on your own has warped your mind. I know it's slowly warping mine.'

My eyes welled with tears, and I began hyperventilating. I had to hold it together before everything crumpled. I drew one long breath. 'Liar! You're a liar, Mummy, and I hate you!'

I sensed Mummy's shock through the phone. 'Mummy? Did you hear what I just said?'

'I heard you, you insensible little bitch. How dare you accuse me of lying? You're the liar, not me. You know what happens to liars, don't you, Sal? You of all people should know.' I heard the hiss of air leaving her lungs.

'You don't want me to be happy, Mummy. You don't!'

I could hear her taking in a deep breath. 'What? Where's all this coming from? This isn't like you at all.'

My anger was at boiling point now. It was time to let the steam dissipate. 'You're afraid, Mummy. You're afraid that I might find the happiness you never had! You don't want happiness for me. You are a wretched person, and I'm determined never to be like you. Never!'

The ensuing silence was so absolute that my breathing was loud to my ears. Mummy was speechless for the first time I can remember.

Not receiving a retaliatory barb calmed me a little. I drew a slow deep breath. 'I went to see a doctor, Mummy. She told me I'm not autistic.'

'Why, Sal? Why burden me with this now just when I'm going to get my heart checked? You can be so insensitive sometimes.'

I don't care about your cold heart; that can never be fixed. That was what I wanted to say. 'All these years, I've been made to feel inferior,' I said. 'And it's all your fault. Why do you hurt me like this?'

Mummy sighed. 'Have you finished? I'm getting rather impatient now.' She sounded angry.

'Do you know just how far a little love could have gone?' I said. 'I felt caught, trapped. All that anxiety and fear made my brain shut down, and I had to hide myself away just to cope. You made me believe I could never fight back. But here I am, Mummy. I'm fighting back now!'

I'd never heard Mummy's whimpering cries before. They were more like soft wails struggling to be let free. She eventually composed herself. 'Don't get me side-tracked now, young lady. Do you hear me? You think you're so smart and have everything worked out. Just because you've found your voice. Well, you're not so smart, and your voice is feeble. You're a failure, Sal.'

My tears flowed unchecked now, and I found myself choking them back. 'You broke your promise, Mummy. You promised to love, to cherish, and to protect me.'

'What do you know about love, Sal? Everything I ever did for you was for love. The past is still alive, my darling. Those lovely scars of yours—they're a reminder of my love. Do you still have them? Oh, of course you do. Do you still look at them from time to time? I think you do. And how's that limp going? I bet everyone notices it.'

I shook my head, unable to speak as a sharp phantom pain invaded my groin and hip areas. I've lost count of the number of times Mummy has insulted me on the phone. She's always had the opportunity to apologise and straighten things out with words that are unbent, but she hardly ever did. If a thinly veiled apology was ever offered, it was always disingenuous. She could never understand the true peace that comes from genuine and heartfelt contrition.

'Have you lost your tongue now? Just when I was starting to enjoy the new Sally Cartwright!'

I'd had enough. My brain was drowning in cold malice. 'You telling me that I had autism—was that for love too?' The words came out of my mouth as hot as a dragon's flame.

'Yes, it was! I was only trying to protect you from the evils of this world, Sal. Don't you get that?'

I didn't know how I was supposed to *get* being told all my life that I wasn't normal when in all likelihood I was and could have had a happier childhood doing the things that normal children do: riding a bike, playing with dolls, going to the playground, having friends over. I never had any of those things. Mummy always said that playing with dolls was not educational and that any friends were unsuitable for me because they would eventually turn out to be evil and that playing outside would make me sick. What did I end up with instead? Healthy doses of abuse, abandonment, and neglect.

Her friends may see sweet berries, but I only see bitter ones. Was I being too judgemental? I didn't think so.

Calm down, Sally.

'Mummy, I hope you get good news at the doctor's today.'

Mummy's sigh was overlayed with a thin wheeze. 'I won't. My heart's already been broken into a million pieces. You've never heard the sound of a heart breaking, have you, dear?'

CHAPTER 17

'HAVE YOU BEEN taking your tablets, Sally?'
'Yes, I have.'
'Any side effects?'
'No, none.'
'Good.'
I didn't need Declan today. I didn't want him with me.

Dr Gail was wearing a navy-blue skirt and jacket with a white shirt and flat shoes, which did nothing to hide her wide bony ankles.

She opened a folder. 'I'd like to start with some breathing techniques to help you relax. Then we can go through some memory-recall exercises to try and help you remember the video of the homeless man and the bomb. Is that alright with you?'

As long as we didn't have to talk about Mummy, it was more than alright. I wasn't prepared to tell Dr Gail that Mummy and I had spoken yesterday. 'Yes,' I answered.

'Okay. Let's get started.' Dr Gail went on to explain why breathing properly is important. 'The way we breathe affects our whole body. Our breath helps to regulate important functions such as heart rate and blood pressure and can mean the difference between whether or not a stress response is signalled.'

She taught me something called the 4-7-8 breathing technique where you completely exhale all your breath through your mouth before closing your mouth and inhaling through your nose for four seconds. Then you hold your breath for seven seconds before exhaling slowly through your mouth for eight seconds. I tried it, and it seemed to relax me straight away.

'Now that you're relaxed, I want you to close your eyes, Sally. Sometimes it's easier to access memories that way.'

I nodded and gently lowered my eyelids shut, imagining myself going off to sleep.

'That's good. Now imagine your body is like a light balloon, floating. If your body floats, so does your mind, Sally. I want you to think back to the day of the explosion. You told me that you hit your head outside your office when the bomb went off, and that was around the time you normally returned from lunch. Is that correct?' Dr Gail spoke in a low, soothing voice.

'Yes, I return to my work duties at precisely one o'clock each and every day.'

'Can you recall where you went for lunch that day?'

'I can. It was at a place called the Fancy Chef, but that's where I go every day.'

I could hear Dr Gail picking up her pen to write something down. 'Do you recall specifically being there that day?'

'Well, yes—I mean no, I don't recall specifically, but I'm sure I was there.'

'Can anyone confirm that?'

I shrugged. 'The staff I suppose.'

Dr Gail sighed. 'I doubt that. There's a concept called repetition priming where the presentation of one stimulus influences the response to a second stimulus. It means that the staff could say you were there that day even if you really weren't because they have been conditioned to seeing you there every other day. Do you follow me, Sally?'

I wasn't really listening. I was thinking of something really crazy. 'Huh?' I said as I opened my eyes instinctively. Dr Gail repeated the repetition priming bit, and I nodded to indicate that I understood what she had said. 'But I must've been there because I don't eat my lunch anywhere else,' I explained.

Dr Gail ignored my last comment. 'Okay, let's move on. You can keep your eyes open now. What's your overriding memory of having lunch at this particular café? Is it the staff, the food?'

'Neither really. It's of watching the people walking by outside. It's a bit like a rolling soap opera. You know, where you can pick up the plot at any time and not have missed anything.'

Dr Gail laughed briefly. 'Yes. I can imagine how it could be like that, Sally. Now tell me, what sort of people do you see walking by?'

'All sorts. Mainly ordinary people going about their ordinary lives.'

'Ordinary. Is that how you see them?'

'Well, yes. They're all like mice on a wheel, repeating the same meaningless routines every day.'

Dr Gail nodded and bit down on her lower lip. 'Do you put yourself in that category, Sally?'

I hesitated. 'No. I'm not like them.'

'Even though you have lunch at the same café every day.'

I could see her point. 'That's different,' I said without elaborating.

Dr Gail looked at me with an expression of indifference. 'Let's get back to the people you see walking by, shall we? Do any of them stand out? For instance, is there anyone who is very tall or short or grossly overweight that you always see?'

'I don't pay much attention to their physical dimensions.'

'What about clothes? I assume some would be dressed in suits.'

'Most are in suits, even the homeless men, but theirs are always shabby and dirty.'

Dr Gail's eyes widened. 'So what's your number one memory of these homeless people? Is it their clothes?'

I thought hard. A whole minute went by.

'No, it's not their clothes. They all stare at me from afar. But they never come close enough to—' Wait, a fragment just flashed before my eyes—something about a man staring at me through the café window. *Think hard, Sally.*

Dr Gail must have sensed something. 'Sally, do you remember any of these men ever coming up to you or to anybody else while you were eating your lunch?'

'I remember moments here and there but nothing specific,' I said. 'No, wait.' I closed my eyes. 'I see a homeless man talking to a mother who is pushing a pram. I remember that.' It certainly wasn't as detailed a recollection as I would have liked, but it was a start.

'Do you remember if that was on the day of the explosion?' Dr Gail spoke softly and gently. 'No rush, Sally. Take your time.'

MARIO BORAZIO

I felt a level of distress, confusion, a churning in my stomach. There was a memory there, somewhere deep, but I was unable to retrieve it. 'I remember that scene vividly, as though it were yesterday,' I said. 'But I have no time frame around it. I'm sorry.'

We sat quietly for a moment. If only I could go back. There was something hidden away, yet I couldn't fathom what that might be. I wished now I had that time machine that Dr Gail had jokingly mentioned in a previous session.

I looked at my phone on the desk. Suddenly my brain felt like it was about to explode. 'YouTube!' I shouted.

Dr Gail saw the shock on my face before I'd even enunciated those last words.

'Excuse me? What about YouTube?'

'It's all clear to me now. I got a phone call, while eating lunch, telling me about the video I'd taken of the homeless man and the bomb going off. It was the same scenario as that terrible accident with the mirror ball the other night.' I rested my elbows on my knees and put my head in my hands. Dr Gail handed me the tissue box, which I rested on my lap. I knew what she was thinking: that I'd gotten the time sequences all wrong again. I must've taken the video and ran away *after* the explosion, hitting my head later on. It was all so logical all over again.

Dr Gail was very calm. 'Don't worry yourself too much, Sally. We'll take this slowly, one small step at a time.'

In a way, I was angry at myself for remembering what had occurred. But I was determined not to get into a slanging match again about what happened when and where and in what sequence. I wasn't going to tell Dr Gail that there was no phone record of that call either. That would only reinforce her opinion that I was as dumb as a box of old rocks. 'Can we talk about something else, Gail? All this recall business has got me on edge a little.'

She looked at her watch. 'Of course, Sally,' she said softly. 'We have fifteen minutes left. Is there anything you would like to talk about specifically?'

There was. I was compelled to bring Mummy into the conversation at this point. I bit the bullet and told her about my circumcision, all the unpleasant and vile detail of it. It was the right time, I thought. And it felt good to finally get it off my chest. She listened sympathetically, nodding the whole time.

'That's a big thing in your life, Sally. At some stage, we need to talk more about your mother and where she fits into all this.'

I nodded almost imperceptibly. 'Okay,' I said and left it at that. Dr Gail was well aware how sensitive a subject that was for me.

'Sally, the only way to silence the inner voices in your head is to face your past head-on.'

I nodded.

She sat back in her chair. 'Let's talk a little bit about female circumcision. The practice was generally based on a now-discarded theory called reflex neurosis where things like depression and other psychological disorders were thought to originate from the genitals. It was also a method for enhancing a girl's purity and cleanliness in anticipation for when she would receive a man later in her life. Thankfully, such practices are now outlawed in this country.'

I'm sure my circumcision wasn't done for the reasons outlined by Dr Gail. No, mine was merely exacted to deny me a normal and happy life by my nefarious mother. It was as pure and as simple as that. 'Gail, I also need to tell you that, because of all this, I'm still a virgin.'

Dr Gail didn't react in any way to suggest that she was the least bit surprised. 'I see,' she said almost offhandedly. 'You shouldn't be put off though, Sally. Most women who have been circumcised still maintain a perfectly normal sex life.'

I looked up at the clock. Our session was drawing to a close, but there was so much more I wanted to say. Having come this far, there was no way I could turn around now. 'I've always been afraid,' I remarked. 'I'm even more afraid now that I've met Declan.'

'You shouldn't be afraid. You have every right to be intimate together if that is what you both want.'

I looked down at the carpet and shook my head. Tears burst forth like water from a dam, spilling down my cheeks as I clumsily tore a handful of tissues out of the box and breathed in the rich aroma of eucalyptus oil. 'How can I even think about being intimate?' I said. 'I haven't told Declan anything about my past.' Dr Gail leaned forward and took my hand.

'And you've never found yourself in this situation before, not even in a casual relationship?'

What Dr Gail was insinuating disappointed me. 'I don't do casual relationships,' I said firmly. She should have worked that out already.

'Do you like Declan?'

'Yes, I think so. He seems to care about me too.'

'Then you've got to tell him, Sally. Just like you told me here today. He'll understand, I promise you.'

'Alright,' I said without sounding too convincing.

Dr Gail sensed this and continued to press. 'Look, Sally, a lot of women, circumcised or not, can relate to how you're feeling. Just being naked in front of a new person can be daunting in itself. We are always our own harshest critics. Declan is attracted to you for who you are. In order to develop your relationship, you've got to discover each other emotionally and physically. Avoiding physical intimacy may stop your relationship from going forward, and that would be a shame because you've just told me that you really care about this person.'

I looked away when she'd finished talking, knowing full well that she was right. I wasn't ready to dive full length into a relationship just yet, but I couldn't just sit on the edge of a cliff waiting to be pushed off. I needed to take baby steps. 'I think what you are saying makes a lot of sense, Gail.'

'Good. I'm glad you understand.' She looked at her watch. 'Our time's up today, but we'll revisit this topic and others next week.'

Next week? Does this woman expect me to open myself up like a can of tuna all over again? After all the work I'd done? And what other topics was she referring to? I could hazard a guess.

I took the bus home and reflected on my session. In hindsight, I think Dr Gail ended it at exactly the right time. I managed to get some of my memory back and unloaded a lot of things. I couldn't have unloaded much more. My body felt heavy, but my mind was as light as a feather probably because it had been relieved of much of its ordure.

Once home, I slumped deep into my armchair. I didn't want to sleep—not yet. I wanted to savour today's little victories, but I felt tiredness creeping up inside me like a battery slowly being drained away to nothing.

A lot of fear had been purged today. I felt at peace. Then I slept a long sleep.

CHAPTER 18

I
T STARTED WITH fists, kicks and yelps in a cloud of dust. Now it was almost totally dark. I felt the cold as soon as I lifted my head. Someone was laughing. Several of them actually. Then something hard smashed against my head, and the laughter suddenly stopped. I realised I couldn't hear or see anything clearly. The silence continued until there was a rumbling, like many voices protesting and arguing. They seemed distant. I tried to roll over, but many hands wrapped around my body like rubber bands. I couldn't move and began to think I must be trapped somewhere underground. Then suddenly there was noise and then light and the feeling of air over my face. I opened my eyes. My enemies were nowhere to be seen. Bruised and battered, I was carried out of the toilet block.

*

As I've mentioned previously, my school days were never pleasant, even less so when they were painfully re-enacted in my dreams. No matter how much I tried to suppress them, they kept reappearing.

I woke in a sweat, the fear rising up and almost choking me off. Thankfully, it was Saturday, and I didn't have to go to work. But this was no ordinary Saturday. It was the last one of the month, which always meant a trip to the hairdresser.

My mood was strange; I felt on edge and tried to arrive at a plausible explanation for this state of mind. I concluded it was most likely a polite request from my brain to shelter from the emotions that had built up from my dealings with Mummy, my emotions regarding Declan, and my purge session with Dr Gail yesterday. To say the past week had been somewhat unique was an understatement.

I needed a circuit breaker. A feeling of recklessness suddenly coursed through me. I had never considered changing my hair before, but I decided it was time to try a new hairdresser and get a different style. Before I had time to renege on this decision, I ran a hand through my locks and tugged at them so hard that my eyes began to water.

Yes, I was ready to do this.

Her name was Charlize or something that sounded similar. I wondered if she was named after the famous actress. 'New mop, eh? A bit of paint work. I think it's a goer!'

Although her phraseology wasn't aligned with mine, I found her pleasant enough to be trusted. Why not go the whole hog? I hadn't been made up properly before. Ever.

Minimalism was about to give way to extravagance for Sally Cartwright.

Charlize explained with gusto what she was going to do. Terms like *stepped layers*, *feathered finish*, and *half-head highlights* with foils poured out of her mouth as if she were reciting prose. It all sounded like an incomprehensible mound of gibberish, but I didn't care. She lifted a handful of my mane and complimented me on how healthy and shiny it looked. 'How short, honey?'

'The length that you think would best suit me, Charlize,' I said with exaggerated enthusiasm.

I finished up with champagne curls that cascaded over my shoulders and ended with what Charlize explained were 'electric blond' tips. My fringe hovered seductively over my eyes, which were ringed by dark eyeshadow. I looked into the mirror and saw a coldblooded assassin or gothic serial killer. The face paint was applied thick and unevenly, which I was informed was the 'modern way'.

The cost of my new look was extortionate. I worked out that if I'd just had a basic cut and purchased the requisite products and tools to recreate a similar look myself at home, more than half of the money I'd outlaid would still be in my pocket.

Just as well, the new Sally Cartwright didn't worry about all that anymore. After all, you can't take your hard-earned with you.

An hour later, I was back in my flat sitting on my bed staring through the mirror. What had I done? What was I thinking? Suddenly

MARIO BORAZIO

I looked like a complete stranger. I stared some more, moving my head from side to side while keeping my eyes straight. Then it all became so clear, like one of those 'magic eye' pictures. I was in awe of just how skilled Charlize had been. The more I kept staring, the more I liked what I was seeing. Dare I say it, I looked younger. It was my Dorian Gray moment.

I decided that my new look was acceptable after all. It actually suited me more than my old one.

I sat back and pondered whether to call Mummy. It was Saturday, but only two days had passed since our acrimonious phone conversation. She would want me to call if only to seize another opportunity to give me an old-fashioned dressing down.

I had come to view Mummy as a tumour, thinking that it might be better to cut out the malignancy so that the rest of me remains healthy. But I can't shut her out; Sally Cartwright can't do that.

'Hello?' I said rather tentatively. I braced myself for the onslaught.

'Oh, so you're still speaking to me, are you?' Her abrasive tone wasn't unanticipated

'Mummy', I began, 'how are you? How did it go with the heart specialist?'

'Really, Sal?' she drawled. 'That's just delightful, pretending that you are interested in my welfare. It sure didn't seem that way the last time we spoke.'

This wasn't going to be easy. Mummy played the sympathy card better than anyone else. If there was an Olympic event for it, she'd win the gold medal every time. 'Mummy, I just want to know if you're going to be alright.'

'Oh, I'll be alright. I believe in the power of one. I have to.' She was at it again, being overly garish.

I decided to take the upper hand and move the conversation forward—unchartered territory for me. 'Mummy, did the doctor give you any tablets to take?'

She was quiet for what seemed an eternity. Her laboured breathing sounded worse than ever. I wondered if it was a put-on. 'He was a nice

Indian doctor, and yes, he gave me some pills.' No elaboration. Her tone was sombre.

'Mummy, is it serious? I really want to know.'

'Oh, Sal, he said I have heart failure. I have to take pills for the rest of my life, and I can't get too worked up about things anymore. Even trivial things. I suppose that means cancelling my bridge-club evenings.'

I steadied myself, suddenly feeling guilty for my tirade the other night. 'Mummy, I'm sorry for what I said last time. I didn't mean any of it, really.' There was no other way to phrase what I felt had to be said under the current circumstances.

I heard Mummy sniff. 'And how am I supposed to know if you really mean that, Sal?'

'I do mean it, Mummy,' I said. 'Hey! I got a new hairstyle done today, and I'd like you to see it. Can I come up next weekend?' Being spontaneous gave me an instant rush.

There was silence for a while.

'You want to visit me? I'd like that very much, but you don't drive, remember?'

I thought the way that Mummy phrased her last sentence was a thinly veiled way of saying that she didn't really want me to visit her. 'I'll get there, Mummy, I promise.'

'How will you do that? I'll let you know that the trains aren't reliable in these parts on weekends.'

'I might be able to get someone to drive me.'

'Oh, is that right?' Mummy's breathing quickened.

I couldn't hide it any longer. I had to tell her.

'I sort of have a boyfriend. His name's Declan,' I said.

She said something, but it was whispered so softly I didn't hear it. Maybe she didn't want me to hear it.

'He's really nice, Mummy. I'd like you to meet him.' That wasn't entirely true. Mummy has what can only be described as a rusted-on judgemental disposition. Her unpredictable and often abrasive behaviour around new people she met wasn't one of her redeeming features. She always had them sized ab initio.

'That's grand, Sal! You know how dearly I'd love you to find someone special. Is he the one, do you think?'

I tried to restrain my voice. 'I don't know yet. We've only known each other for a short time.'

'I'm so pleased we're talking about this, Sal. That's what mothers and daughters should do. So how did the two of you meet? It wasn't on one of those dating sites, was it?'

'No, Mummy. I lost my phone, and he returned it to me.' She didn't need to know any other details.

'How considerate. Good manners are hard to find these days.'

They certainly are. She knows all about that.

'What did you say his name was, dear?'

'Declan.'

'Ah, a good Irish name. Our ancestors were Irish. Did you know that, Sal?'

'No, I didn't.' Of course I didn't. Mummy never talked about her past. I had no idea where she was born or where she lived her early life or even how many husbands she's had. It's pitiful really. No one would ever believe me if I told them.

I've always been afraid to ask her anything about her past. Afraid that I'd uncover sordid things that were best kept hidden forever. Finding such things out would be like peeling layers from a rancid onion.

'So can I come and visit you, Mummy?'

I heard the click of a lighter and then a long-exhaled breath. 'Of course you can. I'd like to meet Declan. That would be nice.'

'You shouldn't smoke, Mummy. Remember what Dr Rickards said.'

'It's not that easy, Sal. Haven't you ever smoked? Oh, that's right. You were always pernickety about things like that, weren't you? Overcautious. Never took any risks.' Her voice was tiresome now. I didn't respond, fearing I'd upset her again if I said anything. 'I suppose I'll have to give your old room a bit of a spruce up. It will be just as you remember it, Sal. Just you wait!'

I didn't want to remember my room: the shouting, the beatings, the going to bed hungry, the feeling of being super angry or super terrified, of being locked up. Dr Gail said that the first step in overcoming the past was to have the courage to face it. This was my opportunity. 'That would be nice, Mummy. Declan and I would like that.' I tried to sound positive.

'Oh, I don't like the idea of you and Declan in the same room, Sal. He'll stay in the spare room.'

What was I thinking? 'Of course, Mummy,' I said.

'I've got to go, Sal. It's time for me to take my pills. Life has sure changed in a hurry for your dear old mum.'

I didn't feel the need to qualify her comments with any form of sympathy. 'Okay, Mummy. I'll speak to Declan and see if he's free next weekend.'

'Declan—that's such a nice name.'

MARIO BORAZIO

CHAPTER 19

WORK TURNED OUT to be a drag the whole week. No matter how hard I tried, I just couldn't concentrate. It was an effort to switch my brain to alert mode for even five minutes. It got to the point where I had to write myself notes. Rob was the first to sense my monkey mind. After initially ignoring me, he came up and gave me that look, the one formed when one senses something amiss. 'Hey, Sal, something smells fishy here. Are you hiding your lunch somewhere?' He leaned over and grabbed one of my Post-It notes. 'That's interesting. I thought you were supposed to be the queen of efficient work practices. At least that's what fat ass tells us.'

'Fuck off, Rob.' The words felt good to my ears. They were like golden honey trickling smoothly from the corners of my mouth. I gave Rob a cold glare and snatched the note from his hand before pressing it back onto the side of my computer screen, my heart pounding.

Rob went as white as chalk. I knew exactly what he was thinking: *Sally Cartwright swearing? Never!* His eyes and mouth were frozen in an expression of stunned surprise. It gave me a gratifying feeling knowing that the roles were reversed for once.

His comments were ridiculous, unnecessary, and just plain dickery. I'm glad I swore at him. He deserved it. He didn't speak to me again for the rest of the week.

Declan met me for lunch. He loved my new hair and agreed to drive me the one and a half hours to Mummy's house on Saturday. 'It's no problem at all. We'll have fun,' he beamed.

I arrived at Dr Gail's office with a spring in my step.

'Have you told Declan yet?' She got straight to the point, ignoring my new locks and the ever-so-subtle increase in my volume of makeup.

I shook my head. 'I was going to, but then, when it came to it, I just couldn't do it. Not yet.'

She sat back on her chair and stared at me with a vexed expression. At that moment, I felt like jettisoned cargo. 'Sally, sometimes we are too quick to judge people. As I said last week, I'm sure he'll understand.'

He may well understand, but I wasn't going to risk his not understanding foiling our plans for tomorrow's trip. 'I'll tell him when the time's right,' I said.

'When will the time be right?' Dr Gail's tone was slightly hostile.

I didn't have an answer. She leaned closer. 'Love is all about trust, Sally. From what you've told me, you have feelings for Declan and he for you too. There are people who spend their whole lives searching for love. But many of them don't allow themselves to love properly because they see things in their past that they perceive as obstacles to achieving happiness. Sometimes we need to take the first step forward even if we can't see the staircase in front of us. Do you follow what I'm saying?'

I didn't entirely but nodded anyway.

Dr Gail opened a new page in her notebook. 'I thought today we'd spend some time talking about your mother and maybe even your childhood if we have time.'

The two were intrinsically linked. There was nothing else to defer to now, nowhere else to retreat. Talking about Mummy and my misplaced childhood was like treading through a minefield. I was too scared to cross it for fear of triggering an explosion. How could I ever speak up about all of my horrid experiences and about my constant shame? I had to build up my courage and direct my mind into places it didn't want to go. But I knew it had to be done. 'Alright', I said, 'I'm ready.'

'Good. Let's start on a positive note. What's the happiest memory you have of your mother?'

I paused for a moment. I have never experienced the release of positive endorphins derived from any experience concerning my mother. Except for the day I left home but I wasn't going to tell Dr Gail that. Even the few palatable memories had dark undertones. 'Mummy's a bad person. She's been a bad influence on me from my first-ever memory I have of her. That's why I moved out. I couldn't deal with the constant maelstrom anymore. She has not one redeeming feature.'

Dr Gail raised her eyebrows and fiddled with her hair. 'They're strong words, Sally. It seems to me that you've made up your mind to disassociate yourself from her not just physically but emotionally as well. That may seem an easy solution, but simply shutting her out because of past angst may not be in your best interests. In fact, it may well be a contributing factor to your depression.'

'But you don't understand. Even taking the circumcision episode out of it, it's all the other things: the fake autism, the constant physical and verbal abuse, the persistent reinforcement that I was completely useless, and her forbidding me to have any friends. I had to *invent* imaginary friends, Gail. Can you imagine how that was for me? It was the only way I managed to stay sane.' I looked down at my clenched fists as I spoke.

'Those are very serious issues, Sally. But remember, you were only a child when all this happened. It's very important to understand that none of this is your fault. You're much different to your mother, I can see that.' She gave me an encouraging smile.

I agreed that I was different to Mummy but always feared I could become like her. The inevitable legacy of awkward genes.

'People talk about nature versus nurture,' I said. 'I know I haven't inherited her nature. But I feel like the more I think or talk about Mummy, the more I could become like her. That scares me. I couldn't live with myself if I became even remotely like her. I refuse to cut myself on my mind's razor-sharp edges the way that Mummy does on hers. I don't want to be like her, Gail. Not in the slightest.'

'You don't have to be like her at all, Sally. What you have to do is try to understand why she is the person you say she is. Then and only then can you begin to mend bridges. Our lives are shaped by our past, but that doesn't mean we can't shape our futures. If you keep looking behind you, you can't see what's up front.'

I began fidgeting with my hands. 'Mummy's had a difficult past, I understand that. But that doesn't give her the right to treat me like she does.'

Dr Gail leaned forward on her seat and adopted a serious expression. 'Sally, I've worked with many young people just like you. It's normal to feel the way you do. The thing is, even after all that's happened, all the resentment, the only way you're going to feel better about yourself is by trying to help your mother, not by bottling everything up and spiralling further and further down a black hole. You have to forgive her, Sally. Only then can you forgive yourself.'

Tears began raining down my cheeks, and it was very hard to continue talking. 'I get angry sometimes.'

'Anger is good, Sally. It's a way of addressing things you have buried way too deep. Everyone has angry thoughts about a thing or a person from time to time. These can seem worse or more intense when we are tired or upset. The challenge is to move out of that negative spiral.'

That was easier said than done.

'It's the guilt too.' I was trying to force out words, but they only came out as faint whispers. 'I don't deserve to be happy. I don't deserve to have a nice life with anybody else.'

'You deserve it as much as anyone, Sally. Have you told Declan much about your past?'

I shook my head as my heart beat faster. 'That's just it. I can't.' My voice was stronger now. 'There's too much emotional trauma there.'

Dr Gail shook her head. 'Oh, Sally, it's the perception of not feeling safe or not having the support mechanisms in place that end up tarnishing our lives. We feel like we're not good enough, not worthy. That belief then drives out behaviours because if you're not feeling worthy or good enough, you develop unhealthy coping mechanisms to mask the pain. You coped by withdrawing from people, but you can't withdraw from the people you love or want to love.'

There was a lot of truth to what Dr Gail was saying, but words were much easier than actions. 'I feel Declan will abandon me if he finds out,' I said.

'You can't think like that, Sally. I'm beginning to sound like a broken record, but you must give him a chance. He likes you for *you*, not for your past.'

Dr Gail didn't say anything else for a long time. Then, when she said something, it was 'Do you have a garden, Sally?'

The question seemed to come right out of left field. 'A what?'

'Do you have a garden where you live?'

'No, I don't,' I answered after realising that she was being serious. 'I live in a flat.'

'Okay. I want you to start one. In your head.'

'In my head? I don't understand.'

'Your mind is like a garden,' she explained. 'Whatever you plant will grow. But it is up to you to choose which seeds to plant. It is the choice of seeds that governs the harvest.'

This was getting a little too philosophical for my humble intellect. 'I'm sorry, Gail. I don't quite see where all this is going.'

'You do, Sally. You don't realise it yet, but you do.'

I was trying to cooperate as best as I could. 'I'm afraid you'll have to explain it in more detail. My brain's a little foggy at the moment.'

Dr Gail continued, 'Of course.' Her eyes were wide and beamed like headlights as they reflected the afternoon light coming in through the window. 'Any negative or judgemental thoughts are like weeds, Sally. They take over the entire garden and make it difficult for nicer things to grow. Your mind doesn't know yet the difference between the seeds that you want to grow and the weeds you want to hold back. You have to choose: beautiful, fragrant flowers or noxious weeds.'

I was beginning to see the picture that Dr Gail was painting. 'So what you're implying is that I should occupy my mind with only positive thoughts. They'd be the seeds.'

Dr Gail nodded. 'Yes. It's called tending the garden of your mind. You have to sift your thoughts for the gold. When you notice a destructive thought about the past running through your mind, simply let it pass through the sifter.'

What Dr Gail was effectively saying was that for my garden to grow, I had to delete any thoughts about Mummy. She was the bad weed, and Declan was the good seed. The new flower in waiting.

'Mummy versus Declan?' I said.

'Don't see them as antagonists, Sally. You can block out the bad past, but that doesn't mean you can't have a better relationship with your mother from this point on. A relationship can start off stormy, but the weather can change. In time, your mother too can become a flower in your garden.'

I nodded through tears and blew my nose. I had to admit that Dr Gail was making a lot of sense. I've been a pessimist for far too long. This weekend could be the start of something special. With all of her mounting health problems, Mummy needed me more than ever. And it was a chance for Declan to get to experience the real Sally Cartwright, warts and all. 'Actually', I said shortly after realising the entirety of my uneven makeup had been deposited onto a wad of eucalyptus tissues, 'Declan and I are going to visit Mummy tomorrow. She's had a few health issues.'

'There you go, Sally. You're doing it without even realising it.'

'Doing what?'

'Mending bridges and tending to your garden. After all that you've told me, it shows you have a kind heart and that you still care about your mother. Sometimes the light of compassion shines brightest in the dark.'

I looked down and smiled, trying to swallow the lump that had formed in my throat. I realised I was safe here even though I was forced to deal with the raw emotions that flamed inside me. 'Thank you, Gail. I'm actually looking forward to tomorrow.'

'Good for you. We'll talk more next week.'

When I looked up, Dr Gail smiled warmly.

*

I should stick pictures on a wall and connect them all with string to make sense of how I got to be who I really am.

When it came to my emotional healing, I realised that it was about understanding how I, as a child, had felt in those dark moments and in the years that followed and using those emotions to drive me forward. How can I give myself now what that little girl had so desperately craved but didn't receive back then?

CHAPTER 20

YOU SHINE A light on the badness, and you strive to understand it, but you don't plant any of that in your garden. That was the take-home message from Dr Gail, and I was feeling rather tense as Declan and I set off to visit Mummy.

We soon left the city behind. Green paddocks started to appear, and my mind began to relax.

'Thank you again for this,' I said. 'I know I should be able to drive at my age.'

Declan gave me a wide smile. 'That's okay,' he said. 'I like driving. Besides, I'm the one who should be thanking you.'

I didn't quite follow. 'Thank me for what?'

'For interrupting my weekend of game bingeing. It can get pretty tedious sometimes, just sitting at home all alone.' Declan was showing a vulnerability I thought was only reserved for outcasts like me. I smiled back, and we drove in silence for a while longer.

He eventually tuned the car's radio to a heavy-rock station. The cacophony of noise emanating from the sound system did nothing to quell the tension in the air. I could sense the unasked question hovering over us like an impending storm. Please don't ask, I thought.

After a while, he turned down the volume. 'You haven't told me anything about your mother yet.'

Okay, not really a question but still daunting. It's like this: I haven't told you anything because some things are best left unsaid.

Declan was persistent. 'What's one word that best describes her?'

I'll give you two: stubborn and authoritarian.

'I'd rather not talk about Mummy, Declan.'

He looked disappointed but not overly surprised. 'It doesn't take a genius to work out that you've been avoiding talking about her.'

I looked out the passenger-side window. Dark clouds were rolling in, and it looked likely we were driving head-on into inclement weather. 'Mummy's not the nicest person all the time,' I said. To his credit, Declan didn't pursue the topic. He instead turned the conversation onto himself.

'Yeah, I know what it's like. My mother can be the same sometimes.'

I was unsure how best to react to that piece of information and opted for a brief nod.

'There are some bad memories there.' His tone was ominous as he turned to face me. 'Sally, do you want to hear about my childhood?'

There was that word again. It seemed to follow me everywhere I went these days, like a clingy child.

Why, now, did Declan want to tell me about his childhood? I didn't really know anything about his family life. Perhaps he felt sorry for me. I suppose the reason doesn't matter in the end. What matters is that, instead of hiding his emotions, he was willing to share them. And therein lay the fundamental difference between us.

'Yes, I'd like to hear about your childhood.'

He turned off the music and cleared his throat. 'My parents divorced when I was 5 years old. My older sister, Carol, went to live with my mother, and I stayed with my father until I moved out a few years ago.'

Carol wasn't really a suitable name for a girl in modern society, I thought. 'Did your father remarry?' I asked.

Declan shook his head. 'Mum's leaving hit him pretty hard. He took to the bottle and that became his crutch for a long time.'

A picture of Mummy lying unconscious on her bed immediately jumped into my mind.

Declan continued, 'School became a mess. I never got good grades. I just couldn't seem to concentrate on anything. There were always thoughts racing through my head about what mood my father would be in when I got home. He'd beat me up if I was ever late, and he never once helped me with my homework.'

He was choking his words as he glared hard straight ahead. I wasn't sure if he wanted to continue. I went to put my hand on his lap but realised I had no idea what to say to him, so I pulled back awkwardly. He gave me a tacit look.

'It's all right, Sally. I don't mind talking about this stuff now. There was a time when it was difficult, but I've learnt to deal with it.'

I smiled to show him I understood. 'Okay' was all that I could manage.

He kept talking. 'The family courts got involved at one point. They wanted to send me to live with Mum, but I knew my sister was having similar troubles there, so I was sort of trapped. In the end, I decided to stay with Dad.'

'That's a terrible thing to have happen to you. You needed help but didn't get it. How did you cope?'

'My friends helped initially. I'd sneak out whenever Dad was asleep after one of his drinking sessions. But then those same friends began turning on me. I didn't seem to fit in with their group somehow, and they shunned me. It was hard. I was in year eleven and didn't have anyone to turn to. So I threw myself into my schoolwork, both as a distraction to my social problems and to keep Dad off my back. In the end, it helped me get good grades and go off to university.'

I shook my head and didn't know what to say.

'In the end', Declan continued, 'what matters is that I survived. I managed to get my life back on track. I got a steady job, moved out on my own, and made some real friends.' He gave me a warm smile. I felt embarrassed and tucked a strand of my new locks behind my ear.

I looked at him, and he looked at me. Neither of us said anything for a while.

'You know it too, right?' Declan said, looking intently into my eyes.

I looked out the window again before turning back. 'I'm going to keep seeing Dr Gail. It helps.'

'Have you discussed your mother with her?'

I sighed. 'A little. We're talking a lot about my past, and Mummy is obviously a big part of that.'

'It's going to take time, Sally, and it's not going to be easy. I know you find it hard to talk about these things, but whenever you want, you can talk to me about them.'

Of course I found it hard; but I also knew that hiding everything away was, for me, a product of fear. Overcoming that fear was the biggest hurdle in front of me. If I could conquer it, my world would open up. 'I'll remember that,' I said.

We drove on in silence as Declan concentrated on the road. The skies were overhung with a blanket of grey; and then the rain came, first splashing small droplets gently onto the windscreen before attacking with bullet-like splotches. It poured down with a roar that forced everyone on the road to slow down. Count one, count two, count three. A low crackle of lightning quickly gave way to a rolling boom of thunder reverberating over a sky as angry as a raging bull.

Thankfully, the weather cleared by the time we reached Mummy's neighbourhood.

Mummy's house is in a public housing estate. When we first moved into the area, there was an embarrassment and a stigma attached to living here but not now. A lot of the housing was recently sold off to private enterprise, which oversaw the development of bigger and more aesthetic dwellings. It has become quite a nice area now.

Declan parked in the driveway and insisted on taking both our bags. We walked up the side path to the porch tucked away from the front of the house. The air was pungent with the smell of jasmine. To my total surprise, the garden was neat and well maintained. Mummy rarely tended to it while I was living here. She was to gardening what most teenagers are to bedroom tidiness: she saw what needed to be done but didn't have the foggiest how to deal with it.

She must have a gardener. There can be no other explanation.

I pushed open the front door without knocking. It seemed like another lifetime when I'd stood in this entrance, too frightened to take another step inside, the dread of having to face another beating for something I didn't do. The same rising terror circled me now as I took a few tentative steps.

We walked into the living room, and Declan put the bags down.

'Hello, Mummy.'

'Just a minute!' All the noise was coming from the kitchen.

Mummy's strident voice was easily audible over the television and the hum of the fan. She came out to the entrance and was dressed in a neat knee-length dress almost entirely covered by a brightly coloured apron. 'Sally, darling!'

She turned off the television and walked forward to kiss me on the cheek before wrapping me up in a clumsy hug. I just stared, open-mouthed.

I think Declan was waiting to be introduced. My focus was broken by Mummy's odd behaviour, and there was the most awkward of silences as she alternated her gaze between me and Declan.

'Well, aren't you going to introduce me to your friend?'

Having never been in a position to introduce anyone before, I became filled with nervous anticipation and felt a little giddy.

I decided to just go for it. 'There's someone I'd like you to meet, Mummy. This is Declan.'

Declan stepped forward and held out his hand. 'Hello, Mrs Cartwright. I'm so pleased to meet you.' Mummy looked him up and down before wiping her hands on her apron and shaking his hand vigorously. Then she turned to me with an impish look.

'Ooh, darling, you didn't tell me he was so devilishly handsome!' She laughed childishly, and her face became flushed.

I couldn't believe it. Mummy was practically swooning over someone she'd just met.

'Lovely to meet you, Declan,' she said after calming herself down. 'I'm always pleased to meet any of Sally's friends. Sit down, please. Lunch is almost ready. You two must be starving after such a long trip.'

I noticed that Mummy had done her hair and applied some makeup to hide her blotchy, saggy skin. She hadn't noticed my new look yet.

I turned towards the kitchen. The large pot on the stove hub emanated a deliciously soupy smell.

'I've made your favourite, Sal. Clam chowder.'

Firstly, I can count on one hand the number of times Mummy has ever made soup. Secondly and more importantly, I have *never ever* eaten clam chowder.

'It smells great, Mrs Cartwright,' Declan said as he sat on the couch, which I noticed looked cleaner and brighter than I'd ever seen it before.

'Oh, please, enough with the formalities, Declan. You can call me

Eve.' Mummy went to sit next to Declan, and I sat opposite. 'She's a good girl, my Sally,' she announced proudly. 'Never given me any trouble. A surprise, but a blessing all the same.'

I had to turn away.

'I would have loved to have given her siblings to grow up with, of course, but it didn't quite work out. That's one of the greatest sources of sadness in my life.'

Now I was going to be sick.

'So you found her phone, Declan. Is that how the two of you met?'

Declan glanced over at me as if asking permission to answer. I gave him a brief nod. 'Yes, she dropped it on the side of a road.'

Mummy shook her head. 'That's the only fault my Sally has. She's always losing things. Lucky, she's not losing her mind!'

Not yet. But at this rate, that was surely imminent.

Mummy continued, 'I bet she didn't tell you about the time she misplaced her favourite hairbrush. We looked high and low for it. That was very amusing and entertaining, wasn't it, Sal?'

It wasn't. Mummy had spotted me combing my hair with one of her brushes and yanked it out of my hands, threatening to scratch my eyes out with it if I ever touched it again.

I was tempted to publicly correct Mummy's distorted recollection of events but decided against it. I'm sure she'd find a way to embarrass me if I did.

I tried to distract myself from her nauseating behaviour by looking around. The house was immaculately clean and tidy. The carpets had been steam cleaned because the intricate floral pattern within it was more easily discernible. Every surface appeared to be dust free. There were pictures of me alone and of me and Mummy together scattered around the living room. I'd never seen them before. Mummy never had any pictures on the walls. Or anywhere else in the house.

The whole scene was making me crazy. The Mummy that I forced myself to speak to over the telephone every week was not the same one sitting here presently.

The charade continued.

'Tell me, Declan, what line of work are you in?'

'I'm a computer engineer, Mrs Cartwright—I mean Eve.' Declan expanded a little on what his work entailed. Mummy appeared to be fascinated, nodding along and pretending to be genuinely interested. Her duplicity knew no bounds.

Declan got worked up after extolling the virtues of computer hardware and design. Then he asked Mummy a question. 'What about you, Eve. Do you work?'

Mummy ran a hand through her hair and tossed her head back. 'Oh, no, dear. You see, I'm not well. I'm sure my daughter would have told you that already.'

I'd informed Declan about Mummy's diabetes but not about her heart problem. Or her drinking. Or her smoking.

'It's a full-time job seeing doctors these days. And I've got nobody to take me. I tell you, not having family around is really hard.'

Declan gave me a concerned look. For a moment, I wondered if he was going to blame me for Mummy's plight.

'You have to do what you can, Eve,' he said.

We eventually sat down to eat lunch, and I must admit the clam chowder was absolutely sublime. Either Mummy had taken a cooking course or someone else had prepared it.

Did she have a cook as well?

The weather turned nasty again, which consigned us indoors all afternoon. Declan amused himself by playing another mindless game—World of Warcraft I think it was called—on his phone. Mummy seemed to take a sudden interest in it. 'That looks like so much fun, Declan,' she said.

Mummy loathed video games, especially violent ones. She said they were a scourge on society. I totally agreed with her, of course, but at the same time found it unfathomable that she had no issue herself with playing the pokies. Wasn't that worse? At least you didn't lose your money playing a video game.

I busied myself tidying up the lunch dishes. Mummy came into the kitchen and closed the door. The high-pitched whistling sound during each of her breaths was worrying.

'Are you alright, Mummy?'

She sat down and rested her head in her hands. 'I'll be fine, Sal. Just been overdoing it a bit, that's all.'

Perhaps I'd misread her in the domestic realm. 'The house looks lovely,' I said.

'I try,' she said while inhaling another long-laboured breath. 'I've even learnt how to make soup.'

So there was no cook.

'The garden looks lovely,' I said as I peered out through the window.

'I spent all day yesterday out there.'

No gardener either.

After I'd put away the dishes, she gave me a full update on her health. Her diabetes was well controlled with tablets, but she'd been diagnosed with atrial fibrillation. 'I had to wear one of those chest monitors,' she explained. 'My heart's electrical circuits are out of whack, and I'm on tablets to even out my heart rate. I'll tell you something, Sal, those pills are leaving me tired all the time.'

I could tell. Mummy looked drained. Her skin sagged more than I remembered. Despite the makeup, her face showed more lines than a corduroy pillow.

'It's not just the physical side but also the mental,' she explained under laboured breathing. 'My brain feels like it's on about ten per cent battery, so if you don't mind, I'm going to lie down.'

I'd already noticed the packet of cigarettes on the bench, and a quick inspection of the bin revealed a couple of empty vodka bottles. 'You've got to take better care of yourself, Mummy. The doctor said to cut down on your drinking and smoking.' I couldn't bring myself to say her doctor's name out loud.

She pretended not to hear me.

'Mummy?'

She had a doleful look on her face. 'I'm trying, Sal. I really am. But now that I'm not getting out as often, I have more time to myself at home. There are only so many times one can clean or dust.'

Mummy had a point. For all her faults, I didn't want her to die of loneliness. 'What about getting a pet?' I said. 'A small dog perhaps.'

She blew out a wheezy sigh. 'You don't know the new Eve

Cartwright, darling. I can hardly look after myself.' Was this a small airing of fallibility or just another veiled attempt to attract sympathy? I suspected the latter.

'A dog can be therapeutic,' I said. 'I read somewhere that pets can improve your health and decrease anxiety and boredom.'

'I don't think so. It's … it's just too hard.' I could tell by her tone of voice that she wanted the subject closed. She was always against me having a pet. 'Too much responsibility,' she'd say. As I reflected back on it, it had nothing to do with responsibility; she just didn't want me to have anything that may have given me a skerrick of happiness.

'I'll come and visit more often, I promise,' I said.

Mummy's eyes lit up. 'You really mean that, Sal?'

'Yes. I'll come with Declan. I'm sure he won't mind driving me again.'

'He's a fine boy, dear. I hope he makes you happy.' This was the first time Mummy had hoped anything good for me. Perhaps her health woes had softened her around the edges.

Or perhaps not. Be wary, Sally.

She went to lie down, and I settled next to Declan. He immediately stopped playing his game, which I thought was a nice gesture. 'Your mother's really nice,' he said.

Don't you see? It's all an act to paint me as the villain. She's doing all this to spite me! That's what I wanted to say.

'It's strange. I think her health issues may have mellowed her,' I said. I didn't really think that.

It was Declan's suggestion that we go out for dinner. Mummy looked decidedly better after her nap and had changed into a nice floral print dress, which I'd never seen her wear before. It wasn't exactly haute couture but nevertheless seemed to fit her perfectly.

She spent most of the night bombarding Declan with more questions: Do you live close to my Sal? Do you have any siblings? Where are your parents? What are they like? And it went on. To Declan's credit, he answered everything honestly and didn't appear to be put out even when discussing his parents' divorce. Mummy shook her head at that but for the most part kept smiling and laughing.

I abhorred such questioning. Apart from the fact that I thought that many of the questions Mummy came out with were too personal to be asking someone you met for the first time, I think that such behaviour is a deliberate ploy to deflect attention from one's self. How would Mummy feel if Declan came out with these gems: How often do you drink? How many times have you been married? Why do you spend all your pension money on the pokies? Why do you treat your daughter like shit?

Perhaps I was just jealous. Opportunities to converse in this manner were something foreign because they were never afforded to me.

Declan seemed to sense my discomfort once our plates had been cleared by the waiter. 'You look tired, Sally. Shall we go home?' I nodded.

I thought Mummy would be angry that I was about to cut short her evening's entertainment. But it was worse than that. She was apologetic.

'Oh, I'm sorry, darlings. You've both had a long day. Can't always be thinking of myself, can I? I think we better get going.' She turned to Declan with a steadfast smile. 'If you ever have children of your own someday, Declan, you'll find out soon enough that you always run a distant second to them.'

If cruelty was the cause of sickness and love was the hopeful antidote, I was in for a long convalescence.

Declan had no qualms about sleeping in the spare room. It was too small to be a bedroom per se. I'd call it more of a drawing room or a sitting room where one would go to read. But when old Mrs Lovell from next door was forced to sell up because of deteriorating health, a trundle bed was made available; and Mummy eagerly snapped it up. It would be ideal for the spare room, she'd said, 'for when people visit.' No one ever did until now.

I was slightly overwhelmed with memories as I stepped inside my old room. Mummy was true to her word. It was just as I'd left it. Melancholy clouded my mind as I looked around. It contained a small bed, neatly made, one straight-backed wooden chair, and a small side table with a single drawer. There were no pictures on the walls and no curtains because the window was boarded shut. I never got the opportunity to glimpse the outside world, never had the chance to stare out at the ever-changing colours of the sky as night followed day. I never got to marvel at the cloud patterns that shifted across and brought their beauty. I never got to appreciate the changing seasons. I never had the opportunity to peer over the tops of trees to the houses across the street, wondering what happy lives were being lived in them.

As I looked around, a dirty big fly was buzzing angrily around the room, desperately trying to get out. Perhaps it too was frightened off by the memories that lingered here.

Then I spotted him. His ear was jutting out from under the pillow. His name was Fuzzy, an old teddy bear that I'd found abandoned by the side of the road when I was walking to the bus stop from school one day. He was 12 inches tall and had arms and legs that could bend. He was fluffy, and his coat had a bedraggled look to it, hence the name Fuzzy. I brought him home and begged Mummy to let me keep him. She was drunk at the time and said yes.

I read somewhere that the dirtier and older a bear is, the more valuable it might be. It may even become a rare collectable one day. But none of that interested me; I could never sell Fuzzy.

Fuzzy and I forged a special bond because we had something in common: we were both abandoned. He became a good friend. We used to take turns at crying all night. Fuzzy would take over whenever I got too tired. He was very loyal. Even though I miss him, I couldn't bring myself to take him with me when I moved out. I felt this was his home.

*

I heard banging and someone shouting my name. It took me a while to realise the banging was real and that I wasn't dreaming. I tried to stand, but my legs wouldn't support me. I looked down; my knees were swollen purple. I don't recall how I got those injuries. I slowly rolled out of bed onto the floor and crawled towards the door. The banging and shouting continued; but no matter how much I tried, I couldn't push myself up to the door handle, which now began to rattle. A volcano of fear and terror built up deep within me. Then I heard a loud clanging noise; and before I could even blink, the door handle had dropped to the floor. The door flew open, and standing above me was Mummy. 'Tut, tut, I did warn you,' she said. 'Now look what you're going to make me do.' At once, I became rigid and frozen. Mummy was holding a kind of iron grille, black and medieval looking. She raised it over her head and, with one almighty pivot, brought it down onto my cowering body. My world went black.

*

I closed the door and went to bed with Fuzzy safely tucked under my pillow. The missing door handle was a stark reminder of the painful past.

CHAPTER 21

THE DRIVE HOME was uneventful. As a way of distracting my mind from the weekend from hell, I began reading the number plates of the cars in front. One stood out: 1MU1AM.

Amusing.

The weather was kind; and to my relief, Declan did most of the talking. I was grateful for his company but not for the subject matter of his conversation. He kept harping on about what a lovely host Mummy was and how he wished his mother could be more like her. For the most part, I listened, content to let Mummy have her fleeting moment in the sun even though she didn't deserve to be in any way eulogised.

Declan looked at me carefully. 'You've got to give her a chance, Sally. She's been through a rough patch and really needs you now,' he said before pausing and leaving me to fill in what he was thinking. If only it was that simple.

'It doesn't work like that, Declan,' I said. 'I know Mummy, but she doesn't know me. Not the new me. I've changed a lot since my sessions with Dr Gail, but she can't see any of that change.' I was going to say that my real turning point was finding out that I wasn't autistic but stopped myself just in the nick of time.

'She didn't even notice my new hair today,' I said.

Declan's eyes moved tentatively to the top of my head, and he smiled before adopting a serious expression. 'So what do you want from her, Sally?'

My eyes filled with tears; I stared out the window, wanting to hide my gloomy expression. 'All I want is love,' I said as I looked out into the passing paddocks. 'That's the only thing that will bring us closer. I don't really care about the hair. I only did that for myself.'

That wasn't entirely true.

'Visiting her more often will help with that,' Declan declared.

I wasn't so sure about that. Mummy's house stirred up so many bad memories, but I did make a promise, and I suppose I was obliged to follow through on it. Declan said he was free most weekends and would drive me, which was more than I could have expected.

We arrived at my flat just as the late-afternoon light was fading. As he parked and cut the engine, Declan turned to face me, and I was suddenly aware of how close we were. I noticed a pinkish glow to his face.

'One thing I've learnt from my own experiences,' he said, 'is that there's love in all of us, that it's a genuine human trait, and it has nothing to do with whether or not you believe in God or in any religion. Everyone is capable of loving and being loved back.'

My view on God is this: if God exists and truly loves us, why does he allow all the suffering in the world to continue? I watched a documentary recently that said that over 9 million children under 5 years of age die in the world each year. That's approximately one death every four seconds. How can any God allow this to happen? He must be either evil or impotent and takes great joy in testing our powers of credulity. When prayers are answered, people see him as a loving God. When they're not, they see him as a mysterious God. I've never followed this flawed logic.

My personal opinion is that God is just a giant set of scales with love on one side and hatred on the other. Each one of us controls our own scales. It's up to each person to balance theirs so that they don't tip over into the hatred side.

Religion has never been a topic of discussion for me. Some people see it as a way of coping with their problems, but I never saw it like that. Mummy didn't either. I can't remember her ever taking me inside a church.

I suppose her views are what shaped mine.

'I'm not religious at all,' I admitted. 'Mummy isn't either.'

Declan nodded. 'Same with me,' he said. 'My parents aren't believers either.'

It was a pleasing thing to know that Declan valued love the same as I did and that neither of us would ever be forced to defend our lack of faith.

He continued talking, 'I believe we all control our own destiny. Sure, you can pray to a God if it helps, but you can't just sit back and hope that your prayers will be answered. You have to make them happen yourself. Do you get what I'm saying?'

I think Declan was giving me a subtle lesson in life management. I nodded as he leaned closer. 'I hope we can do something daring together someday, Sally,' he whispered before kissing me gently. For a moment, I wondered if he somehow had figured everything out about my past.

He pulled me in for a hug and held me. I knew I had to fight my reluctance to take this relationship further. When we broke apart, I gently kissed his cheek, his two-day growth soft and ticklish. 'Thank you for this weekend. I'm glad I visited Mummy.'

Declan started the engine. 'I'll let you get some rest,' he said. 'It's been a long couple of days.' I didn't invite him in. Whether he was genuinely concerned about my physical well-being or he just wanted to get home and spend three hours killing aliens didn't faze me. I really was tired.

I slept soundly that night, making up for the two previous nights from hell.

*

I no longer found visiting Dr Gail a daunting experience. I was beginning to understand the efficacy of process in getting to where I needed to be. She said I had to be patient, but that was easy for her to say.

Her shoulders sagged, and the disappointment etched on her face was plain to see. I had just conveyed to her that I hadn't yet told Declan anything about my past. We sat deep in silence for what seemed an eternity. The drone of the air-conditioner reverberated around the room like an ill wind.

Finally, Dr Gail broke the silence.

'Have you started your therapeutic garden yet?'

I thought for a moment before answering. 'Sort of. I promised Mummy I'd visit her more often from now on.'

She stared at me with her mouth slightly open. 'Okay, that's good. You've planted the first seeds. You should be proud.'

Just when I thought I was immersed in a 'feel good' moment, her expression changed. 'It's time to ramp things up a bit,' she said.

That sounded ominous.

'What do you mean?' I asked.

'Let's talk about the bad seeds.'

I knew exactly what they were.

She continued, 'There's so much in your life you never wanted to think about, Sally. All those things you mentioned last time, I want you to revisit them, but more than that, instead of just talking about what happened, I want you to tell me how you feel about them.'

'I'm sorry, Gail. I'm confused. I've already told you how I feel about them.'

Dr Gail shifted in her seat and shook her head. 'You need to go deeper. I want you to take control, delve into your inner self. That's the only way you're going to overcome your fears. If you bury your inner feelings deep enough and for long enough, pretty soon, you won't feel anything at all. It's only when you can fully deal with these bad seeds that you can throw them out for good, and they'll never appear in your garden again.'

This was going to be new ground for me. I'd never put such deep thoughts into words before, not even in my head. I was scared of what might come charging out. 'There are things … lots of things,' I mumbled. What a useless word *things* is. *Come on, Sally, be brave. Name these 'things'.*

Dr Gail sensed my apprehension as I nervously gulped some water and stared straight ahead. 'You must shun your shame and your doubts,' she said. 'Just remember, none of what happened to you is your fault. And no one is going to judge you, least of all me.'

I broke my stare and looked out the window before drawing a deep breath. 'I get so angry at all that's happened, Gail.'

She nodded gently. 'That's good, Sally. As I've told you before, it's okay to be angry. I would be too if I were in your situation. Now go on.'

'There's just so much pain from my memories of not feeling safe, from having my boundaries invaded time and time again.' I felt a sharp stab of guilt, as if I was betraying Mummy. But I knew I wasn't. I blew my nose, and my chin quivered, but I managed to continue speaking. 'It's all the beatings, the physical scars, of not knowing my father, not being allowed to have any friends, all the horrors of school, being made to feel inferior, and being falsely labelled as autistic. But the thing that hurts me most is not being loved. That hurts way more than all the physical stuff.'

I stopped. I didn't trust myself saying anymore without other things coming out as just pathetic excuses for my predicament. This was new territory, and I felt like I was in a dark tunnel unaware of what lay ahead.

Dr Gail's dark eyes watched me intently as the tip of her pen caressed her lips. 'How do you feel now that you're thinking these things out loud, Sally?'

I really didn't know how I felt. I shrugged my shoulders. 'Relief, I suppose,' I said. 'It's like I've sunk into this chair a little deeper.'

She scribbled something down and looked up. 'That's right. It's the relief of knowing that everything's finally out in the open. All the lies, the trickery, you can't hide them away and keep pretending that they'll magically disappear. Telling someone how you feel about them is the best thing you can do. It's like they've been purged now.

'For far too long, you put up a wall as a way of conserving energy. You were willing to accept the inevitability of cause and effect. In social situations, you instinctively put on a mask. It's time to ditch that mask and take a look over the wall.'

I stared down at my hands, scared to look up to see what Dr Gail's expression might be. She was right again, of course. I had just vented more than twenty years of pent-up anger and frustration, and it felt damn good not hiding behind a wall anymore.

Dr Gail put down her notepad. 'I don't know if you're ever going to forgive your mother, Sally', she said, 'but there is one thing you must do: you need to forgive yourself.'

I nodded through tears. It all made sense now. I felt better already. I'd laid bare my feelings, and the world didn't cave in.

It was time to tell Declan everything and let him know the truth: that Mummy really was a bad person.

CHAPTER 22

I THINK I'M BECOMING addicted to cleaning. Ever since purchasing a treasure trove of cleaning products and eradicating my flat of all its detritus a few weeks ago, I have come to view germs as public enemy number one. They lurk in the shadows oblivious to my end goal. What foolish creatures they are.

I immersed myself in a cleaning frenzy. I read somewhere that cleaning is nothing more than an attitude and that some people begin cleaning to occupy their minds and escape from certain unpleasant thoughts and situations in their lives. This tenet could well apply to me because today is Saturday. It's Mummy day, and I was dreading calling her up. Her indifferent behaviour last week was hard to read. Was she merely trying to impress Declan, or had her health issues really forced her to reassess her outlook on life?

There was only one way to find out. I removed my rubber gloves and sat down on the couch.

'Mummy, how are you?' I said over a crackly line. There was a long pause before she spoke.

'I'm not feeling well, dear. I think I have the flu.' Her voice had a hint of annoying familiarity to it. I'm sure it was more than just flu.

'Are you sure it's the flu, Mummy?'

'Oh yes, I can feel it coming on fast.'

She let out an exaggerated cough followed by the most pathetic of moans. I couldn't let her get away with it this time. 'I think you've been drinking too much again, Mummy,' I said coldly.

She laughed abruptly and then stopped. 'What are you insinuating, young lady? That I'm drunk? Don't be ridiculous.'

'It's not ridiculous, Mummy. I know you still drink too much. I saw the bottles in your bin.'

'Don't you dare tell me how much I'm allowed to drink. You don't own me, Sal.'

'I'm just making sure that you look after yourself. You've got to think of your health.'

'Oh, for God's sake, I admit I may have the odd drink occasionally, but there's no harm in that, is there? Anyway, I was just celebrating a great weekend with my daughter. I'm allowed to do that, aren't I?'

'You mean celebrating a great weekend with Declan.' My tone hung somewhere between sarcastic and annoyed.

There was a pause before Mummy responded. 'Honestly, darling, he's way too good for you. Any fool can see that,' she said bluntly.

Bitch. Just as I'd almost convinced myself that she was glad to see me happy, she stabs me in the heart. 'I think he really likes me,' I said with a hint of defiance in my voice.

'Huh! You're too funny, Sal. What on earth would a handsome young man like Declan want with an untidy, scarred, namby-pamby wench who walks like a clockwork soldier? Let's face it, sweetie, you are quite uncomely.'

Uncomely is a rarely used word in the English language. I considered it a strong one in this context.

'Our brains are hard-wired to like nice people, darling, not nasty ones like you. Declan is only being polite. Trust me.'

Double bitch. Who made Mummy the arbiter of aesthetics anyway? I swallowed my anger hot, and it was burning my insides. I desperately needed a cool antidote. 'You've got it all wrong, Mummy,' I said. 'Why would Declan drive me all the way out to see you if he didn't care about me?'

I heard a heavy sigh. 'Oh, you have a lot to learn, my dear.'

I felt myself getting wound up like a toy.

Mummy continued, 'It's plain to see you're someone very different, Sal. A person can easily get caught up in first impressions, but Declan will work out pretty quickly what you're all about, and then it will be sayonara. I really liked him, though. What a pity.'

If only Mummy could see the anger on my face right now. Maybe then she'd stop. Fires of fury were smouldering in my brain. I was afraid that the pressure of my raging sea of anger might force me to say things that I'd regret later, things I didn't really mean.

Everything was becoming so delicate under my carefully ordered world.

Oh, to hell with it all.

'I'm sick of being a goddamn sheep, Mummy! I'm going to tell Declan everything. I'm going to tell him how you drink too much, smoke too much, and how you beat me all the time and how you never allowed me to have any friends. I'll even show him my scars. Then he'll see you for who you really are. How do you like that?' The release of tension I felt through my body was stimulating.

Mummy started crying. She never cried on the phone. Or hardly ever. If she did, it was usually to make you feel guilty about something. But this was different. Her sobs were punching right through the phone, like they were tearing from deep in her throat. 'I always tried my best, darling. You know that. Sure, I probably made some mistakes, but you didn't exactly help yourself, did you?'

I didn't know what Mummy was insinuating by that last remark, but I was too wound up to ask. 'I mean it, Mummy. I'm going to tell Declan everything.'

'Oh, Sal, you're a bumbling idiot at the best of times. You won't have the courage.'

'I will too. The doctor I'm seeing has given me the confidence I need.' I heard Mummy drying her tears, and then she sighed.

'It's more complicated than that, Sal, isn't it?' she said. 'I think you're—how should I put this?—you're just an attention seeker. Your words will have as much credibility as a crooked politician's.'

'Must you always think the worst, Mummy?' I said in a voice deliberately heavy with disgust. 'People have to be honest with each other. If I'm ever going to have any sort of relationship with Declan, he has to know everything. I'm sure he'll see the truth, and he'll take me seriously.'

There was heavy breathing, and Mummy didn't speak. The breathing slowly morphed into a slow moan.

'Are you alright, Mummy?'

'Don't talk about my health, darling. It's late, very late.' Whether she meant the hour of the day or something else, I don't know. She sounded tired. Perhaps I'd overdone it again. 'Now, if you'll excuse me, I need to take a cold and flu tablet.' With that, she hung up.

My anger was at boiling point. I had to let the steam dissipate into the ether. I still had some cleaning to finish and looked across at my caddy of bottles and utensils. The germs should be extra fearful today.

CHAPTER 23

I SPENT THE REMAINDER of the weekend holed up inside my spotlessly clean flat watching cringeworthy television to try to stop myself thinking about Mummy. All the efforts on Dr Gail's part to engender positive thoughts within me had been rendered futile by one phone call.

You can rot in your rat-infested hole, Mummy, drinking and smoking yourself to death. See if I care!

Declan hadn't called, but I didn't read too much into that. He probably had things to do. Normal people tend to lead busy lives. I was glad he didn't call. He might suggest visiting Mummy again, which I didn't want to do again in a hurry.

I turned off the television and found myself consumed by an uneasy thought; I probably came on too strong with Mummy on the phone. The guilt was beginning to press on my chest like an uncomfortable weight. My timing couldn't have been more out. Knowing full well that the last thing she needed in her present state was a bagful of stress, I still felt justified to vent all my frustrations with both barrels loaded. I should be calling her to apologise, but that would only be playing into her hands. No, I think I'll ride this one out. It will give her a chance to reflect on all the bad things that she said about me. Silence can be a soothing tonic sometimes.

It was five o'clock when my phone pinged. I knew it was Declan from the caller ID. 'Hello, Sally Cartwright speaking.'

'Hi, Sally. How are you this evening?'

I hesitated before answering. I honestly didn't know how I was. My thoughts appeared to be disembodied. That is to say that anything that popped into my head felt like a weed invading my garden. Dr Gail doesn't like to see weeds in my garden.

'Sally?'

'Okay, I guess' was the best I could do.

'Just okay?' Declan's tone smacked of scepticism.

I shouldn't assume that it's Declan's job to make me feel better, to take the negative energy I manage to build up all the time and banish it into oblivion. But I'd tried to cope alone for far too long and look where that's got me. Dr Gail kept harping on about how I should share my problems. A problem shared is a problem halved, as they say.

It was time. 'I need to talk to you, Declan. About stuff I've been avoiding.'

We went for a drive. It was a balmy evening, as calm as the proverbial millpond. We parked at a deserted lookout with a stunning view of the cityscape, which sadly I wasn't in any frame of mind to appreciate. I could feel my heartbeat, every single pound in my chest like a ticking bomb. My mouth was dry, and I was afraid of stumbling over my words.

From somewhere deep within me, I found courage—my call to arms. I unclipped my seatbelt and took in a deep breath before turning towards Declan. He could see my tortured expression. 'I'm listening,' he said softly, as though he anticipated exactly what was coming.

I told him everything, from my tormented childhood and the constant abuse at the hands of Mummy to my sham autism diagnosis, the circumcision, and of still being a virgin. I even told him about my hip surgery and my limp and my physical scars. That part was the hardest, and I felt so ashamed about it that I covered my face with my hands, sobbing. I was expecting at least a gasp, a murmur of astonishment, even a look of shock horror. Instead, Declan stayed quiet and had this look of submission that suggested he wasn't the least bit surprised with what I'd told him.

I wiped my eyes on my sleeve and forced myself to look directly into his eyes, pleading for some response. He looked at me guardedly. 'How do you feel right now, Sally?' he said.

'Better.' I sighed, and then I smiled. I did actually feel better, but I also felt strange because I realised that everything I'd been hiding all these years wasn't my own anymore. It was all out there now. From this moment on, Sally Cartwright's problems will forever be public property.

Declan placed his head on my chest. There was an awkward moment when our eyes floated uncomfortably, and I felt myself blushing. He slowly lifted his head. 'Sally', he said, 'I know I've had issues with my own childhood, but I can't even pretend to imagine what you've been through. You deserve a better life from this day forward. You deserve goodness, freedom, love.'

That last word caused my throat to constrict as I choked back tears. I simply nodded. Declan was sounding quite sensible and rational. 'I'm sorry,' I said as I wiped away more tears. 'I'm a real mess now.'

'Don't be sorry. The tears are necessary.'

There was a protracted silence.

'Declan,' I said. My voice was growing stronger. 'Can you sleep over tonight?'

*

The waiting to have sex—I think that's a self-preservation thing. Obviously, it was something I wanted to experience, but would I feel the same after it? Just as importantly, will Declan feel the same about *me*? Sex should be an expression of love, of the bond that it should form.

Declan would be my first. Would he be my only one? That was an impossible question to answer.

I couldn't afford to let this moment pass.

He came into the bedroom totally oblivious to my racing heart and shaking body. My clothes were on the floor except for my underwear; I didn't want to show him everything just yet. I was underneath the covers. He paused and looked at me before removing his jeans and pulling his shirt up over his head to reveal a ripped torso. He slid quietly under the sheets, and his hands came up to my neck and hair. In that split second, every cell in my body and brain became electrified.

I pulled away just as he touched me. He leaned back with his hands behind his head, staring up to the ceiling. I knew I'd offended him. 'I'm sorry,' I said. 'I just want to enjoy this moment.' He turned to face me.

'Sally,' he whispered. I could hear and feel his desperation to use his hands and the willpower it was taking him to not do so.

A few seconds passed before he gently rested his head into the nape of my neck. At that point, my breathing became rough and fast. His hands came up to my bra, and this time, I didn't stop him; I think I've savoured the moment enough. He didn't even attempt to undo the strap, and I heard the fabric rip as it was pulled off. I felt an arm wrap around my back; and in one gentle pull, our skins were touching, and there was a kind of static between us. My back arched upwards, and my head rocked back hard against the pillow. Before I knew it, Declan's body was covering mine like a blanket. He slid a hand down my thigh; and his fingertips felt like embers, burning me wherever they touched.

I felt my heart pounding like a hammer, and my head became filled with crazy thoughts I desperately tried to erase. I tried to immerse myself in this moment. My scars didn't exist anymore. I was ready. My virginity weighed like a millstone around my neck, and the time had come to remove this weight.

Time was forgotten as our body chemistries went into overdrive. I guess the flood of endorphins was all a part of it.

I can't remember how long it lasted.

CHAPTER 24

"SALLY CARTWRIGHT IS no longer a virgin." If I had a T-shirt with that slogan on it, I might just have been daring enough to wear it on the bus today. On reflection though, I probably wouldn't have. That would have been just plain silly.

What can I say about my first sexual encounter? I think my overriding emotion would be one of disappointment. It was certainly momentous but I didn't really find it all that enjoyable. I was anticipating a sensory tempest to be unleashed or some miraculous change to present itself but all I felt was a sharp pain. I read that pain was pretty normal the first time someone swiped your V-card. There was even some blood. It wasn't a World War II massacre by any stretch and Declan even did his best to pretend not to notice it.

I can't even be sure if it was enjoyable for Declan because I had my eyes closed the whole time.

People keep going back to the well so I guess it can only get better the next time around.

If there would ever be a next time.

It hit me as soon as I sat at my desk: what if I get pregnant? The thought was abhorrent. Declan didn't use a condom. He didn't even ask me. Maybe he assumed I'd taken the contraceptive pill. I believe it should always be the responsibility of both partners to decide on the method of contraception. Those without a uterus shouldn't dictate what those with a uterus should be doing. Part of the problem is the patriarchal society that we still live in and the perception that, since only the girl can get pregnant, it is her sole responsibility to organise the method of contraception. I don't buy into any of that rubbish.

Declan and I should have talked about all this before we had sex, but my mind was too scrambled to even contemplate it.

As much as I loathed the whole notion of pregnancy, I would never consider an abortion if I ever did get pregnant. My mind harked back to an image I once saw in a documentary where teenage girls in the Philippines were wrapping their unwanted newborns in newspaper and throwing them into dumpsters like garbage. I can't fathom how anyone could live with themselves after such a cowardly and abominable act.

I would never go on the pill either. Firstly, I would need a prescription; and that would mean a visit to Dr Maria, which I promised myself never to do again. Secondly, I read that there can be many side effects including mood swings and weight gain. I sure didn't need either of those right now.

I nervously hovered over my screen and did a search. According to Google, you are most fertile at the time of ovulation, which is about twelve to fourteen days before your period. You are unlikely to get pregnant just before or just after your last period. I stared wide-eyed at my desk calendar and did some quick calculations. I sunk back in my seat and heaved a huge sigh; I was safe.

I closed my screen just in time. Consumed by my intense number crunching, I didn't hear Mike's shuffling gait behind me.

'Sally, can I see you in my office?' he said.

The best word to describe Mike's office would be chaotic. 'Sit down, Sally, please.' His tone was serious, measured. I had to shift a pile of manila folders from the chair to sit down. Mike stared at me in a strange way, and I wondered if he somehow knew. *Hey, everyone, listen up. Sally Cartwright got laid last night!* They say you can often tell when a girl has had sexual intercourse. I'd been extra careful this morning to ensure that my appearance was in no way different to any other work day. My hair was neatly styled, and my minimalistic makeup was applied carefully and evenly. I also made sure that I wore fresh clothes that didn't look like they'd been passed through a sausage machine.

'You've been here how long now?'

I've been working here for exactly four years, four months, nineteen days, and thirty-five minutes. I let out a small laugh, more to calm my nerves than anything else. 'Just over four years,' I said.

Mike leaned forward and gave me one of those typical Mike smiles. 'Did you know that Dolores is leaving us?'

I nodded just to be polite. No, I didn't know that Dolores was leaving us. I didn't even know Dolores. 'No, Mr Cosgrove', I said, 'I didn't know she's leaving. Is she all right?' I forced myself to sound concerned.

Mike waved his hand. 'Oh yes, she's perfectly fine. Her husband got a promotion out of town. I also believe that they're planning to start a family.'

Any talk of domestic circumstances and pregnancy wasn't in my wheelhouse today. 'I see,' I said, trying to sound sympathetic. 'I hope it works out for them both.' I really didn't give a rat's and ran a nervous hand through my hair. All this pretending was taking a toll.

Mike fiddled with his pen. 'So', he said, 'I'm going to need a new Accounts girl. I hear you're pretty good with numbers and matters of managing money. And you never have days off sick.'

I nodded and averted my gaze.

'Would you be interested, Sally? I mean, would you at least be willing to think about it? It would be more money for you as well as some added responsibility, but I'm sure you'll relish the challenge.'

I wondered what gave Mike the inkling that I would relish the challenge, let alone need one. For four years, he'd seen me do my job with dependable precision and a sameness that would bore most people to tears. Never once had I complained or hinted that the work wasn't challenging enough. He surely must know that I'm not a twenty-year career-planner kind of girl.

I considered his proposition for a moment. Did I really want the extra responsibility? I'm safe-as-houses Sally, remember? Or at least I have been until now. 'How much more money, Mr Cosgrove?'

Mike opened a manila folder and turned it around to my side. It was a work contract with my name printed at the top of the page and a figure underlined in red on the bottom.

'Wow.' I gasped and found it hard to hide my excitement. It was almost double what I was currently earning.

'It would mean working back some nights as well as sitting in on management meetings,' Mike said. 'It would also mean having your own office,' he eagerly added.

I always thought that getting my private office would forever be unattainable, something that would forever be assigned to the annals of fiction or even magic. I couldn't curb my enthusiasm anymore. 'A private office? That would be awesome.'

Mike shrugged. 'It's an important job, Sally. You'll need your privacy.'

I considered all the possible implications of accepting Mike's offer. Adding to what he just said, it would mean not having to deal with Rob, Wilma, or Casey. They'd all be intensely jealous, of course, but that wasn't my problem. It would also mean spending less time at home alone watching television or reading a book or even cleaning. I'd also probably have to endure a significantly increased degree of interaction with people whom I'd never bothered to give the time of day to in the past. I'd even have to put up with them coming into my office and whingeing about the most trivial of matters. I hate whingers. Was I prepared to tolerate such puerile activity? The extra money was saying I was.

My pulse quickened, and I felt a tiny trickle of sweat run down my back. 'Thank you, Mr Cosgrove,' I said. 'I accept your offer. I won't let you down.'

'Congratulations, Sally!' Mike leaned over the desk and gave me a firm man shake, which I found both awkward and painful. He then handed me a pen for my signature. Was it a poisoned pen? Only time will tell.

It became official; I was to start my new post next week.

When I sat back down at my desk, I stared at my screen for some time, not actually reading or taking anything in. I felt apprehensive. Maybe I shouldn't have rushed my decision. Every fibre in my body was vibrating like guitar strings, and adrenaline was coursing through my veins unabated.

I was suddenly gripped by an uncomfortable level of anxiety, but I quickly recalled what Dr Gail taught me about dealing with this very situation. It was all about becoming self-aware and in control of the moment. The first step was to clear my mind and think of nothing. This wasn't easy to do, but the office was relatively quiet at this hour,

MARIO BORAZIO

which made it a little easier for me to zone out. After a few minutes, I closed my eyes and began taking long deep breaths using the 4-7-8 technique for relaxation. I placed my hands on my chest and became aware of its rise and fall as I continued to breathe. Now that I felt totally relaxed, the last step was to think about all the positive things in my life. I thought about Declan and where our relationship might one day take us. I thought about my bright and clean flat. I thought about the extra money I would earn from my promotion and how I would spend it. I thought about the excitement of getting my driver's licence.

I tried hard not to think about Mummy.

I opened my eyes and felt a rush of blood to my brain as well as a smile growing on my face. I had a good feeling for the future. The winds of change were all at my back. It was full steam ahead.

Nothing else could possibly go wrong now.

CHAPTER 25

THE WEEK DRAGGED by as slow as sticky honey. Declan came over on two nights but didn't sleep over. He said he had early starts, and I convinced myself that this was a legitimate excuse for him not to stay. But his lack of initiative in instigating any form of intimacy had me a little concerned. I naturally assumed that, having visited my well once, he would want to drink from it again.

Or was I just a 'dud root'? I'd heard this terminology used by my colleagues at work on occasions, usually on a Monday morning after what was supposed to be an amazingly grand weekend spent with a member of the opposite sex had turned out to be anything but. They would all be colluding with the lie that things will turn out better next weekend. They invariably never did.

I was willing to give sex another go although I didn't know if Declan felt the same way.

The Friday sessions with Dr Gail had become a natural part of my routine. It was actually nice to leave work early although I hadn't thought how my new role might impact this arrangement.

We did some variations on anxiety therapy and talked a little more about Mummy. These conversations were becoming easier for me now. I was on a roll and decided to fess up to Dr Gail that I hadn't been taking the antidepressants. She didn't appear at all shocked. She agreed that, as long as I was making progress, I could stay medication free. I was pleased about that.

I also told her about my promotion and how I had discussed my past with Declan, but I couldn't bring myself to divulge anything about my first sexual encounter. I viewed it as a memory best kept to myself for the time being.

It was Saturday. I had to purchase extra supplies of cleaning products.

This gave me a euphoric sense of achievement and a renewed fervour to continue keeping my flat looking pristine. Maybe I was becoming obsessive-compulsive about it, but I didn't care.

After cleaning, I thought about Mummy. I decided that, even though she would always keep putting me down, I had to keep my promise and visit her again.

I called her and told her about my promotion. She sounded more upbeat, and I think she was genuinely happy but in the same breath warned me about the 'blood-sucking leeches of upper management'. 'You'll be a target now,' she warned.

I think the new Sally Cartwright is capable of looking after herself a whole lot better than before, thank you very much.

Mummy had gone back to the heart specialist. He must have put the fear of God in her because she announced that she had cut down on her drinking and had also gone off the cigarettes 'cold turkey.' 'That's great, Mummy,' I said calmly. But I'd heard it all before. I'm sure it won't last long; asking Mummy to show self-control was like asking a fire not to keep burning.

As soon as I got off the phone, I made an inspired decision: with my first upgraded pay cheque, I will get my driver's licence and purchase a car. That way, I didn't have to rely on Declan to drive me to see Mummy.

It rained all day on Sunday. The upside was that I didn't have to feel bad about not leaving my flat. Declan had gone to visit his father who apparently wasn't well, so that left me on my 'Pat Malone'. I just used rhyming slang for the very first time! It wasn't that long ago when I would have considered using such a phrase extremely immature.

I felt jittery. Tomorrow couldn't come fast enough. All I could think about was what my first day in my new job would look like. I spent the afternoon configuring a new wardrobe that would adequately reflect the status of my new position within the firm. Overdressing could be seen as trying too hard or showing off, while underdressing would reflect poorly, as though I didn't value my new position enough.

I didn't have much of a range to choose from, but in the end, I decided on pressed tailored pants and a collared white shirt that didn't show any cleavage.

I made myself a hot chocolate with whipped cream and decided to add a small glittery marshmallow as a sort of self-indulgent treat. I took my creation into the lounge room and plopped myself down on the couch. Seeing and hearing raindrops trickling down the window brought a sense of calmness to me. The whispering hum of the rain was a perfect backdrop. This was a moment to savour. With this promotion and my relationship with Declan trending skyward, such nights of solitude may not present themselves very often anymore.

I dozed off. The next thing I remembered was waking up with a crick neck. Bright sunlight poured into the lounge room as I squinted up at the clock.

I was going to be late for work.

CHAPTER 26

I HAVE NEVER TAKEN a taxi to work before. In fact, I have never taken a taxi—period. I sat in the front seat and watched the metre turning over. On first impressions, this mode of transportation appears to be a licence to print money. We had barely travelled a couple of kilometres, and the metre was already showing ten dollars. That's almost a whole week's worth of bus fares.

Why are taxis so expensive? Looking around the cabin, I couldn't detect any luxurious features or expensive bells and whistles that you wouldn't find in any other modern vehicle. I know the driver has to get paid; and you have to allow for fuel, insurance, and maintenance costs. I get all that. But unless there are hidden extras like regulatory fees and higher-than-normal tax imposts, these operations are taking us all for a ride, no pun intended.

In the end, the driver relieved me of close to forty dollars. Lucky I could afford that now. Message to self: never fall asleep on the couch again!

I walked through the front door at precisely two minutes after nine. 'Excuse me, Jenny,' I said as I rested my sweaty palms on the counter. Jenny was the front of house receptionist whose main job was to greet clients. She has been here for as long as I have. We have never spoken in all that time, never once exchanged pleasantries or even a smile.

She looked up wide-eyed and expressionless, as if I'd just spoken in tongues. 'It's Sally. Sally Cartwright. I'm starting in Accounts today. Can you tell me where my new office is?'

Hello, I'm speaking English.

Jenny didn't answer right away. For a brief moment, her face washed blank with confusion. 'You're starting in Accounts?' she eventually said. I nodded. It was obvious that Mike hadn't yet informed all the staff about my promotion.

'Yes', I said in a slightly panicky tone, 'I should have been at my desk three minutes ago.'

'Down the end of the hall then turn right. Accounts is the second door in.'

I thanked her and strode purposefully past the smattering of workers already hard at it over their desks. Not one of them acknowledged my presence.

The windowless office was illuminated by a single ceiling light and was sparsely furnished: a single chair, a small desk, a computer, and a photocopier in the far corner. Mike was nowhere to be seen. I assumed he would have been here for my 'initiation', but my assumption was misplaced. Or was he here at precisely 9 a.m.? I was becoming slightly panicky now.

I contemplated popping my head into the next office just to see who was in there but thought better of it because I was already five minutes late.

Closing the door behind me and sitting at my new desk, I tried to put my tardiness to one side and just savour this moment. I felt like an excited child. Privacy at last! No more snide remarks from Rob and no more having to endure covert and abrasive conversations between Wilma and Casey. Being able to shut out the rest of the world was surely the holy grail of systemised business practice.

Down to it then. There was work to be done. Where do I start? What do I do? I was a little flustered and decided to poke my head out the door. Just as I did so, I noticed Mike tearing down the hallway towards my office with a worried look on his face. He moved like a pachyderm on a bad acid trip.

'Sally ... sorry ... I'm ... late,' he said, panting. If Mike were to collapse right here and now, it would be incumbent upon me to perform some form of cardiopulmonary resuscitation procedure to ensure that he remains my boss for the foreseeable future. The thought of our mouths touching made me gasp and take stock before answering. 'That's okay, Mr Cosgrove. I was just familiarising myself with the computer.'

'Ah yes ... the computer ... of course.' He nodded and drew a long wheezy breath. 'You'll need the password. It's *crumpet*, all lower case.'

I dared not ask for an explanation.

The first few days were somewhat challenging. To my relief, I wasn't required to attend any meetings, and I didn't have any interruptions except for Mike who would come in every now and then to see how I was doing.

I quickly worked out that my main job was to ensure that the correct invoices were going out to the correct people and that the correct payments were being banked and that people, including all the staff, were getting paid on time. It wasn't rocket science. These were all things that any competent secretary could have handled standing on his or her head. I ruminated that this could become quite a tedious job although I tried not to think too far ahead. I did wonder, though, how Dolores endured it for so many years and still managed to stay sane. She must've been a real trooper.

I convinced myself that the extra money would be enough incentive to keep me sane.

One whole week passed, and I allowed myself to reflect. My new job had definitely rekindled my relationship with work, in general. I never had any intentions of shaking things up. Doing my job quietly and efficiently was all the reward I sought. I read somewhere that if you're learning to ride a horse and it feels comfortable, you're probably not doing it right. Starting a new position can be all new and exciting, and you may easily find yourself overlooking imperfections and dismissing signs that may call this new arrangement into question. Would it lose its lustre over time? I honestly didn't know. Nor did I really care because, at this point, everything in my life was heading north—mummy matters excepted.

I continued my lunch affair at the Fancy Chef. Why should I even consider choosing a more upmarket dining locale? Just because I'm on a higher pay bracket doesn't mean my stomach deserves anything different. Even millionaires eat at McDonalds sometimes.

The café had been closed briefly for renovations after the explosion. I must say I was suitably impressed by its fresh and new interior: brightly coloured walls, shiny metallic tables, and a good mix of ambient and decorative lighting. I surveyed the scene. The new look seemed to have attracted a whole niche of new customers.

I was fortunate enough to score my regular window seat. Declan was meeting me for lunch today. All week we'd only been communicating by electronic means, and I knew something was up by the tone of his messages.

His mood was sombre, which was understandable given the unpleasant news he conveyed to me as soon as he sat down: his father had cirrhosis of the liver. Even a layperson knows that this is most often caused by alcoholism. 'They've put him in hospital, Sally.' Declan slurped his coffee, and for the first time, I saw him crying. 'It's silly, isn't it?' he said.

'What's silly?' I asked.

'My crying. After all the suffering he put me through, I should be happy the bastard's getting some of his own back. I shouldn't be crying.'

I had no reply to Declan's comment. I wondered about my domestic situation and what condition Mummy's liver was in. That made me contemplate how I would feel if she ever became really sick. I honestly didn't know how I'd feel. It's not that I took her for granted as such—heaven knows, nothing can be taken for granted in this life—but I knew all too well where Declan was coming from. 'Declan', I said, 'it's not really my place to give you advice, but you should count yourself lucky to have this opportunity to be with your father when he needs you most. I mean, who knows how long he's—' I stopped myself just in time. *You idiot, Sally.* 'I'm sorry. That's so insensitive. I didn't mean that.'

Declan didn't appear to be offended. 'That's alright,' he said. 'Dad wasn't exactly a picture of health before this, anyway. Besides, I had a feeling something like this was going to happen one day. I was sort of prepared for it.'

'What are you going to do?' I asked.

Declan shrugged. 'I don't have much choice. I know Carol won't step up. Neither will Mum. She wouldn't care less about Dad's health. She won't be happy until he's resting inside a pine box.'

My sexual evolution would have to take a raincheck. 'You have a duty, Declan,' I said. 'We can keep in touch by phone or text.' In a perverse sort of way, I was enjoying this experience. Declan had chosen me to share his uncomfortable news with. I felt like a spy privy to top-secret information. I opened my mouth to say something, but nothing came out. He looked at me all serious, and I looked at him back. There was warmth in what wasn't being said.

Back at work, I found it hard to concentrate on anything at all. Declan's news had put a dent in my day. This time, it was my turn to be the sympathiser. Not having experienced this before, I thought about whether I had done enough to support him. I also thought about how long it would be before I see him again. That, of course, would be totally dependent on his father's state of health.

I slumped at my desk and shut my eyes to begin some focus exercises that Dr Gail had said would help me to concentrate better. It's a sort of self-hypnosis.

I was almost off with the fairies when my phone rang. Startled, I sat up quickly, and my heart began racing. The number was unfamiliar. My mind flashed back to the calls I'd received in the past. What calamity was I going to be warned about this time? But hang on. This is my new phone. Surely, it couldn't be that girl from YouTube again. She wouldn't have my new number. Or would she?

With mild panic and a shaking hand, I pressed the answer button. 'Hello.'

'Hello, is this Sally? Sally Cartwright?' To my relief, it was a man's voice this time.

'Yes, it is,' I said in a shaky voice. 'Who is this?'

'My name is Constable John Spiers. I'm calling about Eve Cartwright. Is she your mother?' The man's tone sent a chill down my spine.

'Yes. Eve is my mother,' I said. 'Is anything the matter?'

'Your mother's been taken to hospital. She's had a stroke.'

CHAPTER 27

S ALLY CARTWRIGHT, DO NOT PANIC. The police officer told me that he spoke with the hospital, and they said that Mummy wasn't in any grave danger and that it wasn't necessary for me to rush to her bedside. Nevertheless, as her only living relative, it was my duty to be there for her. I could just imagine it, Mummy lying on a dirty hospital bed all alone and neglected for hours.

I tried using Dr Gail's 4-7-8 breathing technique to calm me down, but it didn't work this time. The panic rose up from my abdomen like a cluster of firecrackers firing simultaneously. All kinds of thoughts were conjuring inside my head. They all crowded together and were jostling for my attention. What should I do? Who should I call? I can't call Declan. His father needs him. My phone was on the desk right in front of me, yet it seemed so far away.

With trembling fingers, I called the taxi company, picked up my bag, and hastily left the building without telling anyone, not even Mike.

As I waited outside for the taxi to arrive, I tried to get answers to impossible questions: Was I somehow responsible for Mummy's stroke? Did I upset her too much during our last phone conversation? Then there were broader questions: Could I have done something to curb her drinking? Was it my fault that she drank and smoked too much and that her health had deteriorated?

I felt like a stone had settled deep inside me and was getting heavier, sinking further and further down.

I rode in the backseat this time. Since my maiden foray into the taxi-hailing scene last week, I'd studied these vehicles more closely and noticed that almost everyone sat in the backseat. If it was okay for these customers to do so, it was okay for Sally Cartwright too.

As the driver negotiated the morning traffic out of the city, I contemplated whether what I was doing was impetuous. I should have at least informed Mike that I was leaving. And I should have gone home first and packed an overnight bag. How long would I be gone for? That was an impossible question to answer.

I couldn't help myself; I slipped out my phone and googled all the possible sequelae of a stroke: difficulty communicating, memory loss, cognitive changes, depression, paralysis, difficulty walking, hearing loss, vision impairment, incontinence—the list was almost endless. It was times like these I wished I was religious. *Please, God, don't let Mummy have any of these things.*

What if she deteriorated and was in need of full-time care? *Don't be daft, Sally. You don't need to think like that right now. It's all hypothetical.*

The driver dropped me out the front of the hospital and cut the engine as the metre took its last click. Two hundred and twenty dollars suddenly seemed like a fair price, and I paid without making a fuss. It's amazing what we're prepared to accept when our emotions take over. It's like if you were in a car accident and the paramedics informed you that they were only prepared to save your life if you handed over ten thousand dollars. You'd be begging them to take your credit card.

I've only ever been inside a hospital once. That was for my hip operation, but I can't remember much of what the place looked like—I don't ever want to remember it.

I perceive hospitals, in general, as being beneficent places of caring and compassion, places where one is sent to recover from an illness and be doted on by dedicated and caring professionals. I imagine soft footfalls of doctors and nurses trudging purposefully down long corridors to help patients in desperate need of tender loving care. I have visions of complicated machines, shiny metal and clean linen, bright lights, tubes, and drips. Kind voices explaining things. Openness and white shiny walls, bright flowers in foyers, the smell of disinfectant, and nurses all immaculately dressed in crisp light-blue uniforms with white piping.

These were, of course, merely assumptions borne in my head but ones that I hoped held true. In the end, though, hospitals are merely places where birth, death, and everything in between coexist.

I took a few tentative steps inside. The reality was a trifle disappointing: The entrance was small, dim, and stuffy; and the air had an undertone of staleness as if I were somewhere deep underground. The carpet looked like it could do with a good dose of my buckwheat cleaner, and the walls showed patches of bare concrete where cream paint had once lived. The whole place had the depressed air of an underfunded public health facility. Even the wandering nurses looked dishevelled and tired. Some looked beyond tired.

I couldn't help but think that this was a place that offered inadequate care and had slipshod compliance across the board with every one of its protocols.

The receptionist behind the information desk looked more plastic than the purified water dispenser that occupied the corner to her left. She was so still and expressionless. Her face was set almost as firmly as a mannequin's, and her makeup could quite easily have been mistaken for thick clumps of plaster. I wondered what had brought her to this robotic half-alive state. Was it the tedium of the job, or had she just given up on life? Either way, I felt sad for her.

'Excuse me,' I said just loud enough to get her attention. 'I'm looking for my mother's room. Her name is Eve Cartwright.' The girl didn't acknowledge me in any way, didn't even look up. Her eyes were drawn to her computer screen like two little magnets. She remained silent, and I wondered whether her pursed bright-pink lips ever came apart. She pressed them together firmly until they disappeared. I was about to repeat my request when she decided to speak.

'Three west, room 10. Take the lift to your left.' Her voice was unmelodious, the kind you often hear on an automated phone message.

I thanked her and made my way up to the third floor.

On Mummy's ward the atmosphere was surprisingly different, more in keeping with my preconceived expectations. The air had a perfumed scent, and every surface appeared dustless. Beautiful framed prints of contemporary art adorned the walls. The nurses' station was unoccupied. On the counter was a hand sanitiser dispenser, which I used liberally. Who knows what germs lurked here or indeed inside the taxi that I rode in?

The floor squeaked as I walked down the corridor towards Mummy's room. All I could hear was the noise of multiple televisions at various volumes. There wasn't a moan in sight.

I drew a deep breath as I stepped into room 10. Mummy's bed was the last one nearest the far wall. It was separated from three others by a thin curtain, which was partially drawn. Before I opened it, I allowed myself to study the other three patients. All of them looked old beyond a natural lifespan. One didn't even look human. Her sallow eyes were the colour of charcoal clouds, and she had her head tilted towards a sun that sadly for her remained on the wrong side of the windowpane. Her face appeared ashen where the sunlight caught it, subdued and greyish. I hope Mummy doesn't look like that.

The old man next to her made a slight gesture with his right hand, a salute of some kind. He had fluttering white hair and a fierceness to his eyes, which was a little unnerving. I waved back and quickly turned away.

The patient closest to Mummy was using a magnifying glass to read a magazine. I don't think he was even aware of my presence. There was an impressive bunch of fresh flowers as well as a packet of biscuits on his side table.

It suddenly dawned on me that it was very much the custom to bring a gift when visiting someone in hospital. I thought about what sort of gift might have been appropriate for Mummy. Cigarettes and alcohol were definitely out. Maybe a packet of nuts, although she may not be allowed to eat them yet. I think the most appropriate gift would have been a care bear, one with a poignant message attached. Something like 'I Love You' or 'Get Well Soon' were messages that immediately sprung to mind.

In the end, I was glad that I didn't buy Mummy anything; she wouldn't appreciate the gesture. In any case, I'd never find a bear near as nice as Fuzzy.

The anticipation was too much, and I pulled the curtain open before nerves could get the better of me. Mummy's hair was whiter, and she looked older. Her eyes were closed, and her face had a contorted expression as it pressed against the pillow. I could see that she'd taken a decent knock to her head. Her upper lip was split in the middle, and her forehead had developed a small blue egg near her left temple. I could tell from the regular way that her chest rose and fell that she was sleeping. It was a relief to know that she wasn't dead. There was a drip in her arm, and her body was tethered to an array of wires all funnelling into a small monitor that displayed a heart rhythm as well as a reading of her blood pressure and oxygen saturation level. The continued activity on the screen was a reassuring sight.

There was a dull ache deep inside me that entwined both empathy and disappointment. It hurt me to see Mummy in this state, but it also made me angry to know that all this could have most likely been avoided if she had listened to her doctors and made some basic lifestyle changes.

I was about to reach forward to touch her hand when I heard someone clear their throat behind me.

'Are you a relative?' The young nurse's ebony skin and impressive long black braided hair stood out against her starched white uniform. She was holding a glass thermometer and a small plastic cup.

'I'm her daughter.' My voice was croaky, and I cleared my throat. 'My name is Sally,' I said.

The nurse didn't bother introducing herself. 'I'm here to take your mother's temperature and administer her tablets.' She burst past me and shoved the thermometer in Mummy's mouth without attempting to wake her up. Mummy flinched a little but didn't open her eyes. The nurse waited a few seconds before pulling the thermometer out and holding it up to the light. 'Just two tablets now, Eve,' she said as she emptied the contents of the plastic cup into Mummy's mouth, followed immediately by a small amount of water. Mummy's head was turned to one side, and I was afraid she wouldn't be able to swallow. An immense relief surged through me as I saw her take one big gulp.

The nurse made to bustle off, but I deliberately blocked her exit point. 'Excuse me,' I said as calmly as I could. 'I've only just arrived. Can you tell me something about my mother's condition?'

She shook her head and arched her eyebrows. 'I've just started my shift. You'll have to speak to one of the doctors,' she said.

I stood as still as a dead slug and adopted a deadpan expression. 'All right then. I'd like to speak to a doctor please.'

The nurse sighed and gave an expression of childish insouciance. She took a quick look back at Mummy, who was still sleeping soundly. 'Your mother has been heavily sedated. She'll be sleeping for a while. There's not much you can do here. I suggest you go home and come back in the morning.'

Did this woman not hear a word I said? Just as I was about to repeat myself, her pager buzzed. She pressed the button and made to head out. This time, I grabbed her arm. 'I would like to talk to a doctor. Please.' The last word was emphasised.

She let out a slow breath. 'You have to remember, there are a lot of patients on this floor, and most are sicker than your mother.'

'I don't care,' I said with as much assertiveness as I could muster. 'I've travelled almost two hours to get here, and I'm not leaving until I find out what is going on with my mother. Now, either you get a doctor, or I will report you to the relevant authorities for failure of duty of care.' My abruptness surprised me, and I hated how I had to sink into this role of pretending to be a hard-nosed bitch. But I couldn't see any other option open to me at this point in time.

The nurse stood stiffly, absorbing my display of anger. 'Alright,' she said. Her tone was as sharp as a steel trap. 'I'll get a doctor to come and see you as soon as possible. Now if you'll excuse me, I have vitals to take, pads to change, and medications to administer.' She gave me a cold stare and walked away with the grace of a six-legged spider, which mirrored perfectly her demeanour.

I hope I never have to see her again.

I sat down and continued watching Mummy's rhythmical breathing. I'd never seen her so peaceful. In a strange sort of way, I was wishing that she'd never wake up.

Time dragged on. The sound of people walking up and down the corridor was assuring, but not one person had entered Mummy's room in more than an hour. The clock ticked just past four o'clock, and it suddenly dawned on me that I had skipped lunch and was ravenously hungry. And I forgot to call Mike. Suddenly my idle time in this hospital room seemed a precious opportunity missed.

I checked my phone, but there were no messages or missed calls. Was Mike even aware that I wasn't at work? I was about to send off a text when a man in a white coat sauntered into the room carrying a folder. He sat on the edge of Mummy's bed.

'Hello, I'm Dr Morton.' His voice was reedy and high pitched but pleasant nonetheless. He was thin with ginger hair and wore round wire spectacles perched over a thin pointy nose.

'Hello, I'm Sally Cartwright.' I offered my hand, but he didn't notice. His gaze was fixed on the folder, which I assumed to be Mummy's file.

'Your mother has had a stroke. I presume you've been told that already,' he said.

I nodded.

'Do you know what a stroke is, Sally?'

I did, sort of. It was something that affected the brain, but I knew very little beyond that. 'I know there's a lot of information out there, but I'm only familiar with the basics. I'd like to know more please, Doctor.'

'Certainly.' The doctor grinned and placed Mummy's file on the side table. He appeared to have a pleasant bedside manner. 'A stroke occurs when an artery supplying blood to the brain becomes completely blocked or bursts. In either case, a lack of oxygen-carrying blood can damage or even destroy previously healthy brain cells, which can, in turn, affect all sorts of bodily functions.'

'Do you know yet how this stroke has affected my mother?'

'Your mother has lost motor control of her right side. That means that she has weakness and limited movement of her right arm and leg. From the other tests we've done, we're pretty sure that her vision and speech haven't been affected. As to whether or not her memory and cognition have also been affected, you'll be the best judge of that when she wakes up.'

I rested my elbows on my knees and looked over at Mummy. Never in my wildest dreams did I ever imagine this moment. Mummy was always the strong one, or at least that's how she portrayed herself. She'd grown a hard shell over many years but never dared show anyone her weaknesses. Yet here she was—vulnerable and helpless.

I turned back to face Dr Morton. 'Will my mother ever recover from this?' I asked.

He shrugged. 'It's too early to tell. We'd just be throwing darts in the dark. Even psychics have to look both ways before crossing the street,' he said sagely. I found that analogy disturbing and just a little odd.

'So what now?' I asked.

'She'll need some rehabilitation and will have to see a physiotherapist as well as an occupational therapist. A full recovery is still on the cards, but it can take a long time, and nothing is guaranteed.'

Dr Morton continued his explanation. 'Stroke recovery can take months or even longer. A lot depends on the caregiver. Does your mother live alone?'

'Yes. I moved out over four years ago.'

'Do you live close by?'

'No. I live in Melbourne.'

'I see.' Dr Morton began scribbling some notes. 'Does she have any relatives close by?'

I shook my head. 'I'm afraid not,' I said. 'I'm the only family she has.'

The doctor stared at me with a worrying and serious expression. It would be inappropriate for him to smile or pretend that everything was going to be okay when we both knew full well that that may not be the case.

I had a fair idea how this was going to play out.

'You've got an important decision to make here, young lady. Your mother will need full-time care once she leaves here.' Dr Morton's pen was poised. 'Tell me, do you have a family of your own, Sally?'

'No. I live alone.'

Dr Morton nodded. 'I see. What about work?'

'I've just been promoted.' I'm sure that wasn't the correct answer.

The doctor twisted his head and looked up at Mummy's monitor before turning back around with a creased brow. 'As I was saying, this will be a very difficult decision for you to make.' His voice was thick with seriousness. 'It's not one you can make lightly or quickly.'

I nodded to show that I understood.

Dr Morton continued, 'You'll have to consider work and if you can juggle things around that. You'll also have to think about the day-to-day tasks that may need to be done, helping your mother with her toileting, eating and dressing, as well as organising medical appointments for her. It's a big responsibility.'

It was. A thousand questions were whirring around in my head, but I only asked one. 'How much care will my mother need?'

Dr Morton again shrugged his shoulders. 'As I said before, we can't yet ascertain the full impact of her impairment. We'll know a lot more when she's able to leave hospital, which probably won't be for a few weeks. Our medical team and social services case manager can work together with you to create a plan for her release based on her needs.'

I couldn't concentrate on those scenarios yet because I was curious about something else. 'What if I am unable to look after her?'

'If you are unable to be your mother's nominated caregiver, we'll have to turn her over to the state.'

I had visions of Mummy trapped inside a secluded institution with locked doors, barred windows, and angry-looking nurses. Despite all her failings, she deserved better than that.

I watched Dr Morton go over Mummy's notes again. Without a word, he leaned over her bed and pulled the blankets down. He did some fiddling with first her arms and then her legs before pulling the blankets back up. Mummy didn't stir. 'Her right limb muscles have already lost some tone,' he said concededly.

A silence followed that made me feel acutely uncomfortable. I suddenly felt devoid of any emotion. Dr Morton sensed my apprehension.

'Can I get you anything?' he asked.

I shook my head. 'No thanks. I'll be fine.'

He closed Mummy's folder and stood up. 'I'll be in touch tomorrow,' he said before leaving the room.

I watched Mummy sleeping for what seemed like another hour, but in reality, it was probably shorter than that. Time seems to warp when

MARIO BORAZIO

you have a lot on your mind. I continued watching her face, which had fallen to almost a scowl. How appropriate, I thought. I reached out with my fingers extended and gently touched her forehead. It was clammy and cold.

I had a choice to make, of kindness or cruelty. It took only a split second to reach a decision. I wasn't born for great things, and I didn't perceive what I was going to do to be anything great in any way, but this was my destiny.

I had to become Mummy's caregiver.

CHAPTER 28

I WASN'T HUNGRY ANYMORE. As I sat back waiting for Mummy to wake up, I contemplated texting Mike. The batteries of both my phones were low. Just as well, I always carried the chargers in my bag.

I plugged the charger of my newer phone into the wall socket and began texting:

Hi Mike, this is Sally Cartwright speaking.
Something has come up. I don't know when I will be back at work.
It will be at least a few days.
Regards, Sally Cartwright.

It was only a few weeks ago that I would have berated myself for even thinking about taking time off work. But I couldn't have ever imagined the circumstances in which I find myself now. Life throws up curveballs, which we all have to deal with as best we can.

I knew I'd be gone for more than a few days, but I felt that I needed to break the news of my absence to Mike as gently as possible. I wasn't prepared to tell him the reason for my desertion just yet. That can wait. It will be like a game show where the contestants are drip fed clues until they have enough information to decipher the full message.

I had just put my phone away when I noticed a pair of eyes staring back at me.

'Sal! How good of you to come to visit your dear old mum!' Mummy was sitting up and spoke with a slight drawl. It was then I noticed that her face was pale and her mouth drooped down on the left side. Her features had developed an ugly twist. Any other time, I might have recognised this as her way of showing scorn towards me.

She was sweating profusely. I quickly looked around for a towel but couldn't find one. 'Wait a minute, Mummy,' I said. I rummaged through my bag and found a small packet of Kleenex. 'I'm just going to wipe your brow.'

She winced as I dabbed a tissue against the bruise on her forehead. 'You must think your mother a right old stumblebum,' she said. 'I suppose they told you that I fell in the garden. That's where the neighbours found me. I must've got tangled up in those blasted begonias. They'll have to go when I get home.' She tried to twist herself up but could only manage to roll onto her left hip. 'Oh dear,' she moaned. 'I must have fallen harder than I thought. I can't seem to put even the slightest weight on my right side.' I handed Mummy a fresh tissue, which she used to mop the back of her neck.

This wasn't the time for small talk. I had to tell her the truth. 'Didn't they tell you what really happened, Mummy?' I said. 'You've had a stroke. That's the reason you fell.'

Mummy looked at me with a mixture of concern and humour, her crooked half smile faltering a little when she realised that I might be serious. Still, she took the approach I was all too familiar with. 'Oh, Sal, I can recall all of the stupid things you used to say, all the lies, but this time you have well and truly outdone yourself. Why do you continue to lie to me?'

I felt wary about saying anything else at this point. It was as though Mummy was giving me some sort of a test. 'It's true, Mummy,' I eventually said. 'Dr Morton was just in here while you were sleeping. He told me that you had a stroke and that you have lost some strength in your right arm and your right leg.'

Mummy shook her head and had a look of haughty disdain. She hauled herself farther up the bed; her hospital gown opened up, revealing a flat stomach and hard ribs, which were more obvious than they ought to have been against her pale skin. She almost looked emaciated. 'You've pulled the wool over my eyes for far too long, Sal, telling tales that were never true. How dare you try to deceive me when I am at my most vulnerable? Have you no heart?'

I tried to shake the negative memories building up inside my head. The bad seeds. These memories always came in like tides, rising and hitting their peaks before slowly and quietly slipping away. 'You've got to believe me, Mummy. I have never deceived you.'

'Huh!' Mummy threw her head back and tried to swipe at me with her right arm, which barely moved. Suddenly there appeared a frightful expression on her face, and she took in a sharp breath. 'Sal, I can't move my arm!' Then she looked down. 'Or my leg!' Tears began to fall down her face as the walls that had held her up to this point suddenly collapsed. Her chin trembled, and her voice became shaky. 'Is it true, Sal? Did I really have a stroke?'

I instinctively clutched Mummy's hand. Now it was my turn to shed a tear. 'You did, Mummy,' I said. 'Everything I've told you is true.' She looked towards the window, her cheekbones and jawbones very prominent. She looked a broken woman, and it was plainly obvious that this news was a huge shock.

'I'm scared, Sal,' she said as she frowned and stared blankly. 'What will I do?'

'Don't you worry, Mummy. Dr Morton is the doctor who examined you. He's going to help you.' I tried to sound optimistic.

Mummy surveyed the room and shook her head. 'I'm trapped in here, aren't I, Sal?' she said.

'What? No. You'll be home in a few weeks, and then you'll start physiotherapy to strengthen your right side. Dr Morton said that, with time, there is some chance you can make a full recovery from this.'

I let go of Mummy's hand, and she pulled her gown back over her chest. 'Time is what I don't have, sweetheart.' Her voice was melancholic despite the drawl. 'What with the diabetes and blood pressure, my clock is definitely ticking. Besides, how can my life ever be the same again? In case you've forgotten, I live alone.'

I felt that wave of familiarity again. Of the 'woe is me' persona rearing its ugly head. I shouldn't be too harsh on this occasion, though. Mummy had every right to be frightened. 'You won't be alone, Mummy,' I said. 'I'll look after you until you're better.'

'You?' Mummy's tone suggested genuine surprise.

I nodded. 'I've already informed my boss that I'll be taking some time off. I've accrued plenty of sick days.'

Mummy sighed dramatically. She appeared shocked and was finding it hard to show any appreciation for my gesture. 'I'm sorry for you.' She searched for her words. 'I've put you in a pickle. But yes, I suppose I could do with some help.' I was resigned to the fact that this was the closest I was ever going to get to a thank you from her. Her crooked smile was even more pathetic now. She was getting animated. 'You were right, Sal. I probably shouldn't be drinking anymore. I'm stopping as of right now. The new Eve Cartwright will be sober for every day, every minute, and every second from now on. We can spend quality time together, just like old times!' Her voice was cheery. She shuffled over onto her left side and closed her eyes.

We were silent for a while until I realised that she had fallen back asleep. I reached down into my bag and checked my phone. The corners of my mouth curled up into a smile.

Mike sent me a thumbs-up message.

CHAPTER 29

THE NURSING STAFF at the hospital informed me that Mummy still needed to sleep and that it was best if I went home to do the same. Fortunately, her house was only a short walk from the hospital, and I was mighty relieved that I didn't need a taxi this time.

The walk stirred up more unpleasant childhood memories. What I'd experienced in that very house all those years ago, I thought I'd buried all that for good. My mind was trying hard not to resurrect those dark memories. Deep down I know those horrors will never leave me.

Spending a couple of nights here was one thing; but the thought of having to stay for considerably longer than that was another challenge I had to rise to.

I was already awake when the birds started chirping just before six. I contemplated sleeping in Mummy's room but in the end decided to sleep in my bed with Fuzzy keeping a safe eye over me.

I wore Mummy's nightgown. The rancid smell of tobacco emanating from its fibres made me feel unclean. Putting that thought to one side, I stole out of bed and shuffled into the kitchen to make breakfast. The remains of last night's meagre dinner, an almost-inedible meat pie, were still on the kitchen table.

One of the nurses told me that Dr Morton usually begins his rounds at around ten o'clock and that I shouldn't be late if I wanted to talk to him again. I peered up at the clock. The four hours till then would afford too much time to contemplate what else I needed to ask him. I should fill my time with things that didn't involve Mummy directly.

I decided to text Declan:

> Hi Declan, it's Sally Cartwright.
> Mummy's had a stroke, and I'm at her house now.

I hope your father is doing better. I don't expect you to visit.

Please message or call me when it suits.

Regards, Sally Cartwright.

I sat at the kitchen table, still in Mummy's nightgown, waiting for a reply. My stomach began to rumble. Casting my eye across a sea of cardboard boxes on the kitchen bench, I picked out a multicoloured one and managed to scrounge up the butter, eggs, and a barely legal bottle of milk to make pancakes. The end result was surprisingly good even though no maple syrup was involved.

Declan had still not replied by the time I stepped into the bathroom and slapped the boiler to life. The water started up with a heaving growl. By the time I stepped out of the shower, the whole room was cast in fog. Wiping the mirror with my hand, I saw my face staring back at me through the steam. What I saw shocked me: The fine, clear skin I remembered had been replaced by dark patches around bloodshot eyes. My hair, not so long ago a glowing masterpiece of reinvention, looked no more edifying than frayed rope. I'm sure if I still had on Mummy's nightgown I'd look just like her.

Putting on the same clothes that I wore yesterday—I dared not wear any of Mummy's—I stepped out into a hazy morning. Whatever sun there was had disappeared behind thick clouds, which threatened to smother the entire landscape.

Inside the hospital, the vibe was decidedly different to late yesterday. The plastic receptionist was nowhere to be seen. In her place were two older women who looked real enough. They were attending to concerned visitors who all wore sad or worried expressions. In the corridors and beyond, there was a great bustle and much activity. Some nurses were attending to patients on trolleys. There were other people moving about and looking busy, but as far as I could tell, they really weren't doing anything in particular, just walking fast. As I made my way towards the lifts, the cries and moans emanating from the patients who were occupying trolleys made me feel uneasy.

Mummy was asleep. The whole room was quiet except for the clatter of a cup on a saucer followed by the scraping sound of a butter knife on a slice of toast, both sounds coming from the bed opposite. Mummy's breakfast tray sat untouched. I was leaning against the bed, listening to her wheeze, when I heard a voice behind me.

'Excuse me.'

I turned around to see a young man with deep-blue eyes looking at me with a broad smile. He was tall and stood upright with a shock of dark hair sticking out in a wild tangle and partially covering his smooth tanned skin. He wore a white coat with the word *Orderly* emblazoned across the left breast pocket. 'Are you Sally?'

'Yes, I am.' I felt my lips curl into a soft smile as I spoke. The young man kept on smiling. He had the most piercing of gazes, and I immediately formed the opinion that he was devilishly handsome. He thrust out his hand. 'I'm Myles with a *y*. I'm the orderly looking after your mother. I'm afraid Dr Morton won't be in today, but I'd be happy to answer any questions you may have.' His hand was warm and firm.

'Um …' I had to catch my breath. It was as though the oxygen had been sucked out of the room. 'I don't really have any questions. I just came in to see how my mother was doing.'

Myles nodded. 'There's not much more to report that you haven't already been told,' he said. 'Your mother is still heavily sedated. We can talk more about her condition when she wakes up. You can hang around here if you like, but I think she'll be sleeping for a while. It might be best if you go back home to your family.'

'I don't have a family. I live on my own.' The words came out awkwardly.

'You don't? How has a woman like you managed to escape the clutches of a man?'

Myles was making some sweeping assumptions. How did he know what sort of woman I was? Did he factor in the possibility that I may be divorced or even gay before forming his opinion?

It was on the tip of my tongue to tell him the truth, but I stopped myself on the premise that he didn't need to know.

I shrugged my shoulders and blushed. 'I haven't had the time for a relationship,' I explained. 'You have to give it time and attention. I

MARIO BORAZIO

moved away from here for work a few years ago and have been too busy concentrating on that.'

'You grew up here? I'm surprised we haven't crossed paths before.' I'm not.

'You must have an interesting job,' he said in an overly enthusiastic voice.

Not really. But he didn't need to know that. 'I've come back to look after my mother,' I explained. 'She doesn't have anyone else, I'm her only child.'

'What about your job?' Myles asked.

I shrugged again. 'If I lose this job, I can easily get something else.' That wasn't entirely true.

Myles appeared to be genuinely interested in what I had to say. He walked around to the end of the bed and pulled out Mummy's chart. 'Your mother may not make a full recovery, Sally. If Dr Morton hasn't told you that already, then I think it's important that you are aware.'

I nodded. 'Yes, he did tell me. He said that I have to be realistic. I know the odds, Myles.' Saying his name sent icicles down my spine.

Myles put down the chart and shook his head. 'I admire people like you. You're a rare breed. There aren't too many 20-year-olds who would do what you have done.'

'I'm 26. Almost 27.' I don't really know why I felt the need to divulge my age.

He looked me up and down as though he were examining me for any faults. *The scar on your thigh—how long have you had that?* I suddenly felt extremely self-conscious.

I would have told him it was from a horse-riding accident had he asked, but he didn't.

'You don't look 26.'

My cheeks went as red as a couple of ripe tomatoes. It suddenly felt very hot in here. I was tempted to ask Myles how old he was but couldn't bring myself to do so. He looked younger than me; I guessed around 22.

He looked at his watch. 'I've got to go now, but here.' He slipped a card out of his breast pocket. 'This is my personal number. You can call me anytime. Anytime you want to discuss your mother's condition.' For a moment, we were both silent as we smiled at each other. I could feel myself still blushing as he walked away.

CHAPTER 30

AS I SAT and waited for Mummy to wake up, I thought about my encounter this morning with Myles. I wondered if he made a habit of giving out his card to every visitor or if that privilege was only afforded to people he took a liking to. Was I secretly wishing that he would flirt with me? He gave me his number. I think that definitely qualifies as flirtatious behaviour.

I shouldn't have let him flirt. I have a boyfriend. Wait, do I? Declan has never officially said that he's my boyfriend. I'm not sure if one sexual encounter qualifies us as girlfriend and boyfriend. I am led to believe that lots of people have one-night stands and never end up seeing each other again.

This was pathetic. I was almost trying to invent excuses as to why Declan could *not* be my boyfriend. He hadn't replied to my text yet, but that was probably because he was too busy attending to his ailing father.

I suddenly felt very tired and could feel the beginnings of a headache coming on.

A couple of nurses came in to check on Mummy. They were much nicer than Ms Airhead from yesterday. I must admit that I was a little disappointed that Myles wasn't with them. Perhaps he'll come back later.

One of the nurses whose name was Brenda explained that they were going to take Mummy away to perform a procedure called thrombolysis where a drug will be injected into one of her veins to dissolve any nasty clots that may still be present in her brain. This will improve blood flow and prevent any further damage, she said. I agreed that this would be a good thing for Mummy to have. Brenda smiled and gave me a courteous nod. 'We'll come back later when she's awake.' She promptly left the room with her colleague.

It was almost lunchtime. Mummy began to stir a little but didn't wake up. I allowed myself a glance through the full-length mirror next to the toilet door and immediately wished I had something nicer to wear. The ensemble I had on wasn't my favourite. It just happened to be the only one that wasn't in the wash when I left for work yesterday.

After they take Mummy away, I think I'll go into town to buy some new clothes. I deserved to treat myself.

Mummy finally woke at twelve-thirty. 'I'm so thirsty, dear,' she said. Her voice was croaky.

I poured her a cup of water from the plastic jug. 'How are you feeling, Mummy?' She gulped the whole thing down in record time and sighed heavily.

'I'm tired,' she said before looking quickly around the room. 'Where am I?'

'You're in hospital, Mummy. Don't you remember?'

Her eyes darted around the room again, and her eyelashes fluttered as she glanced back at me. She rubbed her eyes with the heels of her hands.

'How did I get here, Sal?'

'You had a stroke, remember?'

She stared at me for a while, as if sizing me up for something. The silence pooled between us, and I studied her confused expression. She shook her head and made to sit up before letting out a loud howl and clasping her head in her hands. 'Oh, the pain!' she shouted before slumping back down on her pillow. 'My head hurts so much!'

'Oh good, our patient's awake.' Brenda must've heard the commotion and was standing at the door holding a tray with a single syringe in it. 'How are you doing, Eve?' she said.

Mummy tried to sit up again to see who had entered the room. Her hair was frizzed up at the crown. 'Who are you?' she said coldly.

'I'm Brenda. I have to give you your insulin, and then we're going to take you downstairs, okay?'

Mummy shot me a glare. 'Where am I, Sal?'

'I told you, Mummy. You're in hospital because you've had a stroke.' I turned to Brenda. 'Is it normal for Mummy to be so confused?'

Brenda nodded. 'I'm afraid so,' she said. 'She's had a major traumatic

MARIO BORAZIO

event and has been heavily sedated.' Her face was a collage of pity and empathy as she stared at her patient. 'She'll be a bit dazed for a while. We'll take her down for the thrombolysis soon. I suggest you go home and come back later this afternoon.'

Ten minutes later, I headed out of the hospital and pressed my index fingers against my temples to try to alleviate my headache. Only a short walk away was a main strip full of shops, and I went into the largest of the clothes stores. I was soon wandering through rows of lovely dresses and colourful separates, from casual to evening. A frilly green skirt sprigged with tiny flowers caught my eye, and I flirted with the idea of trying it on. It didn't scream Sally Cartwright at all but—my heart began to race as I whisked it off the rack. I also grabbed a tight brown silk dress and a lacy cream blouse and made my way to the change rooms. The green skirt was far too short, the dress way too tight, and the blouse excessively see-through. I bought all three and left the store beaming with pride and a sense of achievement. There was no time for regret here. Then I ventured into a shoe store and looked at heeled shoes. Feeling reckless, I bought gold ones with bright red tips.

I read somewhere that retail therapy can help you feel better. At this point, my adrenaline was surging and my headache was completely gone.

As I left the shoe store, I realised I hadn't rung Dr Gail yet. She would be expecting me tomorrow. The phone was answered by her secretary who was very understanding after I explained what had happened. She wished Mummy a speedy recovery and told me not to worry about my appointment.

I closed my phone and thought about Declan and how he still hadn't replied to my text message. I tried to put that thought out of my mind as I trudged back to Mummy's house. Her car was sitting idle in the driveway, and it suddenly hit me that I could have driven it if I had my licence.

I really must get my licence when I get back home.

I stood in front of the mirror wearing my new skirt, blouse, and shoes. The woman staring back at me looked very different to the one who stood on this very spot this morning. I'd say she looked more sexy than demure, but that's what I wanted, wasn't it?

Come on, Sally, who are you trying to impress? Images of Myles and Declan simultaneously floated across my vision. No sooner had I savoured it than my phone pinged. It was a message from Declan:

> Hi Sally, sorry to hear about ur mum.
> Hope she's okay.
> Dad is on the mend but I need to still be here.
> Luv U
> Declan

My throat immediately tightened and blocked me from crying or laughing. The abridged version of *I love you* stood out like a neon sign demanding to be noticed. This was it. The moment I'd yearned. Words are only crude tools, yet they can be so powerful, even where shorthand texting is concerned.

I took in a sharp breath and texted right back:

> Thank you Declan. I'll be in touch
> Regards, Sally Cartwright

I winced as soon as I pressed the send key. Should I have reciprocated with an *I love you* of my own? Was Declan expecting one?

> I love you too
> Regards, Sally Cartwright

My finger hovered nervously over the send key. This could be a pivotal moment. There was a feeling in my heart that said, 'Yes, send it', but another in my gut that said, 'No, don't.' In the end, I couldn't bring myself to send the message. I don't know if I was being wise or foolish.

I closed my phone and headed back to the hospital.

I could hear the commotion as soon as I got out of the lift. It was definitely coming from Mummy's room. Her eyes widened as she saw me. 'Sal! Thank goodness you're here!' Her voice was fretful, her skin flushed.

'What's the matter, Mummy?' Myles was standing off to the side with his arms folded. He gave me a sharp look and quickly followed up with a warm smile. I found myself staring back at him and panicked for a moment until Mummy's voice broke the intenseness of the atmosphere.

'Sal, you've got to get me out of here! This man is trying to kill me!' She shot daggers at Myles.

Myles unfolded his arms and stepped closer to Mummy's bed. 'No one is trying to kill you, Eve. We're here to help you,' he said as he rested an arm on the side table and turned to face me. 'Your mother is suffering from paranoia, which is not an uncommon thing to happen in this setting,' he explained in a measured tone. 'Dr Morton's been notified.'

I nodded as Mummy lunged forward and clutched my arm. 'Don't listen to him, Sal! They're going to kill me. I heard them talking.' She tilted her head back and darted her eyes up to the ceiling. 'There are noises up there. They're building coffins!'

My heart lurched in my chest. Mummy had never talked in this way before. I turned to Myles. 'How long has she been behaving like this?'

'Ever since we brought her back from the procedure downstairs.' He gestured towards a chair and pulled it closer.

'Thank you.' I sat down and held Mummy's hand. 'Mummy, Myles is a nice man. He won't let anything happen to you. I promise.'

'Liar! Why do you keep lying to me?'

I stared into her eyes. They seemed dull and frightened, devoid of even the faintest glow. Seeing her like this made me sad. Surreptitiously, I wiped away tears with the back of my hand just as Brenda entered the room with a tray.

'Hello, Sally.' Her tone was upbeat and filled with a bustling urgency. 'I trust Myles has filled you in on what's happened?' I nodded. Brenda sat on the bed and gave Mummy an injection before she had any time to take exception. 'This will help to calm your mother down. Dr Morton will be in to see her tomorrow.'

Within minutes, Mummy was sound asleep. Brenda vacated the

room and left me alone with Myles. I could feel him watching me as I fiddled with Mummy's blankets, pretending to make her comfortable.

'You look smashing. Going anywhere special?'

I believe the word *smashing* in this context was modern slang for one possessing a favourable appearance.

The question caught me completely off guard. How was I supposed to answer it? *Be natural, Sally.* 'Nowhere,' I said almost inaudibly as I tugged on my skirt. 'I just bought these clothes today.'

Myles looked me up and down. 'You have good taste. It wasn't long ago you couldn't buy any clothes of quality in this town. They've obviously picked up their game. But you would have noticed that, having grown up here yourself.'

I wouldn't have. I was never allowed to go shopping.

I nodded without comment. Myles kept staring at me. His luminous eyes were burning right through me. I needed to deflect the conversation back to Mummy.

'Mummy will be all right, won't she?' I said.

'Yes, I think so.' He allowed a brief pause before continuing, 'I hope you don't think this to be too personal a question'—I immediately wondered what was coming and caught my breath—'but why are you here alone, taking on this burden by yourself?' He must have caught my look of surprise because he continued in a hurried tone. 'I'm sorry. I shouldn't have asked you that.'

It was so ridiculous. I should have announced right there and then that I had a boyfriend back in Melbourne and that he couldn't be with me due to personal reasons. That would have put a quick end to this flirtatious line of questioning. But it was as though my voice was buried deep underground. Words left me. I couldn't will my lips to move.

Myles took a sharp glance at his watch. 'I've got a few minutes. Perhaps you can tell me a little more about yourself. And I won't ask any more silly questions, I promise.' His eyes twinkled.

I felt my stomach flip. 'There's not much to tell, really. As I told you earlier, my life is pretty much tied up with my job.'

'What do you do in your spare time, though? Do you go to the movies? Clubbing? See bands?'

A disturbing image of a falling mirror ball immediately filled my mind as I shook my head. 'No. I'm pretty much a homebody. I prefer to stay in and watch television. Nature shows and the like. I'm especially fond of wildlife documentaries.' My mind harked back to the David Attenborough programme I watched recently about the endangered animals.

'I see …' Myles seemed to be considering what to say next. 'I like wildlife too. I have a collection of miniature turtles. Do you know anything about turtles, Sally? They are fascinating animals.'

It felt like I was fighting a wave stuck in time. I searched my mind for something reasonable to say, and to my surprise, my heart answered for me. 'I don't know anything about turtles, but I think they'd be interesting creatures. It would be nice to see one up close.'

'You would? I'd love to show you my collection. I finish my shift at five o'clock. My apartment is literally only a few blocks from here. We can meet in the entrance if you like.'

In the grand old world of gender dynamics, Myles would be categorised as a fast worker. 'That would be lovely,' I replied weakly.

'Okay, I'll see you then.' He smiled broadly and looked at his watch again before leaving the room. I caught the eye of the patient opposite who looked decidedly more alive today than he did yesterday. His expression told me exactly what I knew he was thinking.

CHAPTER 31

CALM DOWN, SALLY. It's not a date. One thing my time with Declan has taught me is that the words *date*, *catch-up*, and *meeting* were more or less interchangeable.

But if it wasn't a date with Myles, what was it?

It was such a strange feeling, going to the house of someone I hardly knew. I stared into the mirror again and straightened my new skirt before nervously playing with my curls. I took Myles's card from my bag and for a fleeting moment wondered if I ought to call it off. All sorts of domestic permutations whirled around in my head: Is he single? He must be, or he wouldn't have invited me. But how do I know that for sure? What if he has a girlfriend and they live together? That would definitely be awkward. Maybe I won't go.

I looked up at the clock. It was almost five o'clock. Excitement quelled my uncertainty. I was ready. Mummy was still snoring. I kissed her goodbye and headed downstairs.

Myles was already waiting for me.

I consciously kept one step behind as we walked the few blocks to his apartment. I could see that he was probably older than I'd first thought. The late-evening light caught his hair and picked up a few grey strands around his temples. I'd say he'd be in his late twenties.

He turned and studied me as we walked. 'How long have you been limping?' he asked. I told him it was the new shoes I'd bought. I think he believed me.

We exchanged a few titbits from our respective lives. I told him about how Mummy raised me on her own, but I dared not say anything about the manner in which I was brought up. He told me that he was born and bred here in Colac and that his parents had a rocky marriage. His mother left his father several times but kept coming back. He said he doesn't know if they're still together because he rarely talks to either of them anymore. He said he got sick of their bickering, and that was the reason why he moved out.

He lived on the ground floor of an old terraced house. Reaching the doorway, he put the key in the lock and turned around to say something but didn't speak. As the door opened, he drew back to let me in, the scent of his cologne invading my nostrils as I brushed past him. He closed the door but didn't turn on the light. A faint glow illuminated the front room. The cheap venetian blinds didn't completely block out the last of the golden late-evening light. I took a moment to look around. The ceilings were high, the living area open plan, and the space was uncluttered, which probably indicated that he spent very little time here.

He showed me into another room and eagerly turned on the lights. The turtles were housed in an enclosed glass aquarium-style tank carefully fitted out with rocks, sand, and twigs of various shapes and sizes. There would have been at least a dozen or so turtles, their tiny shells glistening like beaten metal.

'How long have you had them?' I asked as I peered around the side of the tank to see if I could locate any others.

'About a year. I collect them from down by the riverbank. They are not easy to find, though.' Myles's tone suggested a real passion for his hobby. He continued, 'They are actually more active and less dangerous than keeping snakes or other reptiles. They don't make much noise and are super easy to care for.'

'Do you have names for them all?'

'I do.' Myles pointed out a sheet of paper stuck to the wall above the tank. There were two columns. A name on the left was matched to a letter beside it. 'It becomes more difficult to keep track the more turtles I collect. The letter next to each name relates to the shell colour.'

I watched eagerly as each turtle meandered ever so slowly around the terrain, oblivious to the presence of the other inhabitants, or of me or Myles for that matter. I was finding myself becoming enamoured with these little creatures. A feeling of envy rushed through me. I dared not mention to Myles that Mummy didn't allow me to have any pets. 'What do you feed them?' I asked.

'Not all turtles have the same diet,' he explained. 'It depends on the species. These little tykes can eat most things, though. I could just buy them pre-packaged pellets, but I don't do that because I read up that there can be some nasty stuff in there, which may be detrimental to their health. I usually give them leftover veggies and fruit with the occasional treat of snails and worms. They are not strictly herbivores. The term I would use is *flexitarian*.' He let out a small laugh. I liked the way he laughed. I also liked his kind eyes.

'That's fascinating,' I offered. I didn't know what else to say.

'Hey, would you like a drink, Sally?'

We settled on his couch with a Coke each. He didn't seem in any way shocked when I told him I preferred something non-alcoholic. We began talking about books and films, and it was soon apparent that my knowledge of these subjects was far inferior to his. 'As I've told you, I prefer watching wildlife documentaries,' I said. He listened closely and kept nodding as I told him about the documentary I'd watched on the endangered animals. I felt he was genuinely curious, and he hung on my every word. His stare made me slightly uncomfortable and nervous.

'Wow,' he said. 'It is so good to meet someone with similar interests. I appreciate you coming round, Sally.'

Breathing in deeply to calm my nerves, I could see how unbelievingly good-looking he was. 'Thank you.' I managed a smile despite feeling strung up with excitement.

I smelled his cologne again as he leaned forward and kissed me on the lips and then my temple. I turned my head, his breath entering the whorls of my ear.

I could feel his warm body against mine as he angled his arm around my waist. I should have stopped him there. He inched his fingers under my blouse so he could touch bare skin, sending tiny shockwaves rippling through my body.

Night had well and truly fallen, and the room was plunged into semi-darkness as if it were setting a mood.

I'd never felt like this, so aroused. I'd never wanted to lose myself to anyone so badly, not with Lars all those years ago. Not even with Declan.

I had a decision to make.

MARIO BORAZIO

Myles sensed my withdrawal and loosened his arm. I could hardly breathe now, let alone talk. Eventually, words came up slowly like smoke through a chimney. 'I'm sorry, Myles. I can't do this.' Some may have called it hesitancy. I saw it more as caution.

He leaned back, and my stomach tightened as I glimpsed his expression.

'There's someone else, isn't there?' For the first time, there was despondency in his voice.

'I have a boyfriend back home.'

He didn't say another word as he stared motionlessly straight at me. His disappointment was palpable.

'I'm so sorry,' I said.

'You told me you didn't have anyone. I really believed you.' His voice was laced with frustration.

'I know. I should have told you,' I said. *But I didn't want to.*

He drew closer again and gave me a peck on the cheek. I felt my face flaming. 'I'm glad you told me,' he said. 'Better it's all out in the open. But we can still be friends, though. We can promise each other that, right?'

I nodded like an obedient dog. 'Yes, of course. I'd love to come and see the turtles again.'

'You must.'

As we said our goodbyes and I stepped outside, a cold wind blast hit me and seemed to awaken my senses. I felt a moment of remorse and a rush of guilt. Declan's presence in my life seemed to have built a wall around me, sealing me off from any mechanism inside me that should be reacting to another man's advances. They say that first love can often be blind love. I didn't yet know if that was true.

It felt as though I had already cheated on Declan by going to Myles's apartment, but I was probably being too harsh on myself for thinking that.

A tiny pouch of panic rose up within me as I reflected on the events that had just transpired; things could have ended so differently if I'd allowed my real emotions to shine through.

Tonight was like a pleasant dream, but it scared me to think that

I could easily fall in love with Myles. Even though he was a little flirtatious, he was easy to talk to, and a warm feeling permeated through me every time he was anywhere near.

I walked back to the hospital, wondering whether I'd find Mummy awake.

CHAPTER 32

I T WAS PAST visiting hours, but the night staff didn't seem to mind me taking the lift up to Mummy's floor. She was sitting propped up against a pile of pillows and looked remarkably alert for the hour, her gaze fixed intently on mine.

'Where have you been, Sal?'

'I went for a walk, Mummy.' A tray with a couple of empty plates rested at the end of her bed. I suddenly realised just how hungry I was. 'I see you've had some dinner,' I said.

'I was famished. Can't say the food was too agreeable, but I could've eaten an old shoe.'

She appeared restless, turning her head this way and that on the pillow. 'How can I stay in this uncomfortable bed? I feel well enough to go home.'

'You'll do as Dr Morton tells you, Mummy. He'll let you know when you're well enough to come home.'

'Stuff the doctors, Sal! I'm going crazy in here.' Her expression was fretful. She grabbed her hairbrush with her good hand and threw it across the room. It clattered against the wall next to the door. None of the other patients in the room seemed to notice what had happened. One was asleep, and the other two appeared lost in their own worlds.

I was hoping to avoid the temper tantrums, but that was almost impossible with Mummy. At least this little episode demonstrated that she was back to something like her old self.

Feeling more than a little weary, I retrieved the hairbrush and let out a soft, deflating sigh. 'It's best that you rest, Mummy. I'll be in tomorrow morning.' She raised her eyebrows and looked at me questioningly as I was leaving the room, muttering something under her breath. I pretended not to hear.

Feeling refreshed after a surprisingly restful sleep, I spent the following morning cleaning Mummy's house. I was buoyed by the fact that my newfound skills in this area would be put to good use. There was a lot of clutter. Mummy was a serial hoarder. Ever since I can remember, she had an obsessive need to keep everything and found it almost impossible to throw things away, regardless of functionality or worth.

I flitted from room to room and began clearing out all the stuff that was never going to be used. Who needs a wonky ironing board or broken Christmas decorations? After deciding what to leave alone and what to store away, I went about cleaning up the mess and dirt. It was funny. I had never worried about how the house looked before I moved out. There had been more pressing issues that concerned me back then.

A couple of hours later, I sat down feeling extremely proud of myself. The whole place felt lighter and brighter.

I took a moment to recalibrate.

I thought about Declan. When will we see each other again? Was he still thinking about me? Did I hurt him by not adequately expressing my affection towards him in my last text message? Do I really love him? These were questions for which I presently had no answers.

I thought about Mike and how he would be coping without me. Mike deserves to know exactly what's been going on. He's been a great boss, always upfront and honest with me. I really should call him.

I thought about my money situation. What would happen if all my savings ran out while I was looking after Mummy? I don't know how much she has saved up, but it's probably not very much. I'm assuming the pension doesn't go very far these days, especially for someone with a chronic alcohol and tobacco habit, not to mention a penchant for playing the pokies. I should really know what my leave entitlements are too, but I don't. It irked me to think that I had never bothered to take the time to look into such matters seriously in the past. In truth, I'd never even thought about it. I was always reliable Sally with the best work attendance record in the country; days off were not in my DNA.

I thought about Dr Gail. I miss our sessions together. She'd be the perfect sounding board right now. Her advice would be invaluable. I should organise a phone consult.

There were so many loose ends, but I couldn't afford to dwell on them or anything else right now.

I thought about getting my licence too.

It was time to go to the hospital again. I tried, without success, to dismiss another thought that seemed to have imprinted itself onto my brain: how to behave around Myles if we were to cross paths again. I'd still probably give him a smile and a nod. Would he still greet me politely? I'd like to think so. I expect him to be professional. After all, looking after Mummy is a part of his job.

Mummy was eating toast when I arrived. She appeared rather sombre and was in no mood for idle chat. After five minutes of listening to her moaning, I heard shuffling feet at the door.

'Good morning, Eve. And how are you feeling today?' Dr Morton entered the room and gave me a courteous smile before retrieving Mummy's chart from the end of her bed. Mummy didn't answer as she wiped her mouth with a paper napkin. The doctor sensed her desultory mood and remained silent as he bent down to take her pulse. The silence was only broken by the ticking sound of the clock.

He fixed a blood pressure cuff around Mummy's right upper arm and pressed the button. 'Hmm.' His brow arched as he watched the digital display. 'How are you feeling, Eve? Do you have any headache? Any tummy pain?'

Mummy took a long slow breath but didn't give Dr Morton as much as a passing glance. 'I … I'm fine. I shouldn't even be here,' she muttered under her breath.

Dr Morton got up to face me. 'Her pulse and blood pressure are a bit raised but nothing alarming. I don't think it's serious.'

'She was a little agitated last night,' I explained.

Dr Morton nodded in an exaggerated way. 'That's probably the reason why things are a little topsy-turvy.' He opened the chart and studied it. 'The stroke took a lot out of your mother,' he explained. 'Our tests show that she's had several transient ischaemic attacks, or TIAs, leading up to all of this. Do you know what a TIA is, Sally?'

I'd never heard the term. Dr Morton explained what it was before continuing. 'Each time she has one, she loses a bit of ground physically, but mentally, although her speech is slightly slurred, she still seems quite sharp, don't you agree?'

I nodded.

'I think we can discharge her today.' He turned his attention towards Mummy. 'How does that sound, Eve?' Mummy's ears pricked up, and she swivelled her head to reveal a crooked grin, which I fear may now be a permanent fixture.

'That's just fab, Doctor. Thank you! See, Sal, I told you I don't belong here.'

Dr Morton smiled. 'Bless you, Eve.' He glanced in my direction. 'She's a sweetheart.' I pretended not to hear. 'Will you be looking after her?' he asked.

'Yes, I will.'

'Good. We'll have to organise continuing care. I'll send the physiotherapist up soon. Your mother will need to use a walking frame, at least for a little while.'

Mummy shuddered. I know she'd be too proud to use a walking frame. She will try to convince everyone that she won't fall. I can just imagine myself pleading, cajoling, and trying to reason with her until I'm blue in the face.

Dr Morton put Mummy's file back in its holder. 'I'll also send someone up with the discharge paperwork and instructions about her medications,' he said. 'And we'll have to schedule a review appointment for two weeks.'

I felt like I needed to express my gratitude. Almost everyone here had done a great job in caring for Mummy. It warmed my heart to know that people do care, even though my dear mother can't see that sometimes. 'Thank you, Dr Morton. Thank you for everything you have done.' I smiled warmly and he smiled back.

The doctor skipped out of the room and left me to ponder what life will look like at home with Mummy again. Will she still be the boss?

MARIO BORAZIO

I already knew the answer to that question.

The physiotherapist came in shortly after and showed Mummy how to lift herself out of the bed and the chair and how to use the walking frame, which will be loaned out to her. She reluctantly accepted her fate once it was demonstrated how much more steady she'd be with a frame. I was so relieved.

A short time later, I heard the sound of purposeful footsteps behind me beating against the hard floor. I froze as soon as Myles entered the room. For a moment, I held my breath. I could feel my heart beat ... every single pound in my chest.

'Good morning, Sally. How is Mum doing today?' He was carrying a wad of papers.

I stared, unable to speak. My face felt on fire. This was not the way it was supposed to play out. I felt like running away or jumping into a deep hole.

Myles kept his familiar piercing gaze, not dropping his eyes for a moment. 'Sally, are you alright?'

I nodded almost imperceptibly and then heard Mummy's slurred voice, 'For goodness' sake, Sal, answer the man.' She turned towards Myles. 'Please excuse my daughter. She's a bit shy. Anyway, I can answer for myself. Yes, I'm doing fine, thank you. And I'll be doing even better once I'm out of this hellhole.'

Myles placed the papers on Mummy's bed. 'Now, Eve, you shouldn't talk like that. I'm sure deep down you really enjoyed your stay with us. I bet you'll even miss us!'

Mummy let out a guttural laugh. 'Yes, I will. Like a hole in the head!' Myles joined in the laughter, and it was as if two old friends were enjoying an overdue catch-up. He was behaving so affably, and it appeared so natural for him to do so.

He looked just as gorgeous as he did last night. Without as much as a hint of tension between us, he nonchalantly laid out the papers for me to sign. 'Thank you, Sally. I'll input these into the system right away.' He then handed me a sheet of paper. 'This is a list of your mother's medications. They'll be ready at the pharmacy downstairs later today.'

'Thank you, Myles,' I said as my heart continued to pound. 'I'll come back for them later.'

'Tell you what'—Myles was pensive for a few seconds—'I can deliver them to your mother's house after work.'

I shook my head. 'That won't be necessary. I don't want to put you out.'

Mummy began muttering something in the background. 'Okay, yes, that's a good idea. Do you have our address?'

Myles held out the release form. 'It's on here, Eve.' He glanced at the top of the page. 'We're practically neighbours!'

It was true. Mummy's house was only a few blocks away from Myles's apartment.

I felt like I had to continue my protestations, if only to ease my growing anxiety. 'That's so kind of you, but we can manage.'

Mummy shook her head. 'Don't be so sensitive, Sal. The nice man only wants to help.' She pushed her fingers through her scruffy hair and turned towards Myles. 'Thank you. We will accept your offer.' Her tone sent shivers down my back. Somewhere deep inside her cold heart, she had somehow managed to find a shred of cordiality and bestow it first onto Declan and now onto Myles.

Was there not some in there reserved for me?

I was trying to remain stoic and continued my protestations, albeit in a resigned tone. 'No. I can come back to collect them. I ...' My voice trailed off.

Myles raised his eyebrows. 'Honestly, it's no trouble, Sally.' He looked up at the clock and then at Mummy. 'Anyway, I must get going. You'll have your meds personally delivered this afternoon, Eve.'

I watched Myles as he strode purposefully out of the room. He had his own special swagger. It was impossible to miss and hard not to keep watching.

'You like him, Sal, don't you?' Mummy's crooked grin hadn't moved.

I pretended not to hear.

MARIO BORAZIO

CHAPTER 33

LETTING EVERYTHING BE easy. That's what I'd like, but I didn't know how to make it happen. There aren't any rules for this stuff. At our last session together, Dr Gail suggested I start keeping a journal of my thoughts. It was no substitute for regular sessions, she'd warned, but might well prove therapeutic. I began writing the next day and the day after that, but I didn't feel this was helping me in any way. The words felt meaningless—just ink pressed onto paper.

I burned the pages just to be safe.

'Thank you for returning my call, Gail.'

'It's great to hear your voice, Sally. A phone consult can be almost as effective as a face-to-face meeting. How is your mother doing?'

I didn't know how to answer that. If Dr Gail was asking about Mummy's recovery, I'd tell her that she's just come home and is learning to use her right side again and is making steady progress. But if she was asking about how she's behaving, that's a whole different story.

'I've told you what our relationship is like,' I began. 'I'm trying to help her, but I feel like I'm the one who needs the help, not her. I'm beginning to think that living in Mummy's house again isn't ideal for me.'

Dr Gail allowed a brief pause before speaking. 'Just breathe and relax, Sally. You have to slow down both your physiological and emotional responses. Try to recall the techniques we've been working through.'

'I've been trying to focus on my breathing all morning; but I just can't breathe. Mummy's only been home a few hours, and my chest already burns every time she calls me for something. She just has this awful attitude, and it's suffocating me.'

'Can you elaborate on that?'

'She thinks I just live to wait on her like a personal maid. And she's pushy. Just the sound of her voice puts me in a spin.'

'What does she say to you?'

'She says that I'm annoying and not very good at being a caregiver. But that isn't true. I try so hard.'

'I'm sure you do. But it sounds as though your mother is causing you to self-sabotage, even though she's probably not doing it deliberately.'

'That's just it. I think she *is* doing this deliberately. She's trying to make me feel guilty for abandoning her.' I paused and drew a deep breath. 'I'm sure she blames me for her stroke.'

'Hmm …' There was another pause. 'Self-sabotage can be a way of protecting yourself, Sally.'

I wasn't following. 'Excuse me?'

Dr Gail ignored my question. 'So what's your strategy moving forward? Do you have one?'

Of course not.

Dr Gail didn't wait for my reply. 'I'm trying to help you, Sally. It appears to me that you resent your mother's behaviour but don't know how to make her change it. Thoughts are merely intangibles. You can't grab them out of the air and change them or make them go away. You have to stand up for yourself.'

I didn't know how to stand up to Mummy. I'd been conditioned not to.

'I feel as though she's trying to micromanage every aspect of our lives together. It's like reliving my childhood all over again.'

I could hear Dr Gail leaning back on her chair and slowly breathing out. 'Those thoughts can easily arise, Sally. If someone has experienced abandonment in childhood, they may be easily coaxed into experiencing those feelings again.'

'The pressure she puts me under is not something I can endure anymore.'

'That's good, Sally. I like that description. What you need is a way to remove that pressure.'

'For my small contribution, Gail, that will be fifty dollars, thank you.'

Dr Gail allowed herself a short laugh. 'It's time to get serious, Sally. I want you to close your eyes now. Close them tight.'

I was reluctant but did as I was asked.

'Now imagine that you are walking through mountains and come across a cave.'

First a garden and now a cave. Maybe next time it'll be the moon. As usual, I didn't follow. 'A cave?'

'Yes. A large cave. Can you see it?'

I imagined taking a long drive into the countryside with Declan— or was it with Myles? I imagined discovering a large cave. 'Yes, I can see a cave,' I said.

'Okay, walk far into it and find a place to sit down and then breathe in the air. What can you see? What does it smell like? What does it feel like?'

I didn't know if these were trick questions. 'Do you want an honest answer? Nothing at all. I can see nothing, I can smell nothing, and I can feel nothing.'

'That's exactly what the inside of your head is like at the moment. The darkness, the lack of features. That's what's causing the pressure, Sally.'

Just the thought of being in that dark cave had me choking inside. I needed to get out.

'Now open your eyes, Sally.'

I felt a huge relief as soon as my eyelids lifted. 'Am I out of the cave now?'

'I don't know. Did you find the entrance?'

I imagined coming out and squinting in the bright sunlight. But I still felt trapped in that cave. 'I don't see the entrance,' I said in a mildly panicked voice.

'It's alright,' Dr Gail said. 'Just focus on your breathing and push all your fears and negative thoughts as far away as possible.'

The breathing helped. 'Yes, I'm out now.'

'Good. What is it like, Sally?'

'Well, I can see the sun again. And I can smell the flowers and the trees.'

'Doesn't that feel good?'

It felt liberating. 'Yes, it does,' I said.

'Sally, you've always had a plan but not a good one. Your plan was to coast along, hoping that change would just happen. From what I can see, nothing is going to change unless you are prepared to make that change happen yourself.'

'That's all well and good,' I said, 'but I feel a forlorn helplessness. I think my being back home with Mummy is a bad omen.'

'We're not determined by omens, Sally. Only your actions will set you free, release the pressure, make you breathe again.'

I glanced over at Mummy as I held the phone against my ear. She was asleep in her recliner, looking so feeble. Suddenly I felt emboldened; I really did have the power. 'Thank you, Gail. Thank you for making me see a new way of thinking.'

'It's the only way forward, Sally. Your mother has to know how you feel. Remember, you can set the rules from now on.'

Mummy needed me. The cold logical part of my brain was telling me that Dr Gail's advice had to be heeded. 'I can see everything in a better light now.'

'Good. Now is there anything else bothering you? Anything else you want to talk about?'

Where do I start?

My brain went into overdrive. It was like someone else was answering for me. 'Yes. There are a few things.' I proceeded to tell Dr Gail about my situation at work and how I haven't told Mike the real reason I'm here or even for how long I'd be away. I told her about Declan's father and how his new circumstances have sort of put a hold on our relationship.

I told her about meeting Myles and the attraction I felt towards him.

Dr Gail, in her usual way, listened without once interrupting. 'Hell is other people,' she said soon after realising I had finished talking.

For a fleeting moment, I thought she was addressing someone else. But she was still on the phone with me. 'Excuse me, I didn't quite follow what you just said.'

'*Hell is other people* means that, sometimes, interactions with others can bring about negative outcomes. Every therapist will tell you that human beings are happiest when they surround themselves with other people. I'm telling you it doesn't always work out like that.'

This felt awkward. Was Dr Gail saying that it was best if I went back to being a loner?

I was trying so hard to break the old Sally Cartwright mould.

As if reading my thoughts, she continued, 'I'm not suggesting you cancel these people from your life, Sally. When we first met, I quickly ascertained that you weren't living in a bubble of joy and platitudes. That you were lonely. That was plain to see. What I'm saying is that you have a choice in how you deal with these people in your life. Your actions will either bring them closer to you or push them away. Take Mike as an example. By not calling him and keeping him in the dark, you are pushing him away. If you call him and explain your situation honestly, I'm sure you can reach some sort of agreement regarding your employment, and that will put both your minds at ease.'

This was making sense; I realised I had to be more proactive. 'I can see your point,' I said.

'You alone can influence how this goes, Sally, just like my advice about dealing with your mother.'

Mike would be easy, but I wasn't so sure about how to deal with Declan or Myles. I expressed this to Dr Gail.

'You can do it, Sally. It can seem an impossible situation having similar feelings for two people. The most important thing is to think about who you would rather be with five or even ten years down the track. That may not be an easy choice for you to make right now.'

It certainly wasn't. I could feel tears stinging my eyes and reached for the non-scented tissues on the coffee table. 'So where do I start?' I said through soft sniffles.

'We all know the feeling when everything seems to be working against us, Sally. It can feel like an emotional hurricane. What you need to do is work through these problems one at a time, slowly. And you have to do it when your emotional barometer is low. This is where your calming techniques come in.'

I took a deep breath just as Mummy was waking up. She opened her eyes slowly and was staring straight at me. She looked tired, sad.

I had the upper hand now.

'Mummy's just woken up.'

'Be strong, Sally. Don't let the grey win.'

MARIO BORAZIO

CHAPTER 34

I WAS ABOUT TO start dinner when the doorbell rang. I looked up at the clock. It must be Myles with Mummy's medications!

My heart beat so fast I thought it was going to explode out of my chest. The myriad of thoughts and emotions tumbling around in my brain after my conversation with Dr Gail had completely pushed Myles's pending arrival out of my consciousness. My nerve endings crackled as I took off my apron and roughly fixed my hair.

I shouldn't feel so nervous, but I couldn't help it.

My hand was on the door handle; all I was thinking was not to embarrass myself. *Stay calm.*

'Good evening, Sally.' He was leaning on a push bike and seemed to be catching his breath.

'Good evening, Myles.'

He looked flushed, and sweat was trickling down his brow. 'I thought I was going to finish on time. I normally do, but that didn't happen today.' He inhaled a sharp breath. 'I apologise for my tardiness.'

He handed me Mummy's Webster-pak. 'Thank you,' I said, trying hard not to shake. 'You didn't have to rush over.'

'There are very few things in life that bother me more than being late for something. It rarely happens, but when it does, I feel a tremendous responsibility.'

The sound of Mummy's walking frame scraping across the carpet behind me caught me by surprise. 'Is that you, Myles?' She cocked her head around. 'For goodness' sake, Sal, let the poor man in. He looks like he could use some refreshment.'

'Hello, Eve. Thank you, but I really must be going.'

'What's the rush? A glass of lemonade won't hurt. Come on in, and I'll fetch one for you.'

Mummy really was too much. All day she'd been hammering on

about how she can't do this and needs help with that, and all of a sudden, she's willing to entertain a guest without my help.

Someone please shoot me.

'I'll get it, Mummy,' I said through gritted teeth.

'Nonsense. I'm perfectly capable, Sal. I'm not a silly old woman yet. You can show our guest into the living room.'

It was barely a few hours ago that the living room resembled a war zone. Mummy hadn't yet commented on my decluttering and cleaning efforts.

I wasn't holding my breath for that to happen.

Myles and I sat on the couch in silence as his eyes wandered around the room. He was avoiding eye contact, or so it seemed. It was almost as though I didn't exist. I wondered if he still wanted us to be friends as he'd suggested. I also wondered if he'd ever allow me see his turtles again.

'You have a nice clean house here, Eve.' He raised his voice enough so that Mummy could hear from the kitchen. 'It's very homely.'

Mummy shuffled into the living room *sans walking frame* and was holding a glass in her left hand. 'Thank you, Myles. I always try to keep it tidy for guests,' she said matter-of-factly before settling into her recliner.

Nausea crept up from my abdomen to my head, as if it were somehow teasing me. I was almost sick.

Myles downed the lemonade in three or four gulps and looked at his watch. 'I've really got to go. I have a gym class in fifteen minutes. That's why I rode my bike today.' In my mind's eye, I could picture him pumping weights with beads of sweat trickling down his face and silky-smooth skin.

'You'll come back soon, won't you?' Mummy said quizzically.

Myles hesitated as he reached the door. 'I'd love to, but I'm sure Sally is quite capable of looking after things from here.' He gave me a smile before turning back towards Mummy. 'Everything is going to be okay, Eve. I might see you when you come in for your check-up in a couple of weeks.'

'That would be lovely. Thank you, Myles.' Mummy had a cheeky grin, albeit a crooked one.

'Goodbye, Eve. Goodbye, Sally.'

It was drizzling outside. As Myles pedalled off, lightning cracked the sky, sending a spear of light through angry dark clouds.

The weather perfectly matched my mood.

CHAPTER 35

FOR THE FIRST time since being back at Mummy's house, I overslept. My alarm hadn't gone off, which was a strange occurrence because I was sure it was set. I set it every night before turning off the light.

Why didn't Fuzzy wake me up?

It was almost ten o'clock. Mummy would want her breakfast. I got dressed in a hurry and ran into the kitchen only to find her standing by the stove making pancakes. Her walking frame was nowhere in sight.

She gave me a scornful look. 'Well, look who's decided to wake up! My stomach was growling louder than a pack of ravenous wolves.' Melodrama could easily be Mummy's middle name. She bit down on a cigarette, and it dropped onto the floor. With a sly grin, she bent down and picked it up. 'Oops, I must be mindful of keeping the place clean, especially after all the hard work you've put into it, Sal.'

That was the closest I was going to get to a compliment for my cleaning efforts, but it didn't help because my anger and frustration right at this moment were off the charts. I felt my body physically contorting. 'Mummy, how could you? You promised to stop smoking!'

Mummy looked down, turned back to the stove, and casually flipped her pancakes over. 'I'm done with promises, Sal. I need to live my life.'

My knuckles turned white from clenching my fists too hard. I took deep breaths and tried to clear my mind, just as Dr Gail said I should.

'At least tell me you're not drinking again, Mummy. Are you?'

Mummy sighed heavily. 'Please, Sal. All these questions. They're pointless.'

I gave her a cold stare, pinning her gaze so that she couldn't look away. I was determined not to back down this time. 'They're not pointless. I need to know.'

She was silent for a while, her dull eyes fixed and unblinking. 'The odd tipple doesn't hurt anyone, Sal,' she eventually said.

At that instant, I inwardly chastised myself for not confiscating all the liquor in the house. Like a slide show playing in my head, I pictured all the times I saw Mummy engulfed in a cloud of smoke, all the times I had to clean up cigarette butts from inside and outside the house, and all the times I had to carry her off to bed after one of her drinking sessions.

It was time I grew a thicker skin.

'That's the final straw, Mummy! You need to take some responsibility. I can't look after you if you keep behaving like this!'

Her expression was one of disbelief, probably not so much because of what I said but how I'd said it. 'You're abandoning me again?'

I bowed my head, unsure of how to respond. Depending on how this played out, I could be heading back home today. An image of an elated and smiling Mike welcoming me back to work flashed across my eyes.

Mummy's body suddenly flopped, like one of those huge inflatable advertising stick figures that had suddenly lost all of its air. She gripped the edge of the bench to steady herself. 'Sal, please … please tell me you're not leaving me. You're upset. I can see that. You can't throw everything away for some stupid mistakes you think I may have made.'

It was all too much for me now. I wanted to scream. I wanted to cry. Finally, I just let out a long howl. It sounded feral and tortured—a sound foreign to my ears. Once it started, I had no control over it. It was like an unstoppable force pressing up through my chest and out of my mouth.

Everything I'd held in for so long was finally being set free.

The silence that followed was almost unbearable; it only added to the escalating tension in the already charged atmosphere. Mummy stood with her lopsided mouth agape, waiting for me to say something.

Remember, Sally, you have the upper hand.

'You don't need me anymore, Mummy. You're hardly using your walking frame now, and you can clearly fend for yourself in the kitchen.'

'Oh, but I *do* need you, Sal! I need you more than ever! Who's going to organise all my appointments? What about my tablets?'

'You'll manage.' My tone was cold, measured.

'But I can't … I won't …'

I felt like I was immersed in a mental quagmire, sinking into quicksand. It was time for some clear thinking. I took a deep breath to clear my mind. 'Okay, I'll think about staying, Mummy. But I have to set the rules from now on.'

Mummy's demeanour quickly changed. She nodded like an obedient dog. 'Yes, whatever you say, Sal.'

I'd seen this all before. If Mummy was good at anything, it was acting. I had to be more assertive. 'I need to make it clear to you that I won't tolerate similar behaviours and actions. You follow my rules and don't put me down, or I really *will* leave.' My tone was harsh but necessary. 'I'm trying my best.'

There was an awkward silence as I brushed past Mummy and flipped two slightly burnt pancakes onto her plate.

'I couldn't manage very much on my own, Sal. I really couldn't,' she whispered apologetically, catching my hand as I placed the plate on the breakfast bench. 'You're doing a great job. And by the way, I do like your new hair.'

The morning's tension slowly simmered down. It took me a while to digest Mummy's complimentary remark about my hair. I suppose I should be at least grateful for that.

She didn't say another word after breakfast, opting to sit quietly and watch mind-numbing television instead. I didn't mind. I knew that, if this was going to work, we had to give each other space.

After tidying up the breakfast dishes, I made a point of confiscating Mummy's cigarettes and draining every last drop of alcohol into the sink. It was a big weight off, one less thing to feel anxious about.

I lay on the bed and contemplated calling Mike. Dr Gail's voice echoed inside my head: 'You need to work through these problems one at a time.'

It felt so good to hear his voice again. He assured me that everything was under control at work and that I was sorely missed, but they were coping without me. He also assured me that my job would still be there when I got back.

'It's so good of you to say that, Mr Cosgrove,' I said gratefully. 'I don't think I could have coped here any longer not knowing where I stood with my job.'

'Everything's fine, and every client is still being looked after,' he said. 'Now, how's your mother? Is there any improvement in her condition?'

'She's progressing well. They're talking about physiotherapy next week. From what I've seen so far, I think her chances of making a full recovery are very good,' I said and added almost hesitantly, 'I need to stay for just a little while longer.'

'Then stay', Mike urged, 'and don't worry about a thing at this end. We're managing. Stay as long as you have to, Sally.'

'Well, if you're sure, Mr Cosgrove, I—'

'I'm sure.'

'Thank you. I'll be back as soon as Mummy's better.'

'Take care, Sally, and give my regards to your mother.'

My mind felt more at ease as soon as I hung up. I found talking to Mike the easiest thing in the world and wondered why I'd been so reticent to do so in the past. His reassurance that I still had my job and what I was doing was for the best was the shot in the arm that I needed. There must be a particular star alignment in the sky today looking down and taking pity on me.

The week went by relatively incident free. Apart from complaining one night about the beef stroganoff being too salty, Mummy was relatively well behaved and not once pleaded for a cigarette or a drink. It made me wonder if she had a secret stash somewhere. A quick inspection of her room failed to uncover any evidence to confirm my suspicion.

The physiotherapist who visited from the hospital was a nice young Asian girl who introduced herself as Tran. It was plainly obvious from Mummy's behaviour that she took an instant dislike to her. Without trying to make sweeping generalisations about racial issues, I think this was more a product of her generation's attitudes rather than anything about Tran herself.

Tran, to her credit, ignored Mummy's standoffishness and went about her work with the utmost professionalism. I was impressed with her deft hands. And so was Mummy. She slowly warmed to her. By the end of the third visit, she had all but forgotten about the colour of Tran's skin and the angles of her eyes.

Mummy turned in early tonight, and I decided to do the same.

I lay in bed and felt the most relaxed I'd been for a long time. It was as though the roller-coaster ride I was on was coming to a slow stop.

It was time to re-lay tracks on flat ground.

My phone buzzed as I was about to doze off. The number was unfamiliar. I was immediately struck with mild panic.

'Hello, Sally Cartwright speaking.'

'Good evening, Sally. I'm calling from YouTube Australia.'

The call was on my new phone this time. 'Yes?'

'Congratulations! Your new video has had over one hundred thousand hits already.'

A suffocating feeling of dread rose up inside me like a phoenix rising from the ashes. 'What video?'

'The video of the burning house. Some of those shots are amazing. How did you manage to get so close in all that heat and smoke?'

I threw my phone into my bag and sprinted into Mummy's room. There was no time to pack.

CHAPTER 36

'DO YOU HAVE anyone to stay with?' The police officer handed us blankets as Mummy and I huddled together on the edge of the kerb, watching the last flames being extinguished.

I shook my head. 'No. We don't have anyone.'

The officer, a stocky middle-aged man with a full red beard, took another look at the ashen wreck and shook his head. 'You were lucky you both got out of there when you did. These old weatherboards can come down in the blink of an eye. I understand you were renting?'

'Yes', I answered, 'My mother has lived here for more than twenty years.' Mummy sat quietly beside me. She hadn't said a word since the fire brigade arrived. She was hugging her dressing gown and appeared to be in shock. She'd lost everything.

I lost Fuzzy. For a fleeting moment, I wondered how much a burnt bear would be worth. Probably very little.

By the time Mummy got her dressing gown on, the laundry was already engulfed in flames.

'We'll contact the agent in the morning,' the officer said. 'For now, though, we'd better organise for you to stay at a motel. Did you manage to salvage any possessions?'

I clutched my bag and shook my head. 'Only my phone and purse,' I said.

We sat quietly as the fire crew wound up their hoses and cleared the last of the debris from the road, all done at a frantic pace. I was in awe of their work. Watching them first-hand gave me an appreciation of their dedication and skill set.

As I looked at the house now, barely a charcoal skeleton, and recalled my panicked phone call to triple zero, this still didn't feel real. Except that I knew it was.

I checked my phone. There was no call history. I wasn't game enough to check for 'that' video yet. Not with people around.

Quite a large crowd had assembled behind the blue-and-white police tape. Most people stared suspiciously and whispered amongst themselves.

Then I saw him, out of the corner of my eye, edging towards the front of the taped-off area. He looked animated and started waving his arms as soon as he realised that I'd spotted him.

'Sally! Eve!'

The police officer shot me a glance. 'Do you know that man?'

I nodded. My pulse began to race, and my chest tightened with anxiety. Mummy was crouched close to the ground and seemed oblivious to all that was going on.

'Myles is a friend,' I said.

The officer waved Myles through, and he sprinted towards us. He crouched down so that his face was barely inches from mine. I could smell a faint tang of cologne. 'What happened?' he asked.

I told him exactly what I told the police officer: I smelled smoke and saw the fire starting in the laundry before waking Mummy and dashing outside.

At least a part of that was true.

Myles turned to the officer. 'Has an ambulance been called?' The officer shook his head. 'Why not?' Myles's retort was brusque.

'It's alright, Myles,' I said. 'Mummy and I didn't inhale any smoke.'

'You don't know that for sure. Can you breathe? You should at least be sipping some water.'

Two plastic cups of water were brought over, and I took a large sip. The coldness in my throat and chest was soothing. Mummy gulped hers down.

'Hello, Eve.'

Mummy swivelled her hips around and sat up straight. Myles's voice seemed to shake her out of her lethargy. 'Hello, Myles! What are you doing here?'

'I live around the corner, remember? Besides, it was hard to sleep

MARIO BORAZIO

with all the sirens.' Myles turned and stared at me. 'Do you know how the fire started, Sally?'

I shook my head. 'The fire fighters seem to think it was frayed wiring, but I guess we'll never really know.'

The police officer approached us holding a piece of paper. 'We've managed to get you a room for the night. I can drive you when you're both ready to leave.'

'A motel?' Myles jerked his gaze towards the police officer. 'I think it would be better if they stayed with me, Officer.'

Mummy was the first to speak. 'No. That's too much of an imposition, Myles. We'll stay at a motel.'

'Nonsense, Eve. You and Sally will get a better night's sleep at my place, and then I'll take you into the hospital tomorrow morning to have you both checked out properly.'

The officer shrugged. 'It's your choice, ladies.'

'Mummy's right, Myles,' I said. 'It's far too much trouble.'

'Nonsense. I won't take no for an answer. I can sleep on the couch. Or with my turtles!' He allowed himself a small laugh, and I found myself laughing along. Mummy looked annoyed that she had missed the joke.

I turned to Mummy. 'What do you think? What shall we do?'

She saw it on my face. 'Alright, Sal,' she said before turning to Myles. 'Thank you, Myles. You're a good friend. We are so grateful.'

'Thank you. Thank you so much.' I found myself gushing.

Myles beamed. 'It's settled then.' He helped me up and held my hand.

Now what was I supposed to do with that act of chivalry? Frankly, I didn't know.

CHAPTER 37

RUE TO HIS word, Myles let Mummy and me sleep in his
bed while he slept on the couch, close to his beloved turtles.

I woke at five-thirty after an impossible night's sleep. It had nothing
to do with the bed; it was more that I was unable to shut my brain off.
Any attempt to do so was quickly short-circuited by anxious thoughts.

I made sure Mummy was still asleep before nervously checking my
phone for the new video. It was all there, a tiny billowing of smoke to
begin with, followed quickly by flames rising high into the night sky,
and finally just a mound of ash. How could I have taken this video?
I was sitting on the kerb with Mummy while it was all happening. It
didn't make any sense.

If this wasn't a premonition, then what was it?

I wondered if Mummy would miss the place she called home for
the best part of twenty years. It was probable that she would mourn
something about it. There had to be a memory there in every corner,
even if most weren't pleasant ones. I think she'll miss her recliner and
her television more than anything else.

Every time I rolled over and saw her lying next to me, I couldn't help
but feel anxious. All I wanted to do was curl up in a ball and pretend
that last night never really happened. But I knew that it did. Reluctant
as I was to accept this reality, I knew I had some fast thinking to do.

I lay back staring at the ceiling, trying to shut out Mummy's drawn-
out snoring, which was distracting my thought processes. The question
kept popping up like a looped video: what do I do now? There was only
one answer: I would have to take Mummy back home with me.

At least we didn't have to pack.

I closed my eyes and must have dozed off. When I opened them
again, it was almost eight o'clock. Cooking smells emanated from the
kitchen, followed by an exuberant voice: 'Breakfast is ready!'

I sat up stiffly and swung my legs to the side, careful not to wake Mummy who was still sound asleep.

'Well, good morning. Is your mother not joining us?'

'She's still asleep.'

Myles was already dressed and had on a striped apron. 'Bacon and eggs are my specialty. Would you like some toast as well?'

I hesitated before answering. 'That would be fine, thank you.' I'd never had bacon and eggs before. What would it taste like? I was about to find out.

Hopefully it would be better than pizza.

I noticed a paperback novel on the kitchen bench and picked it up. 'What's this book about?' I said, trying to make conversation.

Myles turned his gaze as he was plating up. 'It's about a girl. It's a pretty good read.'

I looked at the title: *Being Wendy Bateman*. 'What's so special about her?'

'Nothing much,' he said dryly. 'She's not special at all.'

'But you said it's a good read.'

Myles nodded enthusiastically. 'It is. I just finished it. By the end, though, I was left with an odd combination of admiration and sadness because I felt that, even though she was a lonely woman in many ways, she was well liked and ended up having a few relationships but never married. She always felt a little bit out in the cold and eventually wound up alone. In the end, she died in a hospital room with no one to support her. To think of her there, facing the hour of her death alone. That was just so sad.'

It was very sad indeed. Was that the path I was headed down? I didn't want to think about that.

Myles and I sat opposite each other on the small kitchen table. He ate quickly. I opted to take my time, my taste buds savouring the unusual combination of rustic and salty flavours. It was a surprisingly good breakfast.

'So what are you going to do now, Sally?'

I sighed, doubly hard. 'I'll have to take Mummy home with me. What other choice do I have?'

Myles nodded; his eyes cast in a way that told me he totally understood my predicament. 'I agree. It's the only way forward. You don't want to put her in public care. I have seen too many bad things. Trust me, Sally, your mother is better off with you. She will get excellent care with you by her side.'

I forced a weak smile and busied myself by stabbing at a piece of bacon. 'I'm scared, Myles. What if she doesn't like living in the city?'

'I'm sure she will be just fine. How could she not be with you by her side?'

I blushed and averted my gaze. There was a sensitivity and gentleness about this man that I was starting to notice more and more. Especially in the way he spoke. He seemed to know exactly what to say, as though he'd rehearsed everything beforehand. Was he acting? I don't think so. Initially, I couldn't help but think that he was only being kind for personal gain. But that was just my pessimism shining through, borne of my unhappiness and ingrained feelings of unfulfillment. Dr Gail told me to banish all those negative thoughts.

'I'll try my best,' I said in an upbeat voice.

Myles smiled. 'I'm sure you will. Life is short, Sally. You've got to make every day count.'

His words made me feel optimistic, a renewed sense of hope radiating throughout my body.

Perhaps I won't end up like Wendy Bateman after all.

I insisted on clearing the dishes as Myles got ready for work. He reappeared from the bathroom minutes later.

'Promise to come down to the hospital when your mother wakes up? I'll let ER know that you are coming.'

I promised. He gave me a gentle hug. 'I'll see you at the hospital,' he said before smiling again and heading out the door.

I watched as he swung his satchel bag over his shoulder and disappeared down the street.

As much as I was resisting any perceived overtures, I could see myself sliding right into Myles's life like a smooth hand into a silk glove. The truth is that he was probably just being a good friend as he'd promised. At this point, that was exactly what I needed.

CHAPTER 38

WE WALKED THE short distance to the hospital. Mummy seemed to be improving by the minute and was managing quite well without her walker. She didn't mind being seen in her dressing gown. She was surprisingly chatty too. 'See that fancy café?' she began. 'That used to be a sewing shop. I used to buy thread from there to mend your school socks. And that place, the trendy new clothing shop, there used to be a butcher there. I would buy meat there whenever I could afford it. And down that way was a shop called the Big Bazaar …'

Mummy continued prattling on about all the old places that had slowly been replaced by new ones. I tried to reimagine them but could only come up with depressing scenes from my childhood—of narrow passages far away from any butcher shop or sewing store or bazaar.

It must have been some sight: two women, both with slightly odd gaits and wearing slept-in clothes, entering the emergency department of a hospital.

The young nurse who greeted us was already aware of our situation, courtesy of Myles. I looked around but couldn't see him. I thought about asking after him but decided against it.

We were ordered to sit and wait. The room was deserted. Mummy looked anxious, as though something was troubling her. Perhaps the impact of the fire had finally hit home.

'Sal, I need to tell you something.'

Slightly surprised, I leaned closer and faced her. 'Yes, Mummy?'

'It's about the fire.'

'Right.' I bobbed my head to indicate that I knew what she was going to say. 'It's alright, Mummy. The most important thing is that we got out safely. The things you lost can all be replaced.'

She turned her head sharply and looked at me with an expression of disregard. 'I couldn't give two hoots about the stuff I lost. Most of it was worthless anyway.'

How ironic, I thought, for a hoarder to say such a thing. 'What *about* the fire?' I asked.

Mummy looked down momentarily before whispering in my ear. 'I think I know what caused it.'

'What are you talking about?'

'We're all fools, Sal. But forgiveness is what life's all about.'

I wasn't following. 'What's the matter, Mummy? What happened?'

A sheepish expression overtook her face. 'Well, I hid some cigarettes in the laundry behind the washing machine. I went to light one last night and heard some noises. In a panic, I flicked it behind the dryer. I think it was still lit, Sal.'

This admission of fault was surprising, but I suppose deep down I knew that something like this was likely to happen. Mummy was as cunning as she was irresponsible. Still, I wished it not to be true. 'Are you sure, Mummy? The firemen seemed to think it was a wiring problem.'

Mummy shook her head exaggeratedly. 'There's nothing wrong with the wires, Sal. Never has been in twenty years.'

'Why didn't you say something before?'

'I wish I had, but I didn't want to get into trouble with the police. Please forgive me, Sal.'

It all made sense now: Mummy's subdued behaviour during all the mayhem, as well as her not noticing Myles when he arrived a short time later.

She had been caught up in her thoughts, mired in guilt.

I should have castigated her for not speaking up, but I demurred. 'Oh well', I said, my voice unconvincingly optimistic, 'it'll all work out, Mummy. No one needs to know.'

'Oh, thank you, dear. It's done me the power of good to get it off my chest. I was worried that you would tell someone.'

'I wouldn't do that. Anyway, I've decided on something. I want you to come and live with me.'

Mummy blinked at me with a perplexed look and gave a short

MARIO BORAZIO

contemptuous laugh, which quavered into a soft sob. 'Can't I stay here, Sal? I can find another place.'

'I have to get home, Mummy. I have my job to think about. Anyway, you'll be better off in the city. You'll make new friends, and I'll make sure you get the best of care.'

She made to say something but stopped short. The look of resignation on her face was a cathartic moment; I had finally won a battle against my mother.

The doctor who examined us was a tall young man with a delicate slim figure and a haughty smile. He asked both of us in turn about any symptoms of coughing, chest pain, shortness of breath, headache, or eye irritation. We both answered everything in the negative. He also explained that he needed to take some blood to test for the amount of oxygen and carbon dioxide in it.

An hour later, Mummy and I got the all clear and were allowed to go home.

Except that we didn't have one to go to.

Mummy looked restless as we made our way to the foyer. 'Aren't we going to wait for Myles?' she said.

I hesitated before answering. 'I suppose we should.'

I was about to ask someone to call him when I became distracted by shouting coming from behind us. A group of people who appeared to be all members of the same family were dragging a patient away from the clutches of a young man wearing a white coat. I couldn't understand everything they were saying, but I certainly recognised the young man. It was Myles. 'You will force me to call the police!' he said urgently. Talk of police had most of the family scattering, but one tenacious man remained.

The man turned to the smattering of people in the foyer area. 'Can you believe this shit? It's inhumane, not to mention stupid.'

Myles stood between the man and the patient. 'Please, sir, calm down,' he pleaded. 'Your father isn't allowed to smoke in his room. It's against hospital policy and also against the law.'

The man's eyes widened, and flickers of fire seemed to form in them. 'I'm sick of this,' he said. 'There's no need for us to be here.' He grabbed his father by the arm before Myles stood between the pair and the door. A standoff of sorts ensued.

Five minutes later, the angry man was cuffed and taken away by two men wearing blue uniforms. The man's father, whose arms and head were covered in dirty bandages, was quietly escorted back to his room without resistance. He hadn't uttered a word throughout the whole ordeal.

Myles had spotted us a few minutes earlier but waited until the situation had simmered down before approaching. 'I'm sorry you had to witness that,' he said with a flourish. 'We are instructed to get the police involved as soon as we see a situation developing. There have been too many bad outcomes in the past.'

The presence of police officers and talk of cigarettes had Mummy visibly on edge. I couldn't help but curl my lips up into a sardonic smile.

I pointlessly tucked a few strands of hair behind my ear. 'That's quite okay, Myles,' I said. 'I thought you handled it very well.' I went to touch his arm but only managed to pat the air around it.

Myles smiled, and there was a gleam in his eyes. 'Have you seen the doctor yet?' he asked.

'Yes, we have. He said we're both fine.'

'That's great news.'

Mummy chimed in. 'Sal's taking me home with her.'

'Yes', I said, 'I'm taking Mummy back with me to Melbourne.'

Myles nodded and turned to Mummy. 'It will be for the best, Eve. I wish you a full recovery.'

Mummy gushed. 'Thank you, Myles,' she said. 'You can come visit us.' She turned towards me. 'Can't he, Sal?'

I nodded. My face broke into a weak smile as I tried to squash my excitement at the thought of having Myles in my flat.

'I will definitely look you up when I am next in Melbourne,' Myles said.

There was that smoothness again, carefully mastered but not contrived. 'Well, I suppose this is goodbye,' I said in a barely audible voice.

Myles frowned and stretched the corners of his mouth. 'You can't leave just yet, Sally. I want to give you something.'

Mummy and I hung around in the hospital lounge. During Myles's lunch break, the three of us went back to his apartment. He introduced Mummy to the turtles. She was dumbstruck and just shook her head as if to rid herself of a hallucination. 'They're so cute! What a great hobby you have, Myles.' She beamed with enthusiasm and turned towards me. 'It will do you good to have a hobby too, Sal.'

I bit down hard on my lower lip. What had she done when, as a child, I came home one day with a frog? 'That thing has no place in this house. I'm taking it back to the swamp!' she'd yelled before placing it in a plastic bag and storming out of the house.

'Perhaps she will have a hobby, Eve.' Myles ran his finger down the list of names on the wall before plunging his hand into the tank and retrieving a turtle. 'This is Henry. I want you to have him, Sally.'

I thought about this for a second. It would be more embarrassing to refuse Myles's gift than to accept it. 'I've never cared for an animal before,' I said. 'Thank you. I'll take good care of him, I promise.'

After Myles carefully placed Henry inside a small ventilated cardboard box and gave me instructions on how to care for him, I called for a taxi.

A mood settled over us all as we said our goodbyes at the door. Myles hugged Mummy, who apologised for being such a difficult patient. She thanked him for all he'd done to help us. 'It's not about thanking anyone, Eve,' he said modestly. But Mummy insisted it was. For once, I agreed with her.

He turned to hug me. I succumbed briefly but then, feeling uneasy, stepped back and merely offered my hand. He still didn't understand my conundrum, didn't see why I insisted on being aloof even when I knew he was only being friendly. I was still unable to give out all my emotions at once, only rationing out bits and pieces as needed.

But I wanted more than this. Deep in my heart, I knew I could have more.

CHAPTER 39

Henry APPEARED TOTALLY relaxed during the trip home. He didn't move at all from the corner of his box and busied himself with a cabbage leaf. At one point, I dipped my hand in and gently patted his shell. He didn't flinch. The touch was not unpleasant. It felt cold and just a little sticky.

Mummy was as jumpy as the back end of a rattlesnake. 'I've never lived in a big city before, Sal,' she said grimly. 'What if I don't like it?' She looked at me in an accusatory way, which shot tiny pulses of dread down my back. If she didn't like it, I knew it would be all my fault again.

'You *will* like it, Mummy!' I tried to sound upbeat. 'You can help me look after Henry. We'll get a tank of some kind. One with rocks and logs. Maybe even a light.' Mummy stared straight ahead, not saying a word. She looked petulant, like an angry, spoilt child.

We finally reached the city. The concrete jungle was draped in graffiti and cast long foreboding shadows as evening closed in. The buildings of the financial district, tall edifices that announced vast accumulation of power, seemed to be breathing in, like enormous steel lungs. Scores of people, mainly men in smart grey suits, were darting purposefully across roads and between buildings. Our taxi driver had to honk his horn and slam on the brakes several times to avoid them. They glanced up, wide-eyed, and nodded a meek apology before rebooting their devices and reinserting their earphones to continue listening to what was probably trashy music or some meaningless podcast.

It was plain to see how such urban imagery could invoke negative thoughts and could easily overwhelm a country visitor. Mummy caught her breath before sighing deeply. This isn't going to be easy for her. I know that.

The taxi driver heaved an exasperated sigh, obviously not overly experienced driving in these conditions. He looked at me through his rear-view mirror. 'What kind of place is this, miss?'

From the tone of his voice, I formed the assumption that he'd never driven in a big city before. I ignored his question.

The amount I ended up paying him was preposterous but, going on past experiences, not at all surprising. He may even have included some danger money in the overall sum. I wouldn't have begrudged him for that.

I felt a little flat by the time I reached my front door.

The place smelled of dust. Mummy's eyes wandered around the room briefly before settling on mine. Her gaze was like a stranger's. 'Where's my room?' she said hastily. 'I need to rest.'

When Mummy was settled, I sat for a long time. I just sat and breathed. A myriad of thoughts invaded my headspace: I needed to clean. I needed to get dinner. I needed to feed Henry. More importantly, though, I needed to organise a doctor for Mummy. As well as a new physiotherapist. And all this before I could even contemplate returning to work.

Moving back home wasn't going to be as straightforward as I may have initially thought.

I frowned, trying to think back through the labyrinth of the events of the last few weeks. They were hazy, probably as a result of my mental fragility.

I added calling Dr Gail to my 'to do' list.

I turned on the television to try to clear my mind. Without even realising it, I flicked over to the animal channel. David Attenborough's *Planet Earth* series was showing a documentary on termites, on how most are blind and how they live in super-complex colonies of mounds and tunnels, without them even knowing that they are underground, or even that they *are* termites. How bizarre was that? In some ways, I think the human race is similar, especially in the big cities where people's robotic lives can sometimes reflect those of the termites. Automatons in the modern world.

By the time the termites had hibernated underground, I'd put some potatoes in the oven. It was six forty-five, and the sun had already gone down. I went into the spare bedroom to check on Mummy, who was sleeping deeply. Then I realised that I hadn't been out of my current clothes for almost two days.

I went into my bedroom, stripped off my filthy, smoke-infused clothes, and jumped in the shower. Hot water thundered on my head, and I immediately felt more relaxed. I also felt a little faint but pleasantly so. It was as though all the negative energy inside me was being purged.

I dropped the soap and bent down to pick it up, trying to feel for it through a cloud of steam. As I tried to stand, I felt a creeping sensation in my inner thighs. Looking down, I saw a small red fish swim out of me before it slithered down onto the shower base and disappeared in the eddy of water. Getting my period sucks.

It was settled then: Sally Cartwright was not having sex tonight.

I cleaned myself up, went through to my bedroom, and stood at the window, hugging my towel around me and watching the sky turn a leaden colour.

I lowered the blind and looked at my bed. The temptation to crawl under the covers and write the evening off was a real one. But I'd left potatoes in the oven. I imagined the smoke alarm going off and me burning my hand on the oven and later freaking out about it all, and—

There was no way we were going to have a second house fire.

I got dressed and put a comb through my hair before checking the potatoes.

I had dinner alone. Well, almost alone. I had Henry for company. We shared a container of broccoli and bean soup that I defrosted. Myles told me that just because Henry is small it doesn't mean he doesn't have an appetite. It didn't take long for Henry to ratify this assertion.

He seemed quite happy in his little box. Have you ever seen an angry turtle?

I decided to text Declan after dinner. The news of my return home was good-enough reason to do so.

I worked my fingers quickly:

> Hi Declan, it's Sally Cartwright.
> Just letting you know that I'm back home.

Regards, Sally Cartwright.

Almost immediately, there was a message alert:

Hey, that's great! I'm home too

No news of his father? Maybe he's dead. The thought—what should that thought be? *Don't be negative, Sally.*

I decided that Declan should know that Mummy was with me. That she was alright:

I've got my mother living here with me. She's doing
fine.
Regards, Sally Cartwright.

He didn't need to know about the fire.
Straight away there was a reply:

Double great! I'd love to see you both again

Mummy walked in just as I was about to text back.

'I feel so much better now, dear. It's amazing what a good sleep can do.' She bent down and gave me an awkward air kiss. I recoiled. Her breath had an alcoholic twist.

There's no way—I didn't even want to think about it.

'I see you've made dinner,' she said with an enthusiasm that suggested she was hungry.

I left a plate on the table beside Henry's box.

She sat down to eat, and I settled back on the couch.

I don't know how much time had passed before I woke up. Mummy had left her plate on the sink and gone back to bed. I looked up at the clock. Was it too late to text Declan? It occurred to me, fleetingly, that my non-reply could be interpreted as me not wanting him to come over:

We are free tomorrow night.

Regards, Sally Cartwright.

Declan still hadn't texted by the following morning. I was loading last night's dishes into the dishwasher when I heard a tactful cough from behind me.

'Good morning, dear.' Mummy looked more dishevelled than I'd ever seen her before, and her voice was croaky. 'I need to have a shower. Can I borrow some clean clothes?'

While Mummy was showering, I decided to put the washing machine on. As I was shoving her dirty dressing gown into it, something fell onto the floor from the pocket. It was a small piece of cardboard. I picked it up and saw that it was folded in two. On one side was an oval faded brown photograph of a handsome but rather arrogant-looking young man with threatening eyes and what I judged to be a condescending smile. The photograph looked old. I would say at least 25 to 30 years old. What was Mummy doing with it tucked away in her dressing gown?

My heart stopped momentarily as I contemplated who this man might me. Could it possibly be my father?

Questions, questions, and more questions. The ones Mummy should have answered a long time ago.

She had always been steadfast that she couldn't be sure who my father was.

But she lied a lot.

CHAPTER 40

T HE WINDOWS OF the bus beaded up as the rain beat down. I hadn't slept well, and the noise from the roof was making it hard for me to concentrate.

I couldn't stop thinking about the photograph and how things may have been different if I'd had a father around. How different? The answer was obvious. It would have been a huge advantage having someone by my side to help manage Mummy. Why wasn't anyone there?

My curiosity was gnawing away like a dog devouring a large bone. I slipped the photograph out of my pocket and turned it around in my hand to examine it more closely. The back was blank. Not even a name or a message. Nothing.

I stared at the man's face wistfully. I imagined him as my father, teaching me to ride my first bike, helping me with my homework, and coming into my room at night to read me a bedtime story. Just doing all the things I missed out on as a child. I imagined him being a great man too. A man of importance in the world. Perhaps even a descendant from aristocracy.

That would be a crazy fluke, would it not? Why would a man of eminence even think of becoming involved with a woman so far below him on the class ladder?

I tucked the photograph back in my pocket and wiped away tears before getting off at the Royal Melbourne Hospital. Thankfully, the rain had stopped. I didn't bring an umbrella.

It was a circuitous route to reach the information desk. There was a low murmur of conversation in all directions, punctuated by the occasional tinkle of laughter.

The young woman behind the desk had close-cropped bleached hair, deep-set eyes, and pale skin. There was the curve of a tattoo peeking from the side of her neck. I explained Mummy's situation to her, communicating everything as accurately as I could, careful not to omit anything important.

'The wait time for the stroke clinic is four months,' she declared dryly.

I felt sick and looked away. By the time I looked back, the woman was attending to her computer screen. 'Would you like to make an appointment?' she asked.

I shook my head. 'You have to listen to me again,' I explained. 'My mother has come all the way from Colac and—'

'We have people coming from all different places,' was her brusque reply. 'Your mother will have to wait just like everybody else.'

I was trying hard not to hyperventilate. 'What about seeing a physiotherapist?' I said.

'Best to speak to your GP. They can refer you to one.'

The queue behind me was getting longer by the minute. I turned around and noticed people wearing worried expressions and holding sheets of paper.

I thanked the woman for her trouble and left quietly.

So Mummy needed to see a GP. I didn't really want to go back to Dr Maria. Perhaps Dr Gail could recommend one.

This was all part of the frustrations of dealing with the public health system.

I walked down Elizabeth Street to attend to my second task for the day: finding a pet shop. At least Henry would be cared for. The Critter Cove was almost the size of a supermarket. I was completely honest with the young sales assistant. I told her that I had procured a small turtle, my first ever, and needed suitable and adequate lodgings for it. Her eyes widened, and she began talking with great fervour. She explained that turtles require specific living conditions, which include UVB light, a basking dock and lamp, a water heater, a water filter, sponges, noodles …

I looked at her quizzically. Henry seemed to be doing just fine inside a simple cardboard box. 'Is all this necessary?' I asked.

Just as Thomas had done when I purchased my new phone, this

girl had managed to sell me more products than I probably needed. I'm sure Myles doesn't have half this stuff for all of his turtles combined.

I walked to the bus stop, dragging a bag the size of a single mattress. *You've got to get that licence, Sally.*

Thankfully, the bus was nearly empty, which meant there was plenty of room for my large bag.

We were stopped at the lights when there was a knock against the glass. An old woman with rheumy eyes and straggly grey hair leaned closer to peer at me. 'Are you running away?' she said. Her expression was hard and genuinely curious. Not like a confused or disoriented old lady's expression.

I just stared at her.

'Well?' she said. 'Are you?' She alternated her gaze between my face and the bag.

I wanted to ask her, who are you? Why are you so interested in me? But I just kept staring at her, speechless. Her face turned angry when the bus took off.

My stomach clenched with trepidation as I turned the key. I needed to ask Mummy about *that* photograph but wasn't certain how or when to do it. She might become hostile and even deny any knowledge of it.

I had to be prepared for her reaction.

I plonked the contents of Henry's palatial suite in the lounge room and walked into the kitchen. Mummy was sitting at the table with a cup of tea. I surreptitiously peered inside the cup to make sure it wasn't filled with alcohol. It wasn't.

She had an almost-frightful expression. Like a savannah antelope sensing the presence of a big cat. (I watch too many wildlife shows).

'Did anything happen while I was out, Mummy?'

'Do you think this is a safe place to live, Sal?' She spoke with urgency and was looking up to the ceiling.

'Yes … I think so. The neighbours seem friendly enough. I rarely see them and haven't had any trouble.'

'Up there.' She shuffled out of her chair and pointed upwards. 'There are screams, like people arguing. Have you heard them?'

I shook my head. 'I can't say I have. Like I said, we all keep to ourselves.'

'It's not safe, Sal. I mean, what if they come here while you're out? What if … what if they stormed in? How would I defend myself?'

At this point, I wondered whether Mummy was imagining the noises as if she were suffering from some form of paranoia like she had done in the hospital. I read that this behaviour is likely when an older person is suddenly thrust into a new and foreign environment.

I needed to distract her. 'Hey, Mummy, come and look in the lounge room!'

Between the two of us, we managed to assemble Henry's tank and connect all the cords and tubes within an hour. Mummy was buzzing with energy. I think she quietly enjoyed the task. She even managed a smile when we finished.

Henry was fed, watered, and transferred into his new home. The plush new surrounds didn't seem to faze him one way or the other. He stilled pottered around in only one corner. I was still of the opinion that he'd be just as happy inside a small box with holes. I wondered if turtles ever showed emotion. A dog will wag its tail. A cat may lay its ears back. What does a turtle do?

I achieved two more things that afternoon: I made an appointment with Dr Gail, and I also booked in some driving lessons. The man I spoke to wasn't too concerned when I told him that I'd never driven a car before.

Declan still hadn't confirmed whether he would be coming over tonight. Perhaps he's too busy gaming.

I cleaned up the dinner dishes while Mummy sat on the couch. She was staring straight ahead. I could see she was brooding.

I went to sit beside her. One look was all it took to set her off. 'There are so many bad elements in big cities today,' she said. 'Too many rowdies about. They go round with axes and knives, causing havoc. You are too naïve to even notice these things, Sal. I'm telling you, it's the uncivilised who rule everything in this world.'

I knew there was no hope of reasoning with her whenever she got into one of these moods. Still, this was a big move, and perhaps her reaction was tied in with the paranoia. I'll have to remember to ask Dr Gail about it.

This wasn't a good time to bring up the subject of the photograph.

'I've just had a thought, Mummy,' I said. 'Tomorrow we'll go shopping to get you some new clothes. Then you'll see just how safe a neighbourhood this really is.'

I could tell by her expression that she wasn't at all thrilled with the idea. She looked somnolent and continued staring at the television, which wasn't even on.

The doorbell rang.

'Sally!' His lips were askew as he spoke. He gave me a hug as he entered. 'Hello, Eve. Do you remember me?'

Mummy's face suddenly lit up as though she'd been shocked back to life by a defibrillator. 'Hello, Declan! Of course I remember you. What a lovely surprise!'

We all sat on the couch. 'Sally told me what happened, Eve. Do you want to talk about it?'

'Of course.' Mummy spoke with fervour, spittle occasionally escaping the corners of her mouth. She and Declan continued on from where they'd left off the first time they'd met. She talked about the fire and how she'd lost everything, being melodramatic about it all. She was enjoying being the centre of attention.

Declan listened, open-mouthed. 'Wow,' he said as soon as Mummy stopped talking. 'You're so lucky Sally was there.'

We all nodded in unison.

Declan later explained that his father was out of hospital but wasn't out of the woods yet. The doctors told him in no uncertain terms that he had to stop drinking alcohol altogether. 'I know that won't be easy', Declan said, 'but there are nurses that go every day and monitor him.'

'I'm glad he's better,' I said as I squatted down next to Henry's tank. 'Come and meet Henry.'

Declan bent over and peered in. Henry looked at the both of us. I couldn't tell if he was happy or sad.

Declan turned around with an animated expression. 'A turtle! Where did you get it?'

'It's a miniature turtle.' I hesitated. 'A person we met at the hospital in Colac gave him to me.'

Mummy piped up. 'His name's Myles. A fine young man too.'

Declan's expression was now deadpan. 'That's nice,' he said as he pressed his face against the glass once more. 'Henry. That's a nice name.' He looked nervously at his watch. 'I've got to go now. I Facetime Dad at exactly nine o'clock every night.'

We hugged again at the door. Declan's lukewarm demeanour and lack of charm created something sick in me. The imprint of a lost affection. An incompatibility of spirits perhaps. Had our time apart changed how he felt? Maybe I was reading too much into it.

I'm not a psychiatrist.

CHAPTER 41

I WOKE EARLY. LIGHT was streaming in through the blinds, and a bird chirruped loudly to herald in the new day. Mummy was awake too, her legs stretched out, with a collection of things—handkerchiefs, socks, and napkins—all neatly folded and lined up meticulously on either side of her. 'Tran told me to practise my fine-motor skills. She said it will speed up my recovery.'

Despite Mummy's impressive achievement, she spoke with a more pronounced drawl and her eyes appeared sunken. 'You look tired, Mummy. Didn't you sleep well?'

She shook her head and appeared disconsolate. 'There's still too much noise coming from above. Didn't you hear it?'

I didn't answer. I didn't want her to get too worked up about what she thought she was hearing.

I'd slept well except for a brief disturbing dream: I am in a room of a house, the walls crumbling, doors and windows being flung open. I am frantic, searching for something or someone. I can make no sense of it. Perhaps it's an earthquake. And then, just like that, I wake up and can't remember anything else.

Did this mean anything? Probably not.

Henry had moved to the opposite corner of his new home. I wondered if he did this quickly, in the dead of night, or if it was a much slower process. If I really wanted to find out, I should set up one of those infrared night cameras like they do in wildlife documentaries.

Would that be an invasion of his privacy? Henry is the most laid-back creature I know. I'm sure he wouldn't object to being on candid camera, but I decided that it would be too much trouble and cost too much money to proceed with this investigation.

The nature of Henry's nocturnal ambulatory pursuits shall remain a mystery.

The factory outlet stores were only a short walk from my flat. As I'd envisaged, Mummy was reticent to venture out into the 'dark world', but I managed to bargain with her: we would only go a couple of blocks, not right into the city centre itself. Even so, she was still jumpy, walking slowly and craning her neck from side to side after every few steps. Was this paranoia or just due diligence? Fear or astute logic? As we continued walking, I couldn't help but be overcome by a sense of irony. It wasn't that long ago, before I was prodded out of my inertness, when I too feared walking through these parts.

We shopped for less than an hour. Mummy wasn't one to dress to the nines or the type to mull over too many choices. She wouldn't ever contemplate asking for my opinion. *Funky* and *elegant* were words that did not exist in her vocabulary.

She came home with a couple of track pants, a few plain tees, and a fleecy wool jumper, more than enough to see anyone through the unpredictable and fickle Melbourne seasons.

After lunch, Mummy went to lie down while I steeled myself for my first-ever driving lesson. Even though I was familiar with the layout of a typical car—the pedals, steering wheel, mirrors, and gauges—I was still nervous.

My first-ever encounter with a driving instructor wasn't a positive one. In fact, it was downright embarrassing.

'Before we begin, I'll need to see your learner's permit,' he announced.

My what?

He informed me, after a tiresome sigh, that I needed to download a booklet from the VicRoads website, study for a theory test, answer some questions, and then book an appointment to take the learner's permit knowledge test, which I had to pay for.

Only after doing all this was I allowed to take driving lessons.

Obtaining a Ph.D. would be easier.

With everything else going on, I made the executive decision to postpone getting my licence.

*

I strode purposefully into Dr Gail's office, determined to get her thoughts on my most recent 'premonition'. I still preferred the term even if she didn't.

I also needed her to steer me back on course, to get back that feeling of peace within me.

I also needed a referral to a GP for Mummy. And I mustn't forget to ask about her paranoia.

'Hello, Sally. It's so good to see you again.' Dr Gail settled herself at her desk and furrowed her brow as she opened my file. 'Tell me what's new.' There was predictability in the way she did things. I couldn't quite put a finger on it, but it was something about her demeanour and the way she spoke. Almost as if she knew what I was going to say before I said it.

'Do you have any more videos to show me?'

Bingo.

I proceeded to tell her about the fire, about how I'd gotten a phone call beforehand, and how there's a video of it but no record of the call.

She nodded, her fingers entwined. 'I see. It seems your quick thinking saved your mother's life. And yours.'

I wondered if she was taking me a little more seriously this time. 'Mummy's home with me now,' I said. 'She needs to see a doctor to get her prescriptions, as well as a physiotherapist. Can you recommend anyone?'

Dr Gail shrugged. 'Not really. It might be best just to see a GP near your home. They can organise everything she needs, including the physical therapist.'

'Okay. Thank you.'

'And how *are* things with your mother now?'

'She's trying to get used to her new environment. She hears noises, which I'm sure aren't there.'

'That's probably paranoia,' Dr Gail asserted with a small frown. 'It should lessen with time.'

I was relieved. 'That's good,' I said.

'How is your relationship with her now?'

'She's still playing me like a fiddle. I've already informed her that

I need to go back to work at some point, but she isn't too thrilled about that.'

Dr Gail made a point of noting all this down. 'You've got to be clear in your mind how this is going to play out, Sally. When circumstances change, you must adapt. Remember what I told you about being in control.'

'I can handle going back to work, Gail. Mummy will have to realise that we need money to live on.'

'Doesn't she get the pension?'

'I think so,' I said.

Dr Gail smiled through her perfect teeth. 'She can help out then. What else would she do with her money?'

Spend it on alcohol, cigarettes, and the pokies, of course. 'She bought some new clothes yesterday,' I said.

'Good.' Dr Gail made some more notes. 'The point is this: Between your job and taking care of your mother, you have a lot to deal with. You've got to realise that you're not superwoman.'

I imagined myself flying around in a tight-fitting Lycra outfit and a gravity-defying cape. 'Maybe I am superwoman,' I quipped. 'I mean, I can predict the future, remember?'

Dr Gail knew I was half joking but didn't seem at all amused. 'None of us can foresee the future, Sally, because the future hasn't happened yet.'

I pulled my phone out of my pocket and placed it on the desk. 'Here,' I said. 'Take a look.'

She took it and stared at it for a few seconds, turning it over in her hands. 'But this is a different phone, Sally.'

'It's the new phone that replaced the one I thought I'd lost.'

She began scrolling through to the one and only video on it. I found it hard to read her reaction as she watched it. Pity and triumph all mixed up. She pushed the phone back to me. 'I have to ask you something, Sally.' She hesitated momentarily before continuing, 'Do you think it's possible that you're doing all this for attention?'

I clenched my eyes shut, not willing to process the implication of what Dr Gail was accusing me of. I felt a wave of nausea, like flashbacks from my wretched childhood. Rage was threatening to burst out of me.

MARIO BORAZIO

'How dare you even suggest such a thing! I've never been an attention seeker. You should know that.'

Dr Gail flinched. I had never snapped at her before. My outburst caught her by surprise. She looked distressed.

'I'm so sorry,' I said. 'I know you're just trying to get answers. We both are. But I can honestly say that I don't know how that or either of the other two videos appeared on my phones.'

'This isn't a game, Sally. I'm making every attempt to remain objective here. You've gone through a lot of issues. Sometimes clearing the path to discovery means having to eliminate the detours.'

I nodded but didn't quite grasp what Dr Gail was trying to say. 'I'm not keeping any secrets,' I said with tears stinging the back of my eyes. 'I'm trying to figure out the truth myself.'

Dr Gail made a noncommittal 'mmm' sound and stared at me. 'There can only be two versions here, Sally. You're smart enough to know what those are.' The statement was said affably enough but in a subtly accusatory tone.

I felt as though my head was being pounded against a brick wall. Just thinking about that was giving me a headache.

Dr Gail continued talking, 'Maybe you're convincing yourself that this is some kind of magic.'

I shook my head. 'I don't believe in magic,' I said dryly.

'Neither do I.' There was silence for a while before she continued, 'This is what I think, Sally. You were desperate and talked yourself round to believing that what you claimed happened actually happened in the order that you wanted it to. Just like the bomb and the mirror ball. Am I clear enough for you?'

I nodded. The explanation was predictable, as was the next sentence. 'This may all be linked to your childhood.'

Of course. What else would it be linked to?

The conversation was threatening to veer into unpleasant areas.

'Can we stop for today?'

Dr Gail stood up and held her gaze on me for a few seconds. 'I'll see you at the same time next week.'

I nodded and walked out without saying another word.

CHAPTER 42

DECLAN CALLED IN unexpectedly after dinner. I didn't mind. It gave me an excuse to procrastinate in asking Mummy about the photograph. Anyway, I wasn't in the mood for any emotional download tonight.

I reflected that this evening might turn out to be a fantasy. I was so used to living alone and having no visitors. The idea of now having two guests—all right, three if you count Henry—in my house seemed surreal.

Declan's greeting was a little cold. He appeared on edge as he crouched down next to Henry's tank, touching the glass walls with his fingers.

He got to his feet and let out a small laugh. 'He doesn't have a care in the world, does he? Animals are so lucky that way.'

I gave Declan a wry smile as we moved onto the couch. Mummy immediately struck up a conversation. This annoyed me considerably. She would never do that when it was just the two of us.

She and Declan talked about television shows and politics. I knew I was out of my depth in the political realm so just sat patiently and listened.

An hour passed, and Mummy took herself off to bed. She was feeling more and more tired lately. I wondered if it was just her age or something else.

Declan came over and sat next to me. He shook his head and started laughing. 'Your mother's a real card. It's pleasing to see that she's making good progress.'

'Physically, she's doing well. But not emotionally,' I said. 'She's still settling in.' I wasn't in any mood to elaborate, being too preoccupied with studying Declan's behaviour.

He nodded. 'Yes, I can imagine it will take a little time.'

Without even a second's hesitation, he slid his hand round to the front of my thigh and then upwards to my rib cage. I felt desire and immense sadness rising inside me simultaneously. The fire that burned within me just before that first time I had sex was almost extinguished. I flinched and crossed my legs.

'Can't we do this?' he asked, hopelessly overoptimistic.

'No', I murmured, leaning my head against his shoulder and taking a stilted breath, 'I've got my period '

He remembered the pub. I could see it on his face. I'd saved his life that night, and maybe I was going to do the same tonight. 'That's alright,' he said. 'I have to go soon, anyway. Dad will be waiting for me to call him.'

We sat close as he described again his father's battle with the bottle and how he felt it was his responsibility to ensure that he remained sober. 'I'm doing everything I can, Sally. But I can't be with him 24/7.'

'No, of course not,' I said empathetically.

I wasn't game enough to tell him that I had the same sorts of issues with Mummy.

I could tell he was thinking of saying more, but then he stood up. 'Can I use your bathroom before I go?'

'Of course.'

His phone was on the coffee table. He'd been sneaking glances at it all night. I have never had reason, or opportunity, to go through anyone's phone before. Yet I couldn't stop the feeling building up inside me. I felt a vague yet very real sense of impending doom if I picked it up, but I knew I had to. It stood out like a lost treasure. My hands closed around it, and I began shaking. I narrowed my eyes and homed in on the screen. There was an unread text message from a woman named Nicole. A sour aftertaste immediately settled in the back of my throat. Probably just a friend. I had to remind myself that normal people are allowed to have friends.

I didn't click open the message. Instead, I scrolled through his photos. They seemed harmless enough: him with a dog, then with a large group of people around a table in a restaurant, then of a lounge suite, then—I stopped suddenly. The picture showed him drinking from a tall glass and flanked by two scantily clad young blonde women. His bare chest and face were wet, and his hair appeared plastered to his head. His eyes seemed to stare straight through the camera, trying to focus on the screen for the selfie he was obviously taking. He was smiling as if he'd just thought of a joke. The two women looked drunk.

My heart was running a marathon. Without giving too much thought to the consequences, I decided to open his message inbox. Almost every message was from women. Lots of them. Lisa, Megan, Sharni—all young names. Some even had pictures attached. Most of them looked like Barbie dolls. I felt a knot tightening in my stomach.

With trembling fingers, I decided to open the most recent message from the woman named Nicole:

Hi babe, don't forget to buy nappies on the way home.

Misunderstandings don't happen when a situation is either black or white. They only happen when there are shades of grey, when there could be more than one plausible explanation for what you are seeing. There was no grey here.

My eyes welled with tears and were threatening to overflow in a torrent.

I memorised Nicole's number and placed the phone face down back on the coffee table just as Declan re-entered the room.

'Are you okay?' He sat down next to me, his eyes instantly flicking down to his phone. He slowly leaned across me and picked it up.

I raised my hands to shield my eyes. 'I think I've got something in my eye.' I quickly stood up and made a dash to the bathroom.

Shit! He's realised that I touched his phone. And Nicole's message was there on the screen, opened. *Don't panic, Sally. Remember what Dr Gail said. Stay calm.*

I closed the bathroom door and recalled Dr Gail's mental scenario about coming out of a dark cave. I imagined a blinding light followed by a sense of relief, of being freed. I closed my eyes and tapped my foot impatiently, waiting for these feelings to take hold. They didn't. All I could see were the digits of Nicole's phone number buzzing around inside my head like a swarm of bees. My panic rose.

'Sally!' The voice was distant. 'Are you okay in there?'

I sat on the toilet for what seemed an eternity.

'Sally?'

I pulled a fistful of tissues out of the box and strode into the lounge room holding them against my right eye. My face was scrunched up. 'It's fine,' I said. 'I must've got some lint in there from my shirt sleeve.'

Declan nodded, his expression not portraying any anxiousness. He tucked his phone into the pocket of his jeans. 'I've really got to go now, Sally. See you again soon?'

'Hmm, soon,' I said through gritted teeth while hiding my face with the tissues. 'I'll be busy the next few days. I'll call you.'

After his car screeched away, I curled up on the couch, feeling more alone than ever. All the pent-up misery and disappointment of finding out that the first and only man I'd ever been with was a womaniser and a liar had completely overridden every good emotion I could and should have felt.

And he has a baby! How could he do this to Nicole?

Was he married? Did that matter?

It all made sense now. He'd never invited me over. If only I'd had more worldly experience. It is often said that people are like onions. They only reveal themselves to you one layer at a time. You've got to wait until you get to the inner layers to see if they're rotten.

I curled up on the couch and shot occasional glances in the direction of Henry's tank.

I wonder if turtles can sense human misery.

CHAPTER 43

THERE WAS SO much I needed to do today: clean my flat, buy groceries, organise a doctor for Mummy, and call work. Any of these things would have been a welcome distraction from the events of what transpired last night with Declan.

But they had to wait.

It was time to revisit the circumstances of my genetics. With my heart beating like a jungle drum, I thrust the photograph in front of Mummy's eyes. 'I found this in the pocket of your dressing gown, Mummy,' I said with my breath catching. 'Who is this man? Is he my father?'

She looked at the photograph and recoiled. I was waiting for her to speak, but she deliberately allowed the silence to linger.

'Mummy, I need to know who this man is.'

The silence continued until it was broken by a distant thumping beat coming from the floor above. Mummy looked up with a fright. The beat was quickly replaced by soft footsteps. There were no screams.

She looked at the photograph again. 'What are you doing going through my things, Sal?'

'I didn't go through your things. It fell on the floor when I was putting your dressing gown in the washing machine.'

Mummy thrust out her hand and snatched the photograph. I didn't resist. She studied the face of the handsome young man. Tears began welling in her eyes. She looked up at me. 'This is Gerald,' she said shakily. 'I think he could be the one, Sal.'

'My father?'

She remained as still as a statue, not answering my question directly. 'He was the only man I ever loved,' she said. 'He was witty and charming. Could charm the flies off a cow's backside. He always made me laugh. He made promises too, like the rest of them, but I thought he was different.' She stared wistfully into the distance. 'In the end, though, he decided to delete me from his life.'

I had so many questions. 'There are things I must know, Mummy. Was it serious with him or merely a fling? Why did he leave? What else do you know about him? How old was he? Do you know his surname?'

Mummy seemed taken aback by this sudden barrage of interrogation. 'Look, Sal, it wasn't just a fling. At least I didn't think it was. We were together for a couple of months before he left. We were of similar age. And no, I never found out his last name.'

'Did he know you were pregnant with me?'

Mummy shook her head. 'No, I didn't tell him.'

'Why didn't you tell him? You just said he could be the one.'

Mummy fell silent. Right now wasn't the time to pity her. I couldn't care less about her sky-high blood pressure or out-of-control sugar levels. I stared at her with an angry expression. 'Have you any idea how hard this is for me? All the years I spent wondering. And you had that photograph all along. Your dirty little secret hidden away in the pocket of a dressing gown. You should be ashamed, Mummy.'

My stinging remarks made her find a stronger voice. She made an exaggerated expression of appearing to be hurt and offended. 'Stop it! Don't talk about it like that! It wasn't a dirty little secret!'

'Of course it was a secret. Otherwise, you would have told me years ago.'

'I said he *could* be the one, Sal, but I can't be entirely sure. I didn't want to get your hopes up.'

I tried to process what Mummy was inferring. 'You mean—'

'Yes, that's right,' she said sheepishly. The shame seemed to come over her suddenly, and she dropped her head as she spoke, 'I was seeing other men too. At the same time as I was with Gerald.'

She pushed back in her chair as if wanting to disappear. I had to look away to compose myself before speaking again. 'But you just said that Gerald could be the one.'

'I always wished that, Sal. Out of all of them, I wished it would be him.'

'Have you tried to contact him since?' I asked.

'Of course I did. I called him several times over the following year or so, but he never returned my messages. You've got to remember there were no mobile phones in those days.'

'Do you still have his number?'

Mummy shook her head. 'I threw it out,' she said morosely. 'I threw it out because I was so angry with him.'

'I think that you would like it if I tried to find out more about Gerald, where he might be now.' I was testing her resolve.

'No!' she said with a violent shake of her head. 'How much clearer do you want me to make it, Sal? I want nothing to do with this man. Not now. Not ever.'

I stared at her. Her eyes looked fierce, but I wasn't going to back down.

'What about his address?'

'I never found out where he lived. We always met up at a café or a pub.'

It wasn't hard to work it all out. 'Gerald betrayed you, Mummy, just like the rest of them did. He probably had a family.'

'You can't say that, Sal. He would have told me.'

I'm not worldly, but I know that men who have affairs want to keep their domestic situation a secret. Insert Declan into that scenario as proof. 'Gerald was just using you, Mummy,' I said. 'Deep down, you know that's true.'

Mummy sniggered something under her breath. She looked petulant. My anger levels were now off the scale, and my tongue as venomous as a snake's.

'I was a mistake! You've told me on numerous occasions that you wished I was never born, that I was the biggest mistake of your life!'

She shook her head before grabbing my arm. Her hold was surprisingly tight. 'I've tried to be the best mother I could, sweetheart! All that talk about wishing I never had you, that simply isn't true. I only said those things when I was drunk.'

Which was most of the time.

I stopped listening because I'd heard this all before. This kind of talk riled me. My insides felt like they were being torn apart.

Mummy adopted a sullen expression. 'You're trying to put me into an early grave, aren't you?'

'What?' I yanked my arm free from her grasp and turned away.

'Where are you going, Sal?'

'I need some air.' I grabbed my jacket, my phone, and a wad of tissues and slammed the door behind me.

As I breathed in the chilly air and started walking, aimlessly, the conversation I just had with Mummy played on repeat in my head. I imagined going back and screaming at her, asking for more details about Gerald. What if she was lying and he knew about me and was eager to meet me? It could only have been Mummy who would have stopped that from happening. What excuse would she have given him? I bet it was a pathetic one.

An uneasy feeling grabbed in my throat. It was strong enough to cut through the tight knot of pain I was experiencing. I felt as though I was poised on the edge of a chasm—me and Mummy on one side and this man on the other.

Who is he?

Is he still alive?

Is he married?

Should I seek him out?

How would I even do that?

The tears returned suddenly. They were coming from deep inside and had no intentions of abating.

Then it started to rain. It rained heavily. I didn't have an umbrella.

It always rains on Losers' Day.

CHAPTER 44

THIS IS WHAT I'll do: I'll go home, turn on the television, and watch the same old shows I always watch. I'll try to re-read an old book and set my alarm clock to wake up at the same time I always do before mechanically completing the same tasks at work. I'll eat lunch at the same café. I'll go home and eat the same dinner I always eat.

Then I'll repeat the whole thing tomorrow because tomorrow will be Groundhog Day.

The old Sally Cartwright would have been happy with all that.

I was beginning to realise how much solitude and bitterness could lie beneath the surface of perceived happiness.

My phone pinged:

Can we talk? I can call you.

I felt a sensation of cold making its way up my spine as I sheltered out of the rain under a shopfront veranda and read Declan's message.

I shouldn't reply.

I won't reply.

I know it's a shitty thought, but was it possible that he was just having some harmless fun with a bunch of girls online?

Maybe they're just some of his gaming buddies.

I know I can be naïve when it comes to such delicate matters, and I definitely can't prove anything for certain, but I can't turn a blind eye either, especially where a baby was involved.

It was time to act. I'd written Nicole's number down just after Declan had left because my mind couldn't be trusted anymore.

My heart pounded as I unfolded the piece of paper; with shaking hands, I punched in the numbers.

The call went straight to message bank.

"Hi, this is Nicole. I'm not available right now. Please leave a message."

The voice sounded pleasant. Almost businesslike. Young too.

I immediately hung up and drew a long breath. There was no way I could have left a message. What would I have said?

I tucked my phone away and made a U-turn back home. By the time I reached my front door, I felt decidedly calmer.

I decided it wasn't worth revisiting the subject of Gerald with Mummy again today. Her viper tongue would just make matters worse.

I decided to clean instead. Mummy sat quietly and didn't even acknowledge my presence as I got busy. The roar of the vacuum cleaner was a welcome buffer between us.

It had been weeks since I last cleaned, and it showed. The midday light streaming in did an excellent job of highlighting the build-up of dust on almost every surface.

I decided to be extra meticulous today. I cleaned out the bathroom fan, washed all the windows, and even used a bleach pen to highlight the tile grout lines. When I'd finished, they stood out like freshly painted white lines on a brand-new bitumen road.

My flat was now pristine. It gave me great satisfaction in knowing that it was again clean and healthy.

My phone rang as I was putting away my trusty cleaning caddy.

A voice from the kitchen: 'Do you want me to answer that, Sal?' Before I could say anything, Mummy picked up. She told whoever it was to hold on for a second and then shuffled over. 'Her name's Nicole. She said you tried to call her earlier.'

I could hear my heart beating through my ears as I tentatively took the phone and walked to the bedroom. I closed the door and sat on the bed.

'Hello. Is this Nicole?' The words barely came out.

'Yes. Who am I speaking to?'

'My name is Sally Cartwright, but we've never met. I—' My mouth stalled. I should definitely have rehearsed this, maybe even written something down beforehand.

'Are you from Empona?' Nicole asked.

'From where? No, I'm calling about Declan.'

There was a long silence as I waited for Nicole to talk. I could sense suspicion down the line.

'Is he in trouble again?'

'No. I mean, maybe.' This wasn't a good start. 'Nicole, I just need to ask you something.' My heart was firmly inside my mouth. 'How well do you know him?' I wasn't prepared to admit yet that I'd read her message.

There was a brief pause. 'How well? Apart from the fact that we share a bed, a bank account, and a daughter, not very well at all. Who the hell are you, and what do you want?' Her voice was now laced with annoyance.

'Declan and I met a few months ago under innocent circumstances, and we became friends. Not good friends, just acquaintances. We—' I was digging myself into a deep hole now.

Just come out with it, Sally.

'Nicole, I think Declan might be cheating on you. No, *cheating* might be too strong a word. *Messing around* is probably a better term.'

'Uh-huh,' she mumbled. I sensed she wasn't completely surprised by what I'd just told her. There was a pause before she spoke again. 'Did he hit on you?'

I couldn't lie. If I had to do this, I had to do it right. 'Just the once,' I confessed. 'It was a mistake, though. Knowing what I know now, I wish it never happened. I would never have let it happen.'

'And what exactly *did* happen?'

No lies. 'We were intimate.' It was absurd; I should've felt great shame in admitting that Declan and I had sex, but I didn't.

'Thank you for your honesty, Sally.' Nicole's voice was calm and even.

'I'm so sorry. If I knew that—'

She interrupted me. 'You said before that Declan was *messing around*. What did you mean by that?'

MARIO BORAZIO

'I know that he's been texting lots of girls. I saw the messages on his phone.'

Nicole sighed heavily. 'So how did you get my number?'

It was time to lay it all out. 'I read your text message when Declan wasn't looking. It wasn't hard to work things out from there. It's only right that you should be made aware of what's going on, Nicole.'

'I see. Thank you, Sally. That's very noble of you. But believe me, nothing you have said has surprised me in the slightest.'

Declan was being painted as an unfaithful husband, and it pained me to accept that this could be true. I was prepared to give him the benefit of the doubt until now.

I drew a deep breath. 'Nicole, are you saying that he has cheated in the past?'

'He promised he'd stop when Ruby was born. His love for her was more blinding than a thousand suns. Or at least I thought it was. It looks like it's still hard for him to keep to the same nest.' Nicole's voice was now a frayed whisper. 'Listen, Sally, I have to ask you something.'

'If it's about the other messages, I didn't open any of them.'

'It's not that.' She paused. 'Are the two of you still an item?'

It wasn't hard to see how Nicole could have arrived at such a conclusion. I answered emphatically in the negative. 'There was never anything between us. Other than that one time. I don't want to be a marriage breaker, Nicole.'

'I know you don't. You sound genuine.'

A warm feeling rose up inside me. 'Okay, thank you for believing me. But I'd like to ask you something now.'

'Oh?' Nicole sounded surprised. 'Ask away.'

'Is Declan's father ill?'

'What? I wouldn't know. And neither would he. They haven't spoken in years. I believe he still lives interstate somewhere.'

The water was getting murkier. 'So he hasn't been caring for his father?'

'Is that what he told you?'

'I'm afraid so. He said he goes to visit him and calls him every night to make sure he's alright.'

I heard another long frustrated sigh. I knew what Nicole was thinking. The implication was clear. 'It seems he's been caring for someone other than his father,' she said.

'So what are you going to do?' I asked.

'It's, um, it's hard now with Ruby.' I heard Nicole swallow a lump in her throat, followed by sniffles. 'I've been trusting till now. I'd convinced myself that he'd changed for good. But now that he's done this again, it changes everything. I … I don't really know what to do.'

The predicament that Nicole found herself in would have to be one of the most difficult a new mother dealing with a cheating partner could possibly face. Smoothing things over while still keeping the family unit intact for the sake of their young child would be an almost-impossible task.

'We've been married four years,' she explained. 'He was so desperate for a child, and so was I. We tried for a long time. We even did the IVF thing. Then I fell pregnant naturally. I was the luckiest and happiest person in the world. And now this.' Nicole muttered the words through clearly audible sobs. 'What can I do? Just let the chips fall I guess.'

I felt our conversation slipping away. Nicole was clearly an emotional wreck at the moment. There was nothing I could add at this point. Whatever was going to happen now would happen.

'Nicole', I said, 'I'm so sorry for lumping all this onto you. I didn't mean to make things difficult between you and Declan.'

'Don't be sorry. I'm glad you rang. I've always had my suspicions, but it was easier to just stay in denial. This has been a wake-up call. Thank you again, Sally.'

Nicole sounded like the type of person you would like to have as a friend.

'You have my number now,' I said. 'If you ever need anyone to talk to—' Here I was, Sally Cartwright: marriage counsellor. Who would ever have thought?

'Yes, um, thank you,' Nicole spoke despondently and noncommittally.

'Whatever happens, Nicole, I'm sure you'll make the correct decision for you and your daughter,' I said. 'Good luck.'

The call was ended without another word passing between us.

I slumped onto the bed and stared up at the ceiling. The sketchy summary I'd formed about Declan had been filled in with a harsh and poisonous pen. My mind reeled. How could he deceive me like he had? How could he keep on deceiving his wife?

Was there always a queue of adoring women just waiting for him to fall for them? Physical attraction shouldn't be everything, but sadly, for some men, it seemed as though it was.

A psychiatrist told me recently that positive thinking is good for me. 'Be strong, Sally,' she said. It's one thing telling someone to be strong; it's another trying to do it.

What does she know anyway?

CHAPTER 45

THREE WEEKS WENT past, and I hadn't heard anything from Declan. The truth was that I was dreading having to face him in person. Every day that passed made it more unlikely that that was going to happen. Nicole must have told him that I was the one who had exposed his secret. How would he be feeling right now? I'd say he'd be burdened with shame. Shame enough to probably hide himself away for a while. I just hope he believes in redemption and rebirth for the sake of his family.

I hadn't heard from Nicole either; I didn't expect to.

On the home front, I took Mummy to the local clinic. She saw a nice male doctor who was very helpful. He liaised with the medical team in Colac, and she was given a whole new set of medications. He also organised a treatment plan for her that included physiotherapy, occupational therapy, and speech pathology sessions on a weekly or fortnightly basis.

Mummy was getting used to living in the city. She even started to venture out on her own occasionally once she realised that not all city dwellers were crazed psychopaths.

We still hadn't spoken about Gerald again.

Henry was thriving. He was eating well and moving about a lot more. His shell had taken on a green glow, which I read was a sign of good health. He'd grown too. The shells of miniature turtles can grow up to fifteen centimetres in length. Henry had almost reached that milestone already.

I thought about Myles. I suddenly remembered that he had given me his number at the hospital. It would still be in my bag. I don't think it would be appropriate to call him. I figured he'd call *me* if he wanted to come and visit.

It would be nice if he came. I wondered if Henry would recognise him. Can turtles recognise people?

I went back to work part-time. To my pleasant surprise, Mummy didn't make a song and dance about it.

Mike was brilliant as usual. He welcomed me back into the fold like a long-lost relative. 'We missed you,' he beamed as six people stood staring at me. Amongst them were Wilma, Casey, and Rob. They each took turns in welcoming me back personally, but their voices sounded aimless and flat. As they turned to head back to their respective workstations, I could hear derisive mutters.

'Thank you, Mr Cosgrove,' I said after all the others had left. 'I've been looking forward to coming back.'

Mike smiled. 'That's good because at one stage there I thought you were never coming back. Such a scenario would be too awful to imagine.'

A touch melodramatic, I thought. But I actually didn't mind the attention. It made me feel important.

*

I strode into Dr Gail's rooms filled with purpose and ruminated about whether to tell her about the photograph of Gerald. I felt I could trust her enough now. She had become like a surrogate mother. After everything she had done for me, she deserved to know.

We revisited my mental garden, and I told her there were still weeds I needed to clean out, but I didn't elaborate. I didn't mention what happened with Declan.

We talked about mindfulness, and Dr Gail taught me how I could 'zone out' and clear my mind during altercations with Mummy. She instructed me to imagine being whipped into a frenzy by Mummy's razor-sharp tongue and then drawing a big deep breath and walking away to a quiet place to reflect on what a rational solution to the situation might look like. She said it was all about trying to flick a switch in my head and realising that I was capable of being rational and handling things better than I have been.

I couldn't keep the photograph in my pocket any longer. 'I want you to see something.' Dr Gail stared at it without saying a word or moving a facial muscle before eventually sliding it back across the table. 'Where did you get this, Sally?'

'It's Mummy's. She had it tucked away. His name is Gerald.'

'Did she tell you who he is? Is he your father?'

'She doesn't know for sure. I believe her about that.'

'Did she tell you anything about him?'

'A little. She said they dated for a while, but then he just upped and left.'

'And your mother was pregnant at the time?'

It really didn't take a psychoanalyst to work out the sequence of events. 'Yes, but she can't be sure if Gerald is my father.'

Dr Gail saw my strained expression. 'I thought you'd be thrilled, Sally. You told me you desperately wanted to know who your father was.'

'That's true,' I said. 'But Gerald might not be my father. I really don't know if I should pursue it further. Mummy hasn't heard from him since he left. I'd be going on gut instinct, nothing else.'

Dr Gail put down her pen and sat forward with her arms crossed. 'Sally, gut instincts can be powerful starting points. When the police are trying to solve a crime, they usually begin with a gut instinct and then fill in the blanks as they go along.'

I admired detectives. They had to be fastidious, unwavering, and always prepared. I didn't see myself like them at all.

I glared at Dr Gail across the desk. 'I understand what you're saying, but I'm not really the detective type.'

'You owe it to yourself to try to be, Sally.' She held up my file, which was now quite thick. 'Your identity is contained within these pages. Your life has been inexorably shaped by the fact that you have never known your father. I know that has been a confusing and lonely feeling for you. Your father's absence has haunted you your whole life.'

And it will continue to haunt me. I knew Dr Gail was right. This was the missing piece of the puzzle. Without this piece, I will forever be just a collection of parts that didn't make sense.

MARIO BORAZIO

I mustn't be reluctant anymore. 'I'll try,' I said, 'but I'll need some guidance. Where do I start?'

'Do you have his last name?'

I shook my head.

Dr Gail began to explain. 'You'll have to be methodical,' she said. 'You can't just play a game of whack-a-mole, chasing down baseless leads. You'll have to talk to your mother again, jog her memory for something more tangible. That's got to be your starting point. It's only after meeting Gerald that you can get all the facts. Maybe he has a nice life, a wife, even kids. That shouldn't matter to you, Sally. He might be glad to meet you, even be willing to take a paternity test. The fact is that you won't know any of this if you never meet him.'

This was going to take a huge effort on my part, take me out of my routine and my comfort zone.

My routine made me feel safe, but I really needed to step out of myself.

'I'll speak to Mummy again tonight,' I said.

I strode out of Dr Gail's rooms with a spring in my step.

CHAPTER 46

MUMMY WAS STILL in bed, on her back, blankets heaped up on one side. Her hair was like grey wire, her eyes puffy and red, half closed, her cheeks hollowed, skin flushed.

She sensed my presence in the room, and I saw her wince as she lifted her head up. Her lips formed words, which were almost inaudible. 'I've got a sore throat, and my head hurts, dear.' Her eyelids fluttered quickly as she spoke and her face was set in a grimace.

Seeing her like this made me feel sad as well as disappointed. I couldn't ask her anything more about Gerald right now, not in her current state.

That would have to wait.

I touched her forehead. It was on fire. 'I'll make you a tea with honey,' I said. 'And I'll get you some paracetamol for the fever.'

When Mummy was settled, I turned on the television. She had left it tuned to the news channel. I detested watching the news and was about to surf the animal channels when a story aroused my curiosity.

A young woman holding an umbrella was standing on the side of a road.

'Detectives from the Colac crime investigation unit are appealing for witnesses after a man was stabbed during an unprovoked assault in central Colac last night. It is understood the 29-year-old man was walking alone when he was approached by two unknown males on Gellibrand Street about nine o'clock last night. The men punched and stabbed the victim several times before fleeing on foot towards Murray Street. The victim managed to walk to the nearby Colac hospital where it is believed he works as an orderly. He was assessed and treated before being later airlifted to the Royal Melbourne Hospital with stab wounds and head injuries. Police have launched a full investigation and are appealing for anyone who may have witnessed the attack to contact the Colac police station. No motive for the attack has been established. The injured man's name has not been released, but we believe he lives on nearby Manifold Street.'

I refused to believe what I'd just heard: young man, badly hurt, orderly, Manifold Street.

It had to be Myles.

I wanted to suppress the power of painful reality and replace it with a more palatable scenario.

That wasn't going to happen.

Trembling from head to toe, I checked that Mummy was sound asleep before grabbing my coat and bag and heading out into the late-afternoon chill.

I sat on the bus and closed my eyes. An image of Myles hugging me goodbye the day Mummy and I left Colac appeared front and centre in my mind. I recalled restraining myself that day but kept wondering what would have happened if I'd been more affectionate. Things could've worked out so differently if I'd just been brave enough.

A mood of melancholy descended upon me. How I'd love for Myles to hug me now.

I was trying my best to think positive thoughts, convincing myself that he will pull through. But the reporter on the television said that he had sustained stab wounds and head injuries.

Please, Sally, do not have a panic attack. Not here. Not now.

The 4-7-8 breathing technique deserted me again. I tried to time my breathing to the rhythm of my thumping heart: one breath to every four beats—one, two, three, and four—anything to stop the primal urge to scream. In desperation, I conjured an image of Dr Gail's cave and the almost-blinding sunlight waiting for me when I stepped outside.

It worked. My heart rate slowed, and I felt a calmness permeate my body.

I considered Myles a friend. What friend wouldn't gift you a turtle? Still, I took a few seconds to reflect on whether what I was doing was a little impetuous. Here I was, on a bus, on my way to the Royal Melbourne Hospital's Emergency Department to visit a man I hardly knew. His family would probably already be by his bedside. Or would they? I wondered if his parents had been contacted yet.

With trembling hands, I rummaged through my bag and found the card Myles had given me. My heart rate jumped up again as I dialled his number.

"Hi, you've reached Myles. You know the drill."

You can be so dumb sometimes, Sally. What made me think he was going to answer? He was probably attached to a ventilator, a myriad of tubes, or, worse, he was still unconscious.

I entered the Emergency Department and immediately guzzled a glass of cold water from the Neverfail water dispenser. The coldness seemed to soothe my insides.

As I waited in a queue to speak to someone, I took a moment to look behind the reception area. The flash of nurses and doctors zipping in and out of narrow corridors stacked with trolleys was a stark reminder of the seriousness of the work that goes on in here. I watched them scurrying about, helping seriously sick people. A deep surge of gratefulness speared through my body. I felt grateful for their calling and professionalism and toil for their community.

When the difference between life and death is often measured in milliseconds, these superheroes deserve our highest praise. The pressure they are under is immense. I recall watching a medical documentary that stated that, of all the medical specialties, emergency medicine had the highest rate of burnout amongst doctors and nurses. Resilience is a key prerequisite for these jobs, but sadly, that is clearly not enough for some of these people.

'May I help you?'

A grey-haired rather elegant-looking woman of indeterminate age looked up from behind the glass of the reception desk.

'I'm here to see a patient,' I said. 'A young man named Myles.'

The woman scrolled her eyes down a computer screen.

'Myles Bennett? Are you his wife?'

Now I know his surname. 'No. I'm just a friend,' I said.

MARIO BORAZIO

'I'm afraid you can't see him. Only relatives are allowed in at this stage.'

An immediate roadblock. 'Can I at least find out if he's alright?'

The woman stared at her screen again and then back up at me. As she spoke, I sensed she was holding back some vital information. 'He's a little out of it at the moment due to the morphine. He needs a lot of rest. I suggest you come back tomorrow.'

I was disappointed yet relieved. At least he was alive.

I had to do some quick thinking if I wanted to see him. 'I'm afraid that's not possible. You see, I just drove all the way from Colac, and I have to go back tomorrow for work and—'

The woman held up a hand and stood up. 'Wait here. I'll see if I can pull some strings and get you a couple of minutes with him.' A smile spread across her face as she picked up the phone.

A few minutes later, a bright-pink visitor's label with my name neatly printed on it with a black marker was stuck onto my shirt, and I was escorted through security glass doors by a nurse. We strode through narrow corridors and past tiny cubicles taken up by mainly elderly patients. The nurse walked with no real urgency and steeled herself before stopping at a cubicle and turning around. There was worry etched on her face, but then her professional briskness returned. 'He's in there. He won't be able to respond to you. I'll give you two minutes.' She gave me a curt nod before turning on her heels and striding away.

'Thank you,' I said as she disappeared around a corner.

My stomach sank as soon as I entered the cubicle. The man in the bed lay motionless with his back to me. The first thing I noticed was that his hair looked matted and was covered with a dark substance I assumed to be congealed blood. Tubes and wires snaked around almost every inch of his upper body. There were monitors charting his vital signs, and IVs pumping drugs into his veins. The hairs on the back of my neck stood up.

He was alive, just.

Such are the vulnerabilities of life.

I walked around to the other side of the bed just to make sure it was Myles. My limbs turned to jelly when I glimpsed the unmistakable brow line, the rounded nose, and the angled mouth. There was an oxygen mask covering his nose and mouth

I sat down and just stared, unable to bring myself to touch him.

'Time's up.' The nurse stood at the door before reaching for the chart at the end of the bed. She glanced at it before putting it back and checking that all the equipment was still plugged in and functioning properly.

I was escorted back to the reception area before I could query anything with her. My state of mind was such that at this point I was unable to think of anything specific to ask anyway.

Another nurse, whom I hadn't seen before, pushed the exit button on the glass doors and gestured towards two empty plastic chairs in the waiting area. It wasn't exactly the most intimate setup for a sensitive conversation, but it would have to do; I appreciated someone taking the time to talk to me.

She introduced herself as Ophelia and looked at my name tag. 'First off, Sally, I'm only filling you in because no family has come yet for Mr Bennett.'

'Haven't they been called?'

'Yes, they have. I believe his mother is on her way.'

I didn't know where Myles's parents lived or if they even lived together, but I still wondered how much of that bitterness between them that he talked about was responsible for their tardiness. Still, any parent would race to their son's bedside and hold a candle for him in a time of crisis, wouldn't they?

The young nurse, who appeared of East Asian descent, adopted a serious tone. She spoke with a rusted-on Australian accent, which indicated she was either born here or came out at a very young age. 'Mr Bennett isn't out of danger yet, but he's in the best place,' she explained. 'He has a small blood clot in his brain, but the ER doctors are confident that will resolve itself with clot-busting drugs and without the need for surgery. The next twenty-four to forty-eight hours will be crucial. Our best line of treatment right now is to keep him sedated and pain free.'

I felt an immediate sense of relief but couldn't help thinking about Myles's family and how they should have been the first people to receive this news. It made me feel just a little uncomfortable. My being here could be seen as a misplaced sense of loyalty manifesting itself.

I wonder how Myles would react if I am the first person he sees when he wakes up. How will he interpret my concern for him? Just as importantly, how would his family interpret it?

Ophelia dipped her head and took a deep breath. 'My shift is finishing now. The night staff will take over and call you if there's any change. They've got your number.'

'Thank you, Ophelia.'

She gave me a warm smile. 'It's you who deserves the thanks, Sally. Intensive care can be a lonely place. Mr Bennett will be pleased to know you came. Thank you.'

I smiled, and a shiver ran down my back. It made me feel good to know that at least one person appreciated my presence here today.

I shifted in the seat and let out a long sigh as the bus spluttered along on my journey home. From what Ophelia told me, Myles was unlikely to wake up anytime soon. There was no way I could keep a bedside vigil. I had to work, not to mention accompany Mummy to all of her medical appointments. There just wouldn't be enough hours in the day. Strangely, this problematic scenario was a relief—a welcome excuse to stay away from the hospital and the potential ire of his family.

That being said, I didn't really want to stay away.

My heart jumped as a message pinged on my phone.

The hospital? Already? Surely not. A wave of nausea crested over me as I saw who the message was from:

Hi Sally, can we talk please?

It was from Declan.

CHAPTER 47

WHY DID I ever allow myself to think that I could have a normal life? What is normal anyway? Finding out that the person you thought loved you never did at all. Seeing the person you really love clinging to life in a hospital bed. Being constantly at war with your mother. Setting your mind to chasing up some man who may or may not turn out to be your father. And to top it all off, finding out that your shrink thinks you're an attention seeker. If these are things that people who live normal lives have to endure, then there are a lot of miserable and unhappy souls walking this planet.

I honestly thought that I could solve the problem of Sally Cartwright, as if all the wrongs done to her all those years ago could be put right. I yearned to grasp at a random straw and find a magic one.

I'm beginning to see that striving for a normal life can be a real killer. That it can just grind you down.

A famous author once wrote that life is generous to those who pursue their 'personal legend'.

What is my personal legend?

As the bus neared my stop, I thought about Declan. I can only imagine what he would say to me if we were to meet again. He'd probably speak brightly, full of enthusiasm, and tell me that I was 'the one'. When I accuse him of lying, I can imagine him struggling to suppress a reaction, and then he would deny it and respond somewhat mockingly before pouting his lips to feign seriousness.

I can't let that happen.

I decided to solve one of my problems right here and now. I will text Declan back and inform him, no, *tell* him never to contact me again. I didn't need to see him. If anything had been left unsaid between us, let it remain so. I had no regrets:

Please do not contact me ever again.

I know who you are. I know what you are.

That ought to do it.

No sooner had I pressed send and slumped back into my seat than the bus reached my stop.

Mummy said something as I walked in, but I couldn't hear her. She sounded a thousand miles away, but I could see her white slippers through the entrance to the lounge room. She was slumped on an armchair and gasping for air.

'Mummy, are you alright? You're usually in bed by now.'

The last of the evening light caught her face. Her bluish lips twitched each time she drew a laboured breath. 'I couldn't breathe at all lying down. Can you fetch me my puffers?'

Her new doctor had prescribed Ventolin and Spiriva. He was flabbergasted that she hadn't been given these before.

'I think your cold has made your breathing worse, Mummy,' I said. She took two puffs of each medicine, and her breathing improved almost immediately.

Her mouth contorted into a leering smile.

'If I don't die here, Sal, it will be a bloody miracle.' She waited for a response, and I could see the disappointment on her face when none was forthcoming. 'This is when I'm going to meet my God!' she continued.

Mummy found it almost impossible to wash away the deep stains of self-pity.

'Don't be so melodramatic,' I whispered through clenched teeth.

'Did you say something, dear?' Her voice had more volume now.

I shook my head and covered her with a blanket. I thought it best not to mention anything about Gerald tonight. Or about Myles. Such sad news could easily bring on another asthma attack. 'You need to rest, Mummy. I'll bring you some soup.'

She nodded and attempted a smile.

I had one eye on the simmering soup and another on my phone. It felt almost impossible to explain the fierce protectiveness for Myles that had welled up inside me since seeing him so helpless at the hospital. I imagined it to be akin to the protectiveness his mother would be feeling, but I didn't know that for sure.

Why was I feeling this way? Perhaps it was because I had no one else to feel this for.

I couldn't sleep. My thoughts were random. I thought about Mummy and whether she'd feel better in the morning. I thought about Myles. I thought about Gerald.

I thought about Nicole too.

With my phone fully charged and tucked under my pillow, I decided I would go into work as usual in the morning. It would be pointless hanging around here or even at the hospital until I'd heard anything.

An uneasy thought entered my mind: What if the hospital forgets to contact me once any of Myles's family arrives? They know I'm not family. They know I'm not even his girlfriend.

I found my hands curled against my chest when I woke up. I remembered my phone under the pillow and immediately retrieved it. No messages. That was a good sign.

'Mummy, if you swallow these, you'll feel much better. I promise.' I held Mummy's tablets out in front of her. She took the pills one by one and swallowed them with a grunt.

'They're all gone now. Satisfied?'

I didn't have time for this. If I didn't leave right now, I'd be late for work. 'Your lunch is in the microwave. I have to go now.'

After a silence, not too an uncomfortable one because this scenario has played out many times before, I kissed her on the head and headed out.

I found my morning's work surprisingly therapeutic. Strangely, my fears about Myles's well-being had abated. I found myself colluding with the notion that no news is good news even though I knew that that didn't hold true all of the time.

Lunchtime was upon me, and I still hadn't heard from the hospital. I had a decision to make: consume my usual lunch at the Fancy Chef or sneak off to the hospital.

Butterflies had well and truly set up camp in my stomach. I wasn't the least bit hungry and decided to catch a tram for the short trip to the Royal Melbourne Hospital.

As the tram idled along, I imagined Myles's mother and other relatives visiting him day after day, hoping he would get better. Then their visits would slowly ease off, and that would allow me more time with him alone. *You can be so selfish at times, Sally Cartwright.*

As I entered the emergency foyer, I thought about how his mother would greet a total stranger who had come to visit her son. What would I say to her? What *should* I say? It would be far easier for all concerned if he were awake and lucid. 'Hey, Mum, Sally grew up just around the corner from my place!' Such an opening comment would be an awesome tension breaker. Who was I kidding, though? He's probably still hooked up to the max with a breathing tube shoved down his throat.

The girl behind the desk had the whitest knuckles I had ever seen. She had a headset on and was talking to someone about morphine powder. Everything about the conversation seemed extremely serious, as though a life depended on it. It probably did.

'Yes?' Her voice caught me off guard. I didn't realise she'd ended her phone call.

I cleared my throat. 'I'm here to see Myles Bennett,' I said quickly. Saying Myles's full name gave me goose bumps. Remaining silent, the girl lowered her eyes to her computer screen.

'Mr Bennett's been transferred to the trauma ward,' she said matter-of-factly.

That's good. He's still alive

'Can you tell me where that is?'

I was given clear and concise directions and within minutes found myself on the seventh floor of the south-west wing.

I was expecting blood, gore, and pained screams. Instead, I walked into a setting as silent and as still as a photograph. This must be the 'quiet hour' when both patients and staff are afforded simultaneous rest. The nurses' station was deserted. The one thing that did strike me was a pungent sterilised smell that seemed to cling to my nose hairs. It had an air of familiarity about it. It wasn't buckwheat, but it did remind me of my flat after I'd meticulously cleaned it.

I peered along the two long corridors leading to the patient rooms. They too were deserted. With my heart rate climbing and sweat prickling my forehead, I made my way slowly down the longer of the two corridors, stopping at each doorway.

I spotted her almost immediately. She had the same rounded nose and high cheekbones. How could I forget those cheekbones?

She looked older than I expected. Middle age is not defined solely by chronological age but is a product of biological, social, and psychological factors. It appeared that the years had not been kind to this woman. She was petite and slim. Her face was wrinkled and blotchy. She had greying hair pulled back tight into a tiny ponytail, and she was leaning forward in her chair in a manner that strongly suggested a permanently stooped posture. For all these physical shortcomings, she was smartly dressed in a perfectly fitted silk shirt and black slacks.

This wasn't the image of Myles's mother I had formulated in my mind.

With my eyes trained towards the floor and trying to suppress a good dose of nerves, I gently tapped on the door and entered the room. The look of alarm that went across the woman's face wasn't unexpected. She jolted back in her chair and gripped the armrests.

'May I help you, young lady?'

Her voice sounded croaky. I immediately formed the opinion that, just like Mummy, she had been or still was a heavy smoker.

Before I answered, I flicked my eyes across to the bed. The patient was fast asleep and breathing on his own. My heart fluttered as I realised it was indeed Myles lying there. Seeing his chest rise and fall freely without the aid of a tube or a machine made me relax and gave me the strength to talk.

'Hi. My name is Sally Cartwright, and I'm a friend of Myles.'

The woman's eyes widened, and her mouth gaped open. It was hard to miss her perfectly straight teeth. I couldn't help but think that they belonged in another's body or that, more likely, they weren't her own. 'Oh, you're Sally. My son has mentioned you.' Her tone was friendly.

I smiled but didn't answer. Yes, obviously he would have mentioned me. Huh? I could feel vital blood draining from my face.

'Are you alright?' The woman showed genuine concern.

Say something, Sally. 'Yes, I'm fine. Myles and I met at the hospital in Colac when my mother was there.'

The woman nodded. 'Myles mentioned your mother as well. How's she doing after the fire?'

It seems that her son had told her quite a lot. 'Better,' I said with a nod. 'She's living with me now.' I felt lightheaded and could sense my voice outside of myself as I spoke. Disembodied, floating. It was a strange feeling.

The woman got up and offered her hand. She stood military straight—so much for first impressions. 'I'm Anna. Anna Hallsworth,' she said.

The perplexed look on my face was a dead giveaway.

'I've gone back to my maiden name,' she added.

Anna began filling me in on her son's condition and said that he'd improved markedly since her arrival last night. The manner in which she spoke indicated that she was very comfortable talking to strangers. She seemed the type of person who enjoyed having someone to talk to in this difficult scenario. 'The doctors said he could make a full recovery.'

I felt like crying for joy. I'd never felt this emotion before. The only crying I did in the past was when bad things happened.

'That's great news, Anna,' I said, choking back tears. 'Myles has been a great help to Mummy and me. He even took us in after the fire.'

'Yes, I know. He told me that too.'

What I gleaned thus far was that Anna and Myles conversed on the phone, at least recently. I bet their conversations weren't anything like the ones Mummy and I had.

'When I saw on the television what happened, I thought the least I could do was come down and see how Myles was doing.'

'That's very sweet of you, Sally. We don't have much family.' The melancholy in Anna's voice was tangible.

I was feeling so light and free now that I decided to ask her a question that I would never have had the nerve to ask before: 'Is Myles's father coming?'

Anna's dark eyes regarded me thoughtfully. 'I'd be very surprised if he did,' she said disconsolately. 'The last I heard he was staying with friends in Queensland, but we haven't talked for over a year. I tried to ring him this morning, but it went straight to his voicemail.' She turned her eyes towards the bed and adopted a sullen expression. 'We haven't exactly been loving parents.' Then she bent over her son's head and began talking to him. 'It was the worst thing I could do, neglecting you. I'm not even asking you to forgive me. I've gone over this in my head so many times. I'm not pretending, sweetheart. I really am sorry.'

I was in awe of this woman's composure as she poured out her emotions in front of a total stranger. She looked straight at me with a tear-laden face. 'Treasure your relationship with your mother, young lady. You'll regret it if you don't.'

I nodded absently and heard a soft snuffling noise from behind me. Myles was rolling over onto his side. I thought he was going to wake up, but he didn't.

'The doctors have sedated him heavily,' Anna explained. 'There's not much to do now but wait.' Her voice was almost a whisper, as though speaking too loudly would wake her son prematurely.

'I've got to get back to work now,' I said as I picked up my bag. 'Can I come tomorrow?'

'You can come anytime, Sally,' Anna said warmly as she touched my arm. I subconsciously stroked my fringe away from my eyes. There was a brief silence between us that felt so right.

Anna sat back down as soon as I left the room. She looked permanently stooped over again.

MARIO BORAZIO

CHAPTER 48

I FELT SAD AND empty, even though I knew that my decision to visit Myles was the right one to make. Anna seemed nice. I wondered why her relationship with her son hadn't been stronger over the years.

You can't really judge a relationship until you know every single detail of the past lives of the people involved. It's so easy to pigeonhole people. Take Mummy and me, for example. A stranger might think our relationship is as strong as iron bands just because we are living under the same roof.

How misguided that would be.

Back at work, I found it hard to concentrate. I thought about Anna again. Where was she staying? Maybe I should have offered for her to stay with me.

I might ask her tomorrow.

'What's this all about?'

The voice caught me by complete surprise. Rob was leaning against the door jamb, pointing to his watch.

'Miss Perfect is never late back from her lunch. Except for that one time when she almost got herself blown up.'

He never comes in here—ever. *You better watch it. I know how much you earn, and it's less than what I earn.*

Sally Cartwright is not vindictive. She would never think or say that.

I took a deep breath and exhaled heavily. 'Is there something I can help you with, Rob?' My voice was calm, measured.

He didn't answer immediately. I surmised he was here on a fact-finding mission. Maybe he was sent by Wilma and Casey.

Well, Rob, it's like this, I had to go home to attend to my mother who had a stroke. Now I'm back, but a man I care about greatly, who is a far better man than you will ever be, is in hospital and fighting for his life. I went to visit him during my lunch break and got back approximately twenty minutes past my scheduled return time. I apologise profusely for my tardiness because, as you are well aware, Sally Cartwright detests being late. Satisfied?

I felt in no way obliged to explain myself. Not to Rob.

'I just came by to see how you were doing, Sal. That's all.'

I knew that couldn't possibly be true, but I decided to play along anyway. 'Thank you for your concern, Rob. I'm doing just fine. How's it going over there without me?'

He saw my question as an invitation to step inside my office and engage in further conversation. 'Casey and Wilma are being pains in the backside as usual. Take the other day, for example. We got talking about music, and they were going on about how great the Rolling Stones's music is, and I foolishly made a less-than-favourable comment about it. Now tell me, Sal, can't a man object to aspects of a band's music without being burned at the stake for heresy? Aren't I allowed to have an opinion?'

I was about to inform Rob that I myself didn't have an opinion on the topic one way or another but thought it best to ignore his questions and change the subject. 'What about my old job? Have they hired someone new yet?

'Yes, they have. She's just started. Her name's Monique, and she's super smart. Witty too.'

How considerate of him to point out my shortcomings.

I pretended to search through some files on my desk. 'I've got a lot of work to do, Rob. So ...'

My remark seemed to fly right over his head as he slipped his phone out from his shirt pocket. 'Hey, Sal, would you like to see some new photos of my nieces and nephews? They're on my Facebook page.'

I wondered how old these poor children were and if they knew yet what a total imbecile their uncle was. 'Ah, maybe another time. I'm busy right now as you can see,' I said.

He finally got the hint and gave me a curt nod. He was muttering something under his breath as he turned to leave.

*

Mummy looked decidedly better than she did this morning. Her breathing was near normal, and she had the colour back in her cheeks. After dinner, I decided to tell her about Myles.

'That's so awful, Sal. I can only imagine how distraught his mother must be.'

She may be able to imagine it, but I didn't for one second believe that she could ever feel it. Such emotions are way beyond her mental capabilities. 'I think I'll ask Anna if she would like to stay with us for a few days,' I said. 'It would be the proper thing to do, don't you think?'

Mummy hesitated. 'That's very noble of you, dear, but we don't have much room.'

I'd already run this through my head. 'I'll take the couch,' I declared. Mummy stared at me before hastily picking up a magazine and pretending to read it.

I didn't sleep well for the second night running. I kept thinking about Anna. I was nervous at the prospect of seeing her again. Her congenial nature was alluring; but with that came the expectation of engaging in prolonged dialogue, which I wasn't comfortable with. It would be overwhelming and unpleasant, even though we'd be talking mostly about nice things.

I decided to go to the hospital before work. That way, once I negotiated Anna, I'd be a lot calmer for the rest of the day.

My heart almost stopped as I neared the hospital entrance. Anna was standing on the steps smoking a cigarette. She forced a smile and coughed gently as I approached. 'Hello, Sally! I didn't expect you here so early.' She took a long drag, and there was something sinister in her eyes as she did so. Perhaps it was just the effect of the smoke.

'Good morning, Anna.' I pretended not to notice her nicotine-stained fingers. I didn't notice them yesterday. 'How's Myles?'

'Much better. He was so chuffed when I told him you came to visit.'

I thought I'd misheard. 'You mean he's awake?'

'Oh yes,' Anna said while stubbing her cigarette out and flicking it into the bushes. 'He's having his breakfast right now. Shall we go up and surprise him?'

As we walked towards the lifts, I slipped out my phone to text Mike. I decided to call in sick today.

CHAPTER 49

IN LINE WITH conformist rules of social decorum, I allowed Anna to walk in front. After all, she is Myles's mother. As we approached the south-west lifts, I reflected on whether my decision to skip work today was an impetuous one. Sally Cartwright calling in sick would be more fodder for Rob's rumour file. But I was beginning to realise that, to appear normal in this world, you sometimes had to pretend a little.

Today I was pretending to be sick.

Myles was sitting up against the back of the bed with his left hand cradling the TV remote.

'Hello, Sally!' His smile extended up to his eyes, which seemed to twinkle as they met mine. I didn't feel any urge to turn away.

It was hard to believe that this man was unconscious only a day or so ago.

This was an awkward moment. Part of me wanted to lean over and kiss him, but I kept my distance. 'Hello, Myles. How are you feeling?'

'Apart from a slight headache, I feel fine. The doctor said it will take a while for me to recover, but he thinks that I will.'

Anna interrupted. 'It's going to take time, but we have a lot of that, don't we?' She looked at her son in a way that suggested they had already discussed future plans together.

'That's great,' I said as enthusiastically as I could. 'Where are you staying, Anna?'

'The hospital managed to get me short-term accommodation close by until we decide on a place to rent.

'We're going to give the city a shot.'

So Myles was staying in Melbourne! This could be the tonic I needed. No, the tonic I deserved. A brand-new adventure! I tried to hide my elation. 'That's great,' I said in a measured tone. My thoughts were selfish, but I didn't care.

'It's exciting,' Anna said. 'Neither Myles nor I have ever lived in a big city before. I think it's the change we both need.'

Myles sat up straighter and spoke with real fervour, 'I've always wanted to live in the city one day, Sally. I'm sure I can get a job in a big hospital, and Mum can find something as well.'

I wanted to enquire about Anna's line of work but decided not to.

'Do you have any particular area in mind?' I asked.

'I'm hoping you can help us with that,' Myles said. 'Not too far from here would be great.'

Could this be a dream?

'Collingwood's nice,' I said a little too quickly. 'That's where I live. The rent is quite reasonable, and it's only a short ride to get to anywhere.'

Anna leaned over and pressed Myles's right hand. 'I'll start looking today, dear,' she said. Her mannerly behaviour around her son made me wonder if what Myles had told me about their frosty relationship was really true.

Myles didn't say anything, but a warm smile covered his face to suggest that he was looking forward to living with his mother.

I have never known this feeling.

I was in my little world as mother and son talked intensely between themselves. I wondered what it would be like having Myles live near me. I also wondered what it would be like having Myles live *with* me, to see him up close every day. I closed my eyes and pictured myself handing him a towel as he shaved, telling him where he missed a spot. I would make him breakfast before he went to work. I would sew a missing button on his shirt. We would go for long walks together, and I wouldn't be ashamed to be out in public anymore. We would go to the beach and walk along the sand, build a sandcastle together, find some seashells, catch a wave, or just sit and watch the sunset. I imagined hot summer nights spent outside together, lying on the grass and gazing up at the stars or admiring the glowing moon.

I wanted all of that.

'Sally?'

The voice startled me. I opened my eyes and nodded without knowing why.

'We've got to go now.' The voice turned to a whisper. 'They said we can come back this afternoon.'

Anna held my arm lightly as I rose from my seat. Two nurses, one a female and the other a male, were busy changing Myles's dressings and studying medicine charts.

Anna and I boarded a tram. Our mission was to find a real estate agent.

I was looking out the window at the bright sky. The rumble and rattle of the tram carriage created a serene ambience, and I almost fell asleep.

'How's your mother, Sally?'

Anna's question startled me. *It's like this, Anna: My mother is a troubled and unhappy woman. She does bad things to me. To herself even. The seed of her badness was planted long ago. You see, it's my welfare you should be concerned about, not hers.*

I should've told her all that.

'She's doing much better now. Thank you for asking,' I said without elaborating further.

I needed to deflect to another topic before the blowtorch became too hot. 'What kind of place would you like to live in, Anna?'

'Oh, nothing too big. It will only be the two of us.' Anna's voice was tinged with melancholy. I wondered deep down if she was still yearning a traditional family unit.

'I'm sure the agent will have something for you to look at,' I said.

She nodded, but I could tell her thoughts were elsewhere. 'It's kind of strange, don't you think, Sally?' she said as she looked outside and admired the people walking along the footpaths while absently removing a scrap of lint from her shirt.

'Strange?'

'You could even call it a coincidence.'

I hadn't the foggiest what she was talking about. 'Oh?'

'The fact that tragedy has united two mothers with their children. That's serendipity at work.'

Anna may see it that way, but I don't believe in coincidence or in serendipity for that matter.

As if compelled to explain herself, she continued, 'If Myles hadn't been assaulted and if your mother's house hadn't caught fire, the four of us would each be still living separate lives in different places.'

That was true. *At least in your case, Anna, your union is destined to be a happy one. The same cannot be said about Mummy and me.* I almost told Anna this but didn't have the courage.

If serendipity were at play, though, I would definitely view my meeting Myles as a serendipitous event.

But I had to keep reminding myself that I don't believe in any of that stuff.

I spotted a real estate agent's office by accident and pointed it out. 'You can get off here, Anna,' I said.

Anna gave me a puzzled look. The sunlight reflecting off her creased face made her look even older than she'd looked yesterday. 'Aren't you coming with me?' she said.

I shook my head. 'I've got to go home. Mummy will be waiting.'

'Of course.'

I promised to visit Myles again as we said our goodbyes.

I didn't go home, though. I went straight to work.

CHAPTER 50

MIKE SPOTTED ME at my desk and made his way over in his familiar waddling gait.

'You should have taken the whole day off, Sally.'

'It's all right, Mr Cosgrove. I feel better now.'

His smile was faint, and the expression he wore was one of suspicion rather than worry.

This is not the Mike I was used to.

I guessed how this might have gone: Rob would have had a word with him about my dismissive behaviour towards him yesterday, and before you know it, the entire office is talking about me.

Something was up with Sally Cartwright, and Rob made it his personal mission to ensure that everybody was clued up on it. It won't be long before they also knew everything about her shameful past.

Mike asked a question, but I didn't hear. My heart was pounding like a drum in anticipation of … something.

'Excuse me, Mr Cosgrove. I didn't quite catch that.' I could feel my eyes fluttering as I spoke.

He adopted a hard expression. 'Are you sure you're alright? I mean, it's not like you to take time off, Sally.' He stopped short before continuing, 'Is it your mother?'

I needed to explain myself. I needed to come up with a lie that would allay any suspicions that Mike might have. 'My mother is doing fine,' I said. 'I woke up with a headache, but it's gone now, and I am able to resume my work duties as normal.'

Mike's familiar grin returned. 'I'm glad to hear that,' he said in a strong voice. 'It's wages day today, isn't it?'

I nodded.

'Keep up the good work.'

I smiled as he turned and left the room. It was comforting to know that the camaraderie we had developed over the years was still alive and strong. That thought made me feel warm inside.

Did I feel bad about not telling Mike the truth? About Myles? Or about wanting to find my father? Dr Gail told me that sharing our problems was the first step to solving them. But I felt in no way obligated to broadcast my personal affairs to anyone at work. Not to Rob, not even to Mike.

I think I'll keep things to myself for now.

After attending to the distribution of wages, a task that took me just under an hour, I closed the door and googled *how to find a missing person* on my computer. What popped up was a minefield; plenty of sites introduced their services in an optimistic fashion: all I had to do was plug in the person's full name, approximate age, schools attended, and any known past addresses. They would do the rest.

All I had to go on were a first name and an approximate age.

They also suggested looking through local newspapers at the time the person was known to you and to even try social media sites like Facebook, Twitter, Instagram, Google Profiles, or LinkedIn. I wasn't familiar with any of these sites. And trawling through old newspapers would mean a visit back to the library in Colac, which I didn't really want to do.

Suddenly my task appeared insurmountable. As I've mentioned before, Sally Cartwright is not cut out for a career in espionage.

But I'm not giving up.

Dr Gail said that the primary skill in dealing with any situation that seems insurmountable is patience. I can do patience.

A quote I once read immediately sprang into my mind: the pain of regret is far greater than the pain of hard work.

I had to jog Mummy's memory again, even though she said she couldn't remember anything more about Gerald. She had to try harder. Somewhere deep in the recesses of what remained of her grey matter was something that, if extricated, could prove to be life-changing for me.

The world was filled with stories. But the one story I really needed to know about was hidden away. I was scared of never finding it.

CHAPTER 51

D R GAIL WAS in a good mood tonight. I attributed this to the fact that she was going to be away on holidays for a week starting tomorrow.

I've never had a holiday. Even at Christmas.

'Now remember, Sally, even though I won't be here, it doesn't mean you can't reach me. You have my number if you need to talk. You can call me anytime.'

I admired people like Dr Gail, willing to go above and beyond for their patients. That could never be me. You couldn't pay me all the money in the world to be a therapist.

You couldn't pay me anything to be *my* therapist.

'Thank you, Gail,' I said. 'I should be okay. Things are starting to look up now.'

She smiled sincerely. 'Just remember what I keep telling you. You have a choice in life: to control your destiny or let your destiny control you. It's all about channelling positive thoughts.' As usual, she seemed to guess what I was about to say next. 'Thank you, Sally. I will enjoy my holidays. See you in a week.'

Mummy was watching TV when I walked in. The place was as hot as a sauna. In fact, it was stifling.

I turned the heater off and opened all the windows. 'Why is the heater turned up so high, Mummy? It's not that cold.'

She looked up with a feeble expression. Her face looked craggy and rough. I was struck by her sunken cheeks, her eyelids that sagged down in tired folds, and deep lines that framed the corners of her mouth. I hadn't noticed these features before. It was as though I was looking at someone for the first time. A complete stranger.

'Are you feeling ill again?' I asked.

'I don't think I'm right, Sal, but I'll survive.'

I stared at the wall, waiting for the guilt trip to follow: Where have you been? Why are you home late? I need to eat something now, or my sugar levels will drop to dangerously low levels and I might die.

Mummy drew a deep breath but stayed silent.

I went to check on and feed Henry. He was resting in his usual corner, as placid as ever. I read that small turtles don't like hot temperatures. Henry seemed to be his normal self, which I was relieved about. How do you ask a turtle if he's too hot?

Mummy's temperature was normal, which gave me more reason to believe that her indifferent mood was being staged.

She hadn't even asked me about Myles.

We ate dinner in silence. Her strangeness had me sidetracked from my main project: to ask more questions about Gerald. It seemed like every foreseeable opportunity to do so lately was met with a roadblock. I decided to take the upper hand, just as Dr Gail advised me to.

'I thought tonight we might talk a little more about Gerald,' I said calmly.

'For heaven's sake, Sal, do we have to do this?'

Mummy's attitude wasn't the least bit surprising. Her tone was dismissive, bordering on boorish.

I had to stay the course. I was more prepared this time. 'Why don't you want this for me, Mummy? Finding Gerald might give me the closure I need.' My voice was croaky but still authoritative.

Petulant silence from across the table.

I persevered. 'What about you, Mummy? Don't you want to know what happened to him? Wouldn't you want to know what he's doing now?'

Her response was immediate and sharp. 'And why would I want that, Sal? He's the one who left me, remember? Not the other way round. Seeing him again would only stir up bad memories. Memories I've tried to erase over many years.'

'Then why did you keep his picture?' I tried hard to keep my voice calm, only partially succeeding.

No response.

'I think you'd like me to find him. I think deep down you really would.'

Mummy suddenly became animated, any ailments she may have had mysteriously disappearing. 'Okay! Okay!' she spoke brightly now, full of zeal. 'Do what you have to, Sal. But don't do it for me.' She looked away before turning back. 'Besides, what would a man like Gerald want now with a frail old woman like me?'

I took a deep breath. I couldn't let this conversation end here. I had to keep at her. 'Do you mean that, Mummy, that you will help me?'

'If it means that you'll stop annoying me about it, then yes.'

After dinner, I took out a pen and notepad, and we sat opposite each other on the couch. She remembered a lot more about Gerald this time. They met at a dance. She remembers him telling her that he grew up in Colac and went to school there, but she can't recall if he told her which school he attended.

'He was into cars,' she said. 'I think he was a mechanic or something, but my memory for that sort of detail is foggy.'

This was good. I was using the same techniques Dr Gail had used on me to force me to open up about things. She would focus on a piece of information and go off on a tangent to try to develop a new line of questioning around it. 'Did he have any friends, Mummy? Do you remember you all hanging out as a group?'

Mummy stared at me blankly. Her brow creased, and I could sense she was deep in thought. 'I really can't remember, Sal,' she said quietly. 'There were always other people around, but I can't recall any of their names.'

I was pretty sure that Mummy was telling the truth this time. She heaved a long wheezy sigh and looked frustrated, staring at the wall. This was the first time she was actually trying to help me.

I finished scribbling and put my pen down. 'It's okay, Mummy,' I said. 'I think I've got enough to get started.' I smiled to show that I appreciated what she was doing.

She nodded but didn't smile back. Her eyes suddenly sprang wide open 'There's one more thing. Gerald loved dogs. I think he had two but don't ask me to remember their names.'

CHAPTER 52

I DECIDED TO VISIT Myles again before work. This arrangement worked well as it allowed me to go straight home to Mummy after work.

We walked into a huge lounge area with tables, chairs, a couch, a large flat-screen television, and large windows looking out onto a dull and dreary Melbourne morning. Two people were watching television. Another pair sat on chairs and talked conspiratorially in low voices. They shot furtive glances in our direction as we walked past.

We settled on the couch. Myles had a gloomy expression. 'I feel like an invalid,' he said. He was wearing a standard white hospital gown, which barely covered his shoulders and was open at the back. I sensed he was beginning to get frustrated with the whole situation he found himself in.

That's how I usually feel.

'You don't look like an invalid to me,' I said in an effort to raise his spirits. He lifted his eyebrows and smiled broadly.

'Thanks for coming in, Sally. I really appreciate the company.'

Anna hadn't been in yet. Perhaps she was finalising her new accommodation.

'Have the doctors told you when you can go home?'

'Soon I hope. These days they take a much more cautious approach to head injuries.'

I nodded to convey that I understood. A heavy silence fell between us. Myles looked around the room, appearing distracted. 'I can't stop thinking about what happened,' he said. His lips scrunched up in unnatural angles, and he spoke in a forlorn voice. 'I wish I'd done more to prevent being attacked. Then I wouldn't have ended up in here.'

He hadn't volunteered anything about his ordeal before. I wanted to ask him whether he knew his attackers or if he'd done anything to provoke them, but I couldn't summon the courage to do so.

'In the end, what matters is that you'll be okay,' I said encouragingly. 'You survived, and you got to reunite with your mother.'

Myles nodded. 'I suppose I was both lucky and unlucky,' he said.

There was another silence before he spoke. 'What have you got planned for the rest of the week, Sally?'

I took a moment to formulate my answer. I told him about work, about looking after Mummy, and about trying to locate Gerald. It felt good telling someone other than Dr Gail. 'Mummy's given me a few leads, which I intend to follow up,' I explained as enthusiastically as I could. 'I don't know if Gerald is my real father, though.'

'No, you don't, but you've got to find out. All those lost years spent without your father—they were wasted years.' He looked wistfully out of the window and shook his head before smiling light-heartedly. 'You know something? It's kind of ironic,' he said.

'What is?' I asked.

'The fact that I know my father and you don't, and you're trying to find yours but I'm not.'

'But don't you want to reconnect with your father?'

Myles stared down at the floor and didn't answer. *Sally, you didn't need to pry. There may be a host of reasons why he didn't want to associate with his father, and it's none of your business.* I didn't expect him to start digging up his past just for me, talking about things that are obviously difficult for him. I know all too well how that feels.

'How's Henry?' he asked. The question immediately broke the tension.

'He's doing well,' I said. 'He's growing really fast.'

'His shell will probably change colour soon.' Myles spoke authoritatively. This was a subject he never tired of discussing. 'You'll probably see little circles appearing or even stripes, which can resemble hieroglyphics. If that happens, don't think he's sick or anything because it's normal.'

I hadn't thought about it much before, but I wondered whether having an exaggerated interest and intimate knowledge of miniature turtles might render a person slightly insane. Or at least a little strange.

'Thank you for the tip,' I said.

'If you like, I can come around and check on him when they let me out.'

I tried hard to kerb my excitement as I spoke. 'That would be nice. Thank you.'

'I might even bring some of the other turtles over to reunite with him. It will be a sort of a turtle playgroup!'

I wondered who was looking after Myles's turtles. He must have read my mind.

'My neighbour has been feeding them until Varlie can bring them down.'

I felt a hot flush sink down over my whole body, a sudden tightness in my chest, a fluttery panic, a churning in my stomach. My heart jumped. Who was Varlie? Myles hadn't mentioned her before. A female? You can never be too sure with names these days.

There were a thousand ways I could have approached this. I considered what to say but worried that my voice would portray my disappointment. I decided to stay silent and just let things roll. If Myles wanted to elaborate, he would do so without my coaxing.

He stood up and went to the window, staring out at a sky filled with rainless clouds.

'I think I can get used to this city, Sally,' he said. 'I know it's a faster, more intense pace than what I'm used to. But I'm really looking forward to living here.' He cocked his head around and looked at me with arched eyebrows. 'I'm sure Varlie is too.'

'Who's Varlie?' The words came out involuntarily as if spoken by a stranger's tongue.

Myles did not portray any sign to indicate that he was the least bit uncomfortable with what I just asked him. He sat down and began telling me about Varlie. Yes, she was a girl. They met a few weeks ago at the gym where she had recently started as a personal trainer. They got talking; and it turned out that she, like me, was a lover of animals and wildlife documentaries. The next day she was introduced to the turtles and the rest, as they say in the classics, is history.

'She's really smart, Sally. I'm sure the two of you will get along well.' Myles went on to explain how Varlie's position at the gym was only temporary and that she wanted to come to Melbourne for better employment opportunities. 'Isn't it funny how things work out?' There was a distinctive excitement in his voice. 'Who would ever have thought that Varlie and I would end up here together?'

So serendipity really *does* exist. It was rearing its head everywhere.

As Myles continued speaking about his good fortune, an extraordinary calm descended over me, a lucidity beyond anything I'd felt before. It all seemed so obvious. I realised that this secret microcosm of existence I'd manufactured for him and me was never meant to be. He doesn't know the real Sally Cartwright; I hadn't told him any of the stuff that I'd told Declan.

I bared my soul to the wrong man.

I couldn't help thinking that if I'd given into his initial advances, if I'd responded to his suggestive caress, then maybe there could have been a sliver of hope and Varlie would not exist in his life beyond barbells and exercise mats.

All the time I spent with Myles felt natural and uncomplicated by the personal spites and grudges that infected the outside world. But a love that did not advance could never renew itself. Who am I to deny this man happiness, even though I myself couldn't be happy?

Love for me appeared to be just a chemical state—something that was messing with my mind.

It could have been all so easy. But Sally Cartwright doesn't do easy.

I tried to be upbeat. 'That's a touching story!' I said with just a little too much eagerness. 'Will Varlie be staying with you?'

Myles shook his head 'She knows a lot of people here. She'll be staying at a share house for now.' There was a sense of inevitability in his voice, indicating that he hoped she would one day move in with him. 'I haven't told Mum about her yet,' he added.

I nodded but said nothing. My mind was clinging to the faint hope that the reason he hadn't mentioned Varlie to his mother was that he was still deciding between her and me.

That thought would be misguided.

We began talking about the type of apartment he might like. 'Two bedrooms minimum,' he declared. 'Three would be better. And a balcony. I've always wanted a balcony. It would be so cool to just sit out and watch people going about their daily business. City people are so much more interesting than country folk, don't you think so?'

Of course I don't. A little tear formed on the side of my nose and trickled ever so slowly down my cheek. I surreptitiously wiped it away with my finger before Myles had time to notice. 'Oh, I don't know,' I said. 'I've heard that living in the city can make some people miserable.'

Myles looked at me a little disbelievingly. 'Are you serious? You don't look miserable.'

Don't judge a book until you've read it, young man.

He looked through the window again. 'No, I'm going to like it here,' he said.

I imagined him and Varlie exploring the hipster culture of inner Melbourne together and slowly becoming ingrained into its fabric and into each other.

I couldn't compete with that.

Anna appeared out of nowhere, slightly out of breath. She was holding a large shopping bag. 'Hello, dear!' Her tone was overly cheerful as she placed the bag on the floor and leaned over to kiss her son on the cheek.

'You've bought groceries?' Myles leaned over to look into the bag.

She smiled broadly. 'Yes. As well as good news. We've got our very own apartment!' Before her son had time to say anything, she pulled out a small envelope from her handbag and unfolded a map. She explained that the apartment was only a short walk from the hospital and had three bedrooms. Myles gave me a wry smile.

'Isn't it exciting?' Her eyes were as wide as saucers. 'I've got enough saved up for the bond, and we can easily meet the rent once we both find work.'

MARIO BORAZIO

Myles nodded like an excitable dog. 'That's great, Mum!' He turned to stare at me. 'Isn't it, Sally?'

I nodded unemotionally. He came and sat beside me, which made me feel awkward. To be near yet not to touch.

'Oh, Sally, I'm so sorry.' Anna hadn't acknowledged my presence until now. 'I got so caught up with all the excitement of our new place I hadn't noticed you there. How are you?'

'I'm fine thanks.' I should have congratulated her on procuring the apartment, but my emotions were too raw. I was caught between timidity and despondency.

I slowly stood up and took a few steps before stopping short. 'I've got to get to work now,' I said. 'I'm late as it is.'

Myles tugged at his sleeves and adjusted the back of his gown. 'Thanks for coming, Sally. Will I see you again tomorrow?'

Maybe you will. Maybe you won't.

I gave a noncommittal nod and left without answering.

*

Work turned out to be a drag. I couldn't seem to concentrate. My brain was like a cracked vessel that doesn't hold water. I knew I wasn't at my best and was paranoid that my colleagues would notice.

I kept looking up at the clock. The hands were moving as slow as molasses. Mike was soon standing at my desk. He didn't bother sitting down.

'Sally.' His tone possessed no joviality. 'This is the third day running that you're late. It's not like you. Not like you at all.' He folded his arms, awaiting an explanation.

This was my time to shine. My time to make Dr Gail proud. To make myself proud. I should've come clean and told my boss everything about my domestic circumstances. But I was in a moping mood. I don't like it when bad thoughts take over. I can't flip the script. Finding out that Myles had a love interest was definitely a bad thought even though I'd already accepted the fact that that was how it was meant to play out.

I opened the window of my heart to let light in, but all I saw were dark clouds.

'Well, Sally?' Mike's voice was laced with sandpaper. This was not a place I'd been to before, having to explain my actions like this. I felt trapped, helpless. It was like trying to get out of a car with my seatbelt still on.

The camaraderie we'd developed seemed to have been totally dismantled.

I should've apologised, begged forgiveness, and promised to make good from now on. But I didn't do that.

'I'm sorry, Mr Cosgrove. My alarm didn't go off again.'

Mike looked down to the ground before raising his head. His expression was cold, pensive. He leaned forward and rested his fingers on the desk. 'Sally, this is your last warning. I like you, I really do. But I didn't promote you just because I like you. You earned this job because I thought you were the most suitable person for it. Please don't prove me wrong.'

He turned on his heels and walked off without uttering another word. I was breathing heavily and could hear the air whooshing in and out of my nose.

I felt another panic attack coming.

CHAPTER 53

MUMMY SAID SHE wasn't hungry. She had taken to eating in her room lately. I didn't mind this new arrangement. It gave me time and space to think.

She didn't as much as look at the food in front of her and continued to stare straight ahead. She sat still as a statue for what seemed an eternity before letting out a short grunt. I said nothing and tried to ignore her little performance.

'I've had a bad day, Sal.' As she lifted her hand to her forehead, I noticed a dark bruise on her wrist.

'How did you get that bruise, Mummy?'

She folded her arms defensively and locked her eyes on mine with a look that was all too familiar. 'How did I get it? Wouldn't you like to know.'

I hated it when Mummy played games like this. Keeping me guessing was one of her more gratifying indulgences. I stared at her without emotion until she got the hint.

'I'll tell you in a minute,' she said. 'But first I need to tell you something else.'

'Oh? And what's that?'

'I want to go back home. Back to Colac. Before it's too late.'

The statement seemed to float past me and disappear, as though it wasn't meant for my ears. 'What did you say, Mummy?'

I understood perfectly well what she'd said. Her speech was now almost back to normal, the drawl all but gone.

'You heard me. I want to go back home.' She gave me a look of indifference, defiance. I knew she wasn't joking.

'But why? I thought you liked it here.'

Her stymied laugh came out as a chortle. 'Huh, I thought I did. But not anymore. I know I'm a pitiful case, Sal, but let me tell you what happened.' She grasped her bruised wrist with her opposite hand and recounted her tale. She was walking down the street when a young man sneaked up behind her and tried to snatch her bag. Had the strap not got tangled around her wrist, she explained, the perpetrator might well have succeeded in his mission. 'They're all a bunch of rotten half-breeds and degenerates out here, Sal. I don't need to put up with them.

'Not to mention the noise from upstairs. There are clearly some shenanigans going on up there, even if you don't believe me.' She lifted her head as she spoke. 'That's why I have to get out. The sooner the better. Otherwise I'll end up losing my mind!'

I couldn't believe what Mummy was saying. Was she just being a touch melodramatic?

My thoughts felt like they were thrashing around inside a salad spinner. I was momentarily speechless.

'Oh, for God's sake, Sal', she blustered, 'are you going to pretend that you're shocked? This has been coming for a while. You should have seen it.'

'No, I'm not shocked, Mummy. I—' Words escaped me. Maybe I *was* shocked.

Silence followed.

'It's not that easy, Mummy,' I eventually said, trying to remain calm. 'You don't have a place to go to, remember?'

Mummy was working herself into such a state now that she began coughing and gasping. She retrieved a puffer from her bag and began drawing in its goodness. Her breathing soon slowed and became shallower. 'I'll find something', she eventually said, 'Even if I have to end up at the charity wards of the Salvos or Vinnies. I don't care.'

A hush fell over us, and the only sound was that of the clock ticking. Mummy sat staring straight ahead with her hands knotted in her lap. Her shoulders narrowed, and for a moment, she appeared shrunken.

I could see in her eyes that she wanted my approval of her decision. Maybe she was right; going back to live in the country was exactly what she needed. With the help of the occupational therapist, the physiotherapist, and some speech therapy, she had made excellent progress, more than anyone would have ever expected.

MARIO BORAZIO

I don't think she'll have any trouble living on her own again.

They say that couples who get divorced get on a whole lot better afterwards. Maybe Mummy and I needed a divorce.

'Okay, Mummy', I said, 'I think the country is where you really belong.'

'You do? That's great, Sal! But you have to help me look for another place. That stuff about the Salvos, I was only joking. I really need my own place again. Just me on my own.'

Mummy went to her room, and I decided to take a shower. As I undressed, I stared into the bathtub. I rarely take baths because, as I've alluded to, I find them boring. How does one not get bored while taking a bath? I've heard people on television talk about the bathtub being like a cocoon, a place for relaxation and self-care. They talk about meditating while in the bath, of lighting scented candles, and listening to 'healing' music. But what would that achieve? The person coming out of the bath will always be the same one that got in, only a little cleaner.

It will take a lot to heal me tonight. I decided to give the bath one more chance.

I rested the back of my head on the discoloured tiles of the tub and closed my eyes. I had a lot to think about. Finding Mummy a place would mean taking time off work. Given my recent history of unpunctuality, I had to adroitly broach the topic of my leave entitlements with Mike.

And I wouldn't be seeing Myles for a while. This could be a good thing. It would allow him and Varlie some space.

I could even spend a few days trying to trace Gerald while Mummy settled in.

As I wiped the steam from the vanity mirror, I studied the face staring back at me. My face. Twenty-six years, two hundred and fifteen days, fourteen hours, and eleven minutes old. I couldn't help noticing the way my skin stretched across my cheekbones, how my jaw sagged right down to my throat, and how sunken and dull my eyes were. There was something strangely hypnotic about looking into my own eyes.

If I were to ever pen a painful memoir about my damaged life, this moment would have to be included.

CHAPTER 54

UNABLE TO SLEEP again, I stared up at the ceiling and imagined a sky filled with stars. Do stars really have five points? No. They're round like the earth, and most of them are significantly bigger. Our sun is a star.

I imagined the stars scattered like powder across the dark sky. There were so many of them, a stark reminder of our insignificance on this earth.

As I continued staring upwards, I pretended there was a star up there reserved just for me, one I could wish upon. I wished that life could be a whole lot easier. But believing that life could be so straightforward was often a ground pass to dissatisfaction and depression.

I needed my star to guide me away from all that.

I decided not to visit Myles today.

*

Dr Gail's office looked different. To my right, a vase of wilting flowers had deposited its ochre petals onto the desk. Usually, they'd be fresh and bright, but they hadn't been watered for a week. They reflected exactly how I felt: *Don't mind us,* they'd be saying. *Just leave us to die in peace.* To my left sat a small tacky porcelain elephant. It was shiny yellow and spotted all over with tiny purple hearts. I assumed it was a souvenir from Dr Gail's holiday.

Dr Gail appeared refreshed. Her skin had a renewed radiance, which matched her smile. She quickly sensed my gloominess.

'Something's up. Why didn't you call me?'

I didn't answer her.

'How is your garden?'

'Full of weeds again,' I announced despondently.

She shook her head and threw me a tragic look. 'Okay. Do you want to talk about it?'

'I don't know where to begin,' I said.

She slid the tissue box closer. The mild scent of eucalyptus was strangely pleasurable today. 'Begin anywhere you like, Sally.'

I needed to explain that, like a severed head of Hydra, delicate situations kept coming back up, and I was unable to deal with them despite being assured that I had the tools to do so. I felt so lost. I was like a path losing itself in an overgrowth of scrambling shrub. The positivity I was emboldened with had all but evaporated.

I took a deep breath and told her everything, clutching at a fresh tissue every time tears threatened. I told her about how it ended with Declan. I told her about Myles and how he has a girlfriend and how I could have been that girlfriend if only I'd been more receptive to his initial advances. I told her about how I hadn't been able to get any closer to Mummy and how she was going back home to live. I told her about work and how unproductive I'd become. I told her about how I hadn't made any progress tracking down Gerald.

In short, I told her how Sally Cartwright had failed in all the challenges she was meant to conquer, about how her mind was presently a scrambled mess.

I needed the world to know that the positional relationship between the cart and the horse was presently unknown to yours truly.

Dr Gail stared sympathetically and gave me a quick hard smile. 'Aren't you going to ask me about my holiday?'

Part of me wanted to break out into a sobbing fit just to garner some sympathy. But that would be childish. That's what Mummy would do, and I didn't want to be like Mummy. 'Okay', I said in a strained tone, 'how was your break, Gail?'

'I'm glad you asked. We had great fun. Here, take a look!' She spoke excitedly as she opened up her phone to show me some photos. She made the odd comment as she scrolled each picture across the screen. One shot showed a burly man standing in front of an old cottage proudly holding a fishing line with a big fish on the end of it. Another showed two young children in a canoe on a lake splashing water at each other. There was a family picture of two adults and two children. In it, Dr Gail was wearing a white dress, and the reflecting sun was making her squint her eyes and distorting her smile. Behind the family was a pier, vivid against a bright blue sky. All the people look tanned, healthy, happy. I imagined myself in that photo, proud to be standing next to my husband and children.

That was the most outlandish scenario imaginable.

I slid Dr Gail's phone across the desk. 'You must've had a wonderful time,' I said with forced enthusiasm.

'We did. And we needed this break, Sally, believe me. My husband and I both have stressful jobs. He's an architect for a big firm. We work long hours and don't spend near-enough time with our children. This was the perfect time for the four of us to reconnect.'

I never imagined Dr Gail's work to be stressful. She always appeared to be in total control. But I'm not walking in her shoes.

As was her way, she managed to link her holiday to my current situation. 'Think of your helping your mother to find a new place to live as a sort of a holiday, Sally. It can be a real opportunity for the two of you to bond.'

I nodded and felt the muscles on the back of my neck knotted and clenched. I could also feel a headache coming on. Dr Gail kept talking, but I dropped my gaze to the floor, barely able to concentrate. Her words seemed to float past me and disappear into thin air.

As the session came to a close and I stood up to leave, she had a few parting words. 'Just remember, Sally', she said, 'you and your mother can build something special in the next few days. Don't let this opportunity slip.'

As I waited for the bus home, I had an odd sense of relief as well as a lingering sadness. I was relieved to be out of Dr Gail's rooms, but I also felt guilty for feeling so miserable. Between the dying flowers and the gaudy elephant, today's session was mostly unfulfilled. It's so easy for her to say that Mummy and I can become closer after our 'holiday' together. If I could flick a switch to make that happen, I'd do it right now.

It wasn't that simple.

MARIO BORAZIO

My phone buzzed just as I boarded the bus. As I took a seat near the rear and glanced at the number, my face became drained of blood.

It couldn't be, could it?

'Hello?'

'Hello, is this Sally Cartwright?'

'Speaking.'

'Hi, Sally, I'm calling from YouTube Australia. Congratulations! Your latest video post has had—'

I could feel blood rushing to my head and I exploded. 'I'm sick of this, so fucking sick of it! Do you hear me?'

There was a long pause. 'Excuse me? Sally?'

I hung up. With trembling fingers, I checked for any new videos. There was one.

As I began watching, my throat tightened, and I was unable to breathe.

The video was extremely clear. A knife was being held to Mummy's neck.

CHAPTER 55

M Y STOMACH WAS clenched as hard as a rock, and my heart was beating so fast I thought I was going to pass out right there on the bus. I closed my eyes and thought hard about what just happened. Crazy thing number one: according to Dr Gail's theory, I would have got my timelines all mixed up again. Crazy thing number two: if I *did* take the video in real time, why would I not have helped Mummy when she was in obvious danger?

Maybe I didn't want to help her.

I raced home, breathless from running the whole way from the bus stop. Just as I was turning the corner to my block, I slipped on some gravel and skinned my knee. The stinging pain was pushed to one side as I got back up and sprinted to my front door. As I shakily put the key in the lock, my mind was consumed by a horrible blend of apprehension and dread. What will I find when I go inside?

Best not to overthink anything.

Everything was quiet. Eerily quiet.

I took a desperate look around the lounge room. Nothing looked disturbed. 'Mummy! Are you alright?'

She was slouched on the couch, reading a magazine. Her rumpled dress had brown stains on the front.

'What took you so long, Sal? Did you need a double session today?' There was a sarcastic tone to Mummy's voice and a sardonic lift of her eyebrows as she looked up at me with an incorrigible smile. 'My goodness, you look like you've seen a ghost!'

I waited a few seconds for my breathing to slow before leaning over and pulling her up to a sitting position. 'Sit still, Mummy.' Before she had time to protest, I braced my hands around her temples and began turning her head from side to side, examining her neck. Apart from the flaccid skin, it was unblemished. I parted her wispy hair and gently lifted small tufts of hair all around her skull. No head wounds or dried blood. I lifted and examined both arms as well as her chest. Not a single scratch. I took a deep breath and slumped onto the chair opposite, not really knowing what to feel at this moment. Of all the things I'd expected, all the scenarios I'd gone through in my head, this was the ideal outcome: Mummy safe and sound. I felt my temples relaxing, my jaw loosening, and my heart slowing. 'Sorry, Mummy', I said, 'I had to check that you were okay.'

'What …?' Mummy hesitated before continuing. 'What's brought all this on, Sal? Was it something your shrink told you to do?'

I should've told her about the video, but I couldn't bring myself to do it.

I shook my head and shuddered slightly. 'Do you remember when you told me that someone tried to snatch your bag, Mummy?'

'Of course I remember,' she said while rubbing her wrist exaggeratedly. 'How could I forget it? That's a great memory I'll leave this place with, I can tell you.'

'Do you remember anything else, Mummy? Was the person holding anything? Like a knife?'

'What?' Mummy's face hardened. 'No. Of course not. What gave you that idea?'

'I'm sorry. I … I didn't mean to—' I couldn't finish my sentence.

Mummy sat back looking smug. She took great pleasure in seeing me frazzled. I could tell she was holding back a victorious smile. 'Honestly, Sal, I'm beginning to wonder if all those therapy sessions are doing you any good at all. Or if, in fact, they are scrambling things around in that head of yours. I mean, look at you,' I must've looked like one of those homeless people I keep seeing outside the Fancy Chef. My hair was a dishevelled mess, and my shirt had dirt marks all over it. My right knee was bleeding, and my palms had little bits of gravel embedded into the skin from bracing my fall.

Mummy looked mischievous as she lay back on the couch, crooking one knee up and resting a hand on it. She gazed down to my leg, which was caked in dried blood. 'You look like you've been in a fight. Care to tell me what happened?'

I didn't answer. I took a step back to gather my thoughts. 'Mummy, listen to me. I think you were right. I'm getting a bad vibe about this place too. I think you shouldn't go out anymore. I think you should keep the door locked whenever I'm out.'

She propped herself up and smiled, the corners of her eyes crinkling. 'Well, this *is* a change, isn't it? I probably should be grateful for your concern.'

You should be, but I know you won't.

'I'll call the real estate agent tomorrow morning and have you back home soon,' I said. 'I promise.'

'That would be nice.'

I had no idea what I should do, so I just lay on the bed. Sitting with my back against the pillow, I eventually fell asleep and had a dream. I was in an open field looking up at the stars. Suddenly they began to fall like confetti at my feet. The sky became totally black; and as I stared up at it, I felt lost. This made me scared. Scared of the world. Scared of all the people in it. Scared of feeling vulnerable all the time. The only safe haven seemed to be right here on my own.

I woke from my dream, relieved that it wasn't a reality. The clock showed it was almost three o'clock. I tried to go back to sleep, but that was impossible. All I kept thinking about was Mummy and that video.

I looked in the direction of my phone, which sat in its charger. In the dark, all that was discernible was the green charge light.

'You should, Sally,' I told myself. Of course I should. Just to be sure. It would make it right. I picked up the phone and scrolled through my phone records.

The phone call I received yesterday didn't exist.

I scrolled through my videos. The one of Mummy's house razed to the ground was still there.

Yesterday's video was not.

MARIO BORAZIO

CHAPTER 56

MY INABILITY TO focus on my work seemed to be the normal course of events lately. As I sat at my desk and stared aimlessly at my computer screen, my mind was racing faster than ever. I thought about how Mummy would be coping cooped up indoors - I'd double-locked the front door from the outside. At least she had Henry for company. I thought about how I was going to broach the subject of my leave entitlements with Mike. I thought about ringing the real estate agent in Colac. I thought about Myles. I thought about Gerald.

I thought about getting my licence—as if that's ever going to happen.

Most of all, I thought about the video of Mummy and the knife. Where had it gone? It couldn't just float away into the ether. If it did somehow get erased, could I still retrieve it? Suddenly my limited knowledge of the workings of a mobile phone seemed a real bugbear. Then I had an idea. I should ask one of the bright tech guys here at work to look into the problem. I'm sure they can help me.

I ambled over to the tea room and pretended to make myself a coffee. I don't drink coffee. Clutching a cup of plain hot water, I meandered through the front office space. The pain in my right knee only served to accentuate my pre-existing limp, but that was of little concern to me right now. I was searching for someone—anyone who didn't appear overly busy. Most of the staff had their heads buried in their screens and didn't acknowledge my presence. The few who did all gave me perplexed glances. Some put their hands to their mouths and whispered something to a nearby colleague after I'd walked past them. Their behaviour wasn't at all surprising; Sally Cartwright is never seen in these parts.

The hairs on the back of my neck were standing to attention, and nervousness overwhelmed me. I was about to abort my mission when a high-pitched voice pierced my eardrums.

'Sally! What are you doing up here?'

It was the unmistakable tone of Casey's voice. She and Wilma were leaning against a set of filing cabinets, each holding a cup.

I was hoping to avoid them.

'Hello, Casey. Hello, Wilma.' I felt compelled to explain myself. 'I'm just stretching my legs!' I said with forced fervour and a contrived smile.

They both looked down at my bandaged knee. I inwardly scolded myself for not wearing pants today.

'Jesus, are you all right, girl?'

'I'm fine. I had a slight fall, that's all.'

They gave only the barest nods of sympathy. Casey pulled a face and pushed some hair behind her ear. 'This is so cool!' she said animatedly. 'Here we are, back in our old routine, shooting the breeze and talking about life in general. What a blast! It's a pity Rob isn't with us. Did you hear, Sally? He left. Got a job somewhere else.'

Good for him, I thought.

Wilma chimed in, 'Yeah, good riddance I say. But even with Rob gone, it's still shitty where we are, Sal. The new girl's nowhere near as good as you were. Casey and me, we always have to pick up the slack.'

Now they know how I felt.

I should've shown some empathy, but all I could think about was getting someone to look at my phone. 'I'm sure you'll both get through it,' I said. 'You always seem to.' I looked up at the clock on the wall. 'Is that the time? I'd better get back to my office. It was nice talking to you both.' Casey gave a humourless laugh, and Wilma waved a stiff hand as I turned to leave.

Back in the office, the stiffness in my knee began to ease gradually, which was a great relief. I stared at my phone, contemplating my next move. There was no way I was going to risk anyone here looking at it, not now with Casey and Wilma snooping around.

I had a thought: I'll go back to where I bought the phone. What was his name? Thomas. I'll pay him a visit in my lunch break.

It didn't scare me. It used to, but it doesn't anymore. I strode confidently into the department store and made my way to the area that stocked mobile phones and computers. In a sort of perverse way, I was looking forward to seeing Thomas again. We'd left on first-name terms.

I looked through every aisle but couldn't see him anywhere. I can't recall exactly what he looked like, but the pizza face would be a dead giveaway.

I searched the aisles a second time without success. This was indeed deflating. A wash of anger and frustration came over me. I was forced into seeking advice from another shop assistant.

She was young with a bubbly charm and introduced herself as Tamara. I explained my situation as clearly as I could. 'I need to know where my video has ended up. It must be there somewhere. I hope you can help me.'

'You say you purchased the phone from us. Do you have your receipt?'

I glared at her, still clutching my phone. For a moment, I thought she might just walk away. 'I think it's at home,' I said. 'I know who I spoke to though. His name was Thomas.'

Tamara nodded, and I noticed her cheeks were streaked with makeup from where she must've dragged fingers down. I wondered if she'd been crying. 'Thomas no longer works here,' she said matter-of-factly. 'But I may be able to help you. May I have your phone?'

Finding out that Thomas was no longer in the employ of this store rendered me slightly flat, but I couldn't afford to dwell on that feeling right now. I handed Tamara my phone.

'What's your PIN code?'

My what? 'Sorry, I don't know what that is,' I sheepishly admitted.

She stared at me with some incredulity before tapping on the screen and looking up with a wide grin. 'That was easy,' she said. 'You don't have one.'

I could have saved her the trouble.

She began scrolling across the screen, occasionally tapping it again. Watching her was akin to watching an accomplished pianist effortlessly gliding his fingers across the piano keys.

The next few minutes went by agonizingly slowly. Tamara eventually closed the screen and gave me back my phone. 'There's only that one video of a house fire in there. There's nothing else.'

Her words stung like a festering sore. My face must've looked blank, shell-shocked. 'Are you sure, Tamara? I mean, did you look in all the places that you should have looked in?'

She gave me another incredulous look and rolled her eyes. 'I looked everywhere. Even in the cloud.'

I wanted to ask her what the water vapour in the air had to do with my phone but decided against it for fear of embarrassing myself.

'It's not there.' Her tone had a finality attached to it.

I started to cry, demonstrating to this girl with devastating clarity just how delicate a flower I really was. 'I see,' I said dispiritedly through faint sobs. 'Thank you for your help, Tamara.' I was shaking like a leaf as I left the store.

MARIO BORAZIO

CHAPTER 57

M Y PHONE LOOKED dead in my hands. Once it became clear that yesterday's video could not be revived, it felt like all life had been sucked out of it. I could easily make a coffin for it.

Did I dream everything up? According to Dr Gail, when we are most susceptible to stress, depression, or anxiety, our minds can play tricks on us. I certainly hadn't imagined the videos of the blown-up homeless man, the falling mirror ball, or the house fire—they were all there. Still real and accessible at the press of a button. But the calls forewarning me of those tragedies were not. Never were. Maybe, as Dr Gail theorised, it *was* me who took those videos; and the calls from Ms YouTube forewarning me of the impending tragedies were just a figment of my imagination, a way for my brain to contrive a totally fantastical scenario.

What about Declan thanking me for saving him from the falling mirror ball? Was he just being polite? And what about the fresh image of someone holding a knife to Mummy's throat? That could have just been an image my brain conceived. I wondered if there was anything subliminal in that.

And just to add fuel to the already-raging fire, Dr Gail suggested that all this delusional mess might be emanating from my childhood.

Tormenting myself with these thoughts wasn't going to achieve anything. I had other pressing things to attend to. Back at work, I closed the office door and looked up the names of a couple of real estate agents in Colac. Mummy said she wasn't fussed about what her new place looked like as long as it was on the ground floor and not too far from the town centre.

'Are you sure you don't want me to send you any photos?'

'No. What you described is exactly what my mother is looking for. Thank you.' The man had an honest voice. He explained that, to our good fortune, the previous tenants had left a bed and some furniture as well as a refrigerator and a washing machine. This was going to save Mummy thousands of dollars.

I gave the agent my details and arranged the bond. The paperwork would be all settled in a few days, and Mummy could move in as early as next Monday.

My next task was to convince Mike to give me some time off. This could be a frosty conversation given my less-than-impressive recent record of punctuality, not to mention my decreased productivity. In my more optimistic moods, I kept telling myself that he'd understand. I've got credits in the bank, and that should surely count for something.

The timing couldn't have been worse. Mike strode into my office but didn't close the door. 'We are heading into a major restructure next week,' he announced. 'I need all hands on deck. That includes you, Sally.'

Exactly what I didn't want to hear. I nodded, trying not to look too rattled.

I had my hands on my lap under the desk and squeezed them into two tight fists to try to control my tension and to look as normal as possible. 'A restructure?' My voice sounded feeble.

'Yes. It's been on the cards for months. If you had attended last week's meeting, you would have learnt about it.'

I didn't attend that meeting. Or any meeting since my promotion. My attendance at such meetings was a stipulation in my contract, but I hadn't kept up my end of the bargain.

I explained how Mummy needed to go home and how it was all arranged for next Monday. 'She's frail, Mr Cosgrove. I have to help her.'

Mike moved to the edge of my desk and jammed his hands in his pockets in an act of frustration. His top lip curled upward as he spoke. 'Sally, I can't give you any time off. Not next week.'

I smiled tightly, trying to procure some sympathy, but Mike's eyes remained stern and locked on mine for a long time. I could tell he was mulling over something. The silence felt awkward and clumsy. His mouth eventually curled up slightly at the corners. 'When did you say your mother was moving back?'

MARIO BORAZIO

'Monday.'

'I'll tell you what, I'll give you Monday off. But that's it.'

Okay, that was a good compromise. I could get Mummy settled and be home by Monday evening. I wouldn't have time to search for Gerald. That would have to wait.

'Thank you, Mr Cosgrove. I'll be back at work on Tuesday morning. You have my word.'

Mike turned on his heels and walked out with a faint smile. There was a heart-stopping moment as I spotted Wilma heading towards me. She had a condescending smile on her face as she stood in the doorway.

'No, Wilma,' I said with a tired sigh. 'Everything's just fine.'

CHAPTER 58

MUMMY INSISTED ON packing her Anglepoise lamp. Other than clothing, it was the only item she'd purchased since moving in here. She used it for reading in bed.

Her entire possessions, including the lamp, her clothes, and her medications, were accommodated neatly into one suitcase.

'Have you a suitable box to take Henry in, dear?' she spoke like an excited child.

'Yes, Mummy.' Although I was only going to be away for one day, I decided to take Henry with me. He will be housed in his original perforated cardboard box. This will be akin to moving out of the Ritz and into a shanty, but I know he won't mind. If he could speak, I'm sure he'd tell me as much.

Henry would be my security blanket for this trip.

While we waited for the taxi to arrive, I ruminated whether to call Myles. We do share a passion for miniature turtles after all, and he did mention that he wanted to come and visit Henry.

Even so, I had my doubts about calling. I'd invented a scenario as a way of distracting my mind from thinking about him: you meet someone, you feel an attraction, then you spend some time with them, and you realise that the attraction is only skin deep so you move on.

I imagined Myles and I becoming incompatible. Still, I was unable to completely bed down this idea. His memory kept filtering its way back into my brain, and I was helpless to ignore it.

I wondered whether he was still in the hospital or settled in with his mother. I imagined him being all better and taking long walks with Varlie, the two of them walking hand in hand, lost in each other's eyes. I could bleed an ocean of tears at that thought.

Informing Myles that I would be out of town would be the perfect excuse to call.

He changed his message:

> "Hi, you've reached Myles Bennett. Please leave a message, and I'll get back to you when I can."

I've read that most people get nervous about leaving a voicemail. The oft-used term is *performance anxiety*. I knew only too well what that felt like.

First things first: I'd never left a voice message before. There was that one opportunity with Nicole, but I chickened out. That wasn't going to happen this time.

> "Hello, Myles, this is Sally Cartwright speaking. Just calling to let you know I'll be away until Tuesday."

That was it. No goodbye. Nothing portraying my concern as to his well-being. No enquiry about where he was. Pathetic I know, but I'm sure he'll call back. He's a decent human being.

The taxi arrived right on time. It was a crisp and cloudless autumn morning. Mummy was behaving like an excitable child on a school excursion. I'm sure I heard her squeal as she got into the backseat.

We were in Colac by lunchtime. I winced as I read the amount on the driver's metre but wasn't the least bit surprised given my past experiences. I paid without making a fuss.

Taxis truly are a licence to print money.

The real estate agent met us at the front door of Mummy's new place located just a few blocks north of the city centre. It was of modest size and smelled of damp. The floors were bare, and the walls had cracks. The paint was coming off in flakes. There were two bedrooms with a divan bed and a wicker chair occupying the larger one. The lounge and dining areas had a small table with two chairs and a scruffy beige couch. The kitchen looked tired and run-down, but at least there was a dishwasher and, as promised, an old refrigerator. The washing machine in the laundry looked ancient but still worked. The unmodernised bathroom had a small bathtub with a rusty showerhead and a threadbare mat.

It was plain to see that the agent had embellished some of the features of this occupancy.

The whole place was in dire need of some tender, loving care. Was my mother the person to provide it? I doubted it but held on to the faint hope that she might prove me wrong.

Mummy looked truly happy. The first thing she did was go to the window and wind up the blind. It was a startlingly beautiful day. She gasped at the stunning view across a slice of the countryside. The sky was a rich blue, the grass a lush green, and the trees seemed to whisper gently as they swayed in the breeze.

Seeing Mummy smile made me feel both deflated and relieved. Although she tried my patience at times, I will miss having her around. It had been comforting knowing that I wasn't waking up to an empty house, knowing I could take a moment to talk to someone before going to work.

But I knew this was the place where she'd be most happy.

'It's lovely, dear, isn't it?'

I nodded and gave a feeble smile.

Once we were settled, we walked into town to buy some essentials: a toaster, a kettle, some pots and pans, a few plates, glasses, cutlery, some storage containers, cleaning products, essential toiletries, and, of course, groceries. Mummy even insisted on paying for everything.

We had crepes for lunch, and she insisted on paying for them too.

Back at the unit, I fed Henry before organising a doctor's appointment for Mummy. I'd convinced her to give Dr Rickards the flick and start afresh with a new doctor at a different surgery. I collated a list of all her medications and wrote them all down, as best I could, to match each of her medical conditions. This would be more-than-enough information for a new doctor to get started on.

Mummy went to lie down after we'd put away all the shopping. I sat on the couch and checked my phone for messages or missed calls. There were none.

I was still of the belief that Myles will call me back.

Mummy was soon fast asleep. It was still two hours before my taxi was due to pick me up for the long ride home. I decided to take this opportunity to venture into town one last time. With the restructuring happening at work and Mike breathing down my neck, who knows when I'd be back here again.

Instead of walking down Fyans Street directly into the city centre, I decided to cut through the botanic gardens as the day was so glorious.

The gardens were a palette of greens, one that would impress any of the old masters. There was an easy grace in the air as I strolled past couples lying on lush lawns, people sitting on benches taking in the warmth of the sun, and children frolicking and laughing under the watchful eyes of proud parents. The whole scene was one of a joyful community at play.

Mummy never brought me here.

As I was approaching the west side of the gardens onto Gellibrand Street, I spotted an overweight middle-aged man walking his dog. His breath was laboured, and there was a vague expression of pain as well as sweat on his face. I watched eagerly as he almost stumbled onto a park bench and took a crumpled tissue from his pocket before opening it. He took out a small tablet and put it under his tongue. He was still heaving long breaths as he bent over and patted his dog who was staring intently at its master.

'Would you like some water?' I might as well have been invisible because the man took no notice of me and continued staring straight ahead.

'Excuse me, sir, would you like some water?' My voice was stronger this time.

The man flinched and squinted in my direction with an impassive expression. 'No, thank you. I'll be fine once I catch my breath.' His voice sounded wheezy.

My brain stuttered for a moment as I processed the image in front of me. Surely it couldn't be. Mummy's photograph of Gerald was ingrained in my mind. My mathematical brain had memorised the angles and proportions of that face. The face staring back at me now, although weather-beaten and older, bore a striking resemblance. The close-set eyes, the slightly turned-up nose, the curled lips, and the prominent brow. They were all perfect matches. All lines meeting at exactly the right points.

It couldn't be a coincidence.

My face felt like stone as I moved in closer and tentatively offered my water bottle. The man shrugged and begrudgingly took it with a calloused hand.

'Thank you, miss.' He took a gulp and handed it back to me. 'What's your name?' His breath was less laboured, and his voice wasn't wheezy anymore.

'I'm Sally,' I said waveringly as I set the bottle down at my feet.

The man slouched back on the bench and tightened the hold on his dog's lead. 'I'm Gerald Tate. Everyone calls me Gerry.'

MARIO BORAZIO

CHAPTER 59

T HE OLD SALLY Cartwright would've ended things right there, almost twenty-seven fatherless years destined to remain that way. I kept staring at this man's face; the more I stared, the more I was convinced that he was every inch the man in that photograph.

'Are you alright, miss?'

The words were a towline back to consciousness. I must've gone pale. I felt the blood drain from my face as I tried to work out what to say.

Gerry stared at me for a few moments more, waiting for a reply.

'I'm fine thanks,' I stuttered. 'Can I ask you a question?'

Gerry nodded as he wiped his brow, which was bathed in the bright sunlight. 'Now that I've got my breath back, you can ask away.'

I didn't know how to phrase what I wanted to say. Then I remembered something Mummy told me about the man she knew as Gerald. 'Are you a mechanic?'

Gerry looked down and shook his head. 'I used to be. Until those bastards took my shop away. Are you an old client? Is that where you know me from?'

I stood on the walking path and looked around, my heart pounding like a bass drum. 'No, we've never met before, but you may know my mother. Her name is Eve Cartwright.'

Gerry stared straight past me with a neutral expression. 'Eve Cartwright.' The words were enunciated slowly as they usually are when one is trying to recall a person or some event from the past. 'Can't say that I do. And you say you're her daughter?'

My heart was still thudding. 'Yes. I'm a Cartwright too. My mother knew a man named Gerald before I was born. She showed me a photograph, and you look just like the man in it.'

Gerry let out a loud and hearty laugh, his breath becoming a little wheezy again. 'We all look alike around here, miss. It's a small town.'

What are you doing, Sally? Just come out with it. 'Mummy—my mother thinks this man she knew, Gerald, could be my father.'

Gerry shrugged his shoulders, but his expression didn't change. 'Who am I to argue? Anything's possible. Like I said, it's a small town.'

I think this man was subtly telling me that promiscuity was commonplace in his younger days. For men to 'play the field'.

'So you could be my father?' I spoke in a slightly higher voice to pretend that I was half joking, but Gerry didn't buy it. His face was solemn.

'I beg to differ, miss, but it doesn't matter anyway. I never knew your mother.' He brandished his dog's lead. 'Come on, boy,' he said before standing up gingerly and walked straight past me without uttering another word.

He had a dog. He was a mechanic. He could be my father.

My taxi was due in less than an hour. I should just let this go, but my gut was telling me to follow this man. I would only be tormenting myself further if I didn't.

CHAPTER 60

I WAITED UNTIL GERRY was far enough in front of me. He walked slowly, so I had no problem keeping up. He turned right at Hesse Street and then left into Calvert.

His house was, by any measure, not the grandest in the street. It looked similar to many in the area, which appeared to have been assembled on a mass-production line.

I stood behind a large oak tree on the opposite side of the street and watched as he vanished through the front door.

I felt a violent ache of anxiety. This man held my happiness in his hands. Oddly, he was playing God, but I had to remind myself that I didn't believe in deities.

Adrenaline pumped me up as I strode across the street and stood on his front lawn. Fear rose up inside me like a phoenix as I pondered my next move. The blinds were down; and although I knew there was no way he could see me, I felt like I was suffocating. *Get a grip, Sally. You can do this.* I tiptoed to the shadowed side of the house and stood by a large window. The slats of the venetian blinds were half closed, and I glanced around to make sure I was alone before crouching down to the level of the window ledge. Suddenly a light flashed on in the room, and I ducked down. There was a rustling sound, and I waited for it to dissipate before raising my head ever so slightly and peering through the lowest slat. Gerry had his back to me. He scraped out his dog's bowl before filling it with dried food. The dog was wagging its tail and circling its master's feet.

'Here you go, Fido. Eat it all up.'

As Gerry left the room, I positioned myself on an angle to gain a better view. I could clearly see into the next room and watched intently as he sat himself down on the couch and began reading a newspaper. Other than Fido slurping his food, the house was silent.

I contemplated Gerry's domestic circumstances: Did he live alone? Was he married? Divorced? Perhaps widowed? Did he have any kids? All of these scenarios crossed my mind simultaneously. But just thinking about them wasn't going to help me. It wasn't going to help me at all.

I climbed to my feet. An awful feeling was starting to form, but Dr Gail coached me to get past this. I kept telling myself that I'm not being stupid, that I have a right to know.

The front door was set into the right edge of the house. The front path was flanked by two narrow flowerbeds that had a few hydrangeas poking up through a blanket of weeds.

I walked slowly up the path and rang the doorbell. The sound of slow shuffling feet coming nearer caused my breath to quicken. The door opened ever so slightly.

'Oh, it's you. You followed me.'

I stood as still as a statue racking my brain, trying to find the right words. Gerry looked closely at me through the small gap in the door, first scanning me up and down before scrutinising my face for any traces of ill will or anything that might suggest that knocking on a stranger's door was a sort of perverse thrill for me.

'I'm sorry to bother you, but what I said in the park earlier was all true. I believe you have met my mother before. Eve Cartwright. She lives not far from here. I can take you there.' I looked down at my clasped hands as I spoke, too scared to see if Gerry's expression had changed. 'I can show you that photograph. You'll see I'm telling the truth.' This was the best I could come up with.

Gerry opened the door fully and remained silent for a few seconds. He let out a long hissy sigh before talking. 'You strike me as a sensible and honest young lady. Not the type who would go around doing this for a prank.' He looked at his watch, and his breath was becoming laboured again. He slipped out a Ventolin dispenser and inhaled two puffs. 'Smoking is a scourge. You don't smoke, do you?'

I shook my head.

'Good. It's much, much worse for you to smoke than it ever was for me. Please understand that.'

I didn't agree with this line of reasoning but frankly didn't care right at this moment. 'So will you come with me?' I said impatiently.

'I tell you what, I will come with you. But only to satisfy my own curiosity. I must warn you, though. You're going to be disappointed. I am not the man you think I am.'

'You must be,' I said, putting on my most strident voice to stop him from changing his mind. 'My mother knew you as Gerald, and she said you kept dogs and were into cars.'

Gerry was about to laugh but smiled instead. 'Let's be reasonable here, miss. All men like dogs and cars. It's embedded in our Y chromosome.'

My mind was an emotional battlefield as we walked, slowly, to Mummy's unit. Gerry was breathing a little uneasily again as he told me a little about himself along the way. I felt comfortable listening because I hadn't instigated the conversation. His wife died from cancer three years ago, and his two children moved to Melbourne for work. This left him alone with only Fido for company and no other relatives. To cope with the strain of a solitary life, he immersed himself into his mechanics business until emphysema and angina took a stranglehold. The insurance company deemed him too high a risk and jacked up their premiums, which he could no longer afford, so he was forced to shut the business. 'Life can be a bitch sometimes, young lady. You remember that.'

I didn't need reminding.

Gerry's amber-coloured eyes portrayed a sadness that indicated a lot of sorrow buried somewhere deep within. I could tell that he had hurt inside him.

As we walked, I checked my phone which I'd put on silent mode. There was a missed call. Could it be Myles? My heart began thumping hard. I looked at the screen more closely. No. It was Mummy. She never calls me. What could be up? Is she not well? Is something the matter with Henry?

'Excuse me, Gerry, I need to make a call.' I strode out a few metres in front and pressed redial. 'Hello, Mummy, what's up?'

'Sal, where are you?' Her voice was strained with worry.

'I've been for a walk. I'm bringing someone—'

'A walk? What the hell for?'

This was the old cantankerous mummy shining through. 'I needed some air,' I said in a hushed voice so that Gerry wouldn't hear. 'Anyway, is that why you called me?'

'Hell no. Your taxi driver was here to pick you up. I tried to call you, but you didn't answer. I had to pay a cancellation fee! That's a great way to start again, Sal. I'm back only a few hours and already in the bad books with someone.'

Shit! All my efforts into coercing Gerry to come to Mummy's unit had distracted me. The pre-booked taxi had completely slipped my mind. How was I going to get home by tomorrow? I couldn't afford to think about that right now. 'I'll be home soon, Mummy,' I said quickly. 'I'm bringing a guest.' I ended the call before she had a chance to ask me anything.

'Mummy, this is Gerry. Gerry, this is my mother, Eve Cartwright.'

She stood at the door in track pants and a white tee. Her hair was a dishevelled mess, and her crackly skin had nowhere to hide without the security shield of makeup. The lingering smell of smoke hung around her like an inescapable form.

After a short silence, she spoke derisively. 'You brought a guest. Why didn't you warn me?'

I ignored all this as we walked into the lounge. Gerry let out a phlegmy cough before extending his hand. 'How do you do, Mrs Cartwright? Your daughter here seems to think we are old acquaintants, but I doubt that very much.'

Mummy gave me a startled look. 'Is this Gerald? It can't be, can it?'

Gerry's face washed blank with confusion. He suddenly realised that what I'd been talking about wasn't a fabrication.

'Excuse me for a moment, Gerry. I'll be back.' I went into the spare room and rummaged through my bag lying beside Henry's box. The photograph was neatly placed inside my purse.

We sat on the couch, and my heart began racing faster than ever. I showed Gerry the photograph. The shock that registered on his face was immediate and wholesome.

'Wow, I am a little taken aback, as you might tell.'

That was all I needed to hear. He was looking at himself as a young man. Mummy sensed it too. Tears began streaming down his face and glistened against the fading late-afternoon sun. He looked up to face Mummy.

'Eve Cartwright. I honestly can't recall your name, but … did we ever date?'

Mummy looked deflated, disappointed even. She was probably thinking what I would be thinking if I were in her shoes: *I must have left a poor impression on this man.* She nervously brushed a few wispy strands of hair behind her ear. 'Yes, Gerald. We dated for a few months. Don't you remember? I had a full head of auburn hair back then, and you loved my haughty laugh.'

Gerry blinked quickly and twitched his nose. Of course he'd remember. He should remember. But the impassive expression he held seemed to suggest otherwise. 'God, I'm sorry, Eve.' His voice was laced with sadness. He closed his eyes and dropped his head to his chest, his eyes still shut. 'My memory's not what it used to be.'

'I know what you mean,' Mummy said. 'Mine's not the best anymore either. I think it's our age.' She smiled to show Gerry that she wasn't bothered by his forgetfulness. Was it a genuine smile?

Mummy and Gerry talked between themselves, the early tension between them long forgotten. As was the usual custom, I remained silent. The more they rambled the more I felt myself shrinking until I'm sure I was invisible to them both, but I didn't mind. I was glad they were getting on so well. They talked casually about growing up in Colac and some of the sites that had changed over the years, about what they got up to as teenagers, as well as a little about each other's lives. Gerry told Mummy about his wife's passing but not of the circumstances.

Mummy sat back and put her hand to her mouth. 'I'm sorry to hear that, Gerald. Are you on your own now?'

Gerry nodded. 'It's just me and my dog.'

I was hoping that talking about the past might help Gerry recall things about Mummy, memories swarming and teeming forth. But that didn't happen.

'Did my Sal mention that you might be her father?'

Mummy's blunt question didn't seem to faze Gerry. 'I suppose that's possible, Eve. Our moral base wasn't very strong in those days, was it?'

Mummy nodded. 'It was purely fun.' She appeared very comfortable talking to this man who she hadn't seen in twenty-seven years. For someone who was initially dead against any of my attempts to find him, this was indeed a turn up. I hadn't seen her so fervid since that day when she met Declan for the first time.

Loneliness can engender surprising reactions in people.

Mummy and Gerry continued talking as I went into the spare room and called up the taxi company. I was told there was no driver available at this late hour who would accept a fare to Melbourne. I would have to wait until at least the morning. A sudden wave of panic took the strength from my legs, and I was forced to sit down on the floor. I was going to break my promise to Mike. Not only that, I'd already decided that I wasn't going back home tomorrow.

I'm going to stay here and talk to Gerry about taking a paternity test.

CHAPTER 61

'I FOLLOWED YOU! I followed you, but you didn't turn back!'
The sun was almost down now, and Gerry and Mummy were
still in the kitchen in intense conversation as I walked in. Mummy
looked animated as she spoke, and her face was flushed a light crimson.
'He remembers, dear. Gerald remembers me!'

I turned to Gerry who nodded and smiled. He was still holding the
photograph. 'That's right, Sally. Your mother says that I gave her this
picture when we first began dating. I can't recall doing that, but then
she mentioned something that awakened some memories. She told me
about the two of us going to a fair. I have fond memories of that fair.
It used to come every summer. I recall we were at this fair and about
to go on a carousel. It was one of those old-fashioned ones with the
horses that bob up and down. We had an argument just before going
on. That's when your mother turned away and left. I thought she never
wanted to see me again.'

Mummy looked at Gerry a little disbelievingly. 'I can't believe you
thought that at the time.'

Gerry blinked hard and swallowed some tea. 'I thought that you
thought that I was a psycho or something. That you didn't want to
touch me with a bargepole.'

'A psycho? I definitely didn't think that.' There was a pause before
Mummy spoke again, 'I even tried calling you.'

Gerry nodded and placed his calloused hands on the table. 'I
remember that,' he said. 'And I thought about calling you back. I really
did. Eventually, I pushed the thought of you from my mind. Buried it
deep somewhere. That's why I couldn't remember your name.'

'And what happened after that?' Mummy asked.

Gerry ran his finger around the rim of his cup. 'Then I met my wife.' He sniffed hard as a tear ran down his left cheek. He looked so mournful. She might have left his world but clearly not his heart.

Mummy stared hard into his eyes. I could tell what she was thinking: how everything could have been so different if only she'd turned back on that fateful day at the fair, if only she'd been brave enough.

I could tell she didn't want to say goodbye to this man again, not a second time. 'We can give it another shot, Gerald. As friends I mean. What do you think?'

Gerry's expression seemed to soften and he formed a smile. 'Why not? I reckon everyone needs friends, Eve.'

And there it was. A beautiful moment beyond which lay the potential for future happiness. I genuinely felt happy for Mummy.

Gerry shifted in his seat and made to get up.

'You don't have to go yet,' Mummy said.

He shook his head. 'No. Fido's waiting for me. But I can come around tomorrow if you want me to.'

Mummy got up looking like a smitten teenager. 'You can come anytime. I'll be here, but I don't know if Sally will. She has to go back to Melbourne for work tomorrow, don't you, dear?'

More than likely, I didn't have a job to go to anymore; but right at this moment, I didn't care. 'Actually, Mummy, I'm thinking of staying for a few more days.'

Mummy sagged back into her chair with a puzzled look. 'Oh? You've changed your mind?'

I nodded before turning to Gerry. 'There's something I need to ask you, Gerry. I need a favour from you.' My heart rate was escalating at the rate of knots.

'Ask away.'

I stared down at the floor as I spoke. 'There's a test they can do. A genetic test to see if two people are related. If you agree we can—'

'You mean a paternity test.'

'Yes. It can be done by a doctor,' I eagerly explained. 'They take a blood sample and sometimes a cheek swab as well.'

Mummy interrupted, 'That sounds like a great idea. You wouldn't mind doing that, would you, Gerald?'

MARIO BORAZIO

Gerry tapped his fingers on the table and stood up. 'Not at all,' he said. 'Especially after all the trouble your daughter has gone to. In my life, I have tried never to complain about anything and to always do right by others. It has brought me many benefits.'

Gerry came across as a good man, a person whom anyone would be proud to call their father, someone who could provide lasting happiness.

'Mummy has an appointment at the doctors' surgery tomorrow,' I said eagerly. 'Perhaps we could go with her.'

'That's a splendid idea.'

When Gerry left, I prepared dinner and made up my bed on the couch.

After dinner, I contemplated whether to send Mike a text informing him that I won't be in tomorrow.

I didn't want to spoil his evening.

CHAPTER 62

I SLEPT IN MY T-shirt and underwear. It was a fitful sleep, and I had a dream about Gerry. I dreamt it was his birthday, and I made a vegan cake for him. Why vegan I don't know. I was looking into his overjoyed, laughing eyes as he gently moved my head onto his chest and hugged me tight. Mummy wasn't in the dream. What did this all mean exactly? I felt confused when I woke up.

There was a new text message on my phone. I knew it would be from Mike:

Where are you Sally? We're waiting for you.

No pleasantries but I didn't expect any either. I should call him right now and explain the whole situation—how I had every intention of being back today but I met a man who could possibly be my father and how that took precedence over my work. Over everything.

The fact that I'd never mentioned the status of my parentage would raise concerns as to the legitimacy of my excuse.

I won't reply. Let them think that the real Sally Cartwright was—what was she?

Mummy's appointment at the new surgery was for ten-thirty, and I'd arranged for Gerry to meet us there. A small part of me kept thinking that he won't keep this appointment, that he'd wake up and decide he really didn't want a new family in his life. But he seemed a good man, and there wasn't a hint of apprehension in his demeanour when I outlined my plan to him yesterday.

He was wearing a blue sweater, which seemed a touch extravagant given the warmish morning. 'Good morning, Eve. Good morning, Sally. Are we all ready?'

I smiled. 'Good morning, Gerry. Thank you for coming.'

'It's my pleasure. I'm about to find out if I have a beautiful daughter.'

Blush is in my DNA. For a moment I felt completely weightless, aware of my colouring betraying me as blood rushed to my cheeks. In an instant, they were a deep rose colour and burned like fire. I forced myself to smile. 'Shall we go in?'

I'd rung the surgery earlier and was fortunate enough to secure an appointment for both Gerry and me. I explained the nature of our visit and was told that we would need separate appointments. I didn't see why but wasn't going to argue.

We were asked for our particulars by a pleasant young girl on reception before being told to take a seat in the waiting room. Mummy was holding a white envelope on her lap. It contained her entire medical history as well as a list of all her medications and records of her hospital admissions. She was smiling at Gerry, her eyes looking more alive than I can ever remember. A kind of smirk appeared on Gerry's face, like he was enjoying a joke, as Mummy talked and laughed with ease. The big gaping hole of loneliness she'd been trying to deny for so many years was slowly being filled.

The disappointed look on her face when she was called in by her new doctor was impossible to miss. I allowed myself a tiny laugh.

As I waited, I drew a deep breath and decided to check my phone, a task I'd been avoiding all morning. There were two missed calls as well as another text message, all from Mike. I built up a mental image of what would be happening at work: Mike would be all anxious, and Wilma and Casey would be sporting broad smiles after I was admonished for my unruly behaviour in front of everyone. *How could she do this to us? This is so unlike her.*

'Sally Cartwright?'

The doctor was a thin young man of Asian descent, and he wore dark-rimmed glasses. My heart began pounding with anticipation as my eyes fell on the small glass tubes on his desk. He asked me about any pre-existing medical conditions and whether I'd done a home paternity test. I didn't even know there was one.

'No medical conditions. No home testing.'

The doctor nodded. 'Good, because those things are not legally binding.'

He went on to explain the procedure: A blood sample will be taken from the potential father and child. This blood will then be sent to a laboratory for analysis, and the results will be sent independently to both parties via a text message a few days later. As insurance, a swab of buccal cells from the inside of the cheek will also be sent for analysis.

I was done in five minutes and sat in the waiting room as Gerry was called in straight after me.

An hour later, we were all back at Mummy's unit. She explained that her new doctor took some blood from her and changed her blood pressure tablets. She said she liked him and called him Dr Sunshine 'because he smiled a lot.'

I went into the spare room and opened my phone. Nothing more from Mike. A sudden feeling of dread washed over me. This was surely the death knell. I probably didn't have a job anymore. I had become superfluous. Even Mummy was sort of ignoring me, smitten by a newfound friend.

I needed someone to feel sorry for me.

I closed the door and began pacing back and forth, stopping at the wardrobe mirror every few seconds to check my appearance. I'd lost weight. My jeans were in urgent need of a belt, and my T-shirt looked like a drop sheet covering a piece of furniture. My breasts had shrunk too. Sally Cartwright was fading away.

Mummy's laughter from the lounge room where she and Gerry were sitting came in fits and bursts to my ears. Childish laughter in an adult's body. Contented laughter.

I sat on the floor with my back against the wall and contemplated what was happening around me. I couldn't stay here; I had to go home.

I rang for a taxi and booked it for thirty minutes. As I waited, my phone rang. It was Mike.

CHAPTER 63

MIKE SACKED ME, but he wasn't hostile about it. He explained that he was perplexed by my behaviour and had run out of patience. He also said that it wasn't entirely his decision, that the newly formed board of management had no other choice to make. I think I took it pretty well. What other outcome did I expect?

He asked me if there were any issues at home that I wanted to talk about. 'No, I'm fine. I'm busy looking after my mother.' It irked me to say that. To use Mummy as an alibi whenever I felt unhappy or whenever anything bad happened. She didn't run my life.

Or maybe she did.

I said my goodbyes to Mummy and Gerry and promised to come and visit soon. Gerry even offered to give me 'unofficial' driving lessons when I came back. That was a magnanimous gesture, I thought, considering he may not even turn out to be my father.

With Henry's box by my side, I sat in the back seat of the taxi and began thinking about what life will be like for Sally Cartwright from now on: Without a job, there'd be no reason for her to get up each morning. She had no reason to visit the Fancy Chef anymore. The only activity that would require a modicum of responsibility was feeding Henry.

As the taxi neared my flat, I thought about Mummy and Gerry together. Here were two old acquaintances, destined to never cross paths again, but somehow fate decreed for it to happen. Their relationship may remain platonic or could eventually blossom into something more. I wouldn't begrudge Mummy any of this as long as she was happy.

*

Life got boring pretty quickly. I'd wake up tired after a fitful sleep, usually around ten, have breakfast, feed Henry and just sit on my couch, thinking. What did I think about? I thought about cleaning the house. I thought about getting another job. I thought about applying for unemployment benefits if I couldn't get another job. I thought about getting my learner's permit. I thought about all of these things but didn't enact any of them. I even thought about calling Mummy and asking how she and Gerry were getting on. I wasn't in the right frame of mind to do that just yet.

I was in a lethargic funk. Every time I moved, it felt like I was swimming in Vaseline.

My phone pinged. It was a text message from Australian Clinical Labs. My heart almost jumped out of my chest as I catapulted out of bed. My finger hovered precariously over the screen:

> Dear SALLY
> Paternity test on 19/04/2018 by Australian Clinical
> Labs
> RESULT: Paternal match was NEGATIVE
> Pls do not reply to this text message

I've tried to fight back, but there was nothing left now. With Mummy back home ensconced in a new relationship with a man who it turns out is not even my father, I felt like excess cargo again. My life was back to how it used to be. Except that I didn't have a job anymore.

Martin Luther once said that for where God built a church, there the Devil would also build a chapel. As I've already mentioned, I don't believe in God in any of his or her forms. That probably implies that I shouldn't believe in the Devil either. But the way that everything in my life was spiralling downward had forced me to rethink this belief system.

I felt as though the Devil had overpowered God and was exacting his revenge on me.

Once you give up hope, you begin to feel a whole lot better. What was there for me to hope for now?

My life was evaporating.

CHAPTER 64

D R GAIL ASKED me how I was feeling and while I wanted to tell her quite a lot—how difficult it has been—I held back the worst of it because I felt I needed to understand myself a little better first. Does that make sense? I don't really know if this line of reasoning is sound.

I think Dr Gail sensed my ambivalence. 'Do you mind if I record today's session, Sally?' Her hair was dyed black and cut straight above the nape of her neck. Her eyes seemed a darker colour, and she wore a new rose gold necklace and crystal drop earrings. It made her appear years younger. I wondered who she was trying to impress.

I know she's married.

'Okay.' I gave her a perfunctory smile before staring at the vase of fresh magnolias on her desk.

Her index finger hovered over the record button. 'For this to work, though, you have to be completely honest.'

I released a chest full of air. This could turn out to be a real nightmare, but I knew what I had to do.

'I want you to tell me everything that's happened, Sally. You can start in your own time.'

It was weird, but I felt comfortable talking into a machine. More so than talking to a person. I talked about how Mummy went back to Colac and how by pure chance I ended up meeting Gerald. 'He prefers to be called Gerry,' I said. I outlined my disappointment at finding out he wasn't my father. I explained the circumstances behind the termination of my employment as well as my feelings about not hearing back from Myles.

In a nutshell, I enunciated how Sally Cartwright's wilting garden had now ceased to exist altogether. Even the weeds had abandoned her.

Dr Gail pushed a few strands of hair behind her left ear and looked up from her desk. 'How are you feeling?' she asked.

'Okay,' I said. But I didn't. I felt terrible.

She sensed the ambivalence in my response. 'Let me rephrase that. How are you feeling about yourself right now?'

If there was a hole in your office floor, I'd like to fall into it. The deeper the better. That's what I felt like saying. 'I feel like I'm a failure all over again,' I said feebly.

Dr Gail shook her head exaggeratedly, her earrings making a slight jangling noise. 'That's something you definitely are not, Sally. Working towards personal goals and aspirations doesn't come easy for anyone. You've been through a lot emotionally in your life, and at times your self-esteem has taken a battering. But self-esteem isn't something you can physically take in your hand and reshape or fix. It happens internally through your thoughts, and it influences your actions and relationships.' She looked closely at me, scrutinising my face for a reaction to her deadly accurate summation. I kept blinking and looked down at the floor in silence.

'Tell me, Sally, do you ever think about dying?'

I didn't know what to say. The atmosphere in the room was strung taut from the moment I walked in because I knew we were going to discuss sensitive issues. But never in my wildest thoughts did I think we were going to discuss death.

Dr Gail stared at her freshly polished nails as she waited for me to answer. I felt like we were playing a game, and I'd missed all the clues.

'Why is this topic so important?' I asked.

'Because it captures the essence of what is important right at this moment in your life. When you feel down, it is very easy to dwell on negative thoughts, like thoughts about death.'

'To be honest, Gail, this topic has caught me completely off guard. I sometimes think about what happens to us after we die but not about dying itself. Does that make sense?'

Dr Gail nodded, and a small feeling of euphoria rose up inside me as I realised she understood what I was saying.

'How are you sleeping?'

The dark lines under my eyes spoke for me. 'Not well,' I admitted. 'I might get an hour's sleep and wake up feeling restless, and then I'm unable to get back to sleep again for hours.'

Dr Gail pulled out her prescription pad and began scribbling. 'You have complex emotions right now, Sally. When you feel the way you do, the body finds it hard to shut down.' She handed me a prescription.

'What's this?' I asked.

'A drug called temazepam. It will help you fall asleep easier and may even help you stay asleep longer.'

My apprehension was etched all over my face as I stared at the prescription form.

'Don't worry. It's a safe drug.'

I can recall Mummy taking sleeping tablets years ago. They always made her feel drowsy the next day. She eventually ditched them. 'Are they absolutely necessary?' I asked.

Dr Gail sat back and folded her arms. Her head was silhouetted against the sunlit window behind her and her face was in shadow, so I couldn't make out her expression. 'Sally, depriving yourself of sleep will cloud your mind. You can't start to heal your hurt unless you have a clear mind.'

'All right,' I said meekly. 'If you think they'll help, I'll take them.' I tucked the prescription into my bag.

Dr Gail sat forward, and her face suddenly lit up as it caught the strong afternoon sun. 'There's a lot to work through here, Sally. Right now, you may feel that everything that we have done over the last few months has been for nothing, but that's not true. Remember your garden? It's still there, and it can flourish again. You have the tools to make that happen. You have the tools to empower and enable you to carry on a meaningful life. You've got to have perspective. Think about the good you have done. You may not know your father yet, but you have been instrumental in enriching the lives of two people. You are a good person, Sally.'

Of course it was Dr Gail's professional duty to put a positive spin on things. To stay composed in the face of a patient who was mired in doom and gloom.

She continued, 'Remember, this, Sally. None of what has happened is your fault. Gerry not being your father is not your fault. He never was your father, never will be. But he can still be your friend. Everything will work out. Don't be scared. I'll always be here.'

In spite of Dr Gail's reassurances, I *was* scared.

I was scared of being alone.

I was scared of remaining an outsider.

I was scared that I'd had my fair share of chances at happiness and blown them all.

*

When I woke up, my head throbbed and my body ached as if I'd repeatedly flung myself against a concrete wall. I wondered if that was how Mummy felt after taking her sleeping tablets. I don't remember falling asleep. Was this the blankness of drugged sleep? There were no dreams, nothing to tell me what my brain had been doing for the past eight hours.

Tilting my head to glance at the clock, I saw that it was close to eleven. I listened for some sounds of life outside. It was raining. The sound of rain can be loud in the silence.

My heart was racing. I jumped up, gasping for air. I watched the window change from a pale yellow to a silvery sheen as my eyes tried to focus. The room hovered around me as though the walls and the ceiling and the window were all closing in.

I took a cold shower, which seemed to soothe my muscles and empower me. Then I microwaved a tub of my homemade chickpea and mushroom soup. After a few mouthfuls, my appetite withered and died.

I sat on the couch and thought about what Dr Gail said about perspective. But before long, the negative thoughts were gnawing away at me again. I needed to get them out of my system.

I sank back and closed my eyes. Staying idle wasn't helping. I knew I couldn't cope with another idle day.

I cleaned my flat and got a small charge when I looked at what I'd accomplished. I'm sure Henry was impressed too.

Feeling a whole lot better, I decided it was time to call Mummy.

'I knew Gerald couldn't be your father from the moment I saw him, dear. He's too good for you.'

That wasn't the welcome I was expecting. I took a long heaving sigh. 'So Gerry told you?' I said forlornly.

'Of course he told me.' Mummy's tone was brusque. 'He told me as soon as he got the test results. I can't say he looked too disappointed either.'

I refused to believe what Mummy was saying. Gerry would have been extremely disappointed. He would have been over the moon if he'd found out that I was his daughter. It would have been better than winning lotto for him. 'I don't believe you, Mummy. Gerry's a caring man.'

Mummy let out a disapproving hiss. 'You just don't get it, do you, Sal? This is what can happen when you're not worldly. You can't see the forest for the trees. Gerald was just being polite, that's all.'

'I think you're being disrespectful.'

'Respect has nothing to do with it, Sal. It's just the way of the world.'

'I think I've got a headache coming on, Mummy. I'm not feeling that well.'

'Yes, I know you are fragile in that way. You always have been. But it's hard to forget, Sal. It's hard to forget what a difficult child you always were.'

I didn't know how to respond. I should've been angry. Beyond angry. I was at a loss to explain Mummy's hostility. What was she hoping to achieve? She seemed so happy before I left.

All I could focus on were the horrible memories of the past that Mummy's grating words had exhumed. In a way, I'm secretly relieved. Not feeling a connection or a sense of belonging had reaffirmed the status quo of our relationship, which I now realise is destined to never change. When you feel more and more let down by the people who should be there for you, you're no longer ready for battle.

I could feel a sense of finality about something which I couldn't pin down.

I was in no mood for a rant. 'I've got to go, Mummy. Say hello to Gerry for me.'

'I must go too. Gerald's taking me out tonight, and I have to get ready.'

CHAPTER 65

I WAS BARELY PRESENT anymore—wrapped up in the darkness of my thoughts. One moment I'm numb; the next I'm swamped by anger, frustration, helplessness, and resentment.

The weekend was a jumble in my head, and I kept leaping from one memory to another. I thought about Gerry and what he'd be feeling right now. Was he genuinely disappointed with the result of the paternity test, or was he, as Mummy had intimated, not fussed in the slightest? Perhaps she was right, and I had him all wrong.

I hadn't contemplated calling her again, not even for one second. Her caustic diatribe last week completely blindsided me. Was she being protective of Gerry, afraid that I might steal him away from her? That thought seemed absurd, but something like that was always a possibility with Mummy.

My appointment with Dr Gail this afternoon didn't go well. I told her that all week since taking temazepam I'd felt worse. Nauseous, lethargic, dissociated and still unable to get a good night's rest. I told her I didn't want to take the pills anymore. She looked at me with an impassive expression. 'Let me make that decision, Sally,' she declared. It was the first time that I'd detected a coldness and arrogance in her voice. I left her rooms feeling disillusioned, betrayed in some way. Deep inside, I was angry and extremely sad.

The lure of a long and restful sleep was gnawing away at me, lurking around the edges of my subconscious. What relief it would be to find peace. Maybe even oblivion, if only for a short while. The anger and frustration were the hardest emotions to bear, and suddenly the decision took hold in my mind like a leech attaching itself to my skin with no intention of letting go.

As the outside light faded, I got up and headed unnervingly to the bathroom. I sat on the tiles with my back against the bath and stared at the box of pills on the vanity. They could still be my sanctuary. How many would it take to push me over the edge? Three? Four? I didn't know.

I didn't want to kill myself. I just wanted something miraculous to happen to make things better. A handful of pills might just be the answer. Obviously one wasn't enough for me. Why didn't Dr Gail tell me this?

I kept staring at the box. Suddenly my decision felt real, and I was petrified. Did I have the strength to go ahead with my plan? Will I get cold feet? If I did go ahead, how would I feel when I finally woke up? What if I didn't wake up?

The frustrating part was that there was no rule book for this scenario. I felt more and more bewildered the longer I procrastinated.

An hour passed. It was completely dark outside. By now, anxiety had flooded my entire mind. I was frantic. It was time. I took three 10 mg temazepam with the intention of falling asleep and waking up to a brand-new world. Except that I didn't fall asleep. Maybe my anxiety was countering the normal effects of this medicine. I didn't feel the least bit drowsy. It was as though I'd been given the placebo treatment in a scientific experiment.

But they were *my* pills, no one else's.

There were six left. A little voice inside me was screaming with frustration, *You haven't been tough enough, Sally Cartwright. Ever.* My voice was mocking me. I recalled what Dr Gail told me a few sessions ago: 'You're less fragile now. It will take something pretty big to overwhelm you.' I tried to reassure myself of this.

I still have what it takes to do this.

With trembling hands, I prised all six tablets out of their blistered pouches and held them in my palm. I closed my eyes and put them in my mouth before cupping my hand under the tap and swallowing a big mouthful of water.

I started to feel cold almost immediately, and my brain began to throb. With my eyes still closed, I sat back down on the tiles and forced myself to breathe slowly in and out, waiting for my brain to stop throbbing. At first there were no thoughts, no words, no feelings, just the breathing. This mindless state continued for at least fifteen minutes. Then my mind began to conjure tumbling images. I took in a little girl, her small round face, the soft eyes, the tilt of her head, the way the hair fell over her tiny shoulders, the happy smile. In the distance was a man wearing a big grin and taking her picture.

Suddenly my body felt like it was hovering above the floor, and my eyelids were like lead weights. I felt totally exhausted.

Then I slept.

CHAPTER 66

I WOKE UP WRAPPED in tubes. I couldn't believe my luck. I was alive! But I was also terrified. I knew exactly what I'd done, what had happened to me. I can recall everything with devastating clarity—first taking three pills, then another six, and then surrendering to a deep and glorious sleep.

And now I've woken up in a hospital emergency room. How did I get here?

I felt strangely empty and hollow. Every so often, a doctor or nurse would lean over my bed and study me intently. They would talk among themselves in low voices interspersed with silences.

'She is still quite drowsy and has been physically sick on several occasions.'

'She is not quite stable yet, but we have her under control.'

'Blood tests confirm a benzodiazepine overdose. There were no other drugs in her system.'

I could hear everything very clearly but was too exhausted to speak. I mustered all of my strength in my throat to utter words, but none came out. They asked me if I was in pain, and I managed to shake my head. They asked me if I was pregnant, and I shook my head again. Then they told me they had to do a pregnancy test anyway, just to be sure. I was unable to communicate that they'd be wasting their time.

I craned my neck around to the other cubicles and realised that I was the youngest person in here. The other beds were taken up mainly by spluttering and moaning old people. That in itself was depressing.

I was desperate to tell someone that I felt fine except for the fatigue. As I motioned with my hand to get a nurse's attention, a slim young man strode into my cubicle and closed the curtain. He had on a tag that read *Registrar*.

'Good morning, Ms Cartwright. Sally. I'm one of the doctors here.

How are you feeling?' He looked impatient, like he was running late for something. I nodded to signify that I was doing okay. He began reading over my chart. 'Now, what made you go and do something like that to yourself?'

I shrugged my shoulders and could feel myself blushing. A slight smile formed at the corners of my mouth. I don't really know why I smiled. I didn't mean to make light of the plight I found myself in.

The doctor leaned over and began pumping up the blood pressure cuff secured tightly around my left arm. 'Are you on antidepressants?' I shook my head. 'We'll have to see about that once the inpatient psychiatrist examines you.'

I suddenly resented taking all those pills and being dragged into this sorry tale of hospital examination and interrogation. I desperately wanted to tell this man that I wasn't a crazy woman. That there was no need for the psychiatrist to see me. I just wanted to go home and put this unfortunate saga behind me. I was even willing to apologise for taking up a hospital bed, which may have been more efficiently utilised for a far graver case than mine.

I dared not tell him that I was already seeing a psychiatrist.

He kept rambling on about suicide ideation and antidepressants and psych beds and about transferring me to the psych ward. I was becoming overwhelmed. He wasn't sensing my fear. That fear eventually shocked my brain and my mouth into action. Suddenly I was able to speak. 'Excuse me, Doctor.' My voice was croaky but audible. 'I don't think any of that will be necessary. I just need to go home and rest. I'll be alright, I can assure you.'

He gave me a cold and angry stare. 'Sally, if your neighbour hadn't found you when she did, you may still be lying unconscious on your bathroom floor. Or worse. You are in no state to make decisions regarding your well-being right now.' He was sounding like a prosecutor in a courtroom admonishing a defendant for a heinous crime.

'My neighbour?'

He leafed through my file with his head down as he spoke. 'Yes. I have her statement right here. She said that she noticed water on the floor of her bathroom, which adjoins yours. She then knocked on your front door, but you didn't answer. Lucky for you, the door was open. She found you slumped on the bathroom floor in a pool of water with the tap still running. You were unresponsive, and that's when she called an ambulance.'

Old Mrs Hutchings. We've only crossed paths on a few occasions. I always tried to avoid her. 'Is she still here?' I asked.

'No, she isn't. She's gone home. But we've got your phone and have taken the liberty of calling your mother. I believe she's on her way.'

I couldn't imagine Mummy dropping everything to come to see me. There'd be no way she'd do that for me. Unless Gerry talked her round.

The doctor looked straight into my eyes. 'So, Sally, tell me exactly what happened.'

I took a deep breath and swallowed. I made sure my voice was more strident. 'It's not what you think. I didn't take those pills to try and kill myself. I just wanted to sleep.'

He looked at me even more intently. 'All our research tells us that people, especially young people, who try to suicide once will try it again. It's quite normal for you to try to cover it all up. I can see you're anxious. All you want to do is go home and work on another plan.'

I couldn't believe what I was hearing. What did I need to do to convince this man that I wasn't suicidal? That I wasn't being sucked down into a vortex? That just thinking about killing myself was dangerous overreach for me?

I tried to sit up but realised that I was hooked up to a drip. I held the plastic tubing in my hand and gave it a gentle tug in an act of defiance. 'I don't even need this,' I muttered under my breath.

The doctor was unperturbed by my staged petulance. He seemed to have made up his mind about my situation and refused to have a bar of anything more I might actually want to say about it. He made it very clear that I wasn't going anywhere. He stressed that I wasn't allowed to leave the hospital under any circumstances.

This doctor was obviously not listening. I needed to convince someone else that I didn't belong here. A new state of alertness came over me, and a new level of anxiety tightened my stomach as the seriousness of my predicament hit home.

To my relief, the doctor took his leave. A young nurse came in soon after. She was in her early twenties, tall, with long dark hair. She wore thin-rimmed glasses and a furrowed brow. 'We are sending you up to the psych ward as soon as a bed is ready. You will be on twenty-four-hour watch.'

I felt utterly helpless. What was I being watched for? I had to make them understand that I wasn't trying to hide anything. I had to convince them that I was telling the truth. They must be made aware that I was in no danger of harming myself or anybody else. 'Please listen to me.' My tone was desperate, and I was on the verge of tears as I spoke. 'I'm not trying to kill or harm myself in any way. I'm not hiding any dark thoughts. I know now that taking those pills was a huge mistake. I'm capable of making rational decisions from now on.'

The nurse's expression was laden with scepticism. Without saying a word, she walked over to the bedside drawer and unlocked it. 'What about these?' She held up a plastic bag containing my now-empty box of pills. 'Why did your psychiatrist prescribe them for you?'

I could imagine what they'd be thinking: *She must be crazy because she is seeing a psychiatrist.* 'I was having trouble sleeping,' I said. 'There's nothing more to it than that.'

'Nothing more?' The nurse's demeanour was becoming slightly hostile. 'We have already contacted Dr Eisenhuth. She explained your situation to us quite clearly.'

I felt panicked. What did Dr Gail 'quite clearly' explain? Did she mention the imaginary phone calls? The videos I took? It would definitely not help my cause if she did.

I couldn't help but feel at this point that the less-than-amicable ending to my last session with Dr Gail may have worked against me.

Just as I was thinking of a way to persuade this nurse that my therapy sessions with Dr Gail were helping me immensely and that despite the overdose I really was in a good head space, a much older, matronly-looking nurse walked in. 'We're moving you up now, Ms Cartwright.' She took one look at my expression. 'I'm sorry but there is nothing else we can do.'

My last hope was Mummy. She will tell them that I'm not crazy.

CHAPTER 67

THE FEELING OF disempowerment when I was being wheeled up to the psych ward was awful. I felt myself sinking. My desperation to find another solution to this whole mess was fast deserting me.

The rooms in the psych ward had no doors and were ordered into two straight rows on either side of a central nurses' station that had a circular flat desk. In this way, all patients were in full view at all times. It almost looked like a prison panopticon. Was this design cruel or ingenious? I didn't allow myself to dwell on that question.

I guess this arrangement was what the nurse was referring to when she told me I'd be on twenty-four-hour watch.

I felt like an animal in a zoo; my every move was being watched from every perceivable angle.

The room itself was extremely small. The single bed had no blankets, only a thin mattress. It was effectively just a narrow bunk. There was a solitary plastic chair and a call button built into the wall next to the bed. There was no washbasin and no mirror. Just an open toilet.

As I lay down and closed my eyes, I became acutely aware of all the unpleasant sounds around me. There were groans and moans like people were being tortured. From one end, I could hear a repetitive banging sound against a wall, a dull thud every fifteen seconds or so. Someone at the opposite end was yelping like a sick dog. There were cries so guttural it was hard to discern if they were human. Just as everything seemed to have quietened down, a high-pitched primal scream shattered the stillness and made me shudder.

I knew I wasn't crazy like these other people. I wondered if they were like me when they were first admitted and only became crazy afterwards. That thought scared me.

I feared that spending a few days holed up in here might tip me over the edge, and I really would become like them. Or maybe they'd just overmedicate me, and I'd turn into a vegetable.

I had to get out fast.

Suddenly I felt extremely lonely and in desperate need of contact with familiar faces. Why wasn't Mummy here yet?

I think I slept for a while and was woken by a shake of my shoulder. My eyes opened in a flash, and I squinted upwards. Gerry stood over me, smiling. 'How are you feeling, Sally?'

I stared hard at him, making sure that it was indeed his face above mine. There was a short silence, which felt awkward. He might have thought I was ignoring him or that I didn't recognise him, but I was peering over his shoulder to see if Mummy was with him. 'I'm doing fine now, Gerry,' I said as I sat upright with my back against the wall behind the bed. 'Hello, Mummy.'

Mummy was in full view in the doorway. She looked sheepish and didn't say anything.

'They only allow one person in at a time', Gerry explained, 'and the rule is strictly enforced.'

I wondered why Mummy didn't come in first. I knew she didn't like hospital rooms much, especially after her recent experiences, but I was sure that wasn't the sole reason.

As for Gerry, there was a softness in his eyes, which told me that he was legitimately concerned about my welfare. He was someone I felt comfortable talking to. 'I took some sleeping pills,' I explained, loud enough so that Mummy could hear as well. 'I took too many by mistake, and now they think I was trying to kill myself. That's why I'm here.' I spoke in a forthright manner. This wasn't the time to be timid or indulge anyone.

Gerry stared me straight in the eye and gripped my hands tightly. I felt no compunction to remove my hands from the warmth of his. He coughed and drew in a long breath, his lungs welcoming the large intake of oxygen. 'Your mother is a good woman at heart, Sally. She is genuinely concerned about your well-being. We spoke to the nurses, and they think a few days in here will do you good. Might calm you down a bit.'

I drew my hands from Gerry's grasp. I couldn't believe he was siding with the hospital. Was Mummy thinking the same? I had to know. 'Could I have a word with Mummy please?'

'Of course.' Gerry peered over his shoulder before walking out of the room and whispering something to Mummy as she walked in.

'It's for the best, Sal,' she said as she placed her bag on the floor. 'They're only trying to help you.'

Just then a nurse came scampering in. 'No bags in here.'

'I'm sorry.' Mummy surrendered her bag, which the nurse handed to Gerry outside. This place really was just like a prison, I thought.

I waited until we were alone again. 'Mummy, I'm fine. I don't need to stay here. You need to tell the nurses and doctors that I don't belong in here.'

Mummy gave me a stare that said her mind was already made up. 'I can't do that, dear. I only want what's best for you. Besides, you haven't seen the doctor yet.'

I DON'T WANT TO SEE THE DOCTOR! Fear and panic were rising up inside me, and Dr Gail's calming techniques weren't even on my radar. 'Nurse! Nurse! Help!' I was almost shouting. The same nurse who took Mummy's bag appeared as though out of nowhere. She looked annoyed.

'Yes? Is there a problem in here?'

'I can't stay here! Please, can I be in a normal ward instead? My mother will stay with me.'

The nurse looked at her watch. Any hope I may have had of her granting my request was immediately extinguished by the expression on her face. 'The doctor will be here soon,' she snapped. 'You will have to speak to him about that.' She turned on her heels, Nazi-like, before walking briskly out of the room.

Mummy stepped in closer. 'Don't worry, Sal. Gerry and I have decided to stay until you get better. You don't mind us staying in your flat? Besides, someone has to look after Henry.'

I'd forgotten all about Henry, as if he never existed. How could he ever look me in the eye again? Does he too think that I'm crazy?

My will for the fight had well and truly subsided. I resigned myself to the fact that I wasn't going anywhere until at least after the psychiatrist had seen me. 'Okay, Mummy.' My voice was dull. 'I'll be home soon, I promise.'

CHAPTER 68

THE THOUGHT OF having to explain myself all over again to another psychiatrist was almost nauseating. After all the effort I'd put in with Dr Gail, I had to endure more confronting questions about my life and family dynamic: Yes, I'm an only child. Yes, I never knew my father growing up, and I still don't. Yes, I had a very unpleasant childhood. Yes, I don't get on well with my mother. Yes, I still find it hard to fit in anywhere.

But more important than having to trawl through my dysfunctional past, I had to impress upon this doctor that I was making good progress in rehabilitating myself and that I was absolutely terrified about being here. How could I ever get better staying in a place that scares me? I just needed to go home and start rebuilding my life anew.

The psychiatrist didn't arrive for another couple of hours after Mummy and Gerry left. I was beginning to feel quite tired and had to force myself to stay awake.

He was an older man of around 60 with a receding hairline, a long thin face, and a furrowed brow. The hoods of his eyes curved like crescent moons.

He appeared to have the stiff demeanour of one striving for eminence and didn't even tell me his name.

He went through my case notes before pulling up a chair and staring at me with a curious gaze. 'Ms Cartwright, I rang Dr Eisenhuth before coming here. She spoke glowingly about you.'

This was the first bit of positive news I'd heard since being here. Maybe there was a lifeline after all.

'I'm making good progress,' I said enthusiastically. 'She and I get along well.' That wasn't completely true, especially of late, but I wasn't going to admit that to a man who held my immediate future in his hands.

He went through the usual questions, just as I'd expected. My answers were a little mechanical, and I was careful not to sound blasé.

Then came the kick in the guts. He told me in no uncertain terms that I didn't have a choice about being here and that I was to remain in this ward for at least the next few days. 'You took a voluntary overdose of sleeping tablets. There is a standard protocol I have to follow in this situation.'

'But I'm not crazy! Why are you all trying to hurt me?'

He gave me a stern look. 'Ms Cartwright, thinking that everyone in this hospital is trying to do you harm is a delusion. Your best defence right now is to cooperate.'

He then got onto the topic of my medications. 'Dr Eisenhuth told me that she prescribed Tofranil for emotional behavioural disorder, but according to the toxicology report, there was no trace of this drug in your system.'

I nodded. 'That's right. I stopped taking it because I thought the sleeping tablets would be enough.' I didn't want to tell him that I wasn't taking the drug even before starting the sleeping tablets.

The doctor's eyes acquired a hardness to them, no doubt developed over many years of dealing with misfits like me. His stare was cold. 'Ms Cartwright, deciding what medicines and how much of them you should or shouldn't be taking is a dangerous practice. Doctors don't just give you drugs because they feel like it, especially where your mental health is concerned. Your well-being is our priority.'

He wrote out a script for Tofranil as he continued talking. 'Like everything else in here, you have no choice. You will take these tablets. The nurses here will make sure of that.'

At this point, I was willing to accept a few pills to expedite my discharge. 'Okay,' I said. 'But then can I go home?'

He didn't answer right away. 'We'll see,' he eventually said while writing some notes.

This was my last chance to negotiate what was still possibly negotiable. 'But you said I'd only be here for a few more days. Is that still the case?'

The doctor's face stiffened for a second before relaxing again. He seemed to sense that I wasn't trying to be difficult. 'Let's hope it is. It depends on the progress you make.'

I thought about asking what 'progress' I had to make but decided not to. I had no choice but to trust this man.

'Thank you, Doctor.'

'I'll be around again tomorrow.' He collected his notes and began walking out before stopping at the entrance. 'By the way, you're not pregnant.'

Tears overflowed my eyes and ran down my cheeks. There was no more talking to be done, no more negotiating. I had to save the excuses now. My immediate fate had been sealed.

I slept the sleep of the dead and assumed that this was because I'd been drugged to the hilt. The night nurse made sure I swallowed every last pill, even checking under my tongue before leaving my room.

I dreamt about Mummy and Gerry together in my flat. It was a pleasant dream, but I can't remember how it ended.

When I woke, I felt surprisingly alert but had a raging thirst. I swung my legs to the side of the bed and pressed the call button on the wall. Within seconds, someone appeared in the doorway. I could tell it was a man, his tall and slender body framed by the light from behind him.

'Well, hello, Sally.'

My heart jumped, and I stood up. Standing in the doorway was Myles Bennett.

CHAPTER 69

WE STOOD THERE looking at each other for what seemed an eternity. Myles had a grin from ear to ear as he waited for me to say something. I eventually composed myself. 'Hello, Myles.' My voice was flat. 'What are you doing here?' I couldn't bring myself to look directly at him as I spoke. Such was the shock I felt by his presence. My heart was thumping.

He stepped into the room. 'I work here sometimes. This isn't my usual ward, but you know what they say: Pickers can't be choosers.' He looked at me more closely. In his eyes I saw a flicker of confusion. 'And what are you doing here, Sally Cartwright?'

Well, I more than likely wouldn't be here if you'd returned my message. That was a selfish lens to view my predicament through.

'I took a few too many sleeping pills by mistake, that's all. But I'm all good now.'

Myles sensed my uncertain mood. 'I've read the admission notes.'

So he too saw me as an unstable, crazy woman. That seemed to be the general consensus around here. 'I feel so bad causing all this unnecessary trouble,' I said. 'I wish I could turn back the clock.' That wasn't strictly true. *How else would I have found you again?*

Myles was in deep thought for a few seconds before he spoke. 'You know it's not that simple, Sally. But whatever happened, whatever the circumstances were, there is only one way forward from here.'

That was easy for him to say. I still believed there was more than one outcome possible. I was feeling a little provoked and tried hard to compose myself. 'Look, I know what you're thinking, but I never wanted to be on those sleeping tablets in the first place.'

Myles took a long time to respond; but when he did, he spoke slowly, his tone unyielding. 'Your psychiatrist prescribed them for a reason. You didn't tell me you were seeing a psychiatrist.'

That was true. Other than being the caring daughter who looked out for her mother, he knew little else about me. I hadn't poured my soul out to him.

I sighed loudly. 'I should have told you.' Tears began brimming up in my eyes, and I had a funny feeling in my throat. I really was parched.

Myles stared at me with a sympathetic expression. 'The notes also say that you suffer from depression.'

'It's not a typical depression,' I spoke defensively and knew I was skating on thin ice by doing so. 'I feel empty sometimes, that's all. More empty than sad.'

Myles was deep in thought, and he paused before speaking. 'The risk of suicide is intrinsically linked to the degree of depression.'

I closed my eyes and took a deep breath. The anxiousness engendered by this conversation was hitting me with a vengeance. I needed to defend myself.

It was time for Myles to meet the real Sally Cartwright. 'I'm not the perfect girl next door. I had a difficult childhood. My mother is not the nice person you may think she is. Because of her ineptitudes, I've had a lot of adjustment issues in my life, and that's why I see a psychiatrist. But being here now shouldn't have any bearing on any of that.' I managed a feeble laugh. 'I know it's a funny way to put it all in perspective, but I'm not crazy. I never wanted to kill myself. You've got to believe me.'

Myles sat on my bed and was perfectly still. I could tell he was choosing his words carefully. 'You have a lot to live for, Sally. I know you wouldn't deliberately do anything like that.'

I felt tremendous relief at hearing his words. 'No, I wouldn't,' I announced emphatically. 'If only everyone else around here would believe me.'

'Are you afraid?'

I shifted on the bed, pulling my feet up from under me. 'Terrified.'

'You shouldn't be. Dr Cassell is a reasonable man. I'll have a word with him, tell him that I know you.' He smiled. 'Everything will turn out fine.'

I smiled back, pulling at my gown in a gesture of nervousness. 'Thank you,' I said. 'I could really do with a glass of water right now.'

MARIO BORAZIO

Myles returned with a pitcher of water and a plastic cup. He sat on the side of the bed and handed me a full cup. I gulped it down and asked for another. 'Thank you. I needed that.'

We sat quietly for a moment. I was beginning to realise that my time here now with this man was the only brightness in my life, but even that was tinged with sadness. I decided to break the tension building up between us. 'You didn't return my call.'

My remark seemed to catch him off guard. 'You called me? When was that?'

'Just after the last time I visited you in the hospital.'

He frowned and slipped his phone out of his pocket before proceeding to push a few buttons. Then he put it away and gave me a despairing look. 'There's nothing there. Are you sure it was me you called?'

'Yes. I listened to your new voicemail, and then I left a message.'

'Did you wait for the beep before talking?'

The beep? For some reason, my mind jumped to a scene from the Roadrunner cartoon. *As this was my first foray into the world of message leaving, I was not aware of all its intrinsic workings.* 'I didn't hear a beep,' I sheepishly admitted.

'Well, that would explain it.' Myles would have been well within his rights to break out into uncontrollable laughter at this juncture, but he didn't, in part because a nurse had just entered the room.

'It's time for your tablets, Sally. We'll bring you your breakfast in a while.'

After I'd swallowed four tablets and was put through the obligatory tongue test, Myles and I were alone again.

'Dr Cassell will see you this afternoon. I'll try to catch him before that. In the meantime, enjoy your breakfast.' Myles left the room before I had a chance to thank him. Once he was gone, I began to feel uneasy. Was his show of compassion merely a benevolent gesture to lift my spirits, or was he just acting in a professional capacity? How much influence will he have on Dr Cassell?

I'll have to wait until this afternoon to find out.

CHAPTER 70

I HAD TO RUB my eyes to make sure it wasn't a mirage. Dr Gail was standing in the doorway with her bag in one hand and a folder in the other. I had gotten so used to seeing her from behind a desk that for a moment I thought it couldn't possibly be her. But then she opened her mouth, and I knew this moment was indeed real.

'Hello, Sally,' she spoke affably, and I sensed she was happy to see me. 'You're looking well.'

Her positivity was reassuring considering the frosty ending to our last session. 'Hello, Gail. This is a surprise,' I spoke optimistically because I was of the opinion that her presence here was likely going to work in my favour.

'The hospital called me when you were admitted yesterday. They called again this morning, and I was advised to come in.' She walked into the room and sat down. 'Now, just so that there is no confusion, I want you to tell me exactly what happened.'

I was reticent and embarrassed to talk about the incident in question and began twisting the end of the bedsheet around my finger.

Dr Gail sensed my uneasiness and placed a hand on mine. 'Look, Sally, we don't have to talk about this just yet. Not if you're not ready.'

Tears were threatening as I spoke. 'It's hard, Gail. It really is.'

'It must be.' She squeezed my hand tight and told me quite assertively that she knew me well enough to be sure that I wasn't trying to kill myself, that my actions were only a cry for help. 'Suicide is the ultimate act of desperation, Sally. It happens when people find themselves in the darkest of places. I know you don't belong there.'

I felt instantly at ease. 'Yes. And that's exactly what it was, Gail. A cry for help. That's *all* it was. It was an accident,' I eagerly explained. 'The trouble is that Dr Cassell doesn't see it that way.'

'I've already spoken with Dr Cassell. He and I came to an agreement once I explained your situation.'

'I see.' My heart was doing back flips in my chest.

Dr Gail opened the folder on her lap and smiled. 'Your friend Myles put in a good word for you too. You're fortunate that he works here.'

So Myles kept his word. This was my lucky day. 'He was in this morning,' I said.

'Yes, I know. I spoke to him when I arrived. He's a caring man, Sally.'

'What's the agreement?' My voice was slightly loud and impatient. Dr Gail could see I was jumpy.

'Although I told them that you would be completely fine on your own, the top brass in here insisted on what's called a "phased return" to society. It's a condition of your release, which I had to agree to.'

I was a little confused. 'What does that mean?'

'It means that you can get out of here but you have to be supervised. That for three months you are not allowed to live alone. And another stipulation is that we have to continue our sessions during that time, and you must continue taking all your medications.'

I still had this fantasy that everything could just go back to normal with me living on my own. That I could pretend this whole saga never happened. *This was not the time to think selfishly, Sally.*

The scenario that Dr Gail explained made me feel like I was a prisoner about to be released on parole. But I really didn't care because I was getting out of here.

I couldn't hide my excitement. 'So I'm really allowed to go home?'

'Yes. But we have to brainstorm this together, Sally.' She opened another page. 'Is there anyone who could come and stay with you?'

I couldn't have written a more perfect script. I explained how Gerry and Mummy came to visit me yesterday. 'They are staying at my flat.'

'Can they stay with you for the three months?'

I shrugged my shoulders. 'I don't know. Gerry has a dog.' I wondered if he brought Fido with him, just as I'd taken Henry with me to Mummy's place.

'What about your mother?'

What *about* her? The notion of Mummy caring for me would normally be assigned to the annals of fiction. But under the circumstances, it wasn't as stupid as it sounded.

The irony, of course, was almost comical. I could just imagine her bossing me around, drinking and smoking to her heart's content in the knowledge that she had power over me.

'I'll have to convince her to stay, but that shouldn't be a problem.' I didn't really want to talk about Mummy, so I changed the subject. 'What about our sessions?'

Dr Gail placed the folder down on my bed and sat back on her chair. 'I want you to know that when you come back to counselling, I might be able to give you some answers, Sally. Answers to why this all happened.'

I thought about this for a moment. A vague feeling of irritation pervaded my mind. Why didn't she provide me with all those 'answers' before all this happened? I might not be here now, lying on a thin mattress, doped up to the eyeballs and forced to listen to barbaric and animalistic sounds emanating from every nook and cranny in this hellhole.

I thought some more. I was probably being too harsh. Ultimately, I had to take responsibility for my actions.

'I look forward to that, Gail. I'm sure that will be a big help moving forward.'

Dr Gail smiled before handing me a release form to sign. She said I would be released once I proved there was someone to care for me at home.

'I can call Mummy, and you can talk to her.'

Dr Gail rang for the nurse who brought in my phone.

Maybe the drugs I was on were causing me to hallucinate, but she and Mummy spoke like old friends. It started with small talk before Dr Gail proceeded to fill Mummy in on the aspects of my release conditions. The entire conversation was interspersed with sharp bouts of laughter as Dr Gail listened to what Mummy was saying, not once interrupting her.

She closed the phone and ran a hand through her hair. 'It's

settled then. Your mother said that Gerry will be here to pick you up in an hour.'

The anxiety etched on my face was impossible to miss. 'Is Myles Bennett still here?' I asked.

CHAPTER 71

T HE MYSTICS WILL weep; their crystal balls are cloudy. This wasn't the way things were supposed to work out. If only I'd believed in fairytales…

*

I could sense problems on the horizon, all stemming from the fact that I may no longer be relevant. After being so important to Mummy, I imagined myself being unimportant again, just like during my childhood days.

I was scared.

I turned the key to my front door with a healthy dose of trepidation. Fido began sniffing at our ankles as soon as Gerry and I stepped inside. I couldn't believe how nervous I was walking into my own living room. I straightened myself up.

Mummy greeted me. Her face looked pale and drawn, and she wore an apron. A soupy aroma emanated from the kitchen. 'Hello, dear. It's so nice to have you home. How are you feeling?' She stepped forward and gave me a peck on the cheek before I could answer. 'Dinner will be ready soon. I hope you're hungry.'

I wondered how much of this spanking-new motherly affection was real and how much of it was contrived just to impress Gerry. I also wondered if Gerry had a word with her about making more of an effort to be nicer to her daughter. Either way, I didn't care; I was home, away from the nightmarish environs of that hellish psych ward.

The only regret I had about leaving that place was not having the opportunity to say goodbye to Myles. I really wanted to thank him for everything he did.

His phone went directly to message bank.

The beep! I was thoroughly familiar with it now.

"Hello, Myles, this is Sally Cartwright. I'm back home now and just wanted to thank you for everything. If there's anything I can do for you one day, just let me know. Take care."

Certainly a lot better than my last effort for which, thankfully, no record exists.

The first thing I did after settling back into my room was walk around the corner to thank Mrs Hutchings for saving my life. To say that she actually saved me from dying may be a bit of a stretch, but I needed to let her know how grateful I was.

She greeted me with a smile and was extremely friendly. I couldn't help but feel that she was a lonely woman who was crying out for a friend.

I could sympathise.

She offered to help if I was ever in need of anything. 'All you have to do is ask, dear.' The way she spoke reminded me of Mummy except that she was much nicer. Her warmth and generosity warmed my heart and made me feel guilty for avoiding her in the past.

Gerry fitted in seamlessly and helped out with the daily chores wherever he could. He agreed to stay for the whole three months as long as it wasn't going to be an imposition. Mummy and I both agreed that he was being silly. He began giving me driving lessons. We initially went to an empty parking lot in an industrial area and I practised until I got the feel of driving. The whole ordeal wasn't as daunting as I'd expected. I don't think I'll have any problems getting my licence.

I developed a real taste for bacon and eggs which were Gerry's specialty dish. He turned out to be a good cook, and his offerings never disappointed.

I continued seeing Dr Gail weekly as was prearranged. These sessions didn't turn out to be as torrid as I thought they'd be. I think she was deliberately going easy on me. I began resurrecting my mental garden and was feeling more at peace with myself. I had to keep taking my medications but didn't really mind because they were making me feel a lot better.

I hadn't had any more calls from Miss YouTube and regularly checked my phone for any new videos. Thankfully, there weren't any. I kept my old phone even though I had no real use for it; perhaps I was becoming a hoarder like Mummy.

Mummy continued to play domesticated host with unwavering aplomb, and the colour in her cheeks returned. I never saw her pick up a drink and never smelled a trace of cigarette smoke anywhere in the house. Was this demonstration of abstinence purely for her benefit or, again, for Gerry's? I knew it couldn't be for mine, but that didn't bother me one bit.

The three of us had lively conversations almost every night after dinner. These discussions would inevitably become quite animated. They were almost always initiated by Gerry, and he did most of the talking. I soon realised he was an eloquent and a well-read man. He had candid opinions on almost any subject. Some of his charisma seemed to rub off on Mummy too. To my surprise, she was totally comfortable with most of the topics up for discussion and joined in whenever the opportunity arose.

Gerry valued my opinions too.

I helped out with the chores and accompanied Mummy to all her medical appointments. I think my fear of being unwanted and superfluous might be misplaced.

Four weeks later...

Gerry and I took Fido for a walk, and I fed Henry when we got back. Feeling a little tired, I lay on the couch and began watching a documentary on the hidden world and extraordinary lives of suicide ants. They are found in Malaysia and Brunei and can explode suicidally in an ultimate act of self-defence. What evolutionary laws of variation conspired to assign such a fate to these poor creatures? Charles Darwin has a lot to answer for, but I decided it wasn't worth putting too much thought into this mystery. Anyway, the subject of suicide wasn't the most palatable, so I turned the television off.

Mummy's voice from the hall sounded strained. 'Sal, there's someone here to see you.'

I could hear shuffling feet, and then he appeared. It was Myles. He wore perfectly fitting navy jeans and a black T-shirt that hugged the contours of his chest and shoulders. He looked utterly gorgeous. Dapper too (Adjective: neat in dress and bearing; trim).

'Hello, Sally. I thought I'd come by and see how you were doing.' His familiar smile hadn't deserted him.

I stood up and smoothed my jeans subconsciously before stepping back to rearrange my hair. Mummy disappeared into the kitchen without saying a word. She must be mellowing in her old age.

'Hello, Myles. This is a pleasant surprise.' It sure was; he hadn't replied to my phone message, and I'd all but given up hope of ever seeing him again.

'I wanted to surprise you. That's why I didn't return your call.'

When I hadn't heard back, I was beginning to question this whole beep theory. It was pleasing to know that my message had been received.

We sat on the couch opposite each other. My heart rate was through the roof, and my hands were clammy. He had a look that was giving me a rush, a desire. He asked me how I was doing. I told him I was doing fine and that I was still seeing Dr Gail, which was helping a lot.

'That's great. It must be a big help having your mother with you too.' Before I could offer a riposte, he pulled a small box from his pocket and placed it on the coffee table. My heart lurched, and my hands trembled. I dithered, unsure of what I should do or say.

'Aren't you going to open it?'

With my hands still trembling, I took the box and snapped the top open. My eyes began to well up with tears, and I had to wipe them on my sleeve to see what was inside. It was a small butterfly brooch with golden wings that sparkled with tiny sapphire blue and emerald green stones.

'It's beautiful. Thank you.' I couldn't say anything more.

Myles leaned over the coffee table and pulled me into a brief but tight hug before moving back. He explained that, in Roman and Greek times, the butterfly was a symbol of the soul. Of positivity and personal transformation. Of endurance, change, and hope for the future. 'It perfectly symbolises you, Sally,' he said. 'It will help you achieve all your goals.'

I didn't really have any goals anymore other than to be happy. This was the perfect start in achieving that.

Once I'd controlled my shaking hands, I clumsily pinned the brooch onto my shirt and sat back with a hint of awkwardness and embarrassment. 'Thank you again. I'll treasure this.' I found it hard to read Myles's expression, but somewhere in it there was kindness and gentleness.

We spent the next half hour talking. Myles dominated the conversation. I was still coming to terms with the nuances of social interaction; it was still a work in progress.

We talked about my hospital stay. We talked about Mummy. We talked about Gerry. We talked about Henry.

Myles didn't talk about himself. I wanted to ask him about his new job. I wanted to ask him about his mother. I wanted to ask him if he was still with Varlie.

I didn't ask him any of those things. I was happy.

Happy that I had a friend.